BURN THE DARK

S. A. HUNT

BURN THE DARK

TOR

A TOM DOHERTY ASSOCIATES BOOK

NEW YORK

This is a work of fiction. All of the characters, organizations, and events portrayed in this novel are either products of the author's imagination or are used fictitiously.

BURN THE DARK

Copyright © 2019 by S. A. Hunt

A Tor Book
Published by Tom Doherty Associates
120 Broadway
New York, NY 10271

www.tor-forge.com

Tor® is a registered trademark of Macmillan Publishing Group, LLC.

The Library of Congress Cataloging-in-Publication Data is available upon request.

ISBN 978-1-250-30643-2 (trade paperback)
ISBN 978-1-250-30642-5 (hardcover)
ISBN 978-1-250-30641-8 (ebook)

Our books may be purchased in bulk for promotional, educational, or business use. Please contact your local bookseller or the Macmillan Corporate and Premium Sales Department at 1–800-221-7945, extension 5442, or by email at MacmillanSpecialMarkets@macmillan.com.

First Edition: January 2020

Printed in the United States of America

0 9 8 7 6 5 4 3 2 1

This book is dedicated to the fans, the Outlaw Army, because without you none of these books would exist. My best friend Chaser and Katie Fryhover most of all, both of whom visualized so many of the elements of my books through cosplay costumes, font design, fashion, and monster design.

All of you, you are my muses, my rock, and my center. I love you all so much.

BURN THE DARK

A girl perched in the cab of a utility van. In one hand was a baby-food jar full of liquid. In the other was a dagger, silver and glittering in the rusty glow of the streetlight outside. Her hair was a Mohawk of wavy chestnut locks, sides buzzed down to dark stubble.

On the dash was a camera, recording her half-shadowed face as she spoke. "Been trackin' this one for weeks," she said, punctuating *weeks* with the point of the dagger, her voice thrumming with a Southern drawl. "Looking for all the signs. Missin' pets. Unusually lucky lottery plays. Over-population of cats. Weird accidents. And all that shit I told you about, you know, in the video about runes.

"I been huntin' down all the runes in Alabama I can find, and here, in Birmingham, they've started to converge. There are more here than anywhere else in the state." She tucked the jar into a jacket pocket and picked up the camera, aiming it out the window. "Like I told y'all, they always live in 'the bad part of town.'

"But I don't think they choose to live there because it's the 'bad part.' I think it's shitty *because* they live in it. They suck the goodness out of it, they *eat the pride*, devour the *heart* of the neighborhood until the people don't care about anything anymore. There's just drugs and poverty and garbage. And when there ain't nothing left, the witch packs up and moves somewhere else. Like psychic vampires, or something. Tapeworms in the intestines of the world."

She heaved a heavy sigh, much too world-weary for such an ethereally young face.

"If you got any doubt about what I'm doing, you gotta get this in your head right now: these fuckers ain't Wiccans or hippies, they ain't those chicks from *The Craft,* they ain't Sabrina or the chick from *Bewitched.* These bitches are the real deal. Lieutenants of Hell on a vacation to Earth. Soul-sucking hag-beasts. And that's what this one is."

Across the street from the van was a board fence. Someone had spray-painted incomprehensible graffiti on it—could have been an ambigram for all she knew, legible upside-down as well as right-side-up.

"Lot of times they'll hide the runes in the graffiti. Check out that sideways Jesus-fish in the middle—see how it's a different color than the rest of it?" Robin's arm thrust into the shot as she pointed at different parts of the graffiti with the dagger. The symbol she indicated was a simple diamond shape that crossed at the bottom to make the tail fins of a skyward-facing trout. "This is what I'm talking about. That ain't no English letter, that's a rune. It means *home,* or *homelands.* It's there to let you know you're in a witch's territory. And you see that little crown on top of it? Means there's a witch livin' somewhere on this block."

She turned the camera around and put it on the dash again. Tattooed on her sternum, just below the pit of her throat, was a symbol like a Y with an extra limb in the middle:

$$\mathsf{Y}$$

"The runes," she said, "they're there to help them find each other. I mean, there are seven billion people on this planet; even with the Internet—which a lot of them don't use—it's not easy. Taggers don't even know they're doing it, either. The witches, they . . . I don't know, they *influence* them somehow, like they send out a radio signal the kids can't help but catch. Like queen bees and worker drones. Maybe it's . . . hell, I don't know. Whatever it is, it needs to stop."

The witch-hunter opened the door and got out of the van, slipping the silver dagger into a sheath hidden in the lining of her jacket. In vinyl lettering down the side of the white van was a sleek, utilitarian logo: CONLIN PLUMBING. The license plate was HEXTIME. She strode with purpose across the night-dark street, and approaching the board fence, she rounded the corner, holding the camera up so it could see into the front yard of a run-down tract house.

Overgrown grass around a lemon tree, shadowy front porch with no porch light. A rocking chair lurked in the gloom.

The girl in the video crept up the front walk of the tract house. *Hoo, hoo, hu-hu.*

Halfway across the yard, she paused and turned to point the camera up into the branches of the lemon tree, the aperture whirring as she zoomed in on it.

A snowy owl perched in the masterwork of shadows some eight feet up, throat pulsing, *hoo, hoo, hu-hu.* The camera zoomed out as the owl took flight and left the screen stage right.

"Hello, honey," croaked a subtle voice.

She whirled around and the world on camera whipped to the left, revealing the front of the white tract house and its shadowy porch, arrayed with boxes of junk, chairs, yellowed and fraying newspaper. A tribunal of cats sat on their haunches all over the porch, fifteen or twenty of them: calicos, tortoiseshell tabbies, midnight-blacks, two Siamese, an orange Morris with brilliant green eyes.

Someone stood behind the screen door, a smear of gray a shade lighter than the darkness inside the house.

At the top of the faint figure was the gnarled suggestion of a face. "What brings you round at this time of night, young lady?" An old woman, her voice kind but deliberate, with a hint of accent. British? Irish? Whatever it was, it wasn't midwestern or southern.

Motionless cats reflected the streetlight with their lantern-green eyes.

Neva Chandler, said a voice-over from Robin. *The self-proclaimed King of Alabama.* Her voice was soft, introspective, an inside-voice that belonged more at a funeral than a YouTube video. Tinged with a faint southern twang.

The girl threw a thumb over her shoulder. "Ah, my car broke down. I . . . I was hopin' I could use your phone."

"Ah." The old woman paused. She might have been folding her arms, but it was hard to tell. "I thought *all* you young ladies these days carried those—those cellular phones, they call them. With their tender apps and GPS-voices. Go here, go there, and so forth."

"No, ma'am," replied the girl. "I'm kinda old-school that way I guess."

The old woman scoffed. "Old-school."

"Yes, ma'am."

"Well, if you're going to come in, it would behoove you to do so, and get clear of the street," the old woman said in a warning way, even though the girl was fully in her front yard by then. "It's a dangerous place for dangerous people."

The stoop leading up to the porch was made of concrete painted in flaking gray, and the porch itself was as well. Columns of wrought-iron curlicues held up the roof. At Robin's feet was a china bowl with a few pebbles of dry cat food.

"Yes, ma'am."

Stepping up onto the porch, she tugged the screen door open with a furtive hand. The old woman behind the mesh faded into the darkness like a deep-sea creature and Robin stepped in behind her, filling the video window with black.

Click-click. A dingy bulb in an end-table lamp burst to life, brightening a living room positively crowded with antiques.

A grandfather clock stood next to an orange-and-brown tweed sofa, tiny black arms indicating the time was a few minutes to midnight. Four televisions of progressive evolution clustered on top of a wood-cabinet Magnavox, rabbit-ear antenna reaching over them for a signal no longer being broadcast. No less than three pianos filled one end of the room, two player and one baby grand, all covered in dust.

All of a sudden the smell hit her, a wall of rotten musk. Boiled cabbage, farts, cigarettes. Dead old things, burnt hair, burnt popcorn. Cat shit.

Gangs of unlighted candles stood atop every surface, halfway melted into the saucers and teacups that held them. Lines of runic script decorated the windowsills and the threshold of the front door between her feet.

Another cat sat on top of a piano, running its tongue down the length of one leg. Robin let the screen door ease shut. "I'm so sorry to bother you this time of night."

Chandler shuffled over to a plush wingback chair and dropped herself into it, crumpling. She wore a pink bathrobe, with steel-gray hair as dry as haystraw tumbling down the sides of her Yoda face. A whisper of mustache dusted her upper lip. She could have been a thousand years old if a day.

An old glass-top coffee table dominated the space in front of the sofa and armchair. Occupying the center of the table was a wooden bowl, and inside the bowl was a single pristine lemon.

"No bother at all, my dear," the old woman said, peering up at Robin with the baggy, watery eyes of a basset hound. "I'm usually up late. No bother at all." As she spoke, she flashed black gums and the pearlescent brown teeth of a lifelong smoker. "Ah, the phone," she wheezed, curling a finger over the back of the chair. "Over in there, in the hallway, on the little hutch. Do you see it?"

The camera soared past the armchair and toward a doorway in the back of the furniture-crowded room.

As it did so, Robin softly interjected a pensive voice-over. *Sometimes when the witches have completely drained a neighborhood down to the bones and they've used it all up, all the—whatcha call it, the "life," the soul—there ain't nothing left to move with. They can't migrate to a new town, they get stuck, and slowly wither away. They starve. They die from the inside out. The deadness slowly makes its way to the outside. Heinrich and I think that's what happened here.*

The old woman's telephone turned out to be a rotary phone. Robin picked up the handset and pressed it against her ear, listening for a dial tone. She put it against the GoPro in her hand.

After a while they're just a rotten corpse in a living-human costume.

Nothing came from the earpiece but a muted ticking, as if she could hear the wind tugging at the lines outside.

Death masquerading as life.

"So what is a beautiful young lady like you doing in a trackless waste such as this? This is a hobby town—there's nothing to do, so everybody has a hobby. Painting model airplanes, collecting stamps, making meth, *doing* meth. Can't be that, though. You're not around to buy drugs." The decrepit crone sat up, leaning over to pluck the lemon out of the bowl with one knobby monkey-paw hand. "No, Robin dear, ohhh, you don't look like the others. You don't look like shit."

"No, ma'am, I don't do drugs. I mean, other than medication." Robin put the handset down. "I'm from out of town, visiting a fr—"

Chandler's breathing came in phlegmy gasps and sighs, tidal and troubled. Sounded like she'd been running a marathon.

"How did you know my name?" asked the girl.

"Oh, honey, bless your heart," said the crone, "I been expecting you all day." She pricked the rind of the lemon with a thumbnail and peeled part of it away, revealing not the white-yellow flesh Robin had expected, but the vital and fevered red of an internal organ. "It took you longer to get here than I expected. But then Birmingham *is* rather Byzantine, isn't it? I remember when I was a child, when it was all gaslights and horse-drawn carts, the layout was so much simpler then."

Blue veins squirmed across the lemon's surface in time to some eldritch beat.

The lemon had a *pulse*.

Lifting the thing to her mouth, Chandler bit into it, spritzing fine droplets of blood into the air.

Ferocious wet devouring-noises came from the other side of the chair, like wolves tearing into the belly of a dead elk. More blood sprayed up, dotting the wallpaper, the lampshade. The remains of the lemon's rind dangled from the crone's hand like a fresh scalp, bloody and pulpy.

Red dripped on the filthy carpet.

"My last lemon," said Chandler, twisting slowly in the chair.

One twiggish hand slipped over the back, gripping the velvet and cherrywood. "I've been saving it for a special occasion, you know."

Rising, she stared Robin down with eyes that flashed with a red light deep inside. Her teeth were too many for her mouth, tiny canines, peg-like fangs. The wrinkles across the bloody map of her face had smoothed. Her schoolmarm hair had gone from corn silk to black rooted in steel. "You think you're the first to seek me?" asked the witch, her lips contorting over the bulge of teeth. The longer she spoke, the deeper her voice got, dropping in pitch like a toy with a dying battery. "My trees are composted with the rot of a dozen *just like you*."

"There ain't nobody like me, lady. I eat assholes like you for breakfast."

The monstrous witch blinked. "You eat assholes?" She giggled, which coming out of her throat sounded horselike.

"I, uhh—well—"

"If you're gonna be a witch-hunter like your friends, you need to work on your one-liners!" Chandler spidered over the chair, pink bathrobe flagging over her humped back.

"Shit!" Robin ran. "Shit shit shit!"

Darkness swallowed the camera, shredded by light coming in through the witch's window blinds. The image went into hysterics as Robin pumped her arms, running through the house.

Tripping over something, she went sprawling in a pile of what sounded like books. "Goddammit! *Aarrgh!*"

The witch came through the house after the girl, her bare feet thumping the carpet, then bumping against the linoleum, meat clubbing against wood. "God won't save you. You'll not have *me*, little lady," gibbered Chandler, invisible in the dark. "You'll not have *me*, you'll not have *me*."

Robin pushed through the back door of a kitchen, bursting out into a moonlit backyard. Turning, stumbling, she aimed the camera at the house.

Shick, the sound of metal against leather. Robin drew the silver dagger.

The back door slapped open. Something came racing out, a wraith shrouded in stained terrycloth, the lemon-heart blood coursing down her chin and wasted xylophone chest—and then the old woman was gliding across the overgrown yard, reaching for her with those terrible scaly owl-hands.

"*Hee hee hee heeeee!*" cackled Chandler, instantly on her, shoving her into the weeds. Both went down in a heap and Robin lost the camera.

Whirling around, the video's perspective ended up sideways on the ground, obscured by the grass, barely capturing the melee in one corner of the screen. Neva Chandler landed on top of the girl's belly cowgirl-style and raked at her face with those disgusting yellow nails, deceptively sharp chisel-points, laughing, crowing in her harsh raven-rasp of a voice.

Even though Robin was fighting with everything she had, she couldn't push the old crone away. An astounding strength lingered in those decrepit bones. Tangling her fingers in the girl's hair, Chandler wrenched her head up and down, bouncing it uselessly against the grass.

"Get *off* me!" shrieked Robin in her thin, high video-voice, thrusting the silvery dagger through the pink bathrobe and into the witch's ribs—*SHUK!*

Time seemed to pause as the fight stopped as suddenly as it had started. Chandler's arms were crooked back, her fingers clawed in a grotesque parody of some old Universal movie monster. Her face was twisted and altered by some strange paranormal force, her mouth impossibly open until it was a drooping coil of chin and teeth. Robin withdrew the dagger, releasing black syrup. Then she plunged it deep into the old woman's chest again, *shuk,* and twice, and thrice, and four times, *shuk shuk shuk.*

Black liquid like crude oil dribbled out around the blade of the dagger. The witch exhaled deep in her throat, a deathly deflating.

"Knife to meet you!" shouted the girl.

Not my best, said the voice-over. *I'm learning, okay?*

With a shrieking snarl, "*Grrraaaaaagh,*" the witch leapt backward—propelled, more like, as if she'd been snatched away by some invisible hand—and scrambled to the safety of her back stoop, cowering like a cornered animal. A stew of red and black ran down her sloped chin and wattled neck. "That won't work!" she choked through a mouthful of ichor. Chandler had taken the dagger away, and now it glittered in one warped claw. "It'll take more than bad puns and pigstickers to—"

Hands shaking, Robin produced the Gerber jar and threw a fastball.

The jar went wide, whipping over the old woman's head.

Glass shattered against the eaves, showering her with the contents. Chandler flinched, blinking in confusion.

"This ain't *The Wizard of Oz,* honey, I ain't going to melt. You was having more luck with the dagger." She flourished the dagger as if she were conducting a symphony with it. "You want this back? *Come get it, little girl!*"

The witch-hunter reached into her jacket.

She whipped out a Zippo, the lid clinking open.

"What you got there?" The witch sniffed the arm of her bathrobe and grimaced. She looked up. "Oh *hell* no."

Alcohol.

Flick, a tiny flame licked up from the Zippo in Robin's hand, brightening the backyard. "Get away from me!" the witch shrieked, trading the dagger to the other hand and flinging it overhand like a tomahawk. Robin recoiled. The blade skipped off the side of her collar, inches from her throat, a sharp pain just under her ear as the blade nicked her skin.

Chandler turned and ripped the back door open, scrambling through. Robin snatched up the GoPro and followed, camera in one hand and lighter in the other. She caught the witch just inside the threshold, touching the Zippo's tongue to the edge of her bathrobe.

The terrycloth caught, lining the hem with a scribble of white light, enough to faintly illuminate the grimy kitchen.

"*Oooooh!*" screeched Chandler, tumbling to her hands and knees. "You nasty, nasty girl! You trollop! You *tramp!*" The witch stood, using the counter as a ladder, and fumbled her way over to the sink, smearing black all over the cabinets. Raking dirty dishes out of the way, Chandler disturbed a cloud of fruit flies and turned on the faucet. "When I get this put out, I'm going to—I'm going to—" She tugged and tugged the stiff sprayer hose, trying to pull it out of the basin.

Flames trickled up the tail of Chandler's bloody bathrobe, but they were going much too slowly for Robin's liking. She reached over and touched the fabric with the Zippo again. This time the alcohol on Chandler's back erupted in a windy *burp* of white and orange. The flames billowed toward the ceiling, a cape of fire, whispering and muttering.

As Robin lunged in to ignite her sleeve, Chandler reached into the sink with her other hand and came up with a dirty carving knife.

She hooked it at the girl, trying to stab her and spray herself with the sink hose at the same time. Robin jerked away. The plastic nozzle showered the witch's head with cold water, soaking her hair and running down her face, washing away the blood and oil-slime. Chandler maneuvered around, trying to spray the fire on her back, but all she could seem to manage was to half-drown herself and shoot water over her shoulder onto the floor.

"Help me!" cried the flame-ghost, water arcing all over the kitchen. "Why would you do this to an old lady like me? *What have I ever done to yooooouuuuu?*"

"*You witches killed my mama!*"

Flinging the refrigerator door open, Robin flinched as condiment bottles and a stick of butter clattered to the floor at her feet. Reaching in, she grabbed the neck of a bottle of Bacardi. The last bit sloshed around in the bottom.

"What the fuck are you talking about?" Chandler shoved the fridge door closed, almost on Robin's head. "*HELP ME!*" roared the slack-faced creature in the bathrobe. Her jaw had come unhinged, and two rows of tiny catlike teeth glistened wetly in the pit of her black maw. Her eyes were two yellow marbles, shining deep in bruise-green eye sockets. "HELP ME OR YOU'LL BURN *WITH* ME!"

Pressing her ragged stinking body against Robin's, Chandler wrapped her arms around the other's chest in a bear hug.

Prickly, inhuman teeth brushed against the girl's collarbone.

With an incoherent shriek, Robin pushed and slapped at Chandler's shoulders and face. Those horrible teeth scratched at her hands and the witch craned forward, her throat engorged and fat like a python, her great moray-eel mouth clapping shut at empty air.

Crash! Robin clubbed the hag across the forehead with the Bacardi, shattering the bottle.

The liquor inside hit the flames and *exploded.*

"EEEEEEE!" the flaming figure keened, fully engulfed now and stumbling blindly around the kitchen, leaving little puddles and clues of fire all over the cabinets and the little dining table with the checkered Italian-café tablecloth. Stacks of old books on the table caught, the grimoires and cookbooks drinking up the heat, already shriveling.

"Burn, you evil bitch! Burn!" Robin fell back, escaping to a hall-way that would have been too dark to navigate if it hadn't been for the screaming bonfire.

"KILL HER," Chandler howled from inside the flames. "*KIIILL HERRR!*"

Cats appeared from everywhere, squirreling out of gaps and from underneath the furniture—black, white, calico, tortoise-shell. They ran straight at Chandler and kamikaze'd into the flames, igniting their own bodies in a zealous fervor.

In an instant, the kitchen was a meteor shower, a riot of immo-lated cats running in every direction, flailing and shrieking.

Running down the hallway to escape the madcap carnage, Robin came out behind a piano in the living room. She slid over the top of the thing on her belly, plowing through a feathery coat of dust and cat hair.

On her knees and then her feet, she shoved through the screen door and ran out into the front yard.

A crowd of thirty or forty people had assembled in the street.

They stood stock-still and rigid in various states of undress, their hands dangling at their sides, staring at her, eyes shining green in the dark. Unkempt hair, awoken mid-sleep. Some of them slowly worked and flexed their hands.

"*Mrrrrrr*," hummed a man in a hooded sweatshirt. "*Rrrrwww.*"

A burning cat pushed past Robin's feet and out into the front yard, where it collapsed.

She juked left, running underneath the lemon tree and around the side of Chandler's tract house, between the board fence and the clapboard wall. Mud and wet grass underneath the tree almost knocked her on her ass.

"Go go go go go," she growled under her breath.

The pounding of sneakered feet made it clear the familiars were chasing her. The fence ended near the back corner and Robin vaulted the chain-link and jumped the sidewalk, almost losing her footing, then sprinted across the street. She opened the driver door of the CONLIN PLUMBING van and threw herself inside.

Through the window she could see half the neighborhood pouring out of the gap behind the fence like hornets from a nest, and just as terrifying.

Her key was already in the ignition. She twisted it until she thought it would snap off in the steering column. The van chugged a few times and turned over mightily, *GRRRRUH!*

When she went to shut the door, she slammed it on the meaty arm of a fat man in an old Bulls jersey, the collar frayed around his hoary neck.

"Get your own car, shithead! This one is paid for!"

"*Mrrrr!*" he growled. His eyes were green screwheads.

Crazed, yowling people clustered around the van and hammered the panels with their fists, clawing at the windows. Jersey Man's arm flapped into the cab with her, fighting her hands, and he found her throat with the fork of his palm, pressing it against her windpipe.

Her neck was pinned against the headrest. She couldn't breathe.

Thrusting her foot into the floorboard, she found the accelerator and put all her weight on it. The engine snarled, vibrating the van, revving hard, so hard for a second she thought it would come apart, but nothing else happened. The van's cabin filled with an acrid burning smell.

"Fffffk," she gurgled, fumbling for the gearshift.

The passenger window imploded in a tumble of glass and someone reached in at her.

Robin put the van in Drive and stood on the gas again. This time the machine leapt forward like a greyhound busting out of the starting block, pressing her against the seat. The engine coughed once, twice, the drivetrain rumbled, and then the crowd fell away and she was barreling down the street.

Bodies fell in the headlights, astonished faces flashing across the hood, and the van clambered over them, *bonk-badunk-clank-bang*. Driving with her fingertips, she twisted the steering wheel this way and that, trying to shake off the two men halfway inside the cab with her, but only the one hanging out the window fell. The van hauled back and forth, teetering with the gravity of a Spanish galleon on the sea.

"You will die," said Jersey Man, his fingers still clamping Robin's neck to the seat. She could feel her heartbeat in her face. "The Red Lord will find you."

Jerking the wheel to the left, she sideswiped a telephone pole. The wooden trunk slammed into the man's shoulder and knocked him off, his fingernails biting into the skin under her ear. Her tires barked and wailed as Robin fought to keep the van under control, and the telephone pole scraped down the side of the vehicle, beating on the hollow panels with a noise like thunder.

She glanced at the side mirror. Two dozen men and women were running helter-skelter down the street behind her, looking for all the world like a midnight marathon.

She did not stop. She did not slow down. She drove on.

The man's severed arm lay across her chest, speckling the door panel with vivid red blood. She tore its reflexive grip from her throat and threw it out the passenger window, then tried to roll the window up, pushing broken bloody glass out of the gap.

When the camera abruptly cut to a new shot the sun had come up, turning the sky a sickly dawn gray.

Everything was quiet. A couple hours had passed since the chase. A fire truck's silent flasher strobed red across the side of Neva Chandler's house, or at least what was left of it. Black pikes jutted up from shards of siding and electrical conduits.

Robin crept into the backyard and lifted the silver dagger from the weeds, then retreated to her van.

Neva Chandler, the self-proclaimed King of Alabama, said Robin's voice-over, her soft, measured, academic tone incongruous against the chaotic violence that had just taken place. The video faded to black, but she continued to speak. *Almost as old as Alabama itself. My first real kill, my first real fight. There would be dozens more, all over the country, but I'll never forget this one.*

I just keep thinking, she went easy on me. If she was anything like the others that came after, she could have easily killed me. I think she wanted to die. Maybe she wanted one last tussle, one last knockdown-dragout, she wanted to die on her terms, but yeah, she wanted to die.

Well.

If that's the case, I was more than fuckin' happy to oblige.

The camera cut to Robin's point of view as she stood in a car wash, the watery blue dawn peeking through the clouds, spraying the side of the van with a water gun. Blood ran off in pink sheets, coiling and swirling in oily water as it spilled down the drain grate.

"That went well, I think?" she said shakily.

Cut to black.

1

Two Years Later

Robin woke from another nightmare of trees and flame and gulped a deep breath as if she'd surfaced from the ocean. She lay staring at the carpeted ceiling, breathing hard and fast, trembling, trying to mentally scrub off the feeling of being a kid again, the smell of cut grass, the sensation of clutching that wooden hand again—

Condensation dribbled down the curve of the van's rear windows, refracting stony gray light. Her cell phone told her it was a few minutes after ten the morning of October 23. She sat up and lifted a camcorder from its customary place in a tub lined with soft black foam, then wriggled out of her sleeping bag and dug through a tub full of rolled clothes.

The smell of burning bark still floated among the dust, as if the smoke had permeated her skin and hair. She wore nothing but a pair of gray panties and even inside the van, warmed by her farts and body heat all night, the air was graveyard-clammy, so she knew the late autumn morning outside would require something a little more substantial than usual.

Damn Georgia humidity, she thought, pulling on a pair of jeans and a light jacket over a band T-shirt. *Makes the summers hotter and the winters colder.*

The entire back half of the van was lined with rails, shelves, and wire frames in which nested dozens of small plastic bins containing all manner of things:

- packets of trail mix
- electronics parts still in their blister packs
- condiment packets from just about every restaurant under the sun
- barbers' clippers
- toiletries and shaving razors
- USB cables
- name-brand AA, AAA, D, and tiny dime-like watch batteries
- a rats' nest of power adapter cables

One tub held baby-food jars emptied of their contents and refilled with alcohol. Another tub contained handfuls of stacked twigs, another was full of something that might have been ginger root, or perhaps bits of wild mushroom.

A large pegboard occupied one half of a wall directly behind the driver's seat. Several edged weapons had been mounted on pegs and held in place with little clips—a broadsword, a short-sword, a kuhkri knife like a boomerang with a handle, a wicked black tomahawk, a Cold Steel katana painted matte black, the gilded silver dagger from the video.

A fifteen-year-old stuffed animal, a fuzzy blue mosquito peeked over the edge of a tub, his own personal plastic sarcophagus.

Mr. Nosy's proboscis was a lot more limp these days—both of

his glassy wings and four of his six legs had been stitched back on at some point—but he was still whole and had both of his big white Muppet eyes. Robin leaned over and gave her oldest friend a kiss on the nose.

Once she was dressed, she put the camera on a screw-mount in the corner, facing her. There were several mounts around the van, including two on the dash and two clamped to the wing mirrors.

Tucked into the pocket of yesterday's jeans was an orange prescription bottle. She transferred it to today's jeans. Taking a moment to screw the heels of her hands into her eyes again to grind away any remaining sleep, she slapped a bongo beat on her cheeks to redden them, then turned the camera on and started recording.

"Good morning, Internet-Land," she said, her whiskey-and-cigarettes rasp exploding like a hand-grenade in the silence.

She put on her socks and boots as she talked, long green army socks and a pair of comfortable combat boots. "Malus here. You might be able to hear I've got a bit of a sinus thing right now. And I think I might be getting a sore throat. Guess that's what I get for not eating enough oranges?"

She paused, glanced down at the van floor as if to gather her thoughts, then went back to cramming her feet in her boots.

They were like big sneakers, with a padded ankle, an Air Jordan profile, and soles like tractor tires. She'd bought them at a PX in Kentucky earlier that year for almost two hundred dollars, and they had earned the nickname "shit-kickers" before she'd even paid for them. Postmodern punk-rock couture. Her jeans were snug enough the boots fit over them.

"If you've been watching my channel, then you'll know what I've been through. Who I am. My purpose. Well, I'm here. Back where this shit all started." She tied the laces into a big floppy knot, then looked directly into the camera. "Home," she said, as if the word were a hex. "Blackfield." She tucked the laces into her boots and turned the camera to point through the rear window.

Moisture on the windows made a swimmy, crystalline nether-world of the overcast day outside. Crows razzed at each other outside the van, chittering and muttering dark gossip.

She swiveled the camera back around, filling the tiny viewfinder screen with her pale face and the dark circles around her eyes.

Instead of giving her the tough rock-chick look she'd been going for, her wavy Mohawk and shaved scalp made her seem otherworldly and delicate, fuzzy with a week and a half of chestnut stubble.

"*This* girl is going to go find a cup of coffee. Y'all ready for some *BREAKFAST FOOTAGE?*"

Big black crows took flight in every direction when she opened the back door, complaining in their harsh voices. She stepped down out of the van and unscrewed the camera, then grabbed the vinyl messenger bag. As the doors met in the middle with a slam, a blue-and-red logo reconstituted itself: CONLIN PLUMBING.

"I know you ain't here for the food, this isn't a cuisine travelogue channel. But I'm starving." She took some B-roll footage of the area. The van was parked at the edge of a large graveled clearing, and mild white-gold sunlight tried to break through into the day. Several tents had been erected in the grass some thirty yards away, and beyond them was a utilitarian two-story cinderblock building, with doors labeled MEN and WOMEN. From inside came the white-noise rush of hot showers running, and steam poured from PVC pipes jutting out of the roof. Simple graffiti was spray-painted on the walls: BITE MY SHINY LIBERAL ASS. ST. VINCENT. YEE-THO-RAH. Doodles of a monkey taking a shit and a robot on a motorcycle.

To her right, a sprawling split-level cabin lurked in the shadows of the woodline, pumping out the constant smell of cooking food. The back of the restaurant opened up in a large hangar-like seating area with five trestle tables. She scanned the shadows in the back, peering cautiously, looking for a familiar silhouette and staring green eyes.

"The Red Lord will find you," the man had said.

Last time she'd seen what he called the Red Lord was three weeks ago, a jagged figure standing in the tree line on a back road out of Seattle just after dark. Time before that had been two months earlier, a dark shape looming in the corner of her motel room at four in the morning, watching her sleep with luminous eyes.

She sighed with relief.

"Malus inbound. Prepare for impact."

Climbing a hill, she clomped across the front porch, where a smiling gray fireplug of a dog was leashed to the banister.

"Hello there, Mad Max," she said, pointing the camera at him. "How are you today?"

The Australian cattle dog licked his chops and whined.

Miguel's Pizzeria was dimly lit and claustrophobic, with clumps of ropes and climbing gear hanging from the ceiling, and stacks of shoeboxes by the door. A half-dozen booths filled the room, all of them empty.

Robin went to the counter, a glass case containing mementos and historical knickknacks, but nobody was there. A tip jar and a charity jar stood by the register (take a penny, leave a penny), and A4-printed photographs postered the wall behind the counter (take a picture, leave a picture).

The photos were of semi-famous people posing in their climbing accoutrement with the owners of the restaurant, and panoramic shots of the mountains around the valley. She thought she recognized Les Stroud of the TV show *Survivorman* in one picture, and maybe Aron Ralston of *127 Hours* fame in another, his prosthetic arm around Miguel's shoulder.

A Black man came out of the kitchen, wiping his hands on a bar towel. Wearing eye shadow, a silk do-rag covered in purple paisley, and under his apron was an eggplant halter top embroidered with curlicues that looked more suited to a Japanese tea house than a backwoods pizzeria.

Eyeing the camera in her hand, he tucked the towel into his back pocket and leaned invitingly on the counter. "You a bit early for lunch." The nametag on his apron said JOEL.

"That's okay," Robin told him. A glass-fronted mini-cooler stood on a counter behind Joel. She pointed at cans of Monster coffee inside. "I'll have one of those, stick around and wait for lunch time. Cool with you?"

Joel regarded her with a tilted head, rolling a toothpick around and around his mouth. "You look super-familiar. Where do I know you from?" His weary tone and his delicate mannerisms were somehow masculine, yet . . . at the same time stunningly effeminate. He smelled like citrus and coconuts, strong enough to even overpower the burnt-bread smell of pizza crust coming out of the kitchen.

"I have a YouTube channel." She indicated the camera as he took a coffee out of the cooler and put it on the counter. "Called 'MalusDomestica.' Maybe you've seen it?"

Joel rang up the coffee and gave her the total. "No, no, I think . . . I think I mighta went to school with you. Where did you go to school at? You go to high school in Blackfield?"

"Yes, I did." She swiped her debit card and put in her PIN. "Do you have Wi-Fi here?"

"We sure do." Joel printed out her receipt, operating the register in a bored, almost automatic way, not even looking at his hand as he tugged an ink pen out of his apron pocket, clicked the end, and gave it to her. "Password's on the receipt."

"Thanks."

Sliding into a booth, Robin took a Macbook out of her messenger bag and turned it on. She hooked up to the Wi-Fi with the password on the receipt (*pineapplepluspizza*) and went to YouTube, where she signed in and started uploading the week's latest video to the MalusDomestica channel. While it processed, she perused the thumbnails of the videos already posted. Almost three hundred vlogs, most of them no more than twenty minutes long, a few stretching into a half-hour. Her face peeked out from many of them, as if the webpage were a prison for memories, for tiny past versions of herself, as if she continuously shed prior selves and kept them around as trophies. A packrat cicada, dragging around a suitcase full of old skins. She enjoyed browsing through the grid of tiny pictures, each one representing a day, a week, a month of her life—seeing all those chunks of time, those pieces of creative effort, fulfilled her, made her feel accomplished.

Millions of subscribers, millions of viewers' worth of video-monetization ad revenue and MalusDomestica T-shirt sales. Their patronage was what funded her travels, what put food in her mouth, clothes on her back, and gasoline in her Conlin Plumbing van.

She clicked one of the thumbnails, opening a video from a year and a half ago. Past-Robin's hair was dyed pink and she was slightly heavier, pearish, a spattering of blemishes on her cheeks and forehead. Now-Robin clicked to the middle of the video.

A pumpkin sat on a picnic table in a quiet park somewhere. The day was overcast and wind coughed harsh and hollow against the camera's microphone. Past-Robin turned and flung a hatchet with one smooth lunging movement.

The weapon somersaulted thirty feet and planted itself neatly into the rind of the pumpkin with a morbid *splutch*.

"Good one," said Heinrich's velvet voice from off-camera.

Joel slid into the seat on the other side of the table, startling her. His tropical aura of perfume swept in behind him, pouring into the booth.

"Hello," he said.

"Hello, Joel."

"Looked like you could use some company. And by the by, it's not *Johl*, it's . . . *Joe-elle*," he said, poetically pinching the syllable at the end with an A-OK gesture. "You know, like *noel*? Or *motel*? Or *go to hell?*"

She smiled tightly. "Nice to meet you, Joe-elle."

"Likewise."

"Do you always make yourself this comfortable with strangers?"

"Nah, nah—we ain't strangers, hon." Joel turned in his seat, throwing a leg over one knee and his elbow over the back of the bench. "I think I know you."

"Oh yeah?"

"You think ain't nobody gonna recognize you with that Mohawk, that rock-chick look, that extra muscle mass," said Joel, flourishing fingers at her. His fingernails were polished, glittering in the fluorescents. "Which looks really good on you. Very Amazonian. Very punk. I likes. And you got the cheekbones for it." He leaned in close, talking over the Macbook's lid. "Your name is Robin Martine, ain't it?"

She took him in with tightened eyes now, assessing him fully.

"Your mama used to babysit for *my* mama when we was little kids." He sat back again, smiling like a satisfied house cat. "You and me, we used to play together. I know you, yeah, I do. We didn't really ever talk much once we started getting into middle school—"

"My father wasn't too keen on having other kids in the house in addition to—"

"No, honey, he didn't like *Black kids* in the house."

A blush warmed her face, tinged with the heat of anger at the memory of her father. "Well, he's dead now, or so I've heard. So . . ."

"Oh, yeah. I know. Lot of tall tales around this town concerning you and your mama. Some of 'em are even true." Joel took out a pack of cigarettes and packed them against his palm. Some brand she didn't recognize, with a logo in flowery cursive she couldn't read. "You mind if I . . . ?"

She didn't mind. He took one out, but paused, waggling the pack offeringly.

"No." She waved him off. "Tryin' to quit."

Joel cupped the cigarette in one hand with a lighter, lit it and drew on it, then dragged an ashtray over and blew a stream of menthol smoke into the air. "Break a leg," he mused, tapping ashes. "I've quit *many* a time. Not as easy as it looks."

As slow as the Internet was, it would be useless while the video was uploading. Robin studied her keyboard and decided to pay more attention to Joel than the computer.

"So," he said, kicking a toe to an unheard beat, "what does 'Malice Domestic' mean?" He smiled evilly and feigned a shiver. "It sounds so *sinister*." He shivered again.

"*Malus domestica*. Latin scientific name of the common apple tree."

"Apple tree?"

Robin gave a half-wince, half-shrug. "Makes sense if you've watched the videos."

Joel stuck out his bottom lip and nodded as if to say *fair enough*.

She opened the can of coffee with a discreet *snick!* and dug the orange pill bottle out of her pocket, tipping one of the tablets out. Cupping the tablet with her tongue, she swallowed it with a swig of Monster, to be assimilated into the constant swamp-light still humming in the marrow of her bones from yesterday's dose.

Joel took another draw and French-inhaled the smoke up his nose, then blew it back out. "What's it about?" he asked, studying the cherry at the end of the cigarette. "Your YouTube channel."

"It's sort of like . . . a travel journal, I guess."

"Whatcha traveling around doing?"

"Just, ah . . . trying to appreciate America." Robin fumbled for the words. "Roadside attractions, restaurants, that kind of thing."

"Kind of like a homeless Guy Fieri."

Robin chuckled. "Well, I live in my van—but, heh. Yeah, I guess you could say that."

"You are *so* full of shit." He shook his head, the do-rag's ties rustling behind his head like a ponytail. "Look at this thrift-store Lisbeth Salander over here, talking about highways-and-byways. You ain't Jack Kerouac." He leaned in conspiratorially again. "What you *really* up to?"

Robin hesitated, glancing down at the camera. It was still rolling. "Well . . . I hunt witches."

"*Really.*" Joel ashed his cigarette. "*Fascinating.*" He reached over and turned off the camera, surprising her.

"Hey!"

"You need to stop playin'. I assume *huntin'* witches means *killin'* witches, and there ain't no way you're videotapin' *that* shit, cause me and you, we know the truth, but them out there, John Q. Asshole, they don't know shit. They see a video of you shanking somebody, they gonna be all over you. Now, I want to talk to you without this camera here. Backstage, so to speak. Off the record. Cause I can tell you just putting on a show for the people at home. But I want *real* talk." He smiled tightly. "I *know* what you doing. You looking for *them*, ain't you?"

Her breathing had become labored without her realizing it. She felt cornered. "Them who?"

"The ones killed your mama."

"I don't know what you're talking about."

"When it happened, *my* mama lost her shit." Joel squinted in the murk of smoke hovering over the table. "I remember this *vividly*—because she scared the *hell* outta me. This was about . . . sophomore year? Junior year, of high school? She was out of her mind freaked out about it. Shaking, wide-eyed, locking-all-the-windows freaked. Like she thought the sky was falling, like she was afraid the Devil himself was gonna get in the house.

"Asked me all kinds of weird-ass questions about this and that—wanted to know what kind of person Annie was, what kinds of things she did. Why she had a speech impediment, why her tongue was like that. Did she hurt animals, did she do anything to *me* when me and Fish was little . . ."

"She never would have." Robin stiffened. "Mom wasn't like that—"

"Oh, I know." Joel traced imaginary hearts on the table with a fingertip. "Annie was a good woman. A good-hearted woman.

Weird, maybe, but good. I told my mama that. I still remember the way she cooked her bacon when me and Fish came over in the mornings. I cook mine the same way." He illuminated each point with his hands, forming invisible shapes in the air, snapping and wagging invisible bacon. "Crispy, but still floppy. Fatty but not gristly."

Trying to visualize this, eating bacon for breakfast with her mother in their little kitchen, Robin saw two other little faces sitting at the table. Two quiet children, wide-eyed

(*my name is fisher and his name is johl but mama calls him jo-elle*)

and spooked like baby owls. The knot inside her loosened, and her jaw tipped open in surprise. "I *do* remember you."

"Oh yeah?"

"It was the bacon that made me remember."

Joel smiled and made a *Hallelujah!* raise-the-roof motion with his hands. "Ain't nothing in this world good bacon can't make better."

"They made me forget a lot. The shrinks the state made me talk to. They made—or maybe *let*—me think I was crazy, and they brainwashed all the witch stuff out of me. Or tried to, anyway."

Joel glanced toward the kitchen—or perhaps it was the clock—and back at her, giving the scruff-headed woman-in-black an assessing look. Finally, he said in a tentative way, "There was a rumor going around you said witches had something to do with it. I believed it then, and I believe it now."

"Yeah. I told people. But they didn't believe me. That's why I had to talk to the shrinks. They thought I had PTSD or something. Thought losing my mother drove me crazy."

"You ain't found 'em, have you? That's what you been doing ever since the shrinks let you out. You been looking for them witch bitches."

She squinted out the window at the noonday sun.

Joel put both feet flat on the floor and stubbed out his cigarette, leaning on his elbows. He clasped his hands together and spoke around them. "So you for *real*, then. You doing this shit for real. How do you make YouTube videos about this shit? Ain't this incriminating evidence?"

Robin's fingernails dug into her palms. "You ever heard of Slender-Man? Skinny dude with no face, wears a black suit and a red tie, got long arms, creeps people out?"

"Can't say I have."

She did a search on YouTube for "Slender-Man" and turned the Macbook around so Joel could see it. "Half a dozen YouTube channels devoted to this paranormal being Slender-Man. Each one chronicles a different group of people trying to figure out the mystery surrounding him . . . they're all set up as if the events happening in the videos are real. But, of course, everybody knows they aren't—wink-wink. They're each a scripted and acted horror series made to look real. Like, you remember *The Blair Witch Project*? How it was designed and shot to look like somebody found it on a camera in the woods, basically started the found-footage genre?"

Joel nodded. "Yeah. And you doing something like that, but theirs is fake and yours is actually real? But you make it *look* like it's as fake as theirs. Ah ha-ha. Reverse *reverse* psychology."

"Yes."

Another man came out of the kitchen. His hair was going gray and his drawn face was a hash of wrinkles, but Robin recognized Miguel from the photograph behind the register. "Hey," he called. "We got to get ready for lunch."

"Untwist them panties, hero," said Joel, grabbing at the air in a *zip-it* motion. "I'm just doing some catching up."

"Who's your friend?" asked Miguel.

"Her mama used to babysit me and Fish when we was kids." Joel coughed into his fist and took a bottle of hand sanitizer out of his apron pocket, squirting it into his palms and wringing his hands. "Robin Martine."

Miguel's brain seemed to lag like a busy computer program and then he subtly crumpled. "Oh." An awkward silence lingered between them, and then one corner of his bushy mustache ticked up in a wistful half-smile. "I remember hearing about, uhh . . ." His belly bobbed with one hesitant breath. "I'm sorry about your mother."

Robin tried her best to be gracious, but didn't know what to say, so she echoed his expression and dipped her head appreciatively.

"Real big shame, kid. I didn't really know her," he added, "but I heard she was a good person."

"She was." Robin's hand found its way around the can of coffee, and she drummed soft fingers against the aluminum. The two men watched her with expectant eyes, the quiet pause only scored by the sound of furious washing and banging in the kitchen.

Robin looked down at the Monster can. "Five years ago. Decided this year I would come back to town and visit her. This year I've decided I feel like I can finally . . . finally push through the dark and say the things I need to say to her. I guess."

"Well," said Miguel. "Welcome back, Kotter. Mi casa es su casa."

Joel followed him back into the kitchen. "What he said."

2

Their new home cut an impressively Gothic silhouette against the stark white afternoon sky. The house was a two-story Queen Anne Victorian, an antique dollhouse painted the muted blue of a rain cloud. A wraparound porch encircled the front, and the whole thing was trimmed in white Eastlake gingerbread.

In places here and there, it was streaked with black like mascara tears, as if the house had been weeping soot from its seams. "What did I tell you?" asked Leon. He wore a blue thrift-store two-piece and a cranberry tie from Meijer. "Cool, right?"

Wayne unbuckled his seat belt and leaned up, pushing his glasses up with a knuckle. The boy gazed up through the U-Haul's windshield at their new base of operations.

"Looks like the house from *The Amityville Horror* or something," he said, and looked out the side window.

The neighborhood stretched out to their right, a mile and a half of red-brick Brady Bunch ranch houses, double-wide trailers with toys peppered across their lawns, white shepherd-cottages, a few A-frame cabins lurking deep in the trees. Across the road from 1168 was a small trailer park, eight or nine mobile homes marching in rigid lockstep toward a distant tree line. Since his window was rolled halfway down, Wayne could hear the faraway mewling-seagull-cry of children playing.

Coins of light reflected off the lenses of his glasses. A feeling made him look back toward 1168, as if he'd almost been caught off-guard. Empty sashed windows peered down like eyes, darkness pressing against their panes from inside, as if the house were packed to the brim with shadows.

A grin crept across his face. "It's *awesome*."

Leon beamed.

They got out of the box truck and clomped up the front steps. The porch was wider than he expected, four lunging steps across— wide enough to ride his bicycle up and down the length of the porch if he wanted to. A swing was chained to the ceiling where the porch angled around the corner.

A cat stood on the porch, a slender gray shadow with black feet and honey eyes.

Wayne smiled. "Hi, kitty-cat."

"You the welcome wagon?" asked his father.

The cat muttered a hoarse *miaow* and trotted away, re-stationing itself down by the swing at the end of the porch.

"Guess not." Leon waggled his finger for emphasis. "Remind me to get some cat food when I pop into town."

"You mean we can have a cat?"

"I mean we can feed the welcome wagon." A chuckle. "Let's not put the cat before the horse."

"That doesn't make any sense."

"It's a dad joke. It doesn't have to make sense."

Click. The portentous sound of his father unlocking the front door made him twitch. "Check it out, it even locks with an old-timey key," said Leon, showing Wayne the long, thin skeleton key. He pushed the door open with his fingertips.

Disappointingly, it didn't creak open in that spooky, melodramatic way, but the doorknob did bump loudly against the opposite wall. Leon winced and stepped inside, checking behind the door for damage. Wayne went in behind him and stood there, turning in a slow circle, taking it all in. The thick, astringent smell of fresh paint cloyed the air. The front hallway was interminably tall—the ceiling seemed fifteen feet high—but it felt cramped, with only enough room for maybe three men to walk abreast.

To his right, a doorless archway led into a small den. To his left, a stairway climbed to the second floor and a dark bathroom yawned at the foot of the stairs, dim daylight glinting from the teeth of its chrome fixtures. Dead ahead, the foyer hallway went on past a closet door and opened into the kitchen, the floor turning into turtle-shell linoleum.

An intricate red carpet runner had been laid down by the real estate agent, new and clean. Regardless, every shuffling footfall, every little noise they made, and every word they spoke reverberated in short, hollow echoes throughout the house.

"Hello?" called Leon.

For a terrifying second, Wayne almost expected to hear an answer from upstairs. He *loved* it. "Do you think it's haunted?"

Leon tucked his hands in his pockets. "Who knows?"

The den was a cozy space, unfurnished as of yet with anything other than empty bookshelves and a cushioned reading nook in the front window. The walls were painted the same rainy blue as the outside. A modest fireplace occupied one wall, dark and empty.

"Need to see if one of our neighbors might be able to give us a hand with the sofa."

"I can help you."

"I don't know, it's big. Don't want to see you get hurt. We barely got it out of the apartment."

They passed into the kitchen, where the walls had been wall-papered in yellow sunflowers that probably should have looked cheery, but were more forlorn and drab than anything else. Fridge was a new side-by-side slab of black humming efficiently in the corner, and the countertops were dark marble over dark cherry-wood cabinets.

Wayne decided the kitchen would not be his favorite room. Leon went around to all the windows, parting the curtains and letting sunlight in. Dust drifted in the soft white beams.

The pantry was surprisingly large, a narrow ten-foot space lined with three tiers of shelving. He started to climb them to see what was on the top shelf, but his father shut him down with a hand on his shoulder. "Nope. Come on, let's go look at the bedrooms."

The stairs were steep and creaked as if they were made of popsicle sticks, groaning and cracking and thumping.

1168's second story seemed somehow more spacious than the first. As soon as they stepped up onto the upper landing, a narrow T-shaped hallway led some twenty or thirty feet toward a window at the bottom of the T, flanked by a pair of doors. The right one opened onto the master bedroom, unfurnished, with a walk-in closet that stank of mothballs. The left went into a bathroom, with a claw-foot bathtub and a porcelain sink.

The bathroom's wainscoting was done in rose-pink and teal tiles, but halfway up the walls and ceiling became painted drywall. Leon touched it. "I just realized—this is gonna be hard to keep mildew out of. I am *diggin'* this pink, though."

Wayne screwed up his face. A big hoop of metal was bracketed to the ceiling, and a diaphanous plastic curtain hung into the tub. "What kind of bathtub has *feet?*"

Back in the hallway, he stood dejectedly with his hands in his pockets. "Where's *my* bedroom?"

"Ah." Leon searched the hallway, even looking out the window and peering into the master suite again. "Thought I forgot something. I guess you'll have to sleep in the garage, chief."

Wayne's heart sank. "You're full of crap."

His father rubbed his goatee, then thrust a finger into the air and hustled away as if he'd suddenly remembered something. "One last place we haven't checked. There's a closet out here on the landing you can sleep in, if you can fit."

"A *closet?*"

"Yeah, like Harry Potter."

"Harry Potter lived under the *stairs.*" Wayne followed him in a daze back out to the end of the landing, then traced the banister down to a window that cast out onto the back of the house. From here, he could see a rickety tool shed and a huge backyard.

Next to the window was a door, which Leon opened to reveal a set of stairs leading up into soft sunlight and around a spiral, climbing out of sight.

Leon shrugged. "After you."

Wayne ascended them, hitching his knees high, almost clambering up them on all fours. The stairs spiraled once and a half, opening onto a small room inside a dome of windows that made him think of the belfry in a church steeple. The room wasn't a perfect circle but an octagon, with eight walls.

The ceiling was just high enough his father didn't have to stoop, but he stood there with his fingertips pressed against it as if he were trying to hold it up.

"It's called a *cupola,*" said Leon. "What you think?"

The "cupola" seemed small, but as Wayne went from window to window assessing the view, the room proved to be larger than he initially gave it credit for. Plenty of room for his bed, and each of the four windows stood atop a small nook bench that folded open to reveal storage space. He climbed onto one of them to look out the window.

Across the street, a long gravel drive snaked between a trailer park and a series of cottages, climbing a hill to a building that looked like pictures he'd seen of the Alamo. Mud-pink walls topped with Gothic wrought-iron teeth, brown clay roofing tiles. A man drove a riding lawn mower up the hill out front, cropping dull green grass.

"I like it," said Wayne. To the south, he could see the tops of buildings in distant Blackfield, rising over the trees behind the house.

"Then welcome to your new Batcave, Master Wayne."

"The Batcave is underground."

Leon continued his Atlas impression, hands against the ceiling. "Work with me, here. I'm old and out of touch."

"Batman's older than *you* are."

"Keep it up and I'll make you sleep in the garage anyway!"

• • •

As the afternoon wore on, Wayne and his father managed to get most of the boxes and furniture into the house, with the exclusion of the sofa and dining-room table. The most troublesome items by far were Wayne's mattress and box spring, which Leon could handle well enough by himself (with Wayne pushing helpfully from behind) until they got into the spiral stairway to the cupola. That became an arduous trial of swearing, sweating, and banging around in the stuffy space that left them flustered and irritated with each other.

To get the dining-room table in, they carried the table up onto the front porch, then turned it on end like a giant coin and rolled it through the house. Leon ushered Wayne in ahead of the table, confusing him at first, but when his father started humming the *Indiana Jones* theme and pretending the table was the boulder from *Raiders of the Lost Ark,* he couldn't help but run away from it in slow motion.

As they worked, the gray cat maintained its distance, sitting on the porch railing down by the swing, watching them bustle boxes into the house. A curious intelligence glimmered in the animal's brilliant honey eyes, as if it were sizing them up.

"You could help, you know," said Leon.

The cat answered him with a raspy chirp.

Their steel-blue Subaru already sat in the gravel driveway, in front of the U-Haul; Leon had brought it down before the move. They took a break to run to town in the car for hamburgers at Wendy's, and they came back to failing light as the evening came over the trees to the east.

"Hate to bug anybody this late. These rednecks givin' me weird looks," said Leon, unlocking and opening the U-Haul. "But I'd really like to get this truck back as soon as possible. Guess we'll finish tomorrow afternoon."

"Hey," said a husky voice behind them.

A chubby white kid with brush-cut hair was making his way up the driveway, his hands buried in his hoodie's pockets. He seemed to be about Wayne's age, if several inches taller. Wayne thought he looked like Pugsley Addams gone mainstream, or maybe the older brother from *Home Alone*.

"Hey," said Leon.

As if this were the cat's cue to vamoose, it leapt off the railing and trotted across the yard toward the trailer park on the other side of the highway.

Pugsley's voice was the high-pitched rasp of a boy accustomed to shouting. "You guys movin' in?"

"Yep."

"Cool."

A weird silence settled over them. "Nice to meet you," Leon offered, smiling. "Anything we can help you with?"

Pugsley seemed to snap out of a trance. "Oh! I, uhh, wanted to say hi, and . . . maybe see if you needed any help. But it looks like you're pretty much finished." He stepped forward and held out a stubby pink hand. "I'm Pete." Pointing across the street at the trailer park, he added, "Pete Maynard. I live over there. With my mom. I go to school over in Blackfield. Fifth grade."

Leon visibly relaxed, shaking the offered hand. "Nice to meet you, Pete. Leon Parkin. This here's my son Wayne."

Pugsley-Pete shook Wayne's hand and said to his father, "Welcome to Slade."

Leon stuck his hands in his pockets. "Well. I reckon since we got you here, you can help if you want."

3

With much grunting and swearing, the three of them got the sofa down out of the U-Haul, up the front stairs, and into the den. To get it out of the foyer and through the den door, they had to turn it sideways and angle the armrests around the doorframe. Wayne mashed a finger and Leon got pinned against the wall, but they finally managed it.

Once they'd gotten it into the room, screwed the feet back onto the bottom of it, and pushed it against the back wall, the boys sat on it to rest. "So what are you guys doin' out here?" asked Pete, watching Wayne buff his glasses with his shirt. "Don't think I know anybody that dresses up to go to work."

Leon had taken off his jacket and loosened his tie. "I took a teaching position at Blackfield High School."

"Yeah?"

"Gonna teach literature."

"Cool. Maybe I'll be in your class one day. I like to read."

"Maybe. That's good. More kids your age should read. Hey, you had dinner?" Leon took the tie off. "I got us ice cream for when we got done with everything."

"No," said Pete, "but I don't eat dinner most days."

Wayne's head tilted. "Why not?"

"Just . . . not really hungry. My mom says I eat like a bird."

He couldn't imagine that. "Birds eat their own body weight in food every day. That's what *I* heard, anyway." Pete's hoodie was straining at the sides under his love handles. The slope-shouldered boy was taller than the short, gangly Wayne by several inches and outweighed him by a dozen pounds.

The ice began to settle again.

Wayne broke it. "You like *Call of Duty?*"

Pete rubbed his forehead. "I don't know. Guess it depends on which one you're talkin' about. Only got the first one for the Xbox. I haven't, uhh—haven't really played any of the new ones."

"Sounds like you guys have your evening figured out," said Leon, standing up. "Pete, does your mom know you're over here?"

"*Oh* yeah. Yeah—she's cool."

Leon rolled up his tie like a giant tongue, giving Pete the teacher stink-eye. "That sounds suspiciously like a *no.*"

"She knows I came over here. She don't really care when I come back, as long as she knows where I went and I stay out of trouble." Pete sounded noncommittal, lax. Wayne got the feeling he was accustomed to being autonomous. "And I'm not like my dad. I stay out of trouble." He jerked up straight all of a sudden and put up his hands as if to ward off a blow. "Oh, I can head out of here if you guys—"

"Oh *no*, no-no, you're *fine*, man." Leon picked up his suit jacket and beat the dust out of it, laying it over his arm like a sommelier with a towel. "You look like a good kid to me. And Wayne needs friends. He's the FNG. The F-in' New Guy, remember?"

Pete smirked, but Wayne gave his father the side-eye.

"So yeah, hell. Hang out, by all means, this creepy-ass house is gonna need some cheerin' up anyway. Me and him, we can't fill it up all by ourselves. We're from Chicago, we're not used to this kind of quiet, you know?"

"Okay," said Pete, in obvious gratitude.

Leon looked pointedly at Wayne. "Why don't you head upstairs and start on putting your clothes up and make your bed? When you get done, feel free to play video games to your heart's content. Once you start school and start getting homework, your down-time is gonna be at a real premium."

Wayne feigned belligerence. "Do I gotta?"

"How are you gonna sleep in a bed if you ain't made it? At least make the bed. We'll worry about unpacking when that's out of the way."

The two boys got up and left, creaking and crackling up the stairs to the second landing. They sounded like two colonial Red-coats marching across bubble wrap. "I can hook up the TV and Play-Station while you make your bed and stuff, if you want," offered Pete.

"You got a deal."

Wayne led his new friend across the landing. When he opened the closet door to reveal the steep second set of stairs, Pete seemed impressed, if confused. "Wait, your dad's got you in the tower?"

"Yeah. It's the only other bedroom in the house. If you can call it a bedroom." They started up the almost ladderlike stairs. "Why? What's wrong with it?"

"*Nothin'*, man, nothin'. I think it's freakin' awesome. I'm sur-prised, is all."

With the dressers and the bed in it, the cupola was a lot less spacious. Wayne and Pete had just enough room to sit on the floor between the bed and the television, a modest flatscreen set up on one of the windowsills. There weren't any power outlets in the cupola, so his father had bought a dropcord on their dinner trip and run it up from an outlet on the landing. The cord draped down the stairs for now, but they'd use nails to pin it out of the way later.

A lamp was plugged into it. Wayne turned it on.

To get them out of the way, he had already pinned up his posters on the narrow strips of wall between each of the cupola's windows.

One of them was a movie poster for a *Friday the 13th* movie, with a full-body shot of the hockey-masked Jason Voorhees coming at you with a machete. Another depicted the cast of the TV show *The Walking Dead,* with the character Rick standing on top of a school bus aiming his giant revolver. Romero's original black-and-white *Night of the Living Dead.* The popular zombie game *Left 4 Dead 2.*

The mattress was naked and had four cardboard boxes on it. Wayne opened a box and found it full of clothes. The next one had the video games in it: a PlayStation 3, a tangle of wires, and a handful of disc cases. "Here we are."

Pete carried the box over next to the TV and went to work on untangling the adapter and video cords. Wayne opened another box to find his bedclothes.

He was on his hands and knees trying to pull the fitted sheet over a mattress-corner when something occurred to him. "Hey," he said over his shoulder. "Uhm. Do you know if this house is . . . Do you know if it's haunted?"

Pete stared at Wayne as if he hadn't said anything. His eyes were flat in the arcane honey-glow of the lamp, but he slowly reached up and rubbed his cheek as though he had a toothache. The gesture seemed self-comforting, as if he were petting his face. Took him a full seven seconds to answer. "I don't know. Never been in here. But some people say it is."

"Why?"

"Well." Pete got to his feet and pulled the TV cart out, examining the connection jacks on the back. "You really want me to tell you?"

Wayne's curiosity was a bonfire, straining for secrets. "Are you serious? Of course I want you to tell me." He turned over and flopped down on his butt at the edge of the bed, the sheets forgotten. "Let me guess—what is it, there's an Indian burial ground under the house? 'They never moved the bodies! *They never moved the bodies!*'"

"No, there's—"

"A serial killer used to live here?" The more he talked, the more animated he became. He was clenching his fists in anticipation. "And he buried his victims in the basement?" Made him wonder if they even *had* a basement, and what it looked like. He made a mental note to go check in the morning.

"No, dude, somebody *died* in this house."

"Is that all? Man, *tch* . . . people die in houses all the time. Somebody died in the apartment next to ours back in Chicago. If people dying in a place made it haunted, nobody would be able to go into a hospital because of all the ghosts."

Pete grinned a creepy grin. "Why do you think hospitals freak people out so much?"

Wayne deadpanned at him and went back to making his bed.

"Anyway, this one, people say she was a witch."

"A *witch*." Wayne was incredulous. "You're *shitting* me."

Both boys looked down the stairwell to listen for Mr. Parkin, then Pete continued. "No shittin'." He sat down on one of the thin-cushioned windowsill seats. "The cops and the newspaper said it was an accident at the time, but I hear she was pushed down the stairs by her husband."

"A witch with a husband?"

Pete shrugged.

Wayne made a face. "I didn't even know witches could *have* husbands. Anyway, maybe it *was* an accident. Maybe he didn't mean to push her. I can't *believe* Dad didn't tell me about this."

"I don't know," said Pete, going back to untangling the controller cables. "My mom says he used to beat her and her daughter."

"So what happened to the husband?"

"I heard he died a few months later in prison."

"What killed him?"

"Nobody knows. I heard it looked like tubber—ta-bulkyer—"

"Tuberculosis?" Wayne asked helpfully.

"Yeah, that. But they never could find anything. What's this?" Pete held up the tangle of cords so he could see underneath them. He laid the tangle down on the floor and reached into the box, lifting out a Nike shoebox. Wayne abandoned what he was doing and politely took the shoebox, putting it on the bed.

"It's, ahh . . . just some old stuff."

Inside was a pile of photographs, a bottle of perfume, a gold ring with a simple ball-chain through it, the kind of necklace that usually has dog tags on it. Wayne took out the ring and reverently lowered the chain around his neck, letting the wedding band rest on his chest.

"Nice ring, Mr. Frodo."

Wayne looked up. "It was my mom's." He picked up the photographs and shuffled through them with delicate hands.

The photos depicted separate events and locations—one seemed to be a very young Wayne celebrating a birthday in a dark kitchen, everything washed out by camera-flash, his face underlit by the feverish glow of a birthday cake; another was Wayne with his father and a pretty, small-framed Asian woman. She was in all of the photographs, always smiling, always touching, embracing, or pressing against her son.

Presently Pete came out of the funk and went back to pulling at the knot of cables. "What happened, if you don't mind me asking?"

"She died a couple years ago. In Chicago. Cancer. Throat cancer, I think? Lung cancer? But it wasn't really the cancer did it. Dad said, like, 'complications' or something. I don't really know what that means. Something got infected." Wayne lifted the ring to his eye as if it were a monocle and gazed through it, the gold clicking against his right eyeglasses lens. "A couple of months ago, Dad was like 'man eff this shit, we need to get out of here, there's too many memories here, we need a change of scenery,' so he got a job down here and we packed up and left."

"Damn, dude. I'm sorry."

The eye inside the ring twitched toward Pete. Suddenly the soft brown eye seemed a decade older. "When I miss her, I like to look through the ring like it's a peephole in a door. I pretend if I look through it I can see into a—uhh . . ."

"Another time? World? *Dimension?*"

A weird door twelve feet up the lunchroom wall?

"Another world, yeah." Wayne breathed on the ring, buffing a smudge with his shirt. Emotion etched a sudden sour knot at the base of his skull. "Feel like I can see into another world where she's still alive. You know, like Alice in Wonderland, lookin' through the lockin'-glass."

Pete seemed as if he were about to say something, but cut himself off before it could get out of him. Wayne thought he knew what he was about to say. He had thought it himself before, hundreds of times. *What if you look through that thing one day and she actually* is *there?* he thought, peering at his tiny reflection in the gold gleam of the ring. *What* then, *wise guy?*

A glint of vivid red traced across the curve of the ring between his fingers.

Three hundred and six.

Glancing over his shoulder, Wayne expected to see his father's cranberry Meijer tie, but nobody stood behind him.

"What was that about?" asked Pete.

"Hmm?" Wayne blinked, twisting to look down the stairwell. "Thought I saw—thought I saw something."

Tense silence stretched out between them for a brief moment, and then Pete screwed up his face. "Don't even go there, man," he said, and went back to digging through the boxes, gingerly this time, as if afraid to move too quickly in the dusty solitude, and with a few hesitant glances up at the other boy.

4

Robin awoke to birdsong tittering through the windows of her tiny cupola bedroom. The first breezes of June came in through the open screen. Outside, green trees flashed the pale undersides of their leaves as if they were waving dollar bills.

A blue creature lay crumpled in a heap of legs at the foot of her bed. The little girl dragged the stuffed animal over. "Look, Mr. Nosy," she squealed, "it's the first day of summer vacation!"

Mr. Nosy was a felt mosquito the approximate size and style of a Muppet, with big white ping-pong-ball eyes. At the back of his open mouth was a sort of voice box, and when you pinched one of his feet he whined like a kazoo. In her tiny hands, he came alive. She sat him up very carefully on top of the quilt and wriggled out of her nightshirt, putting on a sundress and a pair of sandals. Cradling the puppet, she clomped down the twisting stairway and opened the door at the bottom.

The smell of bacon and biscuits rolled over her in a warm wave.

Robin danced along the second floor landing and down a flight of switchback stairs to the foyer, skipping into the kitchen. Her mother sat at the kitchen table, reading a newspaper and sipping a cup of coffee. Robin arranged her pet mosquito on the counter in front of the bread box and hopped into her chair.

She stared at the back of the newspaper and tried to read it again, but as always in these dreams, it was just a grid of black squiggles.

"Goo morvig," said her mother.

"Good morning, Mama."

Annabelle Martine—Mama to Robin, Annie to everybody else—talked as if she had a mouthful of water. She had a speech impediment that made her difficult to interpret, but Robin had grown up with it and found her as easy to understand as anybody else.

Annie smiled, scooping bacon and eggs onto her daughter's plate. "Did you sleep good?"

"Yep."

"Your birthday is at the end of the month." Annie cut a biscuit open and knifed grape jam into it. "Have you decided what you want yet?"

"No. What about a book?" asked Robin. "I like books."

"Books are the best. Even better than toys and video games, I think. Definitely better than video games."

"I want a Harry Potter book."

Annie sneered in mock disgust. "*Harry Potter?* What do you want to read about Harry Potter for?"

"Harry Potter does magic." Robin rolled her eyes. "I want to read about magic. And swords and kings and dragons and wizards." She waved her fork around as if it were a wand, touching her eggs, her orange juice, the table. "I love wizards. I wish I could do magic."

As she always did when her daughter spoke of magic, Annie smiled bitterly, as if the word dredged some long ago slight from the water under the bridge. "No, you don't, honey."

Tick. Tick. Tick. The clock on the kitchen wall chiseled away at the morning. The short hand and the long hand were racing each other around the dial as though reality were in fast forward. The numbers were unintelligible sigils.

Annie had finished her coffee by the time she spoke up again, cutting through the droning of the lawn mower. "Hurry up and finish, and we'll go down to the bookstore in town. You can pick something out."

After breakfast, they went out the back door, marching down the little wooden stoop. Their backyard was huge, occupied by a stunted oak tree and a lonely gray shed fringed with ragged weeds. A board swing twisted and wobbled in the breeze. In the distance, out by the tree line, Robin's father, Jason Martine, bumped and roared along on his gas-stinking Briggs & Stratton.

"We'll go tell Jason we're going to town," said Annie, referring to Daddy by the secret identity all superhero Daddies had. She started off across the grass. "Don't want him to come in and find us gone without telling him where we went."

You know how he can get.

The backyard was so big. Why was it so big? Seemed like the farther they walked, the bigger it got. The sun bounced up off the dry, prickly grass with a hard, walloping heat, and the tufts of lawn got taller and thicker until they were wading through a thicket of crabgrass, clover, and wild onions.

"Hold on, Mama," Robin said, stopping to search the ground, "I want to find a four-leaf clover."

Annie stopped, took a knee, and swept her hand like a beachcomber with a metal detector. Easy as pie, she plucked a lucky four-leaf and held it up for her daughter to count the leaves. Never failed to amaze Robin that while she could wander the yard for hours stooped over like an old woman and never see a single one, her mother never seemed to have any trouble finding them. "You're so lucky. But you're not as lucky as me." She inserted the clover's stem behind Robin's ear so it flowered against her temple like a hibiscus in a hula girl's hair. "You're not as lucky as *me*, because I have *you*." Annie grinned. Instead of their usual eggshell white, her teeth were made of wood, brown and swirly dark. "I'm the luckiest mommy in the world, you know that?"

Robin stared at her mother in horror. "Why are your teeth made of wood, Mama?"

"What?" Annie threw her head back and laughed. "You're so silly. Such a silly-billy."

Their feet plowed across the interminable lawn, breaking up clumps of mulched grass with a rhythmic swishing. Robin squinted into the heat. Beyond an invisible motion swirling in the air, she could still see her father on his red-and-black-and-green riding mower.

Robin blinked, and her father and his lawn mower were gone. Now there was something else crouched in the tall grass, a gargantuan shape she'd never seen in the sunlight before. And now that solar rays beat down and fully illuminated the creature, she felt both terror at its appearance and a sort of giddiness at its ludicrous proportions. Wind whipped at the coarse, yarn-like hair, it was a *mountain* of red-and-green-and-black hair, prone in the tall grass like a lion stalking its prey. Looked like a mascot costume abandoned to the elements, a baseball jester infested with rot and mold. It reached out slowly, so slowly, with one horrible claw and swept aside the green grains to get a better look at her.

This may have been a dream, but that didn't stop the terror from creeping like ivy into the folds of her brain.

"M-Mama," Robin finally managed to stammer.

"The Red Lord," said Annie. "He's going to find you."

That man at Neva Chandler's house in Alabama, he'd said the same thing. *The Red Lord. He's going to find you. You're going to die.*

Had the witch cursed her?

For some reason Annie seemed to be slowing. Not all at once but gradually as they walked, as if each step were a centimeter shorter than the last. The clipped grass piled around their toes like frozen water at the bow of an icebreaker ship.

"Who is he?" asked Robin.

"He's always been there, ever since the door was opened. Watching. Waiting. A vigilant beast."

Her mother seemed to be the only one succumbing to it, though, like a peat bog, because soon Dear Mama was up to her ankles in the turf. Green ripples bobbed outward from her toes like pond scum, lapping over her instep. "Don't want him to come in and find us gone without telling him where we went," she said, the grass welling around her shins.

"Mama?"

Now Annie was positively forging against the grass; she reached with every step, leaning forward, steaming across the yard.

Looking the way they came, Robin hugged Mr. Nosy against her chest. She wiped her hair out of her eyes. The house was a brick of blue clapboard behind them, as far away as Christmas, the swingin'-tree and woodshed tiny and model-like as if they'd been made of popsicle sticks and reindeer moss.

The lawn had swallowed Annie up to the knees. Her fists pistoned in and out like a boxer working a belly, as if she were walking in treacle. "He'll find you. Wherever you are. I'm so sorry." Her mother was walking so slowly now Robin could overtake her.

Polished cedar. Annie's eyes were made of wood. The sclera were a pale alabaster with streaks of pink, and ragged black knotholes gaped where her irises and pupils should have been. Goatish eyes. "Don't want him to come in and find us."

"What do you mean?" asked Robin, standing in front of her mama, clutching Mr. Nosy. Annie was no longer driving forward, but halted mid-stride. Her feet were rooted in the earth as firmly as any fencepost and her arms were at kung-fu angles, one punched forward and the other's elbow jutting out behind her. She was a statue locked in an action pose.

"What do you mean?" Robin repeated, her voice climbing. Now she was shrieking. "What do you mean? *Goddammit why don't you ever tell me what you mean?*"

She reached out and slapped her mother's motionless face with a six-year-old's hand.

Annie's cheek came loose like a deflated blister, a sag of translucent candle-skin, and the wind flaked a bit of it away, revealing dark brown underneath. Then more came away, and Annie Martine's face began to peel as easy as old paint, spiraling like burning paper into the breeze. Below the flaking skin was bark, smooth black-brown bark, studded with jagged wooden teeth. A lovely wooden skull lurked behind that ivory Annie mask, intricately carved, beautiful, horrifying.

The hulking red thing, still crawling in the saw grass, laughed. *Grrrrruhuhuhuhuh.*

Robin's lungs refused to inflate. Stepping back, she watched as the outermost layer of her mother deteriorated inch by inch, crumbling off and blowing away.

Birch-scrolls drooped from her shoulders, breaking off at the elbow; waxy green leaves spotted with worm-rust sprouted from her hair, and uncurled from her knuckles and the tips of her fingers. Annie's arms and wrists lengthened, reaching out in front of her and over her head, and her legs thickened, elongated, becoming like those of an elephant, covered in cobbly flesh. The terrible sound of rending muscle-fibers whispered underneath Annie's bark as she stretched, reaching for the sky, and then she was a tree, she was a goddamn *tree* towering over her daughter, an apple tree, *Malus domestica,* her skull-carving face buried in her trunk so only her sightless eyes and maniacal Jolly Roger grin were visible.

She had become a Titan's arm, reaching up from the crust and grass, clutching a handful of leaves. Her eyes drooped like empty sleeves, the left one combining with her mouth to make a gaping, C-shaped knothole.

Then the tree that had been Annie burst into flames, all that foliage going up in a bonfire *WHOOSH* of hot light, and the mama-thing inside screamed in pain and terror, and

Little Robin screamed,

and

old women cackled, ceaselessly echoing back on themselves, and—

• • •

Knuckles banged on the side of Robin's van, waking her up with a start.

Fucking nightmare again. Fourth time since crossing the Missis-sippi. Enough, already. She squirmed out of her sleeping bag and opened the door.

Joel stood outside, sidelit by the pizzeria's security lights. He squinted into her flashlight beam. "Hey. Thought that would be you, out here in this sketch-ass van." He had put on a light wind-breaker, his hands tucked deep into the jacket's pockets. "Got any free candy?"

"No, 'fraid not."

"Damn." Joel's eyes seemed to focus more fully on her face. "Hey, you all right? You look like you seen a ghost."

"Maybe." Robin massaged her eye sockets. "No, it's—I had a nightmare. Same one every time. Been happenin' a lot lately."

Joel's face grew softer. She could tell he wanted to pursue that line of thought, to comfort her, but there was an air-cushion, like underneath an air-hockey puck, that the intervening years had pressed between the two of them. They had been close friends a long time ago, but that was a long time ago. In another era. "Uhhm," he began, uncertainly, "I wanted to come tell you, my brother Fish, he owns a comic shop in town? And he does this movie-night thing every Friday. He gonna start it up in about—" He checked his cell phone. "—twenty minutes. You know, if you want to get out of that sketch-ass van for a little while."

"I don't know. I—"

"Miguel usually lets me bring over a bunch of pizza from the shop. Employee discount."

"Jesus, why you ain't say that to begin with?" she asked, flicking on the dome light so she could find her clothes. The sriracha-pineapple-pepperoni slice she'd had for lunch had been amazing, and she was more than ready for Round Two.

"What in the *hell*?" asked Joel, peering into the back of the van with saucer eyes. He reached in and took the broadsword down from its clamp on the wall and struck Conan poses with it. "What is all *this* now? This part of your witch-hunting YouTube channel?"

Robin wriggled into her jeans. "Yep."

He put the sword back and tipped one of the plastic bins so he could see into it. Batteries. "You loaded for bear. You's a badass bitch."

"Witch-hunting is a resource-intensive business."

Shrugging into a hoodie, Robin clambered out of the back of the van and locked it up. As Joel led her out to his car, she turned her video camera on and aimed it at her face, holding it at arm's length. "Hi everybody. It's Malus. I was getting ready to settle down for the night with a good book and a bowl of staple-food ninety-nine-cent ramen when my new best friend Joel—"

She aimed the camera at Joel. "What up, Internet." He blew a kiss.

"—came to invite me to Movie Night. Complete with more of that damn fantastic pizza from the pizzeria. Lady Luck smile on me for a change."

Joel drove a beautiful jet-black Monte Carlo with bicycle-spoke rims and whitewall tires. She opened the passenger door and slid into the plush black interior to find an eight-ball gear shift and an armrest wedge embroidered with a stylized picture of Vonetta McGee in her *Blacula* costume, and the words BLACK VELVET in cursive. She recognized Vonetta as soon as she saw the armrest, because *Blacula* was one of Heinrich's favorites.

"All black." Robin buckled up as Joel tossed himself into the car. "Speaking of badass bitches, I bet this thing is a bitch in the summer."

He turned the engine over with a cough and a beastly, deep-throated *grum-grum-grum-grum*. "Honey, it's a bitch all year," Joel said, throwing it into gear and pulling out of the parking lot.

Speakers in the back howled "Crazy on You" by Heart as he piloted Black Velvet down the twisting highway, his headlights washing back and forth across the trees. The back seat had a stack of cardboard boxes in it, filling the car with the tangy-savory smell of hot pizza. As they came into Blackfield proper, the headlights spotlighted familiar sights that brought back a flood of nostalgia.

"I see you ain't lost ya country accent," said Joel.

Much of the town was different. New Walgreens. The Walmart had become a sprawling co-op. But underneath the shiny new veneer of change were old landmarks saturated with memories.

"Nope. You can take the girl out of the country—"

There was the bridge she used to play under when she was a kid walking home from school.

Jim's Diner, where she had her first piece of cheesecake.

Funeral home with the giant sloped parking lot she'd sledded down one winter and crashed into some spare headstones at the back, leaving a bruise on her ass.

Walker Memorial, where she'd gone to church a few times under the instruction of her therapists in her junior year of high school. Lasted about a month, but she could still hear the vaulted echoes of footsteps, smell the varnish on the pews, the dusty carpet, the faint reek of ancient hymnal books with stiff pages.

"But you can't take the country out of the girl," said Joel, turning down the stereo so he could talk. He took out an iPhone and texted someone, typing with one thumb. "Been a few years, ain't it?"

"Yeah." Robin spoke to the window, the world wheeling past her face like a diorama. They passed the Victory Lanes alley on 7th and Stuart, the neon sign out front showing a bowling ball knocking two pins into the rough shape of a V over and over. "I didn't think I'd ever be back here. Lot of bad memories."

"You said this morning you wanted to pay your respects to your mom?" He attached his phone to a magnetized ball on the dash, *click,* where it perched above the radio.

"Yeah. I might hit up my old house too, if I think I can handle it."

Black Velvet paused at a traffic light and the two of them sat there, listening to the muscle car idle. Joel sniffed, tugging his nose. He glanced out the window and then back at her as if he were about to give her nuclear secrets. "Hey, you want me to go with you?" he said in his own laconic Georgia drawl. *Ay, you want me to go witchu?* "You know, moral support? Or whatever? I don't know when you wanna go, but I got some time off coming."

"I don't know yet." Robin's twang matched it in a way. *Iono yet.* "Maybe some time this week."

"Lemme know. I'll be there with bells on." He flicked the tiny disco ball hanging from his rearview mirror and light danced around the interior of the car. "Jingle jangle." No response from the woman in the passenger seat, so Joel leaned forward to catch her eye. "Hey, you gonna be aight? Must have been a hell of a nightmare. You say they happen all the time?"

"Used to get 'em real bad back when I was in the hospital, after the fire." *After the fire,* she always thought of it, because it was easier to focus on the fire than the sight of her dying mother looking up at her from the floor. "The medication helped. After a while they stopped . . . but by then I was basically a wooden mannequin, so it didn't even matter."

The light turned green, and Joel eased through the intersection, the car's engine grumbling. "Yeah, them anti-psychotics and anti-depressants, they can straight-up turn you inside out."

"You been on that stuff?"

Joel made a flinchy sort of face and said, "Oh hell yeah. Baby, I'm a gay black man in the backwoods south. Even if my mama hadn't lost her mind and drove my brother away and turned me into a fucking basket case, I'd still be on this town's shit list. Some days I'd be fit to be tied if I didn't have something to soften the blow." He flexed a smoothly muscular arm. "Take this python right here, this started when I was workin' for Mr. Barnett fresh outta high school, doing landscaping for his lil shit-ass company. Hard work toting around bags of concrete and big-ass rocks and digging holes all day. After a year and a half of that, I started to get swole. And you know what? I caught a little less shit because of it. People looked at these biceps and it made their bullshit dry up in their mouth."

"You ever get in any fights?"

"A couple. People talkin' shit about my mama. That's why I don't work for Barnett no more."

"You like fighting?"

"No! Not at all. Hell naw. You kidding me? Look at this shit I got on. This is actual silk. I painted my muhfuckin' nails. I hate fighting. I like my face the way it is, and I like my guts *not* full of holes. I'd rather smoke a little good-good and drive my car and play some video games and mind my own business. But sometimes people like to make their circus *your* circus."

He drove on. She noticed that he kept glancing into the rearview mirror, *peering* through it as if it were a mailslot. "And sometimes," he continued, "when they see you get big, they send a few more dudes. That's why I learned how to move out the way, too. How to drive. How to be elusive. Lot of Black folks, we talk about bein' invisible, you know—white people, they can look right through you, like you ain't even there. I judo that shit, right? I make it work for me. I'm like a ninja, I vanish. Ali said float like a butterfly. One minute I'm there, the next, I ain't. Ain't nothing but burnt rubber and a little bit of Forever Red in the air."

"I'm sorry," said Robin.

"For what?"

"That you had—*have*—to put up with that kind of shit."

"Don't be. Made me a stronger person. I made enough money

there to make a down payment on Black Velvet. Either that or a security deposit on an apartment, and after Fish left to make his bones and get rich, I had to stay behind, live in our old house, and take care of my moms." A few seconds passed and then he said, "I wasn't really ever as smart as Fish. I didn't have any choice in the matter." He shrugged, glancing at her. "I do what I can, but I ain't my brother." He patted the dashboard. "But I got my Velvet here, I got gas in the tank and something to eat, and that's enough for me."

They stopped for another traffic light, this one in front of a Taco Bell. Someone had stolen the C off the sign out front so instead of HIRING CLOSERS, it said HIRING LOSERS. Joel leaned forward, catching her eye with a look of concern.

"So: the nightmares," he said. "You wanna talk about 'em?"

Robin gazed out the window, staring her reflection in the face. After a few moments to find the words, she spoke.

"In my dream, I'm a little girl again, and my mom is still alive." She elected not to mention the Red Lord. Seemed a little too heavy for a night like this, and for such a cramped space. "My mom and I go out the back door to talk to my dad while he's mowing the lawn, and she starts acting weird, and then turns into a tree. And then she bursts into flames and starts to burn, and I always wake up before I can put her out."

"Weird."

As they pulled into the diagonal parking in front of his brother's comic book store, Joel leaned over in a conspiratorial way, and murmured, "Well, it's good to have you back, even if being back in town is making you have nightmares. You always welcome to come down to my place and share a bottle of cognac with me. I find the nectar of the gods is most efficacious when it comes to knockin' y'ass out so you can sleep the dreamless sleep of the innocent."

Robin took a moment to study his smooth, open face. "You know, I might takes you up on that."

"Maybe we'll even play a little dress-up like we did when we was kids," Joel said, putting the car into Park and shutting off the leonine engine. "We won't have to borrow your mama's clothes to get gussied up like back then." He flicked an earring. "I buy my own shit now!"

5

Roy was out gassing ant-hills when the sun went down. He slipped a Maglite out of the pocket of his jeans and took a knee, watching the gasoline soak in. Hundreds of ants percolated up from the tunnels, scrambling over each other in the pale blue-white glow of the flashlight beam.

They had found a grasshopper somewhere and dragged it back to the nest, and they had been in the process of cutting it into pieces and pulling it down into the dirt when he'd interrupted them. He liked to imagine the jackboot tromping of their tiny feet, the sound of a klaxon going off as the gasoline washed down into the corridors of the nest, little panicked ant-people running to strengthen levees, hauling children to safety, swept away by the stinking flood into dark confines.

Roy enjoyed watching videos on the Internet of riots and fights, natural disasters, and sometimes people falling off of bicycles and skateboards. Fights were fun as long as they were street-fights. Ultimate Fighting was too structured—he didn't watch fights for the gore or brutality; the unpredictability was what drew him, the chaos and incongruity, the panic and frenzy that was almost slap-stick in a way. Aimless beating, kicking, the rending of shirts and slipping and falling and flopping around, reducing each other to meaningless ragdolls.

If he were a decade or two younger, he probably would have en-joyed playing video games like the *Grand Theft Auto* series.

As it was, behind the wheel he often fantasized about driving off the highway and tearing through backyards and flea markets, plowing through birthday parties and bar mitzvahs. Not so much for the violence of it, but for the strange sight of a car tear-assing through a place you didn't expect to see it. You just don't *see* things like that, and that's what he enjoyed: things "you just don't see."

When he was a kid, he'd gotten his hands on a smoke bomb and set it off in the gym showers after sophomore phys-ed, when he knew it would be full of unsuspecting people. Waiting until the smoke had almost filled the room and was beginning to curl over the tops of the shower curtains, Roy had shouted, "*Fire! Fire!*" and had run outside.

His father had whooped his ass for it, but seeing thirty butt-naked high-schoolers storming through the gymnasium had been the highlight of his high school experience.

He tipped another pint of gasoline onto the ants for good mea-sure and got back on the lawn mower, starting it up and climbing the sprawling hill toward the adobe hacienda. A garage stood open out back where the driveway snaked up out of the darkness and curled around the house like a cat's tail. Roy drove the lawn mower inside, filling the space with a deafening racket.

When he cut the engine off, the silence was even louder. He sat in the dark stillness beside a huge Winnebago, packing a box of cigarettes.

Outside, the evening was tempered by the faint murmur of Blackfield's fading nightlife, an airy, whispering roar washing over the trees. In close pursuit was the constant drone of cicadas and tree frogs.

Southern cities don't necessarily have nightlife. You go up north or out to Atlanta, maybe, or Birmingham—Roy had been to Atlanta twice and didn't care to ever go back, that traffic was horseshit—and yeah, the cities don't sleep. Life runs around the clock. Out here in the sticks, though, a city of six thousand, seven thousand like Blackfield, there's a few creepers after dark. Meth heads, winos, that sort of thing, sometimes hookers. But for the most part the main boulevard is a clear shot from one end of town to the other after dark, cold hollow streets like a John Carpenter movie.

He lit up, wandered back up the driveway and around the house sucking smoke out of the Camel as he went. Standing at the top of the drive, he was treated to a horizon swimming with the red cityglow of Blackfield, and under the jagged rim of the treetops glimmered the windows of the blue Victorian on the other side of the trailer park, a tiny hive of glowing elevens in the darkness.

A gray cat with honey eyes trotted out of the shadows.

As he blew the smoke into the night, multicolored lights flickered in the Victorian's cupola. Someone was watching TV up there. "Looks like somebody's moved into the old Martine place."

An old woman stood by a barbecue grill crackling with flames. She was tall, taller than beanpole Roy even, and lean, broad-shouldered, with feathered gray hair. That and her hawkish nose made her resemble some sort of dour gray Big Bird.

Or a bird of prey.

The ice in her glass tinkled as she took a sip of a Long Island iced tea. Cutty always started dinner with one to whet her appetite. "Know anything about them?" she asked, as the gray cat slinked over to her and darted up onto the patio table.

"Black fella from up north." Roy ashed his Camel and spat a fleck of tobacco. The wind rolling across the top of the hill pushed at his copper hair. He'd once let her make him a Long Island, but it was so strong he could barely finish it. No idea how she could manage it, with her scarecrow figure. She wore enormous shirts and patterned sweaters and dressed in loose layers, so she always seemed to be wearing wizard-robes, even in the heat of summer. Roy was rail-thin and the jeans he wore draped from his bones, but even so he still sweat right through his shirts when he worked.

"Him and some fat chick brought the car down couple weeks ago and the real estate agent showed him around the place. Looked like his sister. Or his wife. Or, hell, his grandmother. I can't damn tell how old any of 'em are anymore."

"Have you spoken to him?" Cutty threw another handful of junk mail on the fire and gave the cat's back a slow, luxurious stroke. The smoke stank, and the ink turned the flames green.

"No."

"Have you got anything for supper?" she asked the flames.

"No, ma'am."

Cutty closed the grill lid and started off toward the back of the house. "Why don't you stay and eat with us, then? Theresa is making pork chops."

"I just might," said Roy. "Thank you."

As soon as the door opened he was bombarded by the aroma of pork rub and steak fries, corn, green beans, baked apples. Theresa LaQuices bustled around the spacious kitchen, buttering rolls and stirring pots.

Theresa was a solid and ruggedly pretty iceberg of a woman, a few years younger than Cutty. Her raven-black hair was dusted with gray. Spanish or maybe Italian or something, because of her exotic surname and olive skin, but Roy never could quite pin down her accent and it never really struck him as appropriate to ask. She was given to dressing like a woman twenty years her junior, and today she had on a winsome blue sundress roped about with white tie-dye splotches.

He couldn't deny she wore it well. Against the well-appointed kitchen, she looked like she belonged on the cover of a culinary magazine. Reminded him of that Barefoot Contessa chick, only a lot older and a lot heavier.

"Well hello there, mister!" Theresa beamed. "Are you gonna be joinin' us for dinner?"

Roy realized Cutty had disappeared. She had an odd habit of doing that. "Yes, ma'am. And it smells damn good. I wasn't even hungry before I came in here, but now I could eat a bowl of lard with a hair in it."

Theresa made a face and gave a musical laugh. "I didn't prepare any lard, handsome, but you're welcome to a pork chop or two."

"I'll be glad to take you up on that."

Roy passed through a large dining room, past a long oak table carved with a huge compass-rose, and into a high-ceilinged living room with delicate wicker furniture. On a squat wooden pedestal was a flatscreen television that would not have been out of place on the bridge of a *Star Trek* spaceship.

Behind the TV were enormous plate-glass windows looking out on the front garden inside the adobe privacy wall, a quaint, almost miniaturized bit of landscaping with several Japanese maples and a little pond populated by tiny knife-blade minnows.

The downstairs bathroom was one of many doors in a long hallway bisecting the drafty old house. The slender corridor, like the rest of the house, was painted a rich candy-apple red, and as the light of the lamps at either end trickled along the wall Roy felt as if he were walking up an artery into the chambers of a massive heart.

He washed his hands in a bathroom as large as his own living room. It was appointed with an ivory-white claw-foot tub, eggshell counters, a white marble floor, and a gilded portrait mirror over a sink resembling a smoked-glass punch bowl.

The vanity lights over the oval mirror were harsh, glaring. Roy was surprised a house occupied by three elderly women would have a bathroom mirror that threw your face into such stark moon-surface relief. Every pit, pock, blemish, and crease stood out on his skin and all of a sudden he looked ten, twenty years older. And he had a lot of them for being in his forties.

His lower lids sagged as if he hadn't slept—which he hadn't, really, he didn't sleep well—and his red hair was fine, dry, cottony, piled on his head in a Lyle Lovett coif. The lights made his face look sallow, made him look melty and thin, like a wax statue under hot lamps.

Junk food, probably. Slow-motion malnutrition. He ate a lot of crap because he didn't cook.

He *could* cook, no doubt—he could cook his ass off, learned from his mother Sally—but he never really made the effort. Not because he was lazy, but because he could never find anything in the cabinets that enticed him enough to cook it (he was a chef, but not a shopper) and he never had anybody to eat with. So he really appreciated the chance for a proper home-cooked meal that left him out of the equation and gave him company to eat it with.

Back in the hallway, Roy passed an open door through which he could see a headless woman in a crisp new wedding dress.

"Hi there," said a woman's voice.

"Hello, Miss Weaver."

An elderly flower child came flowing around the bridal mannequin to him, decked out in layers of wool and linen in muted earth colors. "How many times I gotta tell you?" she said, wagging a knurled finger. "Call me Karen. You staying for dinner tonight?"

Locks of silver-blonde hair tumbled down from underneath a green knit cap and a long curl of yellow tailors' measuring tape was yoked over the back of her neck, draping over her bosom. Karen Weaver had the open, honest face of a grandmother, and eyes as blue as a Montana sky. A silver pendant on her chest twinkled in the light, some obscure religious symbol he didn't recognize.

Could have been a pentagram, except there were too many parts, too many lines.

"Yes, ma'am."

She playfully slapped him on the shoulder. Wisps of Nag Champa incense drifted through the open doorway behind her, accompanied by the sinuous, jangling strains of the Eagles. "Don't ma'am *me*, young man."

"Yes, ma'am," grinned Roy. He flinched away before she could slap him again.

Dinner was excellent. The four of them ate at the compass-rose dining table under the soft crystal glare of a chandelier, Cutty hunched over her plate like a buzzard on roadkill, Theresa with a napkin pressed demurely across her lap. Weaver ate with the slurping-gulping gusto of a castaway fresh off the island.

In the background, the turntable in the living room was playing one of those old records the girls liked so much—Glenn Miller, Cab Calloway, one of those guys, he wasn't sure which. Roy was a golden-oldie man himself, dirty southern rock. Skynyrd fan through and through.

"Cuts like birthday cake," said Weaver, flashing Theresa an earnest smile. "I've been cooking for ages, and somehow I still don't hold a candle to you."

"You get a lot of practice, cookin' for a long line of husbands."

Cutty said in a wry tone, "I wonder why you outlived them."

Theresa feigned hurt at her and went back to feeding herself dainty bites of pork chop with the darting, practiced movements of someone steeped in southern etiquette.

Roy interjected, "Nice dress you're working on, Karen. Where's this one going?"

The old hippie's smile only broadened. "Oh, it's going to a very lovely couple in New Hampshire. They're planning on a November wedding. No expense was spared."

"Too bad it won't be a Halloween wedding. That'd be interesting."

Cutty shook her head. "Ugh. I can't think of anything cheesier than a bunch of youngsters decked out like extras from the *Rocky Horror Picture Show* or something, exchanging their vows in front of Elvis and a congregation of monsters."

"A congregation of monsters!" said Weaver, bright-eyed and smiling. "What a wonderful thought."

"Only you." Cutty eyed the voluptuous Theresa. "And what are *you* doing tomorrow?"

The dark-eyed Mediterranean woman straightened in her seat. "I'll have you know I'm volunteering at a soup kitchen tomorrow evening. The one in Blackfield. I'll be there all evening."

"You? *Volunteering*? At a soup kitchen?" Cutty huffed in disbelief and pushed her food around her plate. "The only thing *I've* ever seen you volunteer is your phone number."

As sullen and stormy as Roy could get, he enjoyed watching the sisters banter. They weren't biological sisters, or at least he didn't think they were. Never talked about where they came from, other than to swap stories and anecdotes about long-dead husbands. They never mentioned children.

"So, it looks like we've got new neighbors. Down the hill, in Annabelle's house."

The other two looked up from their dinner. Weaver was the first to speak. "Oh yeah? Well, are they nice? I think that house deserves someone nice."

"I ain't talked to 'em," offered Theresa. "I saw 'em when I was comin' home from the grocery store earlier today. I was behind them on the road comin' out of Blackfield. Looked like a man and a little boy. Colored folks. They was drivin' one of them Japanese cars."

Sometimes Weaver could be a little eerie, like a gold-miner who'd spent too much time out in the mountains by herself, but when she smiled, the old woman could light up a room. "Oh, that's nice—this gray old neighborhood could use a splash of color, I think."

At that, Cutty dipped her face into one hand and rubbed her forehead in exasperation.

"Say," Weaver added, "why don't we invite them up for dinner one night this week?"

"Like a welcome wagon," said Theresa.

"Yeah!"

"We'll have a barbecue out back and invite the whole neighborhood, and dance around the maypole and sing songs and tell stories," Cutty growled flippantly. "It'll be a regular bacchanalia."

Picking up her goblet, Weaver swirled a splash of wine. "That's the spirit! We'll even have a bonfire!"

Cutty gave her a shrewd glare.

"You *know* how I *feel* about bonfires."

"Oh, right."

"Still," said Theresa. "It would give us a chance to get to know them. After all, they're going to be livin' in Annabelle's house. Like that bunch in Nebraska, they're gonna be askin' questions sooner or later. We might as well lay the groundwork. Establish a little rapport."

"Redirect their curiosity. Yes." Cutty forked a piece of pork chop into her mouth and chewed thoughtfully. "Yes, good idea. Curiosity killed the cat, after all."

• • •

After dinner, Cutty stood at the island in the kitchen and cut an extra pork chop into pieces, then put it in a food processor and chopped it into a dry, grainy paste. Then she used the processor to chop up a cup of green beans, and then a cup of corn.

She assembled all this processed food on a plate with two steak fries and took it upstairs, along with a glass of tea. She put them both on the nightstand in her bedroom and pulled a rope set into the ceiling, hauling down a hinged staircase behind a hidden panel. She carried the plate and glass up into darkness.

A pullchain dangled against her face. Cutty pulled it and a soft yellow bulb came on, revealing an attic.

Years of accretion surrounded her, most of it dusted. Victorian-style lounges and parlor tables with baroque mahogany scrollwork and silk cushions. Steamer trunks full of foxed books, scrolls of paper, yellowed newspapers, movie posters plastered with the faces of long-dead actors. Bookcases with broken glass windows set into them. A clown marionette hung from the rafters, face forever frozen in a loopy laugh. A coin-operated weight scale from 1936. Shelves and shelves of bric-a-brac—toys, coins, bayonets, flintlock pistols.

Cutty walked a meandering path through the labyrinth to a door at the far end.

This she unlocked with a skeleton key.

Inside, a bed faced an old tube television in a dark room. The only window was a tall gothic rectangle looking out on the back garden, and it simmered with Tyrian purple light.

Playing on the TV was the History Channel, which she never failed to find ironic, considering who was watching it. The TV's glow traced the contours of the room with a thin film of blue, and the shape under the thick quilt was only a suggestion in the soft light. The attic's bare bulb filtered through the open door and illuminated the foot of the bed, bisecting the bedroom with dirty gold. The gray cat with the honey eyes lay curled up by the footboard.

The bedridden shape stirred in the shadows. "Evening, cookie." Its genderless voice was a dry croak. Folded up in it was the hint of a sarcastic Brooklyn accent.

"Evening, Mother," said Cutty.

"It *is* evening, right?"

The old woman slept more often than not these days, and often woke in the wee hours of the night. The bedroom was timeless; there was no clock here, digital or analog, which was how she liked it. Mother hated counting down the hours alone in her rare moments of wakefulness, and the constant ticking was maddening, a torturous metronome out of a Poe story.

"Yes," Cutty said. "It is evening."

She put the plate on a vanity and took a bendy straw out of the pocket of her sweater, slipping it into the tea. Sitting on the bed, she helped her mother sit up and drink some of it. The sound of her slurping was like the slow tearing of paper.

"When is it?"

Cutty traded the tea for the plate. "It's October."

She gathered up a spoonful of ground pork chop and fed it to the shape under the quilt. The spoon rattled against her mother's twisted grimace as the meat slid inside. Mother mashed it against the roof of her mouth with her tongue and swallowed.

"What? Already?" wheezed the shape. "Shut the front door."

"Time flies."

"Time flies like an arrow, but bees like a fruitcake."

These garbled aphorisms had long ago ceased to concern Cutty. Considering the crone's state, it was a wonder she could even communicate. She eased some of the chopped green beans into her mother's hard mouth as if she were feeding her through a kabuki mask.

Mother sighed. "Will you hand me the television remote controller thing, cookie?"

"Where is it?"

"I dropped it. It's on the floor."

The shape's shriveled eyes followed Cutty as she put the plate aside and stooped to gather the remote. She put the batteries back in it, put the cover back on, and sought her mother's hand.

"Here you are," she said, putting it in the stiff claw.

Fingers curled around the remote with a subtle crackle. The TV changed channels at a stately pace as Cutty continued to feed her antediluvian mother puréed pork. The gray cat on the quilt looked up, yawned, stretched, went back to sleep.

"I think we're getting close," said Mother, when dinner was almost over. "Finally, finally, finally. After all these long years."

"Yeah?"

"Yeah. Maybe once it's done you won't be keeping me in the attic with the rest of the antiques."

Cutty gave her a wry look.

"What?" asked the shape.

"You *know* you're only up here to keep you safe. Safe from those nasty murdering men and their stolen heartstones."

"Bah. You don't care about me."

"How can you say that?"

"You hardly ever come up here to visit with me anymore." Her mother coughed softly into one dry fist. "You're always downstairs with your friends and that weird Irishman who cuts the grass."

"I've told you before, he's not Irish."

"He's ginger as hell, he does all the lawn work, he drinks, he's Irish until proven otherwise."

"No habeas corpus for you, huh?"

Her mother chuckled, though her face didn't move. "I'm corpse enough for both of us."

Cutty spooned the last of the green beans into her mother's mouth and set the plate aside. Reaching into one of the deep pockets of her wizard-robe cashmere sweater, she brought out an apple. It was the size of a softball and its skin was the liquid, recondite red of a ruby. Rare striations of peach and gold curved down its sides.

Her mother sighed with relief and contentment at the sight of it, like a castaway seeing civilization.

"Almost time for another harvest," said Cutty, handing her the apple. "I think this weekend I'll see to that. Roy and Theresa can help me carry them to the house."

Mother clutched it in her bony hands and lifted it to her lips. Her mouth opened, the corners creasing and flaking, the joints of her jawbone cracking, and she pierced the fruit's skin with her teeth. A soft groan of delighted pain escaped her throat as she bit into the fruit.

Instead of juice, vibrant arterial blood dribbled from its rind and ran down her arms, dotting the quilt.

As the rich carmine ran down her throat, Mother's skin loosened, her fingers fulling and flushing. The corded veins snaking down her neck and across her shoulder plumped, throbbing, and fresh life trickled throughout her body.

"An apple a day," she gurgled.

6

Fisher's comic store wasn't quite on the main drag through town, but it was tucked into a homey little street one block over, a narrow slice of old-fashioned Americana. Knickknack shops, drugstores, a pet shop, boutiques, barber shops, a bar, lawyers' offices, a Goodwill, a soup kitchen. They passed a looming gray courthouse and a red-brick police station.

The Monte Carlo slid into an angled parking spot on the street next to eight or nine other vehicles and Joel got out, taking half the stack of boxes out, leaving the rest for Robin. "Did you say Miguel donates these pizzas?" she asked, picking up the boxes and pushing the car door shut with her foot.

"He sees it as grassroots advertising," Joel said, suggestively tossing out a hip. "Give 'em a taste, they gonna come back for more."

"Sound like the drugslinger method to me." She felt for the curb with her toe and stepped up onto the sidewalk. The windows of the comic shop were painted with intricate images of Spider-Man and Batman in dynamic poses, Bats in his blue-and-gray Silver Age colors. Over their heads was FISHER'S HOBBY SHOP in flowing cursive.

A man came out of the comic book store and held the door open for them. "You trying to hurt me, man," he told Joel, eyeing the pizza. He was brawny but slender, with a swimmer's build and a round face.

"Fish, *you* the one doing it to yourself, don't blame me. *I* eat like a human. You eat like a mule."

The comic shop was dimly lit by bar fluorescents. Comics were only a fraction of the wares on the shelves—there were scores of rare, niche, and run-of-the-mill action figures still in their blister packs, board and card games, Halloween masks cast from various horror movies and superheroes, film props, video game keychains, themed candy. A life-size Xenomorph creature from the *Alien* movies lurked behind a shelf, motionlessly waiting to snag any customers unfortunate enough to step into range of its throat-jaws.

In the back of the store was an open area with booth seats and folding chairs. Arcing over the heads of two dozen people and a small squad of children was a cone of light casting the opening sequence of horror classic *Evil Dead* on a projection screen.

"Fish on that keto diet." Joel put the pizza boxes on a booth table and squirted some sanitizer on his hands, wringing them. The kids immediately got up and came to the table, standing at his elbow like hungry hounds. "He try to tell me it's good and good for ya, but I see that look in his eye when I bring in these pizzas."

"What's the keto diet?" asked Robin.

"Zero carbs. None. Zero, zip, zilch." Joel made that *zip-it* gesture across his face and started putting pizza on paper plates, handing them out. "He don't hardly even eat fruit. He's always been a fitness nut, but this year he's goin' in like a muhfucka. I don't know how he does it." He gave one to Robin and she slid into the booth.

"What *does* he eat?" she asked, placing her camera against the wall to capture the table and its occupants. "Unicorn farts and sunshine?"

"Meat. Vegetables." He wagged his hand. "Bacon all day every day. He cobble together regular food outta irregular bullshit. And the man fry *everything* in coconut oil. I tell you, one time he talked me into coming down to his place, and he made pizza with this dough made out of puréed cauliflower."

"Eww."

Fish, his girlfriend Marissa, and a tall white biker-looking guy named Kenway came to sit with her in the booth. Kenway's Goliath frame was crammed into a black T-shirt and his massive beard made him look like a lumberjack having a mid-life crisis. A riot of color and lines ran down his huge arms in sleeves. Robin helped them destroy the pizza and an army of craft beers while they ignored the movie.

As the evening progressed, she became more and more glad she'd agreed to come. Several sequels into a *Halloween* marathon, she looked up from her beer and realized all the movie-watchers had disappeared. Michael Myers stared blankly out of the screen at a roomful of empty chairs.

"So what do you do?" Robin asked Marissa over the rim of her beer.

"I'm an ER doctor at the hospital here in town." Marissa glanced at her boyfriend with a warm smile. "Fisher here is a computer nerd on top of his hobby shop. Data entry and programming."

"Sawbones and computers. Nice. I don't think I ever had the steel to get through medical school. Just takes something I ain't got. And my Macbook is the extent of my technical wizardry."

"I believe everybody thinks that until they're on the other side, and then they're like, *Holy crap, I did it.*"

"Basic Training was like that," said Kenway. "My mom didn't think I could get through it." He laughed. "Something tells me she didn't think much of me before I went in."

"What?" asked Marissa. "I don't believe that. You're huge."

"I've always been big, but it wasn't always muscle. I was a tubby guy when I enlisted. I lost a lot of weight in Basic and OSUT. When I came home, my mom picked me up at the airport and asked me, 'Where the hell did the rest of you go?' Turns out six months doing calisthenics every day with no beer or hamburgers makes you drop about seventy pounds."

He checked his watch. "Think it's about time I head home," he said, and Marissa let him out of the booth. Robin watched as he unfolded himself and stretched six feet of broad muscle.

She polished off her beer. "Got work in the morning?"

"No, ahh—I don't really work," Kenway said, jamming his fingers into his jeans pockets. "Well, I *do*—" He gestured with a big craggy hand. "—but it's not really your usual nine-to-five."

Marissa smiled. "Kenny is Blackfield's local *artiste*."

"Is that so?" Robin beamed. The smile felt alien and uncomfortable on her face. "What kind of art do you do? Underwater basket weaving? Chainsaw carvings?"

The hulking man laughed and folded his arms. "A little of this, a little of that." It should have looked authoritative, menacing even, but somehow it seemed protective, bashful. "I did the big mural on the wall at the park, and the superheroes out there on the windows of this shop. I have vinyl equipment too, and I make leather stuff."

"Renaissance man. Maybe I can commission you to paint my van."

"That skeezy-ass candy van?" asked Joel.

Robin pursed her lips at him. "Yes, my skeezy-ass candy van. Needs a little style, maybe."

Kenway rubbed the back of his neck. "I'll take a look at it, then. What'd you have in mind?"

"Do you do a lot of vans?"

"A couple. Mostly pickup trucks and hot rods from out of town. Shit-ton of motorcycles for guys out of Atlanta and Chattanooga. Did a big-ass snake on a dude's truck a few years ago. It was pretty freakin' sick, took forever. Went all the way around the back from one door to the other."

Robin tried to picture the van with a new paint job. "How do you feel about doing one of Joel over here, butt-naked, sprawled out on a bear-skin rug in front of a fireplace, with a rose in his mouth?"

The two men traded looks. Marissa burst out laughing. Joel shrugged as if to say, *I'm game.* "You just describing a Saturday night for me," said the pizza chef, striking a pose.

"I'm pulling your leg, big guy," Robin said, grinning. "No, it'd have to be something simple, with stylized artwork. Nothing cheesy."

"Sure I could figure something out."

"*I* think you should take the lady back over there and let her show you her skeezy-ass candy van," suggested Joel, with a devilish smirk. "I live on the other side of town, and it'd be out of my way, so I can't take her home, but your art studio is between here and the pizzeria."

A rush of cold heat shot down Robin's neck in embarrassment. She narrowed her eyes at him. *You planned this all along, didn't you?*

Kenway rubbed the back of his neck. "Yeah, I *guess* I could."

After taking down the projector equipment and cleaning up the mess from the pizza, the five of them regrouped on the side-walk and said their good-nights. Turned out the *artiste* drove a rattletrap Chevy pickup, an antique land-yacht. The paint job was the tired Dustbowl-blue of the sky in old photographs, wistful and cool.

Climbing into the cab, Robin pulled her hoodie's sleeves down to cover her hands and pushed her hands into the muff pockets. She wasn't cold, but it made her feel better. Safer.

A set of dog tags dangled from the rearview mirror, twinkling in the light. She rolled the window down and sat back to listen to the cicadas buzz and whisper in the distance. Kenway got in, filling the driver's seat with his muscular bulk, and turned the engine over with an oily, exhausted *chugga chugga chugga*. He fiddled with the radio, producing a static-chewed gabble.

"What kind of music do you like?"

"Any kind." She smiled as warmly as she could. "Well, I have a special place for death-metal covers of old showtunes."

Kenway snorted.

"Kidding." She eyed him. "I'm game for whatever's on. Just don't expect me to dance. I've got two left feet."

"Me too." The vet knocked on his leg. "They didn't have any spare righties, so I had to settle for a lefty. It's hell for buying shoes." When he caught her look of alarm, he laughed. "Kidding." He settled on a classic rock station—*Revved up like a deuce, another runner in the night,* Heinrich would have liked that—and he looked to her for approval.

Clearest signal on the band, so she pursed her lips in an agreeing smile. "Sounds good."

The gearshift was a twenty-sided die as big as an apple. As he went to put the truck in gear, he noticed her eyes on it. "I won that playing Trivial Pursuit at Fish's shop one night." He chuckled and pushed it across the gearbox, and the engine dropped in pitch. "First time my encyclopedic knowledge of TV shows has ever come in handy. It's actually not a real gearshift, I had to drill a hole in the back of it. Would you believe I've never played Dungeons & Dragons?"

The Chevy swung out of the parking spot and lumbered down the street, passing a tremendous Gothic church that looked as if it were made of sandstone blocks. "Never woulda guessed. You look like the nerdiest guy in town. Total Poindexter over here—"

The thing from her dream stood under one of the stone buttresses, in an alleyway.

The Red Lord.

Luminous green lamp-eyes gleamed in the darkness of its broad face, strobing between the bars of the churchyard fence. A yellow security light on the church wall illuminated it from behind, making a halo of the reddish hair covering its lumpy shoulders and long arms. Years ago, she had pegged it for at least eight feet tall, but next to the monumental columns and buttresses of Walker Memorial it almost looked delicate.

This thing, whatever it was, had been showing up more and more often in the periphery of her life since the incident with Neva Chandler, as if marking the passage of time, or some kind of recurring echo, like a sonar ping.

Boogeyman.

Maybe it was a curse. Or maybe it was real, maybe Chandler had summoned it, maybe pointed her out to it, made Robin more visible to it, in an attempt to distract her from the Job. The Task. The Quest. Of killing every witch she could find.

But see, here's the thing: the being called "the Red Lord" never tried to hurt her. Never came at her in a menacing way, other than silently appearing in her personal space. It just lurked at the edge of the shadows, and in darkened doorways, and outside of cloudy windowpanes. Standing in the trees, just inside the glow of an alleyway security light, motionless, monstrous, staring, the wind tousling that mottled mane. Making that come-hither gesture with one long, gnarled finger.

Come with me, it always seemed to be saying.

I have something to show you.

Maybe the stress of her traumatic shock therapy at the mental hospital, and the strenuous training with Heinrich, and the brutal fight with Chandler . . . well, maybe it all piled up on her until it triggered some kind of a slow-motion mental breakdown.

Hell, maybe she'd been born crazy all along, and the stress had brought it all roaring into her life at full blast.

Perhaps unsettled by the fear on her face, Kenway gave her a side-eye. "You okay? Look like you saw a ghost."

"Y-yeah. I mean, no. No ghosts here." She gave him her best smile.

"You and Joel sound like you grew up together," he said, grinning. "Talk the same way. *Hey y'all, we fittin' to hop on 'at train. Aight.*"

"Like a couple of Podunk country kids?"

"Yeah." He gestured at her in a general way. "So what do *you* do for a living? Must be pretty interesting—"

"Cause of the way I look?" She glanced at herself in the wing mirror and suddenly she seemed outlandish, all dark-eyed and gray-scalped. *You look like an extra from a Mad Max movie.* For the first time in a long time—maybe the first time *period*—she wished she were wearing more makeup. Her fingernails had been black earlier that week, but now they were mostly chipped away.

Kenway scoffed, grinning. "You said it, not me."

"I make Internet videos." She remembered she was holding her camera, and she waggled it indicatively. It was not filming.

"Really. Huh." Kenway stopped at a red light, waiting for cross-traffic that never came. "Didn't even realize you could make money doing that. What do you do in 'em?"

Bet you probably thought I did porn, she thought. *You wouldn't be the first to make that assumption.* The radio was turned so low Robin could hear the traffic light clicking softly in the breeze. Lyrics squirmed at the edge of her hearing like voices on a telephone.

"Vlog."

"Gesundheit."

"No, it's like a video journal. I . . . 'document' things. On YouTube." *You document yourself killing the shit out of things, you mean?* She hesitated. Kenway was good-looking, and she didn't want to jeopardize whatever tenuous thing she could sense hovering in the cab between them with the truth. "Ahh . . . I don't know, it's nothing.

Not really that great. I just talk to the camera a lot. Drive around, visit places, do stuff." *Visit places, do stuff, kill monsters with swords and knives, sacrifice goats. Okay, maybe not that last one, but you're well on your way, aren't you?*

"Cool, cool." The light turned green and the truck grumbled across the intersection. "Anyway, I wanted to tell you, I really dig that Mohawk."

She instinctively brushed a hand across her bristly scalp. "Yeah?"

"Yeah. I'm—I'm really into rock chicks. Biker chicks. That kind of thing. I guess." He rolled his own window down and laid an elbow out of it, leaning away from her. He shrugged. "I don't know. I just . . . wanted to say it, say something. You look good. It's a good look for you."

"Thanks."

"Suits your face."

Robin summoned up her curiosity. "So . . . you don't really look like a local. I don't remember you from when I was a kid." *Good pickup line, doofus. Do you really know everybody in town?*

"Grew up in Washington and California, moved out here a couple years ago. Visiting a friend of mine and decided to stay. I like this town. It's quiet, and I, uhh . . . guess I had some baggage I needed to get rid of. And this place is a good place to lose it." He glanced at her and back at the road. "The baggage, that is. Lose my baggage."

"I know what you meant." Robin stared through the windshield. "I think I brought some back here myself."

You brought an entire cargo ship, girl.

At night, Blackfield was a dead city, an abandoned town painted in shades of the ghastly rust-orange of sodium-vapor security lamps. They only saw two cars, and both of them turned down side streets, heading home. "Y'know, I guess it must not be 'nothing'—" Flicking the turn signal, *tick tock tick tock,* Kenway eased into a turning lane and boated left. "—I mean, if you can make a living at it, whatever it is you do on YouTube must be good enough to pay the bills. Right?"

"Yeah, I guess it's all right. Beats a kick in the ovaries."

"So come on. Out with it, Miss Mysterious. What do you do in these videos, for real?" He smirked at her, lip curling in one corner, white teeth glinting in his beard.

They crossed a small bridge over a canal running parallel to the main drag, and she could hear the faint gurgle of rushing water. On the other side, Kenway turned right and carried them up a street of quaint two-story buildings like some kind of historical business district. A stray dog trotted through the showers of orange lights and patches of darkness, a man on a mission.

"Do you watch a lot of YouTube videos?" she asked.

He shook his head. "No, not really. I don't even have a smartphone. I have a computer at the shop, but I only use it for work. My laptop in my apartment, I don't use it much at all except for watching movies or checking email. Reading the news."

She squinted. "What about that movie *The Blair Witch Project*?"

"I remember, yeah. Came out in like, 1999 or 2000, didn't it?"

"Yeah. My channel is sort of like that. Fake real-life footage of supernatural events in my life. There are actually a lot of channels like mine. Most of them are people dealing with ghosts. Haunted houses. And monsters. Extra-dimensional monsters?"

Coming out of her mouth, it sounded stupid as hell. *Stupid,* she thought. *It sounds crazy, is how it sounds.*

"Mm-hmm." Kenway nodded.

They slowed to a crawl, level with a dark shop front. The plate-glass windows were painted with a gryphon in rampant red, and underneath was lettering in Old English: GRIFFIN'S ARTS & SIGNS. "This is my place. I live upstairs from my shop in a drafty studio apartment. Yep, I'm the stereotypical starving artist."

They drove on. He took them to the end of the median and did a U-turn through the turning lane, going the way they came.

"Do a lot of business?" she asked.

"Not really. But I like it that way. Might have one or two big projects a month. The rest of the time I paint." He tugged his jeans leg up, revealing the sheen of a metal rod. His lower left leg was a prosthetic foot. "VA disability," he said, knocking on it with a hollow *tonk, tonk.* "Gives me a lot of free time."

"I *was* wondering if you were in the army." Robin's eyes flicked to the dog tags hanging from the mirror. She caught one of them and turned it to the light. SFC GRIFFIN, KENWAY. 68W. BLOOD TYPE AB. RELIGION NONE.

"Used to be."

"Mind if I ask what happened?"

He didn't answer right away. His eyes were fixed on some point in front of the Chevy—not the road, but some place in another time. *Good going, idiot. Foot, meet mouth.* "I'm sorry," Robin said. "I shouldn't—"

"It's okay. I was uhh . . . collecting my thoughts." He tipped down the visor and caught a pack of cigarettes, pulling one out with his lips.

He didn't light it, but he put the pack back in the visor and drove with his lighter in his wheel hand. "I was part of an escort for a Provincial Reconstruction Team convoy. They're the ones—they have a lot—*women,* uhh, we brought female soldiers out to the villages where we were building schools and shit, you know, to talk to the Afghan women and kids." The wind played with his hair. His temples were shaved but the top was long, and it whipped in the breeze coming through the window.

A wincing expression had slowly come over his face as if he'd developed a headache. "Anyway. I stopped our vehicle when I shouldn't have. Ka-blooey. End of the line."

"I'm sorry." *Is it possible to deep-throat your own foot?*

Kenway lit the cigarette and took a draw, shrugging. "Oh—do you mind?" he asked, indicating the cigarette.

She smiled wanly. "It's your truck, Joe Camel."

"You smoke? You want one?"

"Trying to quit. Lung cancer isn't good professional branding, and I'm all about branding."

The night blurred past them for a few more moments as they passed lightless storefronts, dead barber's shops, dark alleyways yawning in brick throats. They startled a cat that had been peering into a storm drain and it bounded away, leaping into a hedge.

"You're staying in the rock-climber village next to Miguel's, right?"

"Yep. Roughing it."

A silk sheet of silence settled over the truck as the town tapered away, the buildings rolling into darkness until they coursed along a narrow corridor of trees. Robin became more and more at ease as they rode. Kenway had a calming, languid, ursine presence that reminded her of Baloo the Bear from that old *Jungle Book* cartoon movie. He seemed to operate on a different wavelength; everything he did was slow and lazy, as if he had all the time in the world.

The night vacuumed his smoke away as he drove, his elbow out the window. The trees fell away as well, the blue Chevy bursting into the open, the night sky unfurling above them in a dome of stars. Shreds of gray cloud sailed west under a nickel moon. Hills around them narrowed, enclosing the road in washboard crags of granite, then widened again.

BLACKFIELD CITY LIMITS, said a lonesome green sign. A bit beyond that was a turnoff leading east into the tree line. Kenway flicked the turn signal and the ancient truck slowed.

"Where are we going?"

He looked over at her. "Shortcut? I *always* go this way when I go to Miguel's."

"Oh." The truck angled onto Underwood Road. "Do you like to hike?" The mountains around Miguel's were honeycombed with hiking trails, paths trickling through the forest toward Rocktown.

Rocktown was a clifftop strewn with huge limestone boulders, the local hotspot for college kids, rock climbers from afar, and anybody looking for an out-of-the-way place to burn a bag of weed with their friends. If there's anywhere safe from the prying eyes of Joe Law, it's at the top of a fifty-foot vertical rock face.

"Sure, I like to climb." He smiled. His eyes were the same tired blue as his truck. "Yes, in fact, I *can* climb with this foot, in case you were wondering. Haven't done it much lately, but yeah."

Underwood Road.

Please keep driving. She wanted him to keep on driving to the far end of the four-lane where the freeway overpass arced above their heads, where the Subway restaurant, the bait shop, the Texaco, and the road to Lake Craddock clustered around a secluded rest stop in the wilderness. She didn't really want to come out here yet. *Not yet. I'm not ready. I need a few days to pump myself up.*

Or talk yourself out of it, you mean?

Forest surrounded the truck in a claustrophobic collar of pines and elms, the tree trunks shuttling past in a picket-fence flicker of columns and shadows. She stared out the window at them, the late-summer wind buffeting her face.

"I used to live on this road when I was a kid."

Kenway took one last draw on the cigarette and ashed it in the dash tray, then flicked it outside. "Yeah?"

The trees kept barreling toward them, counting down, becoming more and more familiar. She kept expecting the houses and the trailers with every turn, the memories leaking in like water under a door. There was the NO TRESPASSING sign, shot full of .22 holes. Just there, a faint patch of grungy Heathcliff-orange, the armchair someone had dumped in the woods when she was twelve. *Tried to sit on it once. Found out the hard way there were wasps in it.*

Then, there it was: the forest opened up again and there was the trailer park on her left, all lit up with its sickly white security lights, trailer windows haunted by the honey-red glow of lamps and the epileptic blue stutter of TV shows. A large aluminum sign out front declared CHEVALIER VILLAGE, or at least that's what it seemed to say, under a coating of graffiti.

On top of the angular Old English gibberish was a tiny spray-painted crown.

Suddenly she was sixteen again, she was thirteen, she was nine. Robin sighed, sitting up against her best judgment, and tried to see if there was anything—or anybody—she could recognize. But the night was too dark, and the cars were all too modern, and the yards were strewn with toys, and everybody was inside and had battened their hatches against the dark.

On her right, a double-wide by itself, with a hand-built porch and naked wooden trellis, chintzy aluminum birds with their pin-wheel wings, a deteriorating VOTE ROMNEY sign by the culvert. A wooden-slatted swing dangled by one chain from a rusty frame, the end jammed into the dirt.

Next door, looming on the other side of a stretch of grass, was the monolithic 1168.

"Slow down," Robin blurted. *NO, DON'T, KEEP GOING!*

The Chevy downshifted and the neighborhood lingered around them. The engine protested. Materializing from the deep night like the hull of some sunken ship was the gingerbread Victorian farmhouse she'd grown up in, her childhood home.

The security lamp on a nearby power pole threw a pallid greenish cast across the front so the black windows were more like eyes in a dead face.

"This was my house," she said, as if in a dream.

Familiarity wreathed the window frames and eaves of the house in mist-like echoes as she studied it from afar. Her memories were stale, and far from her groping mental hands. The house was a different color (she knew it as green, the pale green of dinner mints, with John Deere trim), but it was her house. She could feel the splintery porch railing in her hands, the words and runes her mother had carved deep in the windowsills and then painted over.

"Nice place," said Kenway. A U-Haul truck and a blue car sat in the driveway, the car tinted charcoal gray by the watery light. She didn't recognize them. "Looks like somebody else lives there now. Just moved in. Or they're about to move out."

Something drew Robin's eyes back to the trailer park across the street, and she traced the long gravel drive snaking along the east hip of the park to the old mission-style manor lurking on top of the hill.

The Lazenbury House cut a tombstone silhouette against the Milky Way.

All of the lights were off except for one window on the topmost floor. She'd never been up there, but she knew the rest of the house. She knew the blood-red walls, the piano, the Japanese-style front garden with its fishpond. The sprawling, Eden-like orchard out back. She knew the dirt-floored cellar, with its fire-blackened casks of wine and cramped dumbwaiter-style elevator. She'd practically grown up in that house. She remembered stories her mother had told her when she was a teenager, losing sight of little two-year-old Robin and searching the house for her, only to discover she'd wandered over to Granny Mariloo's house for cookies and apple juice. A few times, she'd cried for hours, banging on the door of an empty house. Robin had vague memories of her mother Annie marching resolutely up that long gravel drive barefoot, the wind rippling the hem of her dress, to come fetch her daughter.

Those were the days when her father had been his worst, and her parents had fought with each other the hardest. Disturbed by the shouting, Baby Robin would creep out and seek solace with sweet, maternal Marilyn.

But she'd never been allowed on the top floor.

Did the Lazenbury have an attic? She wasn't sure.

A shadow moved behind the attic window's lacy curtain.

"Okay," she said, startled out of her reverie, and Kenway took that as an indication to keep on trucking.

The forest swallowed them up again, and they followed their headlights down a long, winding two-lane under oppressive branches. Farmhouses sailed past in the cool twilight, surrounded by empty gray pastures tied to the earth with barbed wire and driftwood stakes. Underwood ended at a lonely T-junction watched by a grove of birches, where a single cabin peered through the trees with one yellow eye. Kenway turned left and the Chevy roared north.

A few minutes later, the headlights scraped across the belly of the interstate overpass, and a little beyond, in the crook of a long, shallow curve, was Miguel's Pizzeria. A single security lamp stood vigil by the shower building. Kenway pulled up onto the gravel drive, weeble-wobbling across the jagged ground, and the bicycle in the back thumped in time with the truck's creaking suspension.

"That's me." Robin pointed at the plumber van.

Kenway erupted into laughter. "Aha ha ha, Joel wasn't kidding. That is truly sketch." He must have seen the look on her face, because he immediately stopped grinning. "Oh, I'm sorry. I didn't mean—I mean . . . shit. I wasn't trying to hurt your feelings. I'm sorry."

She waved him off. "It's okay. I know how it looks."

"If you don't mind me asking, why are you living in an old panel van?"

Opening the door, she started to get out but something seemed to press her back into the cab of the truck. Reluctance? Robin slid to the edge of the bench seat, the fabric of her jeans buzzing across the upholstery, but she just sat there. *To hell with it,* she thought, her eyes fixed on the sign out in front, a picture of a cartoon Italian chef perched on a cliff face. I'D CLIMB A MOUNTAIN FOR MIGUEL'S PIZZA! *Might as well go ahead and drop the bomb. It's going to happen eventually, might as well wreck this before it really gets going.*

Instead of meeting his eyes when she turned to him, she fixed on his giant hand, wrapped around the steering wheel. "I bought it with the money in my mom's bank account when I was released from the psychiatric hospital a few years ago."

Kenway nodded, slowly. "Ahh."

She winced a smile at him in gratitude. "Thanks for the ride home. Oh!" Reaching into her pocket, she pulled out a scant wad of cash and peeled off a twenty, thrusting it in his direction. "Gas money. As thanks."

His eyes landed on the money, his eyebrows jumped, and he twitched as if he were going to take it, but he said, "No, that's—it's all right, I'm good."

"No, really. Take it."

He pointed at the dash dials. "I'm full anyway. Filled up on the way to Movie Night."

Folding the money into a tube, Robin stuck it in the tape deck so it looked like the stereo was smoking a cigarette. "There." She slid the rest of the way out of the truck and shut the door, walking through the glare of his dingy headlights.

On the driver's side, she stood in the dark hugging herself. "Drive safe," she said, feeling awkward. "Thanks again for the ride home."

He didn't leave. "You're an odd duck, Robin."

Ice trickled into her belly. *You don't know the half of it, dude.*

"I like odd ducks."

"Quack quack," she replied, with a wan smile.

You are a fucking doofus, Robin Martine. The two of them had a short staring contest, the girl standing behind her van, Kenway sitting in his idling truck.

She was about to bid him adieu and climb into her party-wagon when the man in the truck spoke up. "If you're ashamed about the psychiatric thing, don't be. Lord knows I've spent enough time talking to army shrinks. I shouldn't have any room to talk." Drumming a bit on the windowsill, he added, "So . . . yeah. Don't know what your story is, but you won't find any judgment here."

Robin smiled. "I appreciate that."

"I don't know how long you're going to be in town, but I'll be around. If you want a real bed to sleep on for a night, you're welcome to crash at my place." He crossed his fingers. "No creep stuff, scout's honor. Just . . . you know, an offer. I guess. It's there on the table. I'll sleep on the couch."

"Okay."

She took hold of the utility van's rear door handle and started to open the door and climb in, but then had the idea to tell Kenway good night. Unfortunately, when she turned to speak, he was already rolling the window up and putting the truck in gear. Robin stood there with one foot on her back bumper and watched the Chevy grumble around the parking area, crunching across the gravel and washing the pizzeria with its headlights. Kenway pulled up to the road, paused, then lurched out and disappeared with a roar.

Robin lingered there in the dark for a moment, looking around. She sighed and climbed into the back of the cold van.

Cold, empty, quiet. All of a sudden, her mobile candy-van nest didn't look nearly as inviting as it had before. Robin stripped, kicked her fuzzy legs down into the cold, empty sleeping bag, and lay down with a huff.

Alone again. The inside of the van was deathly silent.

"Shit," she muttered to herself, regretfully wrenching a beanie down over her eyes and rolling over onto her side.

• • •

She was drifting off to sleep when light began to press against her eyelids, pulling her back to the surface.

It's dawn already? she thought, stirring. *I feel like I haven't slept at all.* She checked her phone and discovered it had only been an hour and a half. Robin looked up, blinking in confusion at the shelves and the backs of the front seats. The inside of the van was traced in lime-green light, as if there were a traffic signal right outside the back window, shining through the glass.

The glow faded as she clambered up onto her hands and knees to look outside. "The hell was that?" she muttered, forehead to the rear window.

Nothing out there but the side of Miguel's Pizza and the parking lot. A security light shone through one of the massive oaks next to the building, showering silver coins across the gravel. Beyond was the stygian darkness of the Georgia night, drilled by the constant noise of the cricket serenade. She paused there on her knees, eyes and body motionless, watching for movement.

Only the restless swishing of the oak's leaves. Light gathered in the trees across the highway and a car passed, pushing its high beams down the road and out of sight.

Reaching into a storage tub, she pulled out a combat knife and sighed. "Of course I'd have to go piss. Beer always makes me piss. Thank you *oh* so much for giving me time to get into my sleeping bag and get comfortable."

She climbed out of the van, clutching the knife in one hand so the cold flat of the blade lay against her wrist, and wriggled into her combat boots, tucking the untied laces in alongside her feet. Gravel crunched softly under her soles, almost inaudible under the night-sounds as she made her way toward the cinder-block building out back. She shined her cell phone back and forth, the blue-white light sweeping over gray bushes, gray trees, gray picnic tables, everything traced with the kind of creepy, desolate somebody's-watching-me loneliness that is solely the domain of dark country roads, places where you expect to see things nobody should ever have to see.

Wish I hadn't been the only one to camp out here tonight, she thought, as a moth battered itself against her cell phone. *Could definitely have used a little company.* Her breath coiled white in the beam.

Still resplendent with graffiti, the simple structure towered over her. In the dark, illuminated by a flashlight, the words and doodles had a sinister quality, less like an autograph from the past and more like the scrawlings on the walls of a prison cell.

"Crap." The restroom door was locked. She tried the men's room and found it locked as well.

Maybe I could cop a squat out there in the weeds.

She stared out at the dark forest. *Nah. If something comes out of there after me, I don't want to be standing there with my jeans around my knees and my bare ass hanging out.*

While she thought about it, she paced back and forth on the sidewalk, listening to the crickets. Noise came out of the night in a constant assault, like an eternal tide of bugs, swelling and ebbing, swelling and ebbing. She put her hands in her pockets and found what she'd thought was a balled-up receipt, but turned out to be a pack of cigarettes. She tugged them out and flattened the box. Marlboro Lights. Sigh. Two left. She pulled one out and held it up to the security light. Bent, mashed, but still in one piece. Her other hand plucked her lighter from her pocket and she flicked the Zippo open, the same Zippo she'd burned Neva Chandler with back in ol' Ally-Bammy, and she lit the cigarette with it.

Pay dirt. She sipped at the filter, pinching it as if she were about to throw a dart, and gave a productive cough. Blue smoke clung to her face and smelled terrible. She spat on the ground and growled, "Keep sayin' you gonna quit, and one of these days you'll believe it."

The restroom door unlocked. *K'tunk.*

She froze there in the gloom, the Marlboro perched between her lips.

"Don't do this to me," she said from the corner of her mouth, squinting. The knife came up, shining and sharp, and she settled into a fighting stance. "Not tonight, please."

No one came out. She pushed the door open and found darkness.

"Hello?" Taking one last drag on the cigarette with the knife-hand, she flicked it into the dark, where it extinguished with a hiss in a puddle of water. "If someone is hiding in here, you better sing Happy Birthday or I'm gonna stab your ass. In the neck. Yeah, your ass-neck."

Before she could find the light switch by the door, the fluorescents flickered to life with a soft *blink-ink!* and hummed down at her.

Motion detector.

With a soft hiss, the door eased shut on its hydraulic arm, and the block walls muffled the night-song outside into a subtle whisper. The gently raunchy smell of a public ladies' room ambushed her: dirty mop-water, ammonia, the hot iron smell of old musk.

Could a motion detector unlock a door? She studied the lock and found only a key-operated deadbolt.

Maybe the mechanism was inside the door where she couldn't see it.

Best not to overthink it. Robin padded toward the back of the room with the combat knife clutched face-level in one hand, every footfall and rustle of clothing magnified by the bricks, and began a thorough search of the room. Four shower stalls, curtains pulled across three of them. Five toilet stalls, all the doors closed. She made her way down the line, nudging the curtains open with the blade of the knife. She pushed the toilet doors open one at a time. At each stop, she froze, waiting to be attacked, and moved on to the next.

On the third toilet, she kicked it open and charged in like a madwoman, yelling at the top of her lungs, brandishing the knife. "*AAAAH!*"

She looked down, shining the cell phone into a disgusting toilet. "Eww."

To her relief, the endmost toilet stall was relatively clean. Resting the knife on top of the tampon disposal box, she pulled down her jeans and underwear and sat down on the huge horseshoe toilet seat. Someone had Sharpied a rhyme onto the wall near her face. *Tinkle, tinkle, if you sprinkle, please be neat and wipe the seat.*

Light gleamed on the blade of her knife. *Gurgle, gurgle, if you burgle, please be kind and stay outside.*

She had finished, and was about to tear off a few squares to wipe with, when the lights went out, blinding her.

"Ah, dammit."

The darkness was absolute, as solid as black water against her face.

A moment passed. "Hello?" she called again, feeling stupid at talking to the motion detector. She pushed the stall door open, trying to trigger it again. A few seconds later the bolt clacked against the frame as the door swung shut. She pushed it again. *Thunk.* She pushed it again. *Thunk.* She pushed it again. "Come on, man. Come on."

No *thunk.*

Robin peered blindly into the dark, overwhelmed by the feeling someone was looking down at her.

Something was holding the door open.

Reaching toward the jeans pooled around her ankles, Robin dug in her pocket and pulled out her cell phone, activating the flashlight. As she did, the knife fell off the tampon box and clattered out into the larger part of the room. "Crap, no!"

What she could see: the stall she sat in, a half-square of torn toilet paper lying in the far corner, and the door standing open, halfway between the wall and the stall frame. She must have pushed it far enough to get it stuck on some rust in the hinge or something. While the floor was bare gray cement, the walls were painted an institutional white. Four feet away from her boots lay the knife.

What she could hear: the distant, tuneless *shree-ew shree-ew* of insects. Her own breathing. The soft ticking of the wind blowing early autumn leaves against the side of the building.

"Shit," she grunted, leaning forward to reach for the knife.

Much too far away. "Turn the lights back on, please." She stuck the phone out and waved the light around. Shadows leapt and capered across the wall. "Yoo-hoo." Still holding out the phone, Robin reached through her thighs with the wad of toilet paper and started to clean up. "I can't see. I need to—"

SCREEEEEEEEEEEEE! A shrill, skin-crawling sound like ten thousand knives being scraped across a blackboard shrieked through the restroom. Blood and adrenaline thrummed through her body as she hunched over in pain, shielding her ears from the metallic screaming.

Admittedly, the shock and surprise actually squeezed out a little bit more urine. She dabbed at herself again, dropped the paper into the water, and flushed the toilet, half-rising to her feet. The bowl was still refilling as the lights came on.

In the middle of pulling up her jeans, Robin squinted up at the door and realized it was trembling, like an arm held out too long.

Trying not to freak out, Robin stood and finished dressing. By then the lights were flashing madly on and off, turning the restroom into a Daft Punk concert.

Look, the witches were one thing—she'd been fighting monster-faced hags for a couple of years at this point, gnarled old witches and chubby-cheeked bohemians that could Force-throw furniture like Carrie, fill your car with snakes, and turn themselves into raving gorgons. She was used to that crap. But this was different. There was no witch in here, there was nothing physical to focus on.

Whatever was giving her grief here in this creepy restroom in the middle of nowhere, it wasn't a witch, and she couldn't see it.

"Ghost?" she asked out loud. "You a ghost?"

For a wild second, she actually expected to hear an answer.

She'd never dealt with a ghost before. Wasn't even sure they existed. But after the last few years, anything could be possible. Maybe he was bullshitting her, but Heinrich had told her of even wilder things than witches out there in the shadows, creatures like the *draugr*, the horrifying vampire ghouls of Icelandic legend, and the *tiyanak*, a man-sized fetus that climbed trees, luring people with the cries of a baby until they were close enough to drag up into the branches and devour.

He'd never mentioned ghosts, but how much more far-fetched is a man-eating tree baby?

Her pulse began to even out, her nerve returning. "No such thing as vampires, no such thing as giant man-eating babies, and no such thing as ghosts." Robin grabbed her phone. "Go get it, go get it, come on, you a bad bitch," and she stepped out of the stall into the flashing madness, shining the phone's light toward the middle of the room.

With one final *POP!*, the seizure-inducing fluorescent lights extinguished themselves, bathing her once again in shadow.

She ducked. *"Jesus!"*

The cell phone glinted on chrome fixtures, porcelain sinks. *Right,* said her inner voice as she knelt to retrieve the combat knife. *No such thing. But half a decade ago, you used to think there was no such thing as witches either, did you?*

Blink-ink! The motion detector tripped and the lights came back on, snaggletoothed by two dark tubes.

"Aight, I'm done playing this game. Cram your lights up your ass, Zuul, I ain't your Keymaster." She washed her hands (briefly, barely a wetting) and went for a paper towel, but there was only a hot-air dryer. Not in the mood to have hot shit-air blown all over her hands, Robin flung the door open and stepped outside.

Cold bug-song covered her in a dazzling blanket of noise. In the restroom, the automatic light clicked off.

She wiped her hands on her clothes and marched back across the parking lot, phone in one hand and knife in the other, light from the tree-obscured security lamp pouring kaleidoscope shadows across her face. "Rusty fuckin' door hinges, that's what it was," she said as she went. "Malfunctioning backwater automatic lights. But I'm sure as hell awake now, that's for sure. Gonna take me forever to get to sleep! So thanks a lot for that, you beat-ass electronic piece of shit!"

Behind her, the automatic light clicked on again, bathing her feet in stark white and unfurling her shadow out in front of her so she was stepping on her own heels. Robin turned and walked backward, expecting to see the hydraulic door easing shut and tripping its own sensor, but what she saw turned her blood vessels into rivers of Arctic ice water. Her hands went numb.

The Red Lord was inside the women's restroom.

Through the door behind him, Robin saw the automatic light go out, and the monstrous silhouette became a blind rectangle of black.

Bright green lamps appeared in the doorway as his eyes opened, two milky railroad signals in the dark. His shaggy bulk filled the doorframe from side to side and he bent to step underneath the lintel, unfolding to his full height. And he was *huge,* a stretched-out scarecrow, all hair and sinew and bone.

The two of them stood there in the parking lot of Miguel's Pizza, facing each other.

"You ain't real," she told him.

Those green lamplight eyes gazed listlessly at her from the doorway.

"I know what you are." An anxious sort of confidence wound its way into her voice. "You're some kind of lingerin' hallucination the King of Alabama put on me. I never got to see exactly what her Gift was. It must have been Illusion. That's what's going on here." She scoffed. "Don't know why I didn't think of this sooner. I mean, come on, that's the deal, right? Maybe Neva reached into my head while I was standing in her living room, found my memories of the night terrors and nightmares I had when I was a kid, and she used them to hex me with some kind of worst-fear bullshit before she died."

The creature stared, blinking slowly.

Calming, relaxing, she gave a snide little shrug, and continued walking backward. "All I got to do is find somebody, maybe a *houngan,* that can do a little hoodoo, nix this Illusion hex on me, and we're golden. Au revoir, weirdo. It was nice knowing—"

Leaning forward, eyes still locked on her, the hallucination let out a deep growl, a low, wet, ragged rumble, a drowned engine.

Grrrrrararararuhuhuh.

She ran.

As soon as she took off, she slid out of one of her untied boots, leaving it behind. The gravel bit into the sole of her foot as she ran for the Conlin Plumbing van. She flung the door open, jumped into the back with the sleeping bag and tubs of junk, and slammed it.

"Hallucinations don't make noise," Robin breathed, fogging up the back window as she locked the door. "Do they?" Her voice shook. "I don't know what the hell that thing is, but it's not Illusion magic."

Kneeling in the back of the van, clutching the Glock, loaded with a full mag of hollow-points. Eyes on the back window. Watching for movement.

Staring. Waiting. "Where'd you go, fucker?"

Steeling her nerve, she crossed herself with the Glock—*mammaries, ovaries, wallet, and watch*—and pushed the back door open. Night air rushed in. She pointed the gun, sweeping the parking lot, finger slipping into the trigger well.

Nothing out there.

It was gone.

7

Since there were no curtains or shades in the cupola, the sun pre-empted Wayne's alarm clock. Exhaling faint white vapors, he sat up to discover one of the most beautiful sunrises he'd ever seen in his life. A majesty of royal purple and orange-gold rippled throughout the eastern sky, an explosion of color and light.

Bedroom was cold, surprisingly so. Wind pressed against the north side of the cupola, making the windowpanes crackle subtly in their frames. Wayne pushed back the covers and ground the heels of his hands into his eyes, stretching like a cat. He was trembling by the time he got his clothes dug out of one of the boxes.

Mom's ring lay on the windowsill. He picked it up and was about to drape the chain around his neck when he realized it was warm.

The heck?

• • •

"Freezing up there," he told his dad as he came down, his shoe-laces dragging on the floor. He kissed his mom's wedding band and slipped it into his shirt.

Leon was brushing his teeth, hugging himself in front of the bathroom mirror. He wore only a pair of sweatpants. "You're a Chicago kid, and you wanna complain about the cold?" he asked, and spat a mouthful of foam into the sink. "Be glad it ain't snowing. Hell, this is mild compared to what I grew up with."

"I know, I know." Wayne tromped downstairs. "Barefoot in the snow, uphill both ways, blah blah."

"Tie your shoes before you fall and bust your face," said Leon's voice from the top of the staircase. "You don't wanna start your first day in a new school with a broke nose, do you?"

"I thought chicks dig scars."

"Scars, yeah. Jacked-up nose, not so much."

Breakfast was a bowl of cereal and buttered toast. "So what did you decide about the cat?" Wayne asked his father, in the brief moments when the man bustled through the kitchen.

"Cat?" asked Leon. "Oh, right."

The boy gave him a pointed look.

"I don't care if you feed it and let it hang around the house," his father told him. Leon had found his way into a two-piece suit and was looping a tie around his neck as he spoke. "They're good for catching mice before they get in. I just don't want it coming inside." He deftly wound the tie into a four-in-hand knot and cinched it tight. "Cats're cool and all, but they like to get into shit."

"All right."

Leon paused, eyeing him. "We cool?"

"We're cool."

Leon straightened the tie and laid his collar down, tugging it firm. "How do I look?" he asked, grabbing his suit jacket from where it lay draped over the back of one of the kitchen table chairs.

"Professional as always."

Leon held up the jacket. "Jacket or no jacket?"

"Wear it until you get to work, then take it off and hang it some-where."

Hesitating for a second, Leon nodded thoughtfully and shrugged into it. "My personal fashion guru saves the day again."

"And roll up your sleeves. Makes you look like you're down to clown."

Roll up your sleeves, Mom said a thousand years ago, stooping to look Wayne in the eye. The memory was bathed in golden light, like an antique photograph. They were standing in their old Chicago apartment, late summer breeze carrying the sound of big-city traffic through their open windows.

Why? he'd said.

Makes you look like you mean business, she'd said.

"Down to clown?" asked Leon.

"Ready for business."

"Oh." Leon tossed him a copy of the house key. "Hey, you can keep your phone turned on today, but don't be playing games on it when you're supposed to be paying attention in class."

"I wouldn't anyway," said Wayne through a mouthful of toast. "The games on this fossil suck."

"Attaboy." Leon bustled back out to the hallway.

Reaching into his shirt, Wayne took out his mother's wedding ring and clutched it while he ate. It was still warm to the touch, as if it had been sitting in the sun.

Raising it to his right eye, he peered through the ring at the kitchen, studying the bulletin board his father had installed on the wall next to the now-obsolete landline jack. This early in their new life down south, there were only a few things on it—coupons for the local pizza place, Miguel's; Post-it notes with various phone numbers on them; a to-do list (set up Internet, look into renter's insurance, get oil changed, etc.).

What if you look through that ring one day—

Shut up, Pete.

Like he'd told the other boy, it was a comforting gesture, like twirling your hair around your finger, or folding your arms, or rubbing the fabric of your jeans, something the school counselor called "stimming," or "self-stimulating." Like a heavy blanket on a cold night, something about the solid feel of the gold ring around his eye made him feel surrounded, protected, shielded, like a mask. His father had talked him into playing a few months of baseball several years ago and he had stood in the outfield with his glove over his face, peeking through the gap between his thumb and forefinger, watching the action on the diamond through the crisscrossing leather thongs. He'd known even then he looked like a daggone weirdo, but he didn't care. The smell of the worn leather, the darkness inside, and the feel of it on his cheeks were reassuring.

He took off his glasses and held the ring in an OK gesture, the hoop tight in the circle of his fingers, braced against his bare eye socket. Another spoonful of cereal into his mouth and he sat at the table chewing, looking around the now-blurry room through his makeshift monocle. Yes, he was nervous about his first day at a new school, all alone.

Just remember, Mom had told him, as Wayne rolled up his sleeves. Everybody else is just as nervous about the first day of school as you are. Remember that, okay?

Okay, he had said, barely believing it.

Imagine them all in their underwear, Mom said.

Wayne had recoiled in horror. Gross. He screwed up his face as he slid his arms through the straps of a backpack that would soon be heavy with textbooks. Besides, I don't really know what girl underwear looks like.

Mom had laughed at that.

Wayne froze, ring pressed against his eye, spoonful of cereal halfway to his mouth. Someone stood just outside the kitchen door, motionless.

A broad shadow darkened the hardwood floor and climbed the opposite wall at an angle before it disappeared behind the doorframe.

"Dad?" Wayne said, quietly.

Whoever stood in the hallway didn't move, didn't answer.

"Dad?" A little louder this time. "Dad, you're gonna be late for work." His voice broke a bit. "Did—did you forget something?"

No answer.

Wayne leaned to one side, his chin almost against the kitchen table, trying to see into the hallway. Leaning farther and farther, one foot coming to rest on the floor, he could see the edge of a silhouette in the morning light coming from the living room, a person, maybe, wearing something brown, or perhaps red, standing just out of sight with their arms by their sides. Without his glasses on, the shape was just that—an amorphous red blob.

"You there?" he called again. "Dad, what are you doing? Did you change your clothes? You're going to be late. Don't forget your wallet. You don't want to—"

WHAM. The wall shook with a hard, hollow noise as if a bowling ball had been thrown at it.

Wayne jerked upright in his seat, knocking over his cereal bowl. Pink milk and a few soggy pieces of Lucky Charms spilled out onto the table. He snatched up his eyeglasses and put them on, blinking in the sudden clarity, and scrambled away from the table to look out into the hallway.

Whatever the red shape was, it was gone. "Was that you?" Leon leaned out of the living room.

"No, it wasn't me."

Leon eyed him. "You sure?"

"*Yeah,* I'm sure. I'd tell you if it was me. Besides, when have you ever known me to mess around and make a noise like that?"

"Well, there was that time you put a bowl of ramen noodles in the microwave with no water, and it sounded like a bomb went off in the kitchen. The apartment was full of smoke, too."

Wayne pushed his glasses up on his nose. "That was *years* ago."

"And it stank until the day we moved out. You ruined the microwave."

Wayne sighed. Dad liked to bring up the Ramen Incident whenever Wayne offered to cook. Never let him live it down. But God forbid Wayne ever brought up the times he'd had to watch his father schlep through the front door an hour from bedtime, drunk as hell. Wayne had learned how to make his own dinner, real quick.

"Maybe something fell upstairs," said Leon from the living room.

"Maybe." Wayne went back into the kitchen to clean up the mess he'd made, swabbing the table with a fistful of paper towels.

• • •

He was still licking his lips and burping up cereal as he went out to stand by the mailbox and wait for the school bus.

According to Pete Maynard, the bus ran at seven, but it was six fifty and he didn't see Pete in the small gaggle of children standing on the other side of the road. Two girls, two boys, all of them but one younger than Wayne. The oldest was a tall Black girl in a parachute windbreaker, her hair braided into a slender rope down her back.

As he approached them, they stopped chattering at each other and fell quiet.

"Hi," he said to them, kneeling to tie his shoes.

At first they didn't respond, but then the tall girl said, "Hi," and rapped a knuckle on one of the boys' chest. "Say hi. It's nice to do that."

"Hi," said the boy.

The others glanced at him and chimed in with their own morose greetings.

Wayne tried to think of something else to say.

"You're the one that moved into the haunted house," said one of the boys.

Wayne twisted around to look at the Victorian, and back to them. His puffy jacket hissed and huffed with every movement in the still morning air. "I *did* come out of it, yeah."

The tall girl backhanded the boy in the chest.

"Ow. Why you do dat?"

"That's rude, Evan," she said. She shrugged in a sulky, downcast way. "I'm sorry. My name's Amanda." She poked the two boys in the temple with her fingertips in turn, pushing their heads. They were both white, with cold-pinked noses. "This is Kasey, and this is Evan. They're my step-brothers. The little girl is Katie Fryhover. She lives in the trailer behind us with her grandmama and their dog Champ."

"My name is Wayne. Wayne Parkin. We just moved here from Chicago."

"Amanda—"

"Hugginkiss," said Evan.

Amanda belted him again. "Shut *up*. My name is not Amanda Hugginkiss. It's Amanda Johnson. *God*."

"Have you seen any ghostses?" asked little Katie Fryhover. Her upper lip glistened with snot and one of her front teeth was missing.

"I ate breakfast with one," said Wayne, becoming aware of the warm wedding band lying on his chest. The kids' eyes bugged out of their heads in shock. He instinctively reached up to rub the ring through his shirt. "I eat breakfast with a ghost *every* morning."

"Woooaaah," Evan and Kasey Johnson cooed in unison.

Amanda regarded him warily.

"Really?" asked Katie.

"Yup." Wayne smiled. "My dad and me leave a place for her at the kitchen table. Nobody ever sits there except her." The reverent, mild way he said it had a chilling effect on the kids' excitement, and they fell quiet.

A door slapped shut somewhere in the trailer park, and Pete came huffing and puffing up the gravel drive to join them at the road. He was pulling on a jacket as he went, trading a Pop-Tart from hand to hand, and when he reached them he was still fighting with it, one arm hiked up behind his back.

"What the frick!" he fussed, the Pop-Tart in his mouth. The kids laughed. Pete accidentally bit through the Pop-Tart in frustration and tried to catch it with his free hand, but he slapped it into the culvert. He chewed in anger, the boys laughing even harder. "Are you even *for real* right now?"

Amanda smirked into her hand. "I'm sure it's not the first one you had."

A frown tugged at Wayne's face as he remembered how little Pete actually ate.

"Just hate to waste food." Pete wrenched the jacket on and blew a stream of vapor. "Morning, Bruce Wayne. How was your first night in the House of a Thousand Corpses?"

"It was okay. I only saw a few corpses, though. Nothing special." One corner of Wayne's mouth came up in a smirk. "Nothing like they said it would be."

"Not as advertised, huh? That sucks." Pete gave him a good-natured slap on the back.

The distant snore of the school bus groaned somewhere in the trees, and a car door clapped shut behind him. They moved out of the way so Wayne's dad could back out of the drive.

As the Subaru hooked into the road, Leon paused, rolling his window down. Some morning radio show came out of the car, two guys talking about a pie-eating contest in a place called Rome. "Have a good day at school," he said, turning the radio off. "If you need me, you know how to get me."

The bulge of Wayne's cell phone lay against his chest inside an inner jacket pocket, next to Mom's wedding ring. "Okay. Have a good day, Dad." The phone was a cheapo crap phone half his own age, didn't have any apps or games other than a measly pin-ball game and some kind of game where you made a rabbit jump around and eat carrots, but he could make calls on it and text Leon's number.

"Oh," he said, waving.

"Yeah?" asked his father.

"What was that loud noise?"

"No idea," said Leon. "I went upstairs and looked around, but I didn't see anything on the floor other than the moving boxes that were already there. Maybe it was the pipes. Did you run the water?"

"No. I was sitting at the table eating breakfast."

"I don't know, then. We'll check it out when I get home, maybe. But, you know, it's an old house. Who knows? Fixer-uppers like this place make all kinds of noises." The school bus came wheezing up the road toward them. Leon pointed at the kids and said, "Stay frosty, compadres," driving away.

Wayne rolled his eyes.

They filed onto the bus, a creaky-drafty thing already teeming with noisy kids. As they sorted themselves into the elephant-skin seats, Wayne gazed out the window. Black wings swooped out of the tree line and a crow landed in the grass by the roadside.

Picking up the remainder of Pete's Pop-Tart with its beak, the bird struggled back into the air and flew away.

• • •

After spending his childhood thus far in Chicago, Wayne found King Hill Elementary School almost *too* quiet, funereal in its own country-bumpkin way. The lunchroom burbled with sleepy conversation, puffy-eyed kids mumbling to each other and nuzzling into the crooks of their elbows, trying to catch a few more minutes of shut-eye before the day started.

Most of them were white, he noticed as he and Pete came shuffling in twenty minutes before the bell. He'd sort of expected that. There were almost no races other than white at all, not a single Asian, and other than Amanda, the handful of Black kids he saw were all several years older, a band of gangly boys clustered together in a tight group in the corner, slumped against the wall and fighting sleep like a roost full of pigeons.

To his surprise and relief, the morning went smoothly. When he had to stand up in front of homeroom class and introduce himself to everybody, something he'd been dreading since the drive down, everyone chanted, "Hi Wayne," and except for a few half-hearted Batman and cowboy jokes, that was it.

The classwork was easy compared to what he'd been doing back home—almost a year backward in terms of academic progress. Gave him the feeling of having accidentally been enrolled in remedial classes, or he'd somehow stepped into a time warp that forced him to re-live the previous year over again.

Oh well, Wayne thought, *just puts me a year ahead of the other fifth-graders. I can coast through and blast all the tests.*

Another thing he didn't expect was the claustrophobic closeness of the smaller school population—none of the classes exceeded twenty-five children, and a few of them had under fifteen.

Each period had a strangely informal, floaty atmosphere, as if a bunch of people had decided to congregate in one place for an hour and listen to somebody talk. Instead of sulking menacingly at the head of an unruly class, the teachers turned out to be friendly, engaging, and upbeat. Huge picture windows down the side of each classroom were full of bright sunlight, and instead of being enclosed in the darkness of Chicago's monolithic buildings he could see swishing treetops, but the desks framed him in broad polo-shirted backs and the faint baby-formula body odor of the congenitally rural Caucasian.

Several of the boys showed up in honest-to-God bib overalls and smelled like rotting compost. Wayne felt like he'd moved into an Amish village. Some part of him kept expecting to spot a butter churn in the corner, or for a chicken to wander into a classroom in the middle of a lesson.

To be honest, it was a little creepy compared to Chicago. Idyllic, muted, almost cult-like.

No one would really talk to him except for Pete and Pete's friend Johnny Juan. The white kids were cordial but standoffish, as if Wayne were a ghost that was only physically solid and present when someone was forced to interact with him. The rest of the time he was invisible.

"So what do your mom and dad do, Wayne?" asked Johnny at lunch, spooning chili into his mouth one bean at a time.

"Johnny" Juan Ferrera was a skinny Cuban kid who, according to Pete, had moved up from Florida the previous year. Juan and his extended family lived in one of the more urban neighborhoods on the southeast end of town, where several of his relatives worked at the Mount Weynon textile factory and the Mexican restaurant on the south end of town near the college.

Pete had gone to Johnny's place once for a birthday sleepover. According to what Wayne was told, Johnny Juan had the newest Xbox and possessed more Legos than Pete had ever seen in one place in his life, but Johnny and his brother slept on the floor in sleeping bags because his grandparents slept in his bed.

"My dad teaches literature. He's working at Blackfield High School." Wayne took out the ring hanging in his shirt and stuck his finger through it, rubbing the rough engraving around the inside. "My mom . . . she died a few years ago."

Johnny paused for a brief moment to watch Wayne stare into his chili, then scratched his head and went back to eating. A tray clattered onto the table and a girl plopped into a seat between them.

"Howdy, kids," said Amanda Johnson.

Pete looked up from his shredded cinnamon roll. "How's it hangin', dude."

She leveled a glare at him and picked at her food with a spoon, demurely folding and folding her chili as if it were expensive lobster bisque. Up close, Wayne could see the shotgun-spatter of acne in the middle of her forehead she'd covered with makeup.

"What're *you* looking at?" she asked with mild venom.

Wayne shrugged and went back to eating. His cell phone hummed inside his jacket. A text message from his father. YOU WANNA RIDE BUS HOME OR ME PICK U UP?

"So have you kids heard the rumors?" Amanda asked them

with the panache of a campfire story. "Apparently there's a killer in town."

Johnny Juan sniffed his milk. "Where'd you hear *that?*"

Tap, tap tap, Wayne sent his father a text in reply: I GUESS PICK ME UP

"Day before yesterday, Jeff Beesler's dog brought home a bone that looked like it came from a human." Amanda's eyes flashed conspiratorially as she leaned in close. "You *know* who Jeff Beesler is, don't you? He's that kid in eighth grade, plays football. I've known him *all* this year. He likes—"

Johnny Juan broke in. "No way."

"Bullshit," said Pete. "What kind of bone was it?"

The girl winced in annoyance at being interrupted. "How should *I* know, do I look like a bone scientist to you? They said it was a piece of a spine. Jeff gave it to the police and they sent it to the GBI Crime Lab in Summerville."

"Man, bullshit," reiterated Pete. "Nobody's gonna kill you. It's probably a bone from like a dead deer, or, or something." He gestured with the ice cream sandwich he was eating. "I ain't afraid of no killer. I know how to get home quick and super-ninja, man. Ain't no killer can catch us where I go."

Wayne looked up from his phone. "For real?"

"Yeah. Takes a little bit longer than the bus, but I'm pretty sure I'm the only person who knows about it. Or, at least, the only person who uses it. I know this town like the back of this hand." Pete splayed his thick paw out on the table and played at stabbing between his fingers with his fork. *Thunk . . . thunk . . . thunk.* "We should go my way when we go home from school today. You gonna go with me, or are ya chicken?"

"Man, that crap don't work on me," said Wayne.

Tap, tap tap. CAN I WALK HOME WITH PETE?

Pete tucked his stubby hands into his armpits and made slow wing-beating gestures with his elbows. His grim face made the Funky Chicken all the more imperative. "Is that so? Buckok. Buckok."

ARE U CRAZY? THATS TOO FAR.

"If you're scared, I'll even go with you two." Amanda leaned close. Her spackled-over acne looked like stucco at this range. "As a chaperone, of course. Are you scared? It's okay if you are."

"Cause you're just a wittle guy," said Pete. "Hey, nerd, get off your phone. We're tryin' to peer-pressure you."

PETE KNOWS SHORTCUTS. WELL BE HOME IN NO TIME.

Johnny leaned into the conversation. "Hey, *I'll* go with you. *I'm* not scared."

NO.

"You don't even live out there," said Amanda. "How you gonna get home?"

"My uncle can come get me. He works first shift, he gets off at like five." Johnny tossed a shoulder dismissively. "Besides, it's not like they're gonna miss me. They don't even know I'm there half the time. And it's Friday anyway. I don't have anywhere to be until church Sunday morning."

YOU SAID TO MAKE FRENDS DAD. THIS ME MAKIN FRIENDS.

No answer from the elder Parkin. The lunchroom monitor started to corral all the children, and Wayne shuffled into line with the other kids to leave. He was in the middle of an argument with Pete over the comparative tensile strength of Batman's sky-hook and Spider-Man's webbing when the cell phone in his pocket vibrated.

ALRIGHT. BUT U GO STRAIGHT HOME. LOCK AL DOORS. GOTA WORK L8 ANYWAY. B HOME SOON.

"Your dad spells like crap for a literature teacher," said Pete, peering over his shoulder. "Looks like we're walking home."

8

She stood in the restroom behind the pizzeria, staring at the toilet stalls, eyes wide, her guts churning with a horror that seemed to lie inside her bones like a cold, bitter marrow of river-water. A toothbrush stuck out of her mouth, forgotten, her mouth full of Colgate foam. The lights weren't flashing this time, but several of them refused to illuminate, and most of the light came through the restroom door, which had been wedged open with a rock.

"Oh my god," Robin said under her breath.

Turning, she opened the tap and cupped a double handful of water into her face, rubbing her eyes hard enough to see cigarette-burn mirages and occult-looking phosphenes behind her eyelids. She bent and sipped some of the water, swished it in her mouth and spat it out, sipped some more water, spat it out.

When she stood straight again, there it remained, visible in the mirror behind her, large as life. "Ah, Jesus. Jesus Christ," she said, wiping her face with her T-shirt. *Hallucinations don't do that.*

Four jagged scratches across two of the steel stall doors, including the one covering the toilet she had relieved herself in the night before. Six feet long and several inches apart, deep, white paint chipping off around them and speckling the floor at her feet. Must have been the source of that ear-splitting knives-on-metal shriek that had driven her out yesterday.

She ran wet hands over her bare scalp and fled the bathroom.

• • •

Miguel's Pizza teemed with the lunch-time crowd, out-of-towners and locals both trying to get in their climbs before the weather turned. Robin was forced to take her stuff out back to the patio, a large conglomeration of trestle tables under an aluminum awning. It was airy and clammy, but she sat at the end of the enclosure where warm sun fell on her and it could have been August again.

She was halfway through a chicken salad when Kenway Griffin appeared and sat across from her with a meatball sandwich and a bottle of breakfast stout. In light of last night's revelation, she was impressed by the ease with which he moved on his false leg—if he hadn't told her, she wouldn't have even guessed.

"Good morning," he said.

Low-key glad to see him, Robin shaded her eyes and peered at the clock on her Macbook. The sun felt good, but made it a little hard to see fine details on her screen. "It's noon."

"Well, morning for me. I don't sleep well and I tend to get up late." He crammed the end of the sub in his mouth and bit through the crusty bread with a crunch, talking with his mouth full. "Haven't eaten actual breakfast in years. Unless you count lunch as breakfast."

"I'm sure there's a word in German for that."

"Brunch?"

"That's not German. Besides, 'brunch' is what comes between breakfast and lunch. You're having lunch *for* breakfast."

"*Sprechen ze brunch?*"

She shook her head, smirking. She gestured to the beer by his hand. "So you a BYOB bruncher?"

"I like to get an early start on my self-medicating. Early bird gets the tequila worm, so they say."

"What are you doing out here, anyway? Don't you have pictures to paint?"

"Today's my day off."

"Oh yeah?"

He washed the sandwich down with a sip of beer. "Yup."

"You're off every Friday?"

"I'm off when I *say* I'm off. Nice thing about being a freelance artist."

"*Artiste.*"

"No, just an artist. I haven't reached *artiste*-level proficiency yet, I don't think."

"Sounds like a fancy way to say 'retired' to me."

A floppy pickle-spear wagged in his hand. He took a bite out of it and pointed with the stump. "Are you saying I look old enough to retire?"

"If you were a silver fox, I wouldn't protest."

"So what are you up to?"

"Editing yesterday's footage." Robin paused, leaning back to brush imaginary crumbs off of her jeans, stalling for time. She took a deep breath. Finally she said, "If I show you what actually happens in these videos, do you promise not to laugh or think I'm crazy?"

For a second she thought he was going to say, *I already think you're crazy,* but all he said was, "I promise."

"I hunt witches," she said, saving the footage progress and opening a browser window. "And I videotape it for the Internet." She clicked the bookmark for her channel and hunted through the video thumbnails as if she were rifling through a filing cabinet. "I monetize the videos with ads and sell T-shirts and hats and things like that." She pulled up a video she'd done and turned the computer around so he could watch it. "Neva Chandler. My first solo witch."

According to the upload date on the page, the Robin in the video was a couple years younger, sitting in the cab of her Conlin Plumbing van. "I've been tracking her for weeks," said the girl's tinny voice.

Kenway picked up his sandwich and went back to eating it, but his eyes were locked on the Macbook's screen as he chewed. Taking a pull off his beer bottle, he said, "Intense. You say you do this for a living?"

"Yep." Robin leaned over, resting her chin on her folded hands, looking up at him. "For a few years now. I have around four million subscribers, give or take a few thousand."

His eyebrows jumped. "Wow. Hell of an audience." He sipped from the beer again and set it next to her elbow. "It's probably rude to ask, but I'm dyin' to know." He burped into his fist. "What kind of money do you make doing this? YouTube videos, I mean. It *can't* be enough to pay bills, much less car insurance. It's why you're living in the van, right? You know, other than the fact that you travel around to shoot this stuff."

"You wouldn't believe me if I told you."

"Try me."

Robin sighed and mumbled, "A little under three hundred . . . a day."

"Three? What—" Kenway's brain seemed to slip gears, and he leaned forward, gripping the table with both hands as he groped for words. "Three hundred dollars a *day?*"

She nodded, blushing.

"Are you *kidding* me? I didn't even see that kind of money in *Iraq.* I don't think *any* enlisted soldier ever has in the *history of modern warfare.*" He did the math in his head, staring up at the ceiling as if God could help him. "Uhh . . . that's about a hundred grand a year."

Robin looked away and coughed, then dug into her salad and pushed a forkful of it into her mouth as if she could chew the math up and swallow it. She felt about three inches tall. Wished she *was* so she could climb into her salad bowl and hide under the lettuce. Her breakfast turned to bitter grass in her mouth, the ranch saline and sour.

Kenway's forehead wrinkled and his eyes searched the table. He glanced up at her and paused the video. "You make six figures pretending to kill witches on the Internet?"

Luckily they were alone on the patio. A brisk wind leapt the fence and ran under the trestle tables, chilling her through her thin sweater.

"Yes," she said, chewing, thoroughly embarrassed.

"Holy god*damn*." Today he was wearing a blue-plaid sort of Western shirt, with curlicues across the chest. Kenway rolled up his sleeves to reveal the tattoos running up his arms. In the sunlight she could finally make them out: robed Japanese samurai battling each other in a froth of hibiscus flowers and green leaves, katanas raised, screaming silently forever. Graceful red foxes darted in and out of the scenes on his arms. "I mean, god, *damn*." He pressed his palms against the edge of the table as if he were going to push away. "Sitting on a secret like *that,* you didn't have anything to worry about, you know, with the shrink thing. I don't think you've . . ."

She ate her salad quietly, not knowing what else to say.

Kenway seemed to deflate. "I'm sorry, it's just a lot to take in, you know?"

"I understand."

"Well, hey, at least you know I'm not interested in you for your money," he lilted. "I liked you even *before* I knew."

Robin nodded, staring down into her food.

"What I meant was, what I was saying, with that kind of a nest egg, it's not like you've really got to worry about what anybody thinks of you." Kenway rubbed his face and picked up his sandwich. "I don't know, I mean, you're sort of 'above the fray,' you know what I'm saying? Above reproach." He took a big bite of the sandwich and stared at the wall, chewing, and said, a little quietly, "Hell, out of my *league,* maybe."

A cold shock ran down the middle of Robin's chest.

"*No,* not at all," she told him, not meeting his eyes. "Money doesn't make me better than *anybody.* Doesn't make *anybody* better than anybody else. Besides . . . I've only just now gotten to that point recently, viewer-wise. It's taken a lot of scrimping and saving to get to this level. I haven't technically made that kind of money yet. And I won't unless I keep swimming." She pointed at the Macbook with her fork. "The videos are passive income, but only so many people can watch them so many times, and if you don't keep producing content you'll start losing subscribers. So it's kinda like being a shark: you have to keep swimming if you want to survive. Lot like being an author, I think."

Kenway regarded her thoughtfully for a moment, not saying anything, and then pressed the Play button on the video with his pinky finger.

As the sounds of her first expedition started back up, the real Robin sitting behind the Macbook thought about how Chandler's house stank. She remembered the fog of funk like it was yesterday, a thick stench that had seemed as solid as Cheez Whiz. "The phone," wheezed the old woman in the video, "is over in there, in the hallway, on the little hutch. Do you see it?"

The monologue about the witches came in over the scene. *They starve,* said the voice-over. *They die from the inside out.* One shoulder came up as a chill of disgust grated through Robin's guts, made her back tense up. *The deadness slowly makes its way to the outside. After a while they're just a rotten corpse in a living-human costume. Death masquerading as life.*

"Jesus," said Kenway. As the battle between past-Robin and the King of Alabama began in earnest, he put down his sandwich and wiped the marinara off his fingers with a napkin. "What the hell." His mouth hung open.

Behind Miguel's Pizza, two years after the events in the video, Robin tried to ignore the screaming coming from the video Kenway was watching. Every sense-memory, every smell and pain, they all drifted in her mind like flotsam, always there, always accessible. Every time she watched one of her own videos, the sensations came rushing back. She realized her folded arms had become a protective hug, her nails digging into her own ribs. She tried to go back to eating.

In the Georgia sun, the faint scars on her arms gleamed pink.

"Get *off* me!" shrieked the Robin in the video in her tinny video-voice. She threw the baby-food jar over the witch's head, where it smashed against the lintel and splattered alcohol all over her bathrobe.

"Oh *shit*," said Kenway, leaning back. "Wait, I totally thought that was gonna be holy water in that jar or something. Righteous." He was entranced by the action taking place on the screen. "What in the balls is even going on right now," he said, leaning over the Macbook, eyes fixed on the video. "Is he—is that guy growling like a house cat?"

"Her familiars," Robin told him, not looking up from her salad.

"The Red Lord will find you," said the man who tried to choke her in the van. His voice was thin and scrapey coming out of the laptop speakers, making it sound more like an insidious whisper than the growled declaration it had been.

As the video faded to black on an image of the blood washing off the utility van and down the car wash drain, it became a grid of links to related videos. Kenway clicked the link that took him back to the main *MalusDomestica* page and then clicked through to the list of Robin's video thumbnails. Most of them had demonic-looking witches' faces on them, yellow-eyed and snarling, or Robin herself with a scratched-up face, with titles like *Mission 12—I Almost Died,* or *Hammertown 5—Knife Training.*

The Red Lord, thought Robin, shuddering. The thought of encountering that thing again did not appeal to her. *It has to be real.* Her mind flashed on an image of those huge clawmarks across the toilet stall doors. *Not a hallucination caused by Illusion magic from Neva Chandler.* She slipped a hand into her laptop satchel to touch the unforgiving security of cold steel. Her combat knife lay hidden in the bag. *Maybe the Red Lord is something related to witchcraft, but not a curse.* What if the creature could sense witchcraft? What if killing Chandler had alerted it to Robin's presence?

If the Red Lord is real, what the hell is it? And where did it come from?

• • •

Kenway sat quietly, scrolling through page after page of YouTube's *MalusDomestica* videos. He didn't watch any of them, but he was hunched over the computer like a Hollywood hacker, gazing intently at each thumbnail as if he could divine its contents by osmosis.

Turmoil spun in Robin's head like hot bathwater going down a drain, leaving her cold and empty and apprehensive inside. *What does he think? Is he scared of me now? No, not possible. He's a vet, his leg's been . . . Does he think I'm a flake? A fake? A nerd?*

Nerd. I can live with nerd.

Finally, he looked up from the computer and regarded her with a wary, squinty eye. A battle was taking place in his head too, she could tell. She could almost hear the mental gears clanking.

She couldn't take it anymore. "Well? Did I scare you away?"

"*Hell* no," Kenway blurted, looking away and talking to the screen with a weird nervous chuckle. "That was bad*ass.* The most badass thing I've ever seen on YouTube. Up till now I thought it was all just—just cat videos and people crashing bicycles." His eyes darted back up to her. "Now I know why you make the big bucks. You're a one-woman production company. You do all your own special effects and everything?"

Caught off-guard, Robin tilted her head. "Yeeeah, you could say that," she said with a coy wince. Her mouth screwed up to one side. "Sure."

His mouth twitched, his face softened.

"I hate to interrupt you," she asked, reaching out to tug the Macbook in her direction with a finger, "but do you mind if I get back to work editing today's video?"

"Oh. *Oh!* Yeah. Yeah, here you go." Kenway turned the laptop around and watched her face over the Macbook's lid as if he were waiting for some kind of tell. *Does he think it's an elaborate joke?* She closed the web browser and pulled up the video-editing console.

Noticing the sandwich on the table by his hand, Kenway seemed to remember he had food and picked it up, eating and staring into the middle distance.

"I want to be on your channel," he said when he finished, startling her. He wiped his mouth with a napkin and wadded it up, shooting at the trash barrel from his seat. The balled-up napkin bounced off the wall and landed on the ground. "I want to fight witches too."

Robin was speechless. "You *what?*"

"I'm tired as shit of hanging around doing what I do. Being the starving-artist cripple that spends all his time up in his studio painting." Kenway got up and went over to the trash, leaning against the wall to snatch the paper off the ground and toss it.

When he came back to her, he leaned on the table with both hands as if he were about to make a business proposal. "The painting thing: it's okay I guess. I mean, it's better than sittin' around with my thumb up my ass. But I do the car stuff because I'm good at it, not because I have a passion for it. And the paintings, ehh. I thought I wanted to be a painter a long time ago. I'll be straight with you, it's wearing kinda thin." Kenway thrust a hand at the Macbook. "Shit! Look at these videos! *That's* passion!" Sitting down, he threw back the last of the beer in the bottle and busied his hands with squeezing the cap into a clamshell shape. "That's different, man. I wanna do something *different* for a change."

"I don't know if that's such a good idea."

He sat there peeling the label off the bottle for a little while, just long enough to give her time to finish the final touches on the video. She went to YouTube and started the transfer.

Kenway wadded up the sandwich wrapper, pitching it into the garbage, and he was about to get up and probably say his see-ya-round.

Don't let him leave without saying something. She reached across the table as if to touch him. *He's a good dude, you idiot. Don't let him be the one that got away.*

In the sunlight, his eyes were the pale, dirty blue of a shallow lagoon, almost gray. He nibbled the corner of his mouth, studying her face, and his eyebrows rose expectantly.

"Look, okay," she said, glancing at the progress bar on her video upload. Two percent. The battery in her laptop would die before it ever got to twenty. "Umm. You're already in this video I'm trying to upload. You can be in the next one too. You don't have to leave."

Ugh, she thought. *Desperate much? Tone it down a little, yeah?*

Fetching a deep, deep sigh, he stroked his beard, smoothing it down. "So what's on the agenda for the rest of the day? Doing any witch-hunting?"

"Right now I'm trying to upload this video, but it's taking forever. And I don't have forever."

"I live in the middle of town." He tossed a thumb over his shoulder. "So my Internet's great. Fast as hell. You're more than welcome to come over and use mine."

• • •

As soon as the back doors of the van came open, Kenway recoiled in surprise, his eyes wide. The swords hanging from the pegboard glittered in the sunlight. "Good lord, you've got an *arsenal* in here. *Look* at all this."

"Part of being a witch-hunter. Thought you would get a kick out of seeing this stuff." Robin gathered her power adapter and— "Actually . . ." She had planned on riding with him in his truck, but it made more sense to just take the van over there. No sense in leaving it here unattended. "How about I just follow you to your place?"

"That'll work."

Apparently when he was alone in the truck, Kenway drove like a maniac. She had trouble keeping up with him in her lumbering panel van. The GoPro was mounted on the dash, facing out the windshield, recording the chase. *One of these days I'm going to have to have an actual car chase,* she thought, grumbling up Highway 9. *The subscribers will love that.*

Traffic was light when they got into town a few minutes later, the lunchtime rush winding down for an afternoon of work.

At the end of his block, Kenway whipped into a parking lot on the corner and she slid into a slot next to him. A sign standing in front of her grille said PARKING FOR STEVEN DREW D.D.S. OFFICE ONLY. One just like it was in front of his Chevy.

As soon as they pulled in, she opened her door and said, "Heavens to Betsy, Action Jackson. Who in the hell taught you how to drive?"

"The army."

"Fair point." She eyed the sign in front of her van, the one that said she couldn't park there. "What about this?"

"I painted the mural in his waiting room for free. He lets me park here so I don't have to use the parallel parking or the angled parking in front of the shop. Backing out into the road makes my ass itch."

"Oh." Robin gathered her Macbook and charger, put them in her messenger bag, and unhitched the GoPro from its mount.

"Doing some filming?" Kenway led her up the sidewalk. As she walked, Robin panned the camera around, shooting B-roll of the street and all the buildings they could see. His art shop was four buildings down, past two empty shopfronts, a Mexican cafe called El Queso Grande, and a DUI driving course office.

"Yep. I like to get as much footage as I can. Makes for a lot of variety and plenty of videos. The more videos you have, the more visible you are on YouTube."

"Makes sense."

I can make today's video a clip episode, like they do on TV shows, she thought. Kenway took out a jingling keyring and unlocked the front door of his studio, pulling the glass door open. *I can tell him my story, and I can illustrate it by splicing in bits of earlier videos. Nice late-season recap episode for new viewers.*

Lights came on and a forest of angular shadows turned into a small office, a computer workstation with two monitors, and several enormous machines of mysterious purpose. One of them looked like a giant laminator, or maybe something that pressed trousers for elephants.

A large table stretched to her right, and both the walls and the table were covered in hundreds of vinyl appliques: sports logos, automobile logos, clothing logos, tattoo designs of gryphons, dragons, tigers; mottos like NO FEAR and ROLL TIDE ROLL and ADVENTURE HURTS BUT STAYING HOME KILLS. A huge cutout of a running football player. Big floppy refrigerator magnets and a couple of coffee mugs with promotional artwork for local businesses. She followed him through a door in the back, coming out into a huge industrial garage and a set of steel stairs leading through a hole in the ceiling.

The garage was strewn with all manner of work trash, bits of vinyl, pieces of broken easel, scraps of canvas, a disassembled foosball table, sheets of plywood and pressboard, and four wide boards with holes cut in them.

The boards made her think of Skee-Ball games. Two legs were bolted to their sides so they stood up at an angle. "What are these?"

"Cornhole."

"*What?*"

"Cornhole," Kenway said again, walking over to a wobbly drafting table and picking up a green beanbag about the size of a baseball. He turned and lobbed it high; she watched it with the camera as it made an arc just under the garage rafters and slapped against the cornhole board, inches from the hole.

"Oh."

He tossed her a beanbag. "You give it a shot."

Robin caught it and fired it across the room. The beanbag hit the wall and landed on top of an electrical conduit some ten feet up.

"Well, shit."

Kenway laughed, climbing the stairs. "Three points." They were impossibly high, climbing twenty feet up the wall and passing between the steel rafters. There were no acoustical tiles, so the ceiling was just gray-green-brown wood that looked like it had been salvaged from a shipwreck.

Emerging from the stairwell, Robin found herself in a space somehow majestic and quaint at the same time. The entire second story was one big open space like the garage downstairs, with a naked fifteen-foot ceiling. Taken as a whole it resembled some kind of modernized tribal lodge, all polished dark wood and hard angles. The south wall was plate-glass windows, looking out at the back of the building behind them and a vast blue sky.

Green marble countertops, steel fixtures, and black appliances made a sprawling kitchen to her left. Directly in front of her was a coffee table made out of a front door, with a short pole jutting up through where the knob used to be.

On top of the pole was a flatscreen TV, the wires running down through the door's deadbolt and into an outlet on the floor. Two park benches made a right angle around the other side of the table.

"Wow," Robin said, still standing at the top of the stairs. A queen-sized bed pressed against the wall to the right, covered in a cream fleece duvet. "*Who* makes the big bucks, again? This place is amazing."

"Most of it was already here when I moved in, except for the bed and the TV." Kenway went over to the kitchen and stood at the island, pouring a glass of what appeared to be tea. "The apartment was part of the deal when I took over the art shop from John Ward, the guy who used to run it before he retired. The VA loan covered most of it; I bought whatever else I needed with my savings. Combat pay makes for a nice nest egg when you're single. To save on power, I don't run the heat, which is why it's cool in here. If I get *too* cold, I haul my little firepit up here and build a fire in it. Lord knows I have enough crap downstairs to burn. Ward used this place for restoring antique furniture too—sometimes I do—and there's a lot of old wood left over."

"You don't have issues with smoke?"

Kenway pointed at vents in the ceiling. "Ventilation for aerosol chemicals. Those, and the vent in the bathroom, they pull the smoke out before it gets too bad."

Above the bed and above the kitchen, the walls were covered in three or four dozen paintings, without frames, just naked mounted canvas. Impressionistic renderings of forests at strange angles, birds in flight, animalistic women in provocative poses with lustrous eyes and bodies hash-marked with cat-stripes. Men and women running with mysterious machines in their hands that could have been rifles, could have been construction equipment, could have been thin shards of stone. Bokeh, the circular lights that appear in out-of-focus photos, dominated the pictures, giving them all an element of dreamlike wonder.

A few other paintings depicted pale nude men standing alone in foggy fields. Hands cupping blood. Grimy faces, always half-obscured by shadow. The bokeh made them nightmarish; they were hung off to the side, as if to marginalize them.

Robin put her bag on one of the park benches and opened her Macbook on the door-table, connecting to the Wi-Fi. Luckily, there was no password, so it only took a minute to get to the channel submissions page. While it uploaded, she walked over to the wall of glass. Peering down into the alleyway behind the building, she could see a large aqueduct running east to west, water trickling along the bottom. "I guess if we're going to be hanging out like this, I should tell you the truth. Tell you how I came to do what I do for a living."

Kenway's answer was grim but somehow warm. "You don't have to do that."

"I want to. I *need* to."

He joined her at the window. "You haven't told your subscribers on YouTube?"

"Yeah. I did in one of my first few videos. But it's not the same, you know? Talking to a camera. It's impersonal. You don't get the same kind of catharsis. And besides, you'll be the second one I've told face-to-face, and I need someone who will believe me. Because what I've finally come back here to do is going to require someone to believe me—believe what I have to say. I need somebody on my side. The more, the better. Shit is going to go pear-shaped real quick, and I need people on my team who are cool with pears."

"The second person?" asked Kenway. "Your therapist?"

"He wouldn't have believed me. He *didn't* believe me. He brainwashed it out of me, as a matter of fact. The whole reason I ended up in the psych ward is because I told the cops the truth about what happened. And for telling the truth, I got the third degree—hypnosis, electroshock therapy, everything short of waterboarding." She spoke to the window, looking down into the aqueduct. "No, I had to tell Heinrich everything if I wanted his help, but if I wanted them to let me out of the loony bin, I had to keep my mouth shut."

"Heinrich?"

"Heinrich Hammer."

"Who is that?" asked Kenway, with a disbelieving chuckle. "Sounds like a fighter in the UFC."

"My mentor. Guy who taught me everything I know about hunting witches." Robin smiled. "He could probably fight in the UFC if he wanted to, but he might be too violent for MMA." She rolled up her sleeves, revealing scars running halfway up the outsides of her forearms. Much too haphazard to be self-cutting scars—they were nicks and cuts from knife-fighting. "I went with him that day in Medina Psychiatric because I'm going to need everything he taught me, and all those weapons in my van—"

"And a bunch of pear experts?"

Robin grinned. "Yes, and a bunch of pear experts. I'm going to need all of that if I want to go head-to-head with the witches who murdered my mother."

Four Years Ago

A shabby ghost sat on a concrete bench in the sun, listening to birds sing in the willows. As pale as the driven snow, her heart-shaped face was spattered with acne and her lips were chapped and thin. Matted brown hair streamed down her cheeks and back. Her hands were cradled in her lap, her fingernails chewed to the quick, a pencil stuck between her fingers like a cigarette.

The teenager was dressed plainly, in a pair of sweatpants and a hoodie. On the back was stenciled MEDINA PSYCHIATRIC HOSPITAL.

It was a nice day, or so she'd been informed. Other patients milled around, playing catch with a little rubber ball, or shuffling through the many clover patches strewn across the courtyard looking for a lucky four-leaf. The nurses said it was good for her to get out and get some fresh air, but the sertraline and aripiprazole in her system dulled everything—the sun on her skin, the breeze in her hair, the sound of it rustling the whiplike branches of the weeping willows around her, the smell of fresh-cut grass.

Indoors or outdoors, it was all the same to a robot. She licked her lips again and looked down at a notebook.

Dozens of rectangles were drawn on the topmost sheet, and within them were more rectangles, creating small self-contained grids of five boxes. Rectangles within rectangles. Each of the boxes were bisected by a snaky, wandering line. Charlie, one of the other patients, had shown her this unfortunate puzzle just after she'd been admitted here, and she'd been singlemindedly pursuing the solution ever since. You were supposed to envision each grid as a "house," and each of the five inner boxes as "rooms." Then you had to draw a continuous line through every wall of each "room" without (a) crossing your own path, or (b) passing through a "wall" more than once. She had the feeling it might have been impossible to solve, but that didn't do anything to mitigate its addictive nature.

She turned the notebook page. Dozens of room puzzles. Turned the page again. Dozens more. In some of the puzzles' "rooms" were written the words *yee tho rah*.

Several pages of scrawled puzzles deeper into the notebook, she found a blank page. She stared at it for several moments before turning the pencil around and putting the lead to paper.

> *dear diary*
> *Fuck this place*
> *fuck green jello with peaches in it*
> *peaches are fucking gross*
> *fuck instant potatoes*
> *instant potatoes are fucking gross*
> *But who gives a shit*
> *I wish I could get a decent cup of coffee in here*
> *welcome to Hell*

She punctuated the missive with another impossible puzzle, guiding the lazy line through each of the walls. She thought she was about to solve it when she realized she'd missed a line in the middle. Rats. Foiled again.

"Hey," said a voice behind her. The teenager sighed and licked her lips, her eyes feeling hot and grainy. "Guess what?"

"What?" she asked, closing the notebook.

"I'm getting married today."

The teenager turned around to face the owner of the voice. It was Mike Hurley, a tall, balding thirty-something who looked a bit like a young Dwight Yoakam. Unlike the girl, he was wearing a two-piece suit, and a tweed overcoat with leather elbow patches.

"Yeah?"

"I'm wearing my Sunday best." Mike dusted his sleeves in a self-satisfied way. "Hey, wanna hear a joke about a ghost?"

"Not really."

"That's the spirit."

"How much will it take to make you go away, Mike?" the teenager asked in her lazy Georgia drawl, hugging the notebook to her chest.

Her feelings about Mike usually vacillated between annoyance and genuine fear. He had some kind of schizo-bipolar issue—she wasn't sure exactly what, and she couldn't get a straight answer out of him about it—and it made him talk in an unfiltered, train-of-thought sort of way. This resulted in an unending kaleidoscope mishmash of ten thousand different topics, and they were almost always some combination of grotesque and silly. Sometimes they veered into vague threats and conspiracy theories, or veiled references to suicide, and that coupled with the way his hands shook and he always seemed wound as tight as a guitar string made the girl anxious. It didn't help that once he got going, he could talk for an hour or more. He also liked to lurk around corners and ambush her with off-the-wall statements, like the getting-married thing, or an anecdote about teaching a dog how to whistle. She'd come walking out of the restroom in the dayroom once, and he'd come at her with the revelation that his dick felt sour.

"It's Mark."

"Whatever."

"Ten thousand shillings in a potato sack." Mark stooped to pluck a piece of grass from the lawn and stuck it in his mouth hillbilly-style. "Did you know, only one out of every seventeen hundred blades of grass has a trace amount of dog urine on it?"

"Yeah?"

"You're statistically more likely to be speared by a swordfish on a deep-sea fishing vessel or run over by a steamroller than you are to put a piece of grass in your mouth a dog's pissed on." The way he spoke, in a measured and articulate tone, seemed at odds with his high-strung manner. He acted as if he were full of nitroglycerin, and the slightest movement would blow him to smithereens. "It's almost time for my meds. I have a goldfish in my room. What are you writing in that notebook? Can I see?"

"I'd rather not," said the teenager. Whether she had intended to or not, the pencil in her hand had revolved so the point jutted out of the bottom of her fist.

"Okay," said Mark. "That's fair." He didn't leave. "Do you remember me? From when we went to high school together?"

"We didn't go to—" she started to say, but thought better of it.

"I guess you don't remember me." He stuck his hands in his pockets. "I don't blame you, I look different now. I used to have red hair, but I cured it by shooting myself in the head." To demonstrate, he took one of his hands out and made a finger-gun, putting it to his temple. "You have no idea how many kinds of cheeses there are. Do you know why the army circumcises all of their drill sergeants? It's because they use the foreskins to create an eyelid for the third eye behind their forehead, so the enemy can't hear what they're thinking. All right, I'm going to leave now. Be good to yourself and be good to your reptilian overlords."

With that, he pulled a demonic Jack Nicholson grin, arched eyebrows and all, and walked away.

A knot in the teenager's guts slowly loosened and relaxed. As soon as Mark/Mike was out of earshot, she got up and headed back inside. Fresh air or not, she didn't want to be sitting in the courtyard when he got an urge to start talking again.

As she opened the dayroom door, she peered over her shoulder. Mark/Mike was goose-stepping enthusiastically up and down the sidewalk in the middle of the area, snapping a salute at every turn. Suddenly he broke into a sprint for the other end of the courtyard, angrily wrenched the nearest door open, and ran through it.

She slipped inside as quickly as possible.

The dayroom was peaceful. Most of the other patients in this wing were outside, so she more or less had the place to herself. She made her way over to the couch, an ancient and very homely thrift-store haul, and plopped down on it to watch TV. There was a movie on, an old one set in the seventies or eighties, with cops and cars, but she couldn't be bothered to expend the mental energy to figure out which one it was.

Someone shook her awake a little while later. A short, stocky lady with frizzy hair. Jennifer, one of the second-shift nurses.

"You doin' okay?" she asked.

"Yeah, I'm fine," said the teenager. The nurses checked on you like this every half an hour or so. Annoying, but not as infuriating as it would have been if not for the medication dulling her temper. "Is it almost time for supper?"

"You got a couple of hours." Jennifer tossed a thumb over her shoulder. "Art therapy is in twenty minutes. You wanna go to that, or you wanna keep napping on the couch?"

The teenager scanned the room. Mark/Mike wasn't here, but a few of the patients from outside had wandered in, and were watching TV while she dozed. "I'll stay in here, thanks." She rummaged around in her head and came up with something that might have passed for a smile. "Not much in the mood to paint fruit today."

"Your call."

The nurse left her alone, spoke quietly to one of the other patients in the room, and made her way toward the hallway door. As she approached it, however, the wing's head nurse came out of it, followed by the tallest, rangiest Black man the teenager had ever seen. Looked like he was eight feet fucking tall. Dressed in a natty blue suit, his collar open to the second button to reveal a pale pendant on his chest.

Even through the med haze, she could tell he wasn't used to wearing snappy garb. His walk was heavy, weary, slow, like an old giraffe, and his eyes were hard and cold.

The head nurse and the stranger spoke for a moment, and then they scanned the room from the door. The nurse spotted the teenager first. "Here she is," she said, approaching. The man did not join her.

"Hi, sweetie." Nurse Anderson was a snake dipped in honey: sweet at first, and all venom on the inside. She was pretty in a 1960s-Hollywood-starlet kind of way, sharp features and slender frame, like a human stiletto. "How are you today?"

"Been better. Looking forward to supper."

Anderson nodded. "Me too. I didn't eat much of a lunch today, and boy, my dogs are barking."

Oh, boo-hoo.

"Well, anyway. Enough of my whining." Anderson smiled her patented smile. Her voice was birdsong, overly congenial, as if she were talking to an idiot. "This nice man here says he'd like to talk to you. Says he knew your family when you were a baby. Says he knows someone named Cutty?"

Ice tumbled into the teenager's veins, as if she'd been injected with Freon. *Cutty. Witch. Cutty. Witch.* Her mother's last words echoed through the hollows of her mind, cutting through the Zoloft and Abilify as easily as the aforementioned stiletto.

"What?" she asked. She felt like the cold had spread to her face and mouth, rendering her lips stiff and mushy.

"He says his name is Heinrich. Friend of your family, before, you, ahh—" A index finger to the nurse's upper lip. "—before you graced us with your presence. He says he wants to talk."

The teenager's eyes darted over Anderson's shoulder to the man standing by the door with his fingertips in his jacket pockets. This Heinrich guy had a monolithic poise and was the king of Resting Bitch Face. "I don't think I like him," she said, drawing her legs up onto the couch, bundling them underneath her, her knees to her chest.

Anderson gave a subtle shrug to the man.

He sauntered over to them. "I can take it from here, ma'am," Heinrich said in a low voice, soft and rough at the same time, like aural corduroy. If he'd had a cowboy hat he would have been holding it to his chest. The teenager got the feeling he had one stashed somewhere, probably in his motel room.

Anderson's lips pursed as she straightened, and she shot the teenager one last exasperated look before she left them to talk.

Heinrich sat on the couch next to the teenager, between her and the patient at the other end, and gave her a moment to either grow accustomed to his nearness or be intimidated by it, she wasn't sure which. Finally he said quietly, "Your name is Robin, ain't it? Robin Martine. I came to the right place, yeah?"

She eyed him. "Maybe."

"My name is Heinrich," he said, offering a hand to shake. She didn't take it. He withdrew it, the hand gently pinching into a fist, as if he'd reached out and taken something from her. "Heinrich Hammer. I knew your mother way back when. We were good friends."

"I think you're full of shit," Robin told him. "My mama didn't have no friends. And that's a weird name."

"She had Miss Cutty, for a little while, didn't she?"

"You don't know nothing about Marilyn Cutty," said Robin. "You don't know shit about me. I don't know who you are, but you're barking up the wrong tree."

"Oh, I very much think I have the right tree." Up close, his face was saddle leather, and a beard of charcoal-colored wool grew on it like moss on a rock. As he spoke, he darkened a bit, if that was possible. Then he lightened again. "I knew your mother, I know who Cutty is, and most importantly—and I think this is most relevant to your interests—I know *what* Cutty is."

Robin's heart skittered in her chest, a cockroach in a can.

"She's a witch," continued Heinrich, "and you—"

"Witches ain't real. Witches ain't real." Adrenaline dumped into her bloodstream. Under her sweatpants, goosebumps trickled across her skin, racing down her thighs. Her bladder threatened to open the pod-bay doors. "Witches ain't real." She looked down and realized she was scrunching up her notebook. "Cutty was just some lady

(go ahead and look, littlebird)

that lived across the street from us. My father murdered my mother. He's a son of a bitch, and witches ain't real." *Witches ain't real witches ain't real witches ain't real witches ain't real witches ain't real—* "I don't know why you're here, but I don't think I want to talk to you anymore." *Witches ain't real witches*

(Mom made me forget)

ain't real witches ain't real witches ain't real. She heard the sound of tearing paper, a snapping pencil. A sharp pain welled up in her left hand, but she barely acknowledged it. *Witches ain't real witches ain't*

(the woman had a gap for a face)

real witches ain't real witches ain't real.

The man's face lightened and his eyebrows rose, as if he realized he'd gotten himself into a mess. "Hey, whoa now," he said softly, placatingly. "I'm sorry, kiddo, calm down, okay? The shouting, it ain't necessary here."

Shouting? Who was shouting?

(even though I walk through the darkest valley, I will fear no evil)

Witches ain't real witches ain't real witches ain't real witches ain't real. Nobody's shouting here.

(I need to protect myself.)

The patient sitting behind Heinrich began to rock back and

forth, bunching his fists against his ears. Someone behind them moaned in a quavering voice. *Witches ain't real witches ain't real witches ain't real witches ain't real.* Anderson came through the door and hesitated, her eyes flicking around the room at the increasingly agitated patients. Clutched in one fist was a hypodermic syringe.

"No!" said Robin, fear turning into anger. "Don't you come over here with that fuckin' thing!" She bared yellow teeth, her greasy dreadlocks parting to reveal a face twisted into a mask of alarm. "You stick me and I swear to God I'll bite your fingers off!"

The man grabbed her shoulders. His hands were strong, iron-strong, but he didn't squeeze her. Just enough pressure to restrain her, as if she were in manacles bolted to the wall. Heinrich looked over his shoulder at the nurse and shook his head. "No! No chemical restraints. I can handle this. Just do what you have to do with the rest of them. I got this."

"Sir, it looks like you don't 'got' anything. You're disturbing our residents."

"I do—I mean, I'm not. Look, I just—"

"Okay, whatever, just take her outside, all right?" Anderson demanded, marching over, the syringe needle still jutting from between her fingers. "Away from the others. You can talk to her out in the courtyard." She and the man named Heinrich lifted Robin by her arms and escorted her out the dayroom door.

Out in the sunshine and vivid green grass and warm breeze, everything seemed a little less imperative, a little less ominous.

"Shut the fuck up for a minute," said Heinrich, depositing her on a bench, obviously becoming some mixture of alarmed and irritated. Robin immediately went to the grass. She pulled up her feet and hugged her knees to her chest, the squished notebook caught against her thighs, and the grass under her face was cool, comforting, fragrant.

"Sir," Anderson said sharply. "That kind of language is quite unnecessary." She paused. "And look, she's hurt herself. What are you trying to do here?"

In breaking the pencil, Robin had pierced the palm of her hand, and rather deeply. Blood trickled down the heel of her wrist. She looked up at the nurse with pleading eyes, squinting in the sunlight. "It's nothing, it's nothing, I don't need to go to the infirmary, it's nothing, I'm fine."

She caught a look from Heinrich communicating frustration, disappointment, understanding, and appeal, all in one. *Come on, work with me here, kid,* it seemed to say. *I drove all this way to see you and I expected more from you, not this caterwauling and batshittery.*

Anderson took her hand and turned it over, inspecting the puncture wound. "I think it needs some Neosporin and maybe a bandage, at least."

"I'm fine. This is fine. I'm calmin' down, I think."

She rubbed the blood off on her sweatpants. Anderson very visibly did not approve.

The man whipped a handkerchief out of a pocket in the breast of his jacket and wiped off the remainder of the blood, and then deftly tied it around Robin's wrist. "There. Mission accomplished," he said, squeezing her hand so hard she could feel her heartbeat in her fingertips.

Away from the patients and the other nurses, Anderson's façade seemed to slip. Both of her hands had evolved into fists. "*Are* you calm now?" she fumed, capping the syringe. "Are you going to make me stick you?"

"Yes. I mean, no. I mean, y-you ain't got to do anything."

Heinrich knelt in front of Robin, still holding the bandaged hand. "We're cool, ain't we? We can be friends and talk about some stuff, right?"

Robin nodded.

Heinrich rubbed the back of his neck and sighed. "I think we're good here." His eyes pinged up to the nurse and back down again, then over at Robin's pale face. "We're good. You can go."

"I hope you *do* take her with you like you said," said Anderson, dropping the needle in her scrubs pocket. "She's been a handful and a—"

"I said you can go." His voice became stone.

Anderson turned and walked away. "This attention whore, I swear to God," she grumbled under her breath. Her pink-and-purple New Balance sneakers scuffed across the sidewalk as she bustled across the courtyard in her busy-bee way, and she disappeared back into the dayroom.

"Now," said Heinrich, still crouching in front of her, "as we were saying."

"Witches." Little more than a whisper.

He paused, and the slightest of smiles touched the corners of his mouth. "Yeah." He squeezed her hand a little bit. "Yeah, we were talking about . . . them." They shared the moment, sitting there in the sunshine, the light glinting on his bald brown head. Cool grass prickled Robin's elbows.

Then he reached into his jacket liner pocket again and took out something like a cigarette rolled with dead leaves. "Mind if I smoke?"

· · ·

They traded the cigarillo back and forth, smoking it by the half-inch, sitting on a bench half-hidden by an enormous magnolia tree. She had only started dabbling in smoking when everything went to shit, and at first the smoke had choked her, but it was smooth enough she didn't have much trouble picking up the habit again. It was coconut-flavored, which to her, after spending so much time in a drab mental hospital smelling nothing but Simple Green and feet, was like being transported to a tropical paradise.

"So you're telling me I'm not crazy. The woo-woo shrinky-dink 'therapy' the psychiatrist put me through, the brainwashing, the meds, the denial, it was all bullshit." Robin sat cross-legged on the end of the bench, Heinrich hunched over with his elbows on his knees. That two-piece suit of his was deep sea–blue and pinstriped, made him look a little like a railroad conductor. But he wore black combat boots with it, spit-polished half to hell and back. "None of the things I've been claiming to have witnessed are delusions brought on by—as the psych calls it—a psychotic break caused by the trauma of witnessing my mother's death. The last year or so, the involuntary committal, the being cuffed to a bed, that was . . . for nothing? There's nothing wrong with me?"

"Yep. You're not crazy." Just then Heinrich had the cigarillo. He ashed it on the ground between his shoes. "Well I mean, if you are, then I guess I'm crazy too."

She wanted to cry, honestly. She wanted to, but thanks to the blunting effect of the Zoloft, she couldn't quite muster the tears. There was relief at the idea she'd been right the whole time, but it was subtle, like getting a pebble out of your shoe. And to be frank, it was sort of tempered by the academically terrifying idea she was right—witches were real.

"So . . . what?" she asked. "What does this mean for me?"

He took a draw off the cigarillo, seemed to mull it over in his head for a moment, and said, "Your mother was murdered," in his customary blunt way, squinting in the smoke. "By your dear darling daddy."

"Yeah, no kidding. Tell me something I don't know. My asshole piece of shit father pushed her down the stairs and broke her neck." She hated calling her father Dad. The name *Dad* was reserved for men who gave a shit, men who raised you right, men who took you fishing and bought you ice cream on the way home, men who picked you up after the prom because you were too trashed to drive or be alone with a boy. Men who didn't murder your mother.

She was in the kitchen when it happened, Robin, a sophomore in high school, making a pitcher of iced tea. Came running out of the kitchen and basically went into shock. Her mother was lying on the floor in a heap of twisted meat, a ragdoll in a dress, her head canted at a weird angle, facing the ceiling.

Her daughter sat beside her and held her, frantic, confused.

A few minutes later, her father snapped out of it. *One of us called 911, but I don't remember who.*

The tea, I remember . . . I left the kettle on and almost burned the house down. The kitchen—and part of the living room—was on fire when the police got there, but the volunteer firefighters managed to put it out, or so she was told. She didn't remember much of that night, or that month, for that matter. "The state of Georgia charged my father with murder," she said quietly. "Third-degree, second-degree, premeditated, I don't know, I wasn't at the trial. By then I was a ward of the state—the cops had taken me away. And thanks to my story about witches and puking up cats, the psychiatrist at the trial said I was mentally unfit to serve as a witness."

"Your father killed your mother because *they* made him do it," said Heinrich, his voice cutting through her reverie.

"Cutty," Robin murmured. "Witch."

My mother's muddled last words, the last thing she ever said to me, as I sat there on the floor holding her useless body.

Her father had come down the stairs, walking all stiff and slow, not saying a word, one hand sliding down the banister . . . and when he got to the bottom, he fell on his hands and knees, arching his back, dry-heaving like he was coughing up a hairball.

He started throwing up blood.

It was really coming out, I mean spewing all over the runner, and then he was choking. He was choking and horking and then he vomited up a cat. His neck bulged out like a cantaloupe, and this gray-striped tabby cat came wriggling up his throat, coming out of his mouth yowling and hissing, with its fur and ears all slicked back with blood so it looked like a waxed weasel. Even lubed up like that, it got stuck. It fought the whole way.

Before he could suffocate, Robin's father had to grab that striped tabby cat by the head and pull it out like a . . . like a birthday-party magician, pulling scarves out of his mouth.

"He was their familiar," said Heinrich.

"Familiar?"

"The women living in that house up the hill from the one you grew up in. Marilyn Cutty, Theresa LaQuices, and Karen Weaver. Those women are probably the oldest and most powerful coven in America. I've been looking for 'em for years, looking for a way to nail their asses."

Cutty, weird, quaint Marilyn Cutty, who she thought of as the equivalent of her grandmother for so many years, whose house she'd played in as a child. Robin remembered lying on the floor in Cutty's living room, reading the Sunday comics and petting her calico Stanley, a little high from the scented markers she'd been coloring with. When Robin escaped during one of her parents' frequent feuds and toddled over to her house, Marilyn would take her shopping and they'd come home with these complex Lego sets. God, she loved Legos. *You don't have to buy me nothin'*, Robin would tell her, and old Marilyn would say, *I know. That's why I do it*.

How could this old woman who regularly loved and spent money on a little girl be this kind of evil?

"See, cats will do anything a witch tells them to," continued Heinrich. "That's not a total stereotype—witches really do have black cats, and white cats, and gray cats, all kinds of cats, but it's a little more complicated."

He passed Robin the cigarillo and she pinched it to her lips as if it were a joint, sucking a lungful of smoke out of it.

"Witches can command cats, you know, like the rats in that movie *Willard*," said the gangly stranger. "They can do this because cats belong to, and are minions of, the Mesopotamian goddess Ereshkigal—they're creatures *of* the afterlife, which is why they can see spirits."

Robin stiffened, giving him a *you're shitting me* look. She handed him the cigarillo.

"Yeah," he scoffed, "*ghosts.*"

His voice was hard, but his eyes were compassionate. "Whole 'nother can of worms we'll maybe have time to get to some day." He took a drag off the cigarillo and smoke curled out of his nose like a dragon. "Right now, you ought to know something: your mother is a witch."

Stunned. Speechless.

All she could do was sit there, trying to compare her sweet, pretty, good-natured mother, that tiny curly-haired housewife

(*Mom made me forget something*)

with the goofy speech impediment and the deep and abiding love for Christianity

(*I need to protect myself*)

against the sinister image of witches she'd built up in her mind during the months she'd spent in the mental hospital. She'd known all along, though, hadn't she? She eyed the scars down the insides of her forearms, the chicken-foot symbol, the *algiz* carved into her skin. Mom tried to make her forget the things she'd seen and heard when she was little, and there were holes in her memory like a moth-eaten sweater, but in the end, she had managed to cling to a few of them. And there, in the back of her mind, those suspicions had lingered, even through the institution's electroshock therapy.

Mom was a witch. Heinrich's declaration pulled at those old mnemonic scars. *You know it's true.*

"There are good witches, and there are bad witches," said Heinrich. Sometimes, it seemed, a witch could be both. "Your mother was a good witch, and she was a *new* witch. Cutty probably talked her into giving up her heart only a couple years after you were born." Heinrich aimed those flinty eyes at Robin. "You can console yourself with the knowledge Annie waited until after you were born to give her heart to Ereshkigal. Witches can't have kids, you know. To be a mother, you have to have a heart."

"What's all this got to do with my father and the witches' cats?"

"There's this fungus called Cordyceps," Heinrich said quietly and measuredly, as if he were confessing to something. "That's the scientific name. It infects ants' brains and it makes them do things they wouldn't normally do, like climb up a tree, where the fungus bursts out of their head and spores out into the air. Reproduces.

"Cats themselves can carry a parasite called *Toxoplasma gondii*, and it can infect the brain of its host, influencing its behavior. When it infects a mouse through contact with cat feces, that mouse contracts an illness called toxoplasmosis and behaves erratically. Gets real screwed up. Real friendly to cats. So you can imagine what happens next: the mouse ends up in the cat's bowels. The only place that particular thing can reproduce. And hakuna matata, the circle of life rolls on."

He took another puff and handed it over. "The witches figured out how to metaphysically 'implant' a cat into a human the same way the Cordyceps inserts itself into an ant's brain, the same way *Toxoplasma gondii* infects mice's brains. They yowl and hiss and claw at you like a cat. It's because they're cats in human bodies. Body-snatchers. Pod people, I suppose. These parasite-cats lie dormant inside their human hosts like hairy unborn children, sleeping, waiting, until the witches need them."

"So that's what was wrong with my father the night he pushed my mother off the upstairs landing," said Robin. "He'd been familiarized. He had a cat in him."

At some point the weight of their conversation had broken through the meds, and tears welled up in her eyes at the sensation of having been right. Robin scraped her face with the inside fabric of her hoodie. God almighty, right as rain, she was *right*. She wasn't lying, she wasn't delusional, she wasn't either of those things. Fuck her therapist. Fuck art therapy. Fuck Anderson.

All of a sudden the air seemed sweeter. It was like being let out of a locked chest she'd been shut up in for a year.

"Why did they do it?" she asked.

By then they had smoked the cigarillo about as far as they

could smoke it. "Why did they murder Annie?" Heinrich mashed the cigarillo against the end of the bench to put it out, then turned and flicked it into the bushes. "They needed her to make a dryad."

"What is that?"

"A dryad is at its most basic a soul trapped inside of a tree. Or, well, technically it's the name for the tree-prison itself, but it also refers to the tree-and-soul combined. Anyway, dryads don't occur naturally, so you have to make one—provided you know how, of course. Now, if you make a dryad out of a normal person . . . take Joe Schmoe off the street, kill him, siphon his spirit into a tree, all you have is a self-aware tree. Pretty shitty existence for poor Joe, livin' out the rest of eternity with squirrels shovin' acorns up his ass, but there ain't nothin' special about it.

"But if you make a dryad out of a supernaturally endowed person, for example, another witch, you end up with what's called a *nag shi*. Like the person it was created from, this kind of dryad is an energy-absorber. And with a little coaxing and a bucket of human blood twice a week, it will become a sort of spiritual black hole. The tree's roots draw up life for miles around, and if it's in a town like Blackfield, it will tap that town for nourishment.

"The soul-tree pulls the will-to-live out of the town and converts it to fruit. Peaches, apples, lemons, whatever the dryad happens to flower. Where does all that give-a-shit go, you ask? It goes into the dryad's fruit. Flora de vida—the fruit of life. The fruit of immortality."

• • •

"You may have a chance to save your mother, you know," Heinrich told her. "She may not be *actually* dead. Not completely. She is a nag shi. She is somewhere, there inside their dryad."

A thrill went up Robin's spine at the thought she could see her mother again.

Her strange benefactor put one of those rough, bony hands on her shoulder, and she fought the urge to shove him. It must have showed on her face, because he immediately withdrew the hand. "But it ain't going to be easy," he said. "You're gonna have to train. Have to learn how to beat 'em." He leaned over toward her. "How would you like to get out of here?"

At first, a splinter of fear tried to worm its way into her. A certain feeling of vulnerability flowered there, like a mouse being invited into the open, where all the owls and eagles and falcons could see it. When she'd first arrived at Medina Psychiatric, Robin had been terrified that since she'd seen them murder her mother, seen them do whatever they did to her father, they'd want to come after her too. Eventually, as she began her meds, and the fog of fear and mania and paranoia had cleared, and she got used to her new environment, the concrete walls of the mental hospital had engendered a feeling of safety, of protection.

She blinked. She was becoming institutionalized, like the old guy in that prison movie. *The Shawshank Redemption.* What was his name? Books? Hooks? Brooks?

"I'd like for you to come with me," he said, "back to my place in Texas."

Texas, she thought, licking her chapped lips.

Mental images of wide-open desert, dry breezes, bristly sagegrass, sand, tumbleweeds . . . it was intoxicating. So different from the sweltering, claustrophobic forests of Georgia. "I can train you," Heinrich was saying. "I can teach you what I know about witches—and," he scoffed, "what I know could fill a book."

The gangly stranger got up off the bench and tugged his jacket straight, dusting off the seat of his pants. "I been working on getting you out of here for a while. Behind the scenes, like. You come with me, you can get 'em back for the shit they did to you. If you want, you can get *all* them witches."

All them witches.

"How many witches *are* there?" Robin asked, threatening to retreat into her shell. She looked around with guarded eyes. The sun was starting to go down, and the shadows mingling with the infinity of pine trees around them seemed to be getting longer and deeper.

"A few."

"How many is a few?"

"I don't know, a few hundred?" Heinrich made a dismissive gesture, as if trying to wave away the question. "Listen, they're weak shit. Most of 'em ain't worth chasing. Little more than palm-reading hippies and crazy cat-ladies. Now, some of 'em are bad news. But the big fish is Cutty's coven." He tugged his cufflinks, adjusting his sleeves. "After you train with me, you can cut your teeth on the small fries before you go back to Blackfield and do what you need to do. I'll make sure you're ready before you face off against any of them. By the time I'm done with you, you'll be a killing machine."

In the middle of his spiel, Mark (or perhaps Mike) Hurley came out of the dayroom door, still wearing his a-size-too-big Sunday-morning-church suit and tweed overcoat. He began to make grand, sweeping motions in front of him, as if he were smoothing out the lawn. Then he held up his hand and made pinching motions in front of his eye, looking at Robin and Heinrich. "I'm crushing your head! I'm crushing your head!" he shouted, his voice echoing off the building. "Look on these works and despair, proletariat! I'm the oppressive specter of free market capitalism, and I'm crushing your head!"

Robin and Heinrich looked at each other.

"I had a bowl of Quaker oatmeal for dinner," said Mark/Mike. "The oats in it were picked by slaves who are the descendants of the people who came here from Neptune in 1962."

"I have papers releasing you into my care," said Heinrich.

"Give me a minute to pack my shit," said Robin.

• • •

He held the front door open for her as Robin stepped outside of Medina Psychiatric for the first time in more than a year. She still wore the team hoodie, so to speak, and the sweatpants, but the gym bag hanging by the straps from her right hand had clothes in it, salvaged by the cops from her bedroom at the house on Underwood. Unfortunately, they were a bit tight on her now—after spending all that time either strapped to a bed or sitting around in the dayroom, she'd developed a muffin top and the clothes no longer fit.

In her other hand was a stockpile of meds in a Ziploc freezer bag, along with a pill cutter.

"We'll stop somewhere on the way out of Georgia and get you some new clothes," said Heinrich, checking out the stencil on the back of her hoodie. He led her down the front stairs and into the parking lot. "I can tell you now, though, you're gonna be losing some of that baby fat when you start training. So the clothes in that bag will probably fit you again."

"That's good, I think," said Robin. Her chest felt tight, her heartbeat thundering in her neck. "I like this stuff. I'd like to be able to wear it again." Though would she? The clothes in the gym bag were flowery, girly—sundresses, T-shirt dresses, jeans with Bedazzler gems on the butt. She wasn't that person anymore. She'd examined all the clothes as she'd packed them, and had the unmistakable impression she was packing clothes meant for a child.

The man's car was a Ford Fairlane, a sleek, monumental cruiser with flair to spare. Deep devil red, almost burgundy, and the chrome was spotless.

"Sweet ride, mister," she said, as he unlocked the trunk. She tossed her bag inside.

"Thanks. Inherited it from my father. He was a preacher. Drove it to service every day for almost thirty years."

"It's nice." She peered through the back window at the leather seats. "Very clean."

"I try to take care of it."

They got in and he started the engine. It roared and rampaged, just waiting to break free and tear shit up.

The man, concern in his eyes: "You good?"

He watched her as if he were waiting for her to start screaming about witches again, his hands resting on the steering wheel. Robin took a deep breath and let it out in a shaky sigh.

"Yeah," she said, pulling on her seatbelt. "Yeah, I think I am."

Pulling out of the parking lot, Heinrich eased them down the long, winding driveway that would take them away from Medina Psychiatric forever. Twenty thousand pine trees buffeted the windshield with shadows from the setting sun. She rolled the window down and let the wind ruffle her greasy hair.

Man, I look rough, she thought, grimacing as she caught a glimpse of her own face in the side mirror. She looked homeless and destitute—Sasquatch hair, grody teeth, dark circles around her eyes, chapped lips from the constant licking caused by the anti-psychotic meds.

The car seemed sturdy. The door felt strong, heavy, solid.

"What if—" she murmured out the window.

"Hmm?" asked Heinrich.

"What if this is a new start? What if this is my life startin' over?"

"We'll call it a mulligan," said Heinrich, turning on the radio. Low, barely a susurration of static and music. "Take two, like they say in the movies. Yeah?"

"Yeah."

She reached over and turned the radio up, trawling through the stations until she found something other than country. Shinedown's "The Crow and the Butterfly" filled the car with music.

"Not what I would have gone for," said the man. "But I can dig it."

"What you into, then?"

"Rock. Oldies. Creedence, Cash, AC/DC, Skynyrd, Hendrix." He twisted the station dial until something with a little more vintage came in: Aerosmith. *Dream on, dream on, dream on, dream on.* "There we go. Can't go wrong with KZ106 Tennessee."

"My mom likes this station," said the teenager.

A smile spread across the man's face, and he turned it up until she could feel Steven Tyler's voice through the seat. "Rock on, then, baby, rock on then."

• • •

Thirteen-hour drive between Georgia and Texas. Almost nine hundred miles. They drove until it was past midnight, then stopped in Jackson, Mississippi, for the night and got a two-bed room at a rundown motel in the middle of nowhere. The next morning Heinrich changed out of the navy two-piece and into something definitely more his style: black jeans, white old-fashioned pioneer shirt, black vest. Over that went a black trench coat and a black gambler hat. The shirt's collar was open a little bit, and she could see the pendant swinging around down in there.

"Like black much?" Robin asked, sitting cross-legged on the bed, eating an IHOP omelet. Best thing she'd ever eaten in her life.

The man tied an avocado-green paisley handkerchief around his neck and stuffed it into his shirt collar for a cravat. "If it's good enough for Johnny Cash," he said, checking himself in the mirror, "it's good enough for me."

"You look like you were born about a hundred years too late."

"Got me fair and square. Felt that way all my life."

She couldn't shake the feeling she was in the wrong place, going the wrong way with the wrong man. She'd spent her whole life to date in Blackfield, and now she had that eerie, queasy sensation you get when you wake up on the bus and you realize you'd missed your stop.

She voiced her concerns to Heinrich, who chuckled. By then they were on the road again. At a nearby Target, Robin picked out a bunch of black clothes herself: T-shirt, ripped jeans, military jacket. "It's called a 'leap of faith,' Robin Hood," he told her. "You're moving forward into the unknown. Shit is scary, I'll give you that. I been there. But you're in good hands now. You been knocked down, kiddo, but old Hammer is gonna pick you up and dust you off."

The landscape slowly transformed from green forest to swampy delta to grassy plains, and slowly they were swallowed up by arid scrublands, which gave way to the open desert of Texas. Gave them a lot of time to talk, and Heinrich did most of the talking. He took the opportunity to continue his history lesson.

"There have always been witches. According to my research, the first witch's name was Yidhra. She was a priestess of Ereshkigal, the Mesopotamian goddess of the land of the dead, Irkalla. Yidhra became a witch by sacrificing her own heart in exchange for a piece of Ereshkigal's power.

"The goddess replaced Yidhra's heart with what they called a *libbu-harrani,* Sumerian for 'heart-road,' to Irkalla, or more specifically, perhaps a sort of conduit—sort of like how a power outlet in a house pulls its electricity from the electric company. Her heart had been exchanged for a direct line to the afterlife. From this conduit, Yidhra derived her powers: divination, sorcery, necromancy, speaking with the dead, the familiarization of animals, that kind of shit.

"Over time, Yidhra became the Biblical 'Witch of Endor,' a minor celebrity in ancient Mesopotamia, a notorious sorcerer, oracle, and cult figure who drew in acolytes, followers who also sacrificed their hearts to Ereshkigal.

"By the time she was living out her twilight years in the village of Endor, she had convinced hundreds of women to give up their hearts to the goddess of the dead."

Around lunchtime the Fairlane wound through Killeen, passing the desolate reaches of the army base of Fort Hood, where Heinrich stopped for gas and got Robin a Vanilla Coke, and they continued on.

On the other side of town, the environment got real sparse, real fast, looking like something out of the old Western movies she used to watch with her dad. Robin watched it pass by them, imagining John Wayne hurtling across the stony sand on his horse, cycling his lever-action Mare's Leg rifle with one hand. Heinrich drove them onto a two-lane meandering almost all the way to Mexico, through stands of tall, scratchy bur oak and red cedar. He diverged from this down a rocky dirt road and came around a particularly large oak, parking in front of what looked like an old Mexican village. Or, at least, it would have if not for the weird script painted on signs nailed to the façades and the half-assed graffiti Kryloned all over the walls.

"Welcome to Hammertown," said Heinrich. "It's a facsimile of a Middle Eastern village. Those signs are in Arabic. It's a 'MOUT' course—Movement Over Urban Terrain. Army built it for training purposes when Desert Storm kicked up, then built a new one on the fort and gave this one to the Killeen police. They eventually opened up the one on the fort to civilians, and abandoned this one."

"You live here?"

"I sure do."

"Nobody gives a shit?"

"They haven't so far." Heinrich opened the trunk and pulled out Robin's gym bag, carrying it through the front gate. "Come on, I'll show you where you're gonna be sleeping."

Her arrangements turned out to be at the top of a rather barren four-story cinder-block structure that, according to her new guardian, was used to train firefighters. She had a cot curtained off from a large, open room with a dusty Oriental rug in the middle of it. Place looked like the studio apartment of some small-time drugrunner, with enormous windows looking out over the Texas desert and posters of seventies blaxploitation movies and kung-fu flicks on the walls. A sectional couch that looked like it had been through the bombing of Hiroshima, a glass-top coffee table with a crack running diagonally across it, shelves upon shelves of military novels and Louis L'Amour adventures and gunsmithing books. The windows had mosquito netting instead of glass, so as the wind blew through they made weird soft thrumming noises.

A turntable sat on a beat-up nightstand. The man put on a record and Earth Wind & Fire began to tell them what would happen if they wished upon a star. "Make yourself at home, Robin Hood," he said, pausing in the makeshift kitchenette to chug water out of a jug in the fridge. "I'm gonna go pick up some food and some other stuff. I'll be back in a little bit."

With that, Heinrich trotted back down the stairs again, disappearing into the darkness.

A few minutes later, she heard the distant sound of the Fairlane starting up, and then there was just her and the music. She sat on the couch, trying to will herself, to center herself, to find her Zen and take stock of what kind of situation she'd gotten herself into.

After a while the song ended, and then the record ended. Robin took it off and found another one. Needle scratch, pop, crackle.

"I keep a close watch on this heart of mine," sang Johnny Cash.

Robin stood at the window for a long time, the Texas breeze showering her in dry, odorless air through the black mesh. Crickets sang softly in the chaparral outside.

Plastic chests lay on the floor around Heinrich's bed—a foam mattress on steel milk crates—and Robin went to them, started picking through them. One was full of military fatigues, or at least that's what she thought they were. One was full of his underwear and socks. She opened another and found a rifle encased in gray foam.

Big. Tactical. Wicked-looking. This thing looked like it belonged in the hands of a revolutionary, or an insurgent. Her heart thumped. The situation hit her like a ton of cold, hard bricks—she had jumped in a car with a man she'd never met before, on the flimsiest and most fantastical of promises, and driven hundreds of miles to the middle of the desert to this burnt-out fortress of papier-mâché and plywood and cinder blocks, where now she knelt in the dust, looking down at a unmistakable tool of incredibly violent death.

Lying on the nightstand next to a dirty ashtray was an enamel lapel pin: green, with gold accents. It depicted a dog's face, or perhaps a wolf, in profile, on top of a golden circle inscribed with a long sentence in an unreadable language. Looked paramilitary, or maybe one of those secret societies, like the Freemasons, or the Illuminati. Around the dog's neck was a bow—not a cutie-pie bow, but the kind that fired arrows.

Whoa. Her hands went cold. She didn't know this man at all.

"These things shall pass so don't you worry," sang Cash. "The darkest time is just one hour before dawn."

She closed the trunk on the weapon and opened another one.

This one contained bundles of blankets and what she discovered to be electric clippers in a heavy plastic bag, along with a small collection of different-sized trimmer heads. She took it out and scanned the walls for a power outlet. One by the sink in the kitchenette. She plugged in the clippers and turned them on. The sound was startling in the solitude of the tower, a loud, venomous, live-wire hum.

Putting the blade to her temple, Robin began to shave her matted hair into the sink.

She was almost done when Heinrich returned just after lunch. He had armloads of grocery bags. He deposited them on the counter and watched her buzz her scalp as he put them away.

Soon, all that was left was a stripe of hair on top of her skull, a slightly crooked Mohawk of wavy locks. With little more than a meaningful glance, the man took the clippers from her and touched up the edges of the Mohawk, then washed the shorn-off hair into the garbage disposal and ground it up.

"Looks good. Welcome to the new you." He pulled a pint of Ben & Jerry's out of a plastic sack and slid it across the kitchen island like a wild-west bartender. "Hope you like ice cream." He took out another pint, tore off the lid, and plunged a spoon into it. "I have two vices in this world: ice cream and not dressing like shit. And my car. Three vices. I bought you a carton of this because if you touch my ice cream I will kill you and leave your body for the coyotes to pick clean."

They locked eyes for an interminable moment in which Robin

thought she might scream and fling herself through the window and mosquito netting. Heinrich's face was so incredibly intense it was horrible—soulless, cold, all full of unfeeling steel and veiled evil. In that instant she considered the fact she might have had a serious lapse in judgment in coming here.

Then his eyes fell from hers and the man laughed into his ice cream, a low, throaty belly laugh communicating more warmth and humor than she thought she had ever heard from a grown man.

"The look on your face," he said, still laughing.

And that got her to grinning like an idiot, and when she looked for a spoon the first drawer she pulled open was full of silverware as if she'd lived here for years, and as she dug out a spoonful of Chubby Hubby and stuck it in her mouth she decided being a guerrilla witch-hunter had the potential to be a pretty sweet gig after all.

• • •

"And that's when I started training with Heinrich," said Robin. By the time she'd finished the tale, they had migrated to the kitchen. She sat on a stool at the island while Kenway cooked burgers on a griddle set in the island next to the stove. Her camera stood on a bendy-legged tripod at the end of the counter, next to a splat of postal envelopes.

"Was it like in the movies?" he asked, flipping a burger. *Kssssss.* "You know, like a montage with a music backing, and you're beating up a kick-bag and throwing wooden stakes at a dummy?"

"That's Buffy the Vampire Slayer." Robin gave him a dark eye. Noticing a glass vase full of coffee beans, she slid it over and took a sniff. "And . . . well, there were things like that I guess. It was mainly porin' over esoteric texts. Library books, microfiche, photocopied newspapers, stolen documents. . . ."

"Stolen?"

"Heinrich was the type, he didn't let a little thing like the law stop him from doin' what he needed to do. Most of them he stole from the cult he used to belong to before he escaped. Never told me much about it, just that they're nasty pieces of work."

"I see." He flipped another patty. *Kssssss.* "I assume you haven't had to do anything like that, since you don't seem to be hiding from the law." Unwrapping a piece of cheese, he added, "You *aren't* running from the law, are you? Living in the van would make a lot more sense if you were."

"Heinrich had already gotten all the stuff he'd needed by the time I met him," said Robin. "Of course there's probably a couple dozen unsolved cases of arson out there." *As well as assault cases, vandalism, manslaughter, and God knows what else. Need-to-know info.* She put a finger to her lips. "But I won't tell if *you* don't."

Kenway sighed thoughtfully and put the cheese on the meat as it sizzled. "You're really something, lady. I don't know what to do with you."

You could kiss me, she thought, but didn't say. "Thanks for giving me a place to hang out for the evening that ain't my van or the pizzeria. And for the Internet."

He smirked up at her. "And the burger."

"And the burger. I love pizza, but I think I'm overdosing."

"So how did the YouTube thing start?" Kenway asked, putting some buns on plates and scooping up the burgers onto them.

"You know how in football, the team keeps the game recordings and goes over them later? Heinrich used to do that so we could watch them and fine-tune our techniques. I was the one who suggested we could put the tapes on the Internet and make money on 'em." Her stomach growled at the smell rising off the griddle. "At first, he was dead set against it, but after I showed him how much like some of the other YouTube series it was, and how much money we could make on it, he warmed up to the idea. As long as I made sure he didn't appear in any of them, and if he did, his face was censored out."

A noise came from Robin's jeans, startling both of them. She dug in her pocket and took out her phone. Alarm set to go off at six. She put it away and slid down off the stool, opening a cabinet. "Where's your glasses?"

"I don't wear glasses."

She grinned awkwardly. "Drinking glasses, you dingus."

"Oh. Yeah." Kenway opened one of the other doors. Robin took down a glass and filled it at the sink, then went to her laptop on the coffee table and dug a prescription bottle out of her messenger bag. She tipped out a tablet and swallowed it with a gulp of water.

He watched her with curiosity, but didn't say anything.

Putting the bottle away, Robin went back to the island to sit down and drink the rest of the glass. Kenway gave her a curious eye.

"The pills are for, uhh . . . well, the shrinks say I got delusions, or something. Hallucinations. Nightmares. PTSD. I had night terrors when I was a kid, and I guess the things I been through just made them worse." She picked at a fleck of color in the marble counter. "The medication helps. I did have Zoloft too, but I stopped taking it when I ran out of the bottle they gave me at the psych ward. I don't like it. I mean I'm not a big fan of the Zoloft zaps, but I like being a robot even less."

And to be honest, I'm not one hundred percent sure I'm even having hallucinations. At this point, taking the meds had become force of habit . . . but after the encounter at Miguel's Pizza, her faith in the anti-psychotics had been shaken. And having her faith shaken in something she'd been relying on to maintain her sanity made her feel vulnerable.

Kenway seemed to be uncomfortable. He rolled his shoulders and tugged on his shirt as if it didn't fit right.

"Guess that probably put you off me, didn't it?" Robin murmured, folding her arms. "It usually does. Guys. Hell, girls, even. I've . . . tried to date before, but as soon as I break out the pill bottle, they're out the door. Confucius say, *don't stick your dick in crazy.* Even if you ain't got one, I reckon."

Pursing his lips, Kenway looked at her—*really* looked at her, a burning, assessing, ant-under-a-magnifying-glass stare—and then he put down the spatula and rolled up one of his pants legs, revealing the prosthetic foot. He unbuckled it, a laborious process with grunting and pulling and ripping of Velcro, then pulled the foot off, leaving a nub wrapped in a bandage.

As big as Kenway was, the false leg looked as if it were three feet tall, with an articulated ankle and a silicone cup. Had a shoe on it, of course, the match to his other Doc Marten.

"If *you* don't run away from *this*—" He stood the leg on the counter in front of her. "—*I* won't run away from *you*."

10

"Here's the school, where we are," said Pete, his finger pressed against the paper. Pete, Wayne, Johnny Juan, and Amanda Hugginkiss-née-Johnson stood in front of the huge map of Blackfield hanging in Mr. Villarubia's classroom. A clock ticked quietly on the wall over their heads: ten minutes after three in the afternoon. They were alone.

The map was as tall as the teacher himself, five feet across, representing several square miles of the territory of the town, reaching clear out into the surrounding counties. This included Slade, the area north of town where the kids lived.

According to Mr. Villarubia's Social Studies class, Slade was either referred to as a "unincorporated township," a "district," or a "suburb," depending on who you asked. As far as he was concerned, it was basically the northeastern arm of Blackfield, a civilized wilderness reaching up to the interstate freeway that ran between Atlanta and Birmingham, Alabama. Unlike the urban grid of avenues and streets in town, Slade was thick forest and cow pastures, chewed up into a hundred wandering feeder roads. They all branched off of Highway 9, a two-lane ribbon dropping like a rock from the freeway into the heart of Blackfield.

Wayne felt like Lewis and Clark looking at this thing, plotting out tracks and trails. A feeling of adventure swelled in his chest, *safe* adventure, welcoming, inviting adventure, nothing like the streets back home.

They'd find no gibbering crackheads demanding money, or trying to sell them stolen watches, coins, car stereos. There'd be no haggard, barefoot women offering to "make a man" out of him, no Bloods looking to recruit a new pusher. No cops stopping him on the sidewalk to ask him what he was doing, where he was going, what he had in his pocket, *no sir, it's just an action figure, no sir, it's just a piece of candy, see?*

Only him, a warm sun on a cool fall day, and a bunch of trees. He found a reassurance and confidence in that the other children would never know. *They literally can't see the forest for the trees,* he thought rather suddenly, a realization dawning on him. *They grew up here. They'll never know what this place really is because they've always known it.*

"And here's Chevrolet Trailer Park," Pete said, pointing to a nondescript part of the woods. His fingertip stood an inch to the right of the 9, and a few inches north of the river running across that end of Blackfield.

"*Chevalier Village,*" corrected Amanda. *Sha-vall-yay.*

"Whatever," Pete said, grimacing.

He pointed to the school again and traced their route. "Okay, what we're gonna do is cross Gardiner, cross the baseball field, then take Wilmer up to Broad, and then we're gonna follow Broad up to here." He looked over his shoulder. "That's where Fish's Comic Shop is. Have you been there yet, Batman?"

"No," said Wayne.

"It's fuckin' awesome. We'll have to stop there on the way. They got a life-size Alien and a Freddy Krueger claw. Guy that owns it does movie nights on Thursdays."

"I love that place," Johnny Juan said to no one in particular.

Amanda rolled her eyes and sighed through her nose. "I wish you would stop swearing so much. It's not right."

Pete winced at her. "*You* ain't right." He went back to his explanation. "Okay, whatever, when we're done there, we'll go up Broad Street for about a block and then there's a bridge you can go under, into the canal next to the street. It's about eight foot deep. Runs under Highway Nine."

"What about the water?" asked Johnny.

"There ain't no water. Well, not really. There's a little bit. There's not a lot in there unless it rains. Nothin' to worry about."

"Oh, okay."

"Anyway, we follow the canal this way." He traced the dotted line east to where it hooked up at a shallow angle, and then he followed it northeast. "Up to the river, and there's a bridge there we'll have to cross. Or we can walk across the big blue pipe that crosses the river next to it. We'll come to the pipe first. The bridge is a little farther down."

"I'll take the bridge," said Amanda. "You guys can fall in and drown without me."

Pete ignored her jibe, tracing a path from the river bridge into what Wayne assumed by the blotchy outline were trees. The blotch was a massive crescent of forest lining the north side of Blackfield and accompanied another highway going north. "Then we'll cut through these woods here and take this trail going north." His finger drew an invisible line up into the forest and on up to a trembly, jagged path labeled UNDERWOOD RD. "From there it's a straight shot to Chevrolet."

"*Chevalier.*"

"That's what I said, Chevrolet. Anyway I've got a surprise for you back in those trees."

"A surprise?" Amanda asked, her eyes narrowing. "What *kind* of surprise?"

"Something I found last summer."

"It's not like those old porno magazines you found on top of the ceiling tiles in the boys' bathroom, is it?" asked Johnny. He wiped his hands on his shirt as if the memory alone was enough to soil him. "Those were so gross. So much *hair*."

Amanda held her stomach and feigned a dry-heave.

The band of explorers headed out the front door, threading a path through the kids outside waiting for the buses and car pick-ups. When they got to the edge of the parking lot, a police officer in the middle of the road stopped traffic to let them across.

"Y'all be careful goin' home," said the cop, a slender man with a weasely face and *Men in Black* Ray-Bans. His jet-black uniform was impeccable, ironed smooth, and he wore a patrol cap with a badge over the brim that glinted in the sun.

"Yes sir," grinned Wayne.

"I ain't no sir," the officer called to him as he stepped up onto the curb. "Sir's my old man, I'm just Owen."

"Thank you, Owen!"

The officer waved them off and went back to directing pick-up traffic.

King Hill Elementary was three blocks west of the main drag through town, a sprawling complex on a hill at the edge of a wooded suburb. The kids marched resolutely across the school's front lawn toward the baseball field. The only other sound was birdsong and the tidal wheeze of poor Pete's horsey panting.

As Wayne walked alongside the gaggle, the feeling of adventure only swelled. It was a real *hallelujah* moment. The remoteness of Blackfield was already starting to grow on him.

The cloudless sky was a thousand miles wide and twice as high, and if he stared hard enough at the airliner carving a whispering contrail across that blue dome, he thought he could almost make out the faces in the windows. It was as if God had reached down and smoothed the world out like a blanket, leaving only him, his new friends, and the tall blue. He made a mental note to thank his dad for dragging them out here to "the middle of nowhere," as he'd been thinking of it all day. With the warm sun on his bare head and healthy green grass under his feet, he found it hard to keep talking trash and playing the pouty transplanted kid.

Children hung out in the baseball diamond, chatting in the bleachers and dugouts, and throwing balls to each other out on the dirt. Pete led them around the back of the risers, passing a blue Porta-Potty.

"Heard one of the high-school kids got trapped in this potty by a mountain lion last year," said Johnny Juan.

Amanda watched her feet eat up the grass, her thumbs tucked behind the straps of her *My Little Pony* backpack as if they were suspenders. "There's no mountain lions out here, dummy."

"There's bobcats."

"There's Bigfoots too," said Pete.

Amanda's ponytail flounced back and forth like an actual horse's tail. Wayne found it as hypnotic as a metronome. "No such thing as Bigfoot."

"Sure there is." Pete looked over his shoulder at Wayne. "What do *you* think? Do *you* believe in Bigfoot?"

"I don't know. Maybe. I'd *like* to."

"See? Wayne believes in Bigfoot."

"I think I'd crap my pants if I ever saw Bigfoot," said Johnny Juan. "Have you ever seen him, Pete?"

"No. But I know about a website that tracks sightings. Bigfoot Research Organization. They had like forty reports right here in Georgia."

Wilmer Street was on the other side of the baseball diamond. They jumped a deep culvert and followed the road's shoulder to where the sidewalk materialized under their feet, assembling itself out of broken slabs where the weeds and mud had started to reclaim it.

That took them up a long valley of nameless brick buildings with wooden house-doors and metal doors without knobs, roll-up garage doors and glass doors with sun-faded signs taped to their insides: OUT OF BUSINESS and CUSTOMERS ENTER AROUND SIDE and MOVED TO VAUGHAN BLVD. Wayne quit paying attention to where they were going and let his feet carry him along behind the plodding Pete in a sort of autopilot.

At one point they passed an open café where two men were perched in a large window cut in the side of a twenty-foot shipping container. A hand-painted sign over the dining-area awning said DEVIL-MOON BEER & BURGERS and had a picture of two disembodied red hands cupping a crystal ball.

Despite Johnny Juan's good-natured beggaring, the men wouldn't let them have a beer, but they had cans of something called Firewater, a locally made cinnamon sarsaparilla, for a dollar. They each bought one and continued up Wilmer drinking them. Amanda had bought some fried dill pickles and let Wayne have one. He thought they were the best things he'd ever eaten in his life, and made another mental note to talk Leon into bringing him back to the Devil-Moon.

Means he'll have to go to a bar, though, he thought.

Johnny Juan pulled some berries off of a holly bush in front of a lawyer's office and chucked them one by one at the back of Pete's head.

You keep on and they're gonna fire your ass, lil brother, Aunt Marcelina had said to Leon.

This conversation had taken place back in Chicago, but Wayne could remember it as if it had taken place that morning. She and Leon stood behind the car, almost nose-to-nose, while Wayne sat in the front passenger seat reading the latest Spider-Man comic book.

I know life's been tough since you lost your old lady, Aunt Marcelina told Leon, her hands on her hips. Her tone was soft but reproachful. *But you can't carry on like this. You keep showing up to work tore up and they're gonna let you go. And you know what's gonna happen then?*

Leon had said nothing, but his arms were folded. Normally a Leon Parkin with folded arms meant you were about to get an earful about something or other, but this time he was hunched over as though the wind were chilling him, even though it was August and the armpits of his shirt were dark. He looked more like a kicked puppy, sweaty and diminished.

This time he was the one getting an earful. *Nobody else is gonna hire you.* Marcelina pointed at the school with an open hand. *Ain't nobody gonna hire a drunk-ass teacher.*

What do you want me to do? Leon had asked.

His necktie was loose, his collar open. His hand drifted up to his mouth and he pulled his face in exasperation, wiping his hand on his slacks.

You need to get right with God, Marcelina told him.

God? scoffed Leon. *God needs to get right with me.*

Don't you start, Leonhard Louis Parkin. Marcelina's broad shoulders hulked over him when she handled her hips like that, like she was using them as leverage to make herself even bigger, and she was already built like a bear. Her lips pursed under flaring nostrils. *I'll tell you what we're gonna do.*

What we gonna do?

I'm gonna give you a little money, and you can get out of town. Get outta your head, get outta that apartment, get away from here and go somewhere you can get clear. Somewhere quiet you can dry up.

Leon stood a little straighter in his surprise. *Get outta town? What is this, Tombstone? You runnin' me outta town now?*

If that's what it takes to fix you.

Marcy, Leon had said, *I can't take your money.*

Yes, you can, she told him, *and you will. Look, you can pay me back whenever.* She pointed at Wayne sitting in the car. The nail on the end of her finger was bright sports-car red. *I want you to think of that little boy sitting in there. Do you love him?*

Leon recoiled. *Of course I do.*

Then get outta here, get away from these memories, away from this city, and get right with God. Baby brother, don't make me have to raise my own nephew. I got three boys of my own. Marcelina hitched up her purse where it'd slipped down her shoulder and took out a wadded-up tissue. *You know she would want you happy, dammit.*

Leon peered through the back window at Wayne, biting his lip in apprehension. His eyes were pink, and his face was twisted like something hurt deep inside. The boy could see the pain sticking out of him like a knife-handle.

I've been talking to Principal Hayes, said Marcelina. *There's a job down south he wants to recommend you for. It's close to Atlanta. Trisha lives in Atlanta. Your cousin, Aunt Nell's granddaughter, you remember her? She's all right, you know? You two used to play together before her mama moved them down there to go to school.* She craned her head forward to look up into Leon's face. *Will you think about it?*

Sunshine glinted on something lying in the cupholder.

Wayne reached in and pulled out a gold ring. An inscription on the inside said, *Together We'll Always Find a Way.*

Instinctively he thought about leaning out the window to ask his father whose ring it was, but he and Aunt Marcy were still talking. *Wait,* he thought, holding it up to the light. *Isn't this a wedding ring? Grown folks wear rings like this when they get married. And Dad never takes his off, even when he goes to bed.*

So it must be Mom's.

He held the ring up to his eye and gazed through it. The back of the school loomed over the windshield, a shadowy brick wall some two stories high.

There were no windows on this side; Wayne wasn't sure why, but he vaguely remembered the cafeteria was on the other side of the wall, and the windows in there were high and wide, like the casement windows in the cellar of Aunt Marcy's house. There were huge fans, too, and before they moved out of Chicago he would learn the fans and high windows were meant for sucking heat out of the often sweltering-hot lunchroom.

Leaning forward, he craned his neck to peer up at the wall. To his surprise, there was a door halfway up, some twelve or thirteen feet off the ground.

What the heck? he'd thought.

Freestanding, with no stairs leading up to it, no platform underneath it. If someone opened it from the other side and walked through it, they'd fall out and face-plant on the asphalt right next to Leon Parkin's car. It stood in a shallow rectangular alcove, embedded into the bricks a few inches. Painted matte brown, the color of well-creamed coffee, with a brushed-steel handle instead of a knob, and there was a gold number affixed in the middle of the door. 306, like an apartment, or a hotel room.

The weirdest thing. The two of them moved soon after, and it never occurred to him to bring the strange door up to his father—he didn't talk to his father about a lot of things after Mom died—but he never forgot about it.

11

Marilyn found Roy out back in the garden beating up the board fence with the Weed Eater, his eyes shielded by his cheesy wrap-around redneck sunglasses. *WHEEEER, WHEEEER,* the trimmer-line cut through crabgrass and wild onions, tinting the air with a bitter green scent.

The secluded garden was massive, cutting deep into the encroaching forest. Impeccable landscaping occupied most of the space, a field of five one-hundred-yard wire fences, each one tangled in grapevines. Flanking the vineyard were shallow hillocks of purple dahlia and lavender, watched over by trees drooping with Texas mountain laurel. The girls didn't make their own wine anymore, too much of a hassle; these days with the Internet they could very easily purchase much better wine, older stock, and to be honest Roy was a bit of an idiot and couldn't be trusted with the delicate processes of producing a fine red.

The aforementioned idiot was at the very back near the dryad, the bright late-afternoon sun shining on his copper-and-salt hair. He cut the Weed Eater off as she approached, pulling plugs out of his ears. "You look like you've had a hard week, dear," she told him, her long hands clasped together over her belly like a gentleman vicar. "Why don't you take the rest of the day off? Get started on the weekend a little early."

"Must admit I am a mite run-down today." Roy pushed his iridescent NASCAR sunglasses up, revealing his pale, ocean-bleached eyes. Putting down the trimmer, he beat the grass off his jeans with his gloves.

As always, his eyes cut over at the tree. *The* tree, the tallest one on the property.

Marilyn relished the hint of old fear in that anxious glance. She smiled ingratiatingly. "I would like to ask you one favor before you go, though."

"What?"

"Mother tells me there is . . . well, it seems our new neighbors have . . . *disturbed* something in Annie's house. I'd like to go investigate with my own eyes while they are gone for the day, but I would like a chaperone. Karen and Theresa have gone to the forest to look for wild mushrooms, and I would appreciate the company."

Even if it's you, she thought.

Roy rolled his shoulders uncomfortably, his head bobbing as if he could duck the request. He tugged his sweaty T-shirt to air out his chest and Marilyn caught a whiff of him. Pickled asshole.

"Yeah, sure."

"When you've put away your tools, I'll be in the kitchen, making you something to drink—it's surprisingly warm for October, isn't it?"

"Warmest year on record so far." Roy hefted the Weed Eater and headed for the garage. "How about that global warming, huh?" Marilyn watched him track across the back lawn, slipping between two grapevine fences, disappearing.

Standing in the absolute rear of the property, a stone's throw from the back fence, was the apple tree that made Roy so nervous.

Underneath the lush, brilliant green foliage was a sinuous violin trunk, with its suggestion of an hourglass shape, as if it had grown tall constricted by a ring around the middle. Two main branches thrust up from the top of the trunk in a great Y, bristling with smaller boughs and twigs. Apples studded the tree's endmost fingers, gleaming red under the indigo sky. As if the branches and leaves were an unbearable burden, the trunk seemed almost to kneel like Atlas carrying the globe, as twisted and bent as a bonsai.

A knothole resembling an eye carved into a deep fold in the bark seemed to watch as Marilyn reached up with both hands and took hold of one of the apples—huge, fat, like heirloom tomatoes. She pulled on it.

The bough resisted, bending right down to her waist before the fruit finally ripped free. She buffed the apple on her sleeve and toasted the dryad with it in gratitude.

"Thank you, Annabelle," said the witch, heading back to the house.

• • •

He had changed into a fresh shirt while he was in the garage, significantly reducing his stench. Marilyn approved of this. She handed Roy a glass of iced tea and they went out the back door and down the driveway.

They said nothing to each other on the way down the hill. Neither of them was much for small talk, and besides, they'd said pretty much everything that needed to be said a long time ago when she and the girls had found him living on the streets in rural New York.

She contemplated New York City as she crossed the dirt and gravel on her horn-hard bare feet, her skirt curtaining around her ankles in the breeze.

The city was nice—the buildings, they'd grown so tall since the last time she was there, and it was a sight to see. But all those ugly new cars were so noisy and horrible, and the air stank, and there were so many new witches and their stunted, half-assed dryads. Suckling like piglets at the teat of the Big Apple, sucking it dry until its core was rotten with consumption, apathy, darkness.

She hated it. The poverty and large-scale drain made the people mean, insolent, resistant to influence. Hard to live with. Hard to control. Cows driven mad by flies. Marilyn preferred small covens in small cities like Blackfield, a town with a population under ten thousand.

You only really needed one tree and as long as you had plenty of cats you were always protected. One tree meant you had a sort of bottleneck push, instead of the constant pull of the piglets. It was why Annie's apples were so fat and rich—Blackfield *surged* with life, stupid red-blooded American hillbilly life, and Marilyn and her girls gorged on its underbelly like ticks on a dog, unseen, unnoticed. A bit like having a secret fishing-hole, really.

They were halfway across Chevalier Village when Roy started belting out a country song to himself.

"Shut up," rasped the old woman.

"Yes, ma'am."

A slate-gray cat loped out from under one of the mobile homes in Chevalier, and a little dog lying in the yard jumped to his feet and took off after it.

Marilyn held out her hand and the cat ran up to her, clawing its way up her sleeve and perching on her shoulder. As soon as the terrier crossed the Chevalier property line, he stopped short of the man and the old woman, gave a furtive whimper, and ran back to the safety of his territory.

She was sure deep down Roy knew what they were, even if he couldn't quite put his finger on it. Roy had never been one to ask questions; he was a worker ant, a drone, and they were his queens. But even he wasn't stupid enough to overlook their eccentricities, the creepy tree in the backyard, their too-intimate regard for each other, and then there was the off-limits third floor, of course, where Mother lived.

Are you looking into the disturbance, cookie? The velvet gray cat rubbed his wet nose on her face. His muffled purring oscillated in her ear.

Yes, Mother. That's what I told you I was going to attend to. Marilyn reached up and stroked the cat's back. *What did you see, anyway?*

Something was asleep in there. They woke it up.

Marilyn pursed her lips.

The cat gave a rusty meow. *Did you take Sling Blade with you? He's a freak. He's full of plans and low thoughts. He's always looking up here at the windows. I don't trust him around the silverware.*

Yes. Oh, you're one to talk about stealing silverware.

Don't forget to water the tree.

I won't.

The two of them crossed Underwood Road and started up the driveway toward the old Victorian, the cat still perched on Marilyn's shoulder like a pirate's parrot. Deep in the folds of her burnoose-like sweater, the dryad's apple thrummed and shifted warmly.

"Ain't nobody home," said Roy.

Marilyn bit her tongue. "That was the whole point of coming over here while they were out for the day."

"Right."

She padded up the front walk, her bare feet plopping on each stepping-stone, and climbed up the front stairs onto the porch. Taking a deep breath, she tested the air—nothing but her own lavender, and Roy's briny miasma—and took hold of the doorknob.

Some heady, electric warmth welled from the knob in her hand, like touching an electric fence with an oven mitt.

Marilyn let go. "Mother's right, something is inside." She peered through the parentheses of her hands, face against the glass, trying to see through the window in the door.

The foyer, wreathed in darkness. Nothing else.

It's been here all this time. The cat looked through the window too, its little gray head shifting from side to side, green eyes shining. *Maybe it wasn't the colored folks what woke it up after all. It's been hiding, waiting for something.*

Roy leaned over and rattled the doorknob. Locked.

Arching his back, the gray cat with the honey eyes hissed. *Oh, cookie, I can feel it from here!*

Marilyn rubbed the cat's scruff, thinking.

She went to the end of the wraparound porch and down the side, trying to see in through all the windows, but they were all obscured by the bride's-veil curtains, giving her a look only at angles, shapes, glints of reflected sunlight. Stepping down into the grass, she went around back and up the rear stoop, pressing her hands against the window in the door and looking through them into the kitchen.

The same swelling of strength emanated from the doorknob on this side, too. Even the glass hummed against the edges of her hands, so lightly she almost doubted it, the wingbeats of a trapped butterfly.

Kitchen table. Magazine, salt-shaker, pepper, envelope.

The fridge was new, but it didn't belong to the new occupants. Annie's fridge was an avocado Frigidaire with alphabet magnets all over it; this one was a big black monolith with a water-and-ice dispenser in the door.

Nothing else was in the kitchen.

The hallway on the other side of the kitchen door, however, was another story.

Marilyn couldn't *see* anything back there, technically, but she received a sense of size, of scale. Something *big* was standing in there, something tall and heavy. The floor and walls almost groaned with the strain. The house itself was like a cage, containing some ancient bear just awoken from a decade of slumber, and even though she hadn't been a child since the Louisiana Purchase, Marilyn felt like a little girl peering in at it.

Whatever it was turned and looked right at her, sending a chill down her carrion spine.

This was old power, *nasty* power, dirty cheating stinking power, an ace up the sleeve, a blast from the past. She had stolen, killed, and eaten, she'd done and wrought terrible things, black unspeakable things, but this beast was . . . *deep,* was the best word she could think of. *Deep.*

Was this Annie's? Did she put this here?

The cat licked a paw and combed its ears. *I think it must have been.*

What is it—

Before she could complete the thought, the presence in the house moved up the hallway and through the kitchen, rushing the back door. As it passed through a sunbeam, Marilyn got a sensation of deformed, muscular arms.

"Shit!" she gasped, leaning back. The invisible beast slammed against the locked door hard enough to bang it in the frame. *CRASH!*

Roy flinched. "*Jesus!*"

The windowpanes crunched, but stayed intact. A low bass growl came from the other side of the threshold, deep enough to make the glass buzz. Marilyn felt compelled—no, *drawn* toward the door, as if some force were pulling her inside. She braced one hand against the doorframe, and then the other, and her face felt as if she had pressed the end of a vacuum-cleaner hose to it, sucking, pulling her out of whack.

Whatever was in there, it wanted to *eat* her rotten body like a buzzard, pick her worm-dirt bones clean until there was nothing left but a grin and two holes for eyes.

"The hell they got in there?" asked Roy. "A mastiff?"

She came down and stood next to him, her toes clenching the grass in surprise and aggravation. "Did you hear it barking?"

"No?"

"Then what makes you . . . oh, forget it." Marilyn threw a hand at him in exasperation and started off back around the house, the cat in tow. *I've never seen anything like this in all my years,* she thought. *What is this? How could Annie, little newborn-witch Annie, just a baby next to us, how could she conjure something like this?*

Catching up, the cat ran ahead of her and trotted through the dry autumn grass. *There are more things in Heaven and Earth, Horatio, than are dreamt of in your philosophy—Shakespeare, you know. I gave him that one.*

"Mother, you are so full of crap," Marilyn told the cat.

Mock me at your peril, lovely daughter. No doubt Annie summoned it to kill you before you could craft the dryad. She knew you had your eye on her. The question is, what woke him up? It weren't Parkin. That thing in there couldn't give less of a shit about some Yankee Negro. No, he's responding to someone else. Someone else is here. Someone directly connected to Annie.

Who do you know fits that bill?

Marilyn halted so quickly Roy almost ran into her. "I know who's here," she said, staring at the forest in thought.

"What?" he asked. "That thing in the house?"

She scowled at him. "No no, not that, but I know why it's upright and sniffing the air. I know who woke it up."

The gray cat gazed up at her expectantly.

"Annie's *daughter*," said Marilyn, a slow smile creeping under her Big Bird nose. "That's it, that's it . . . her little girl is back in town. My littlebird. She's come back to the old haunting grounds. Annie's conjuration knows she's here, she's got Annie's blood in her. He can smell it." Her hands found each other and she wrung them together. "We should put together a welcome-home party."

Roy grinned. "I like parties."

• • •

After she sent Roy home, Marilyn went back to the Lazenbury House and stepped into the pantry, where a glass decanter with a cork lid stood on a shelf. Inside the jar was a heap of sun-dried tree frogs, all tangled together like electronics cables. She wrestled one of the frogs out, put it into a food processor, and ground it into a coarse powder that resembled cilantro. Then she put the powdered frog and two Earl Grey teabags into a kettle with some water and set it on the range.

While she waited for the tea to boil, Marilyn went into her office, retrieved a book of stamps, and went back to the kitchen, where she grabbed a can of Fancy Feast from the pantry.

The gray cat with the honey eyes had followed her into the house.

As she tore one of the stamps off the book, it sauntered over to the cat-food can and sniffed it. There was no creaky voice darting into Marilyn's skull like a slow-creeping fog; Mother had retreated from the cat. Probably asleep. She slept a lot these days.

"Did I say that was for you? Get your ass down," she said, brushing the cat down onto the floor.

Marilyn put the LSD stamp on her tongue and opened the Fancy Feast with a manual can opener, then sat at the island and ate it out of the can with a silver spoon stolen from Adolf Hitler's tea service. The swastika on the handle glittered in the track lighting over her head, but the spoon's beauty did nothing to lessen the foul meatloaf-in-brine taste of the cat food.

The acid had just kicked in when the tea-kettle began to whistle. She made a cup of it and sat back down to drink it (black, of course—sugar always screwed with the alchemic makeup of the scrying mixture), staring blankly out the window at deepening colors, listening to intensifying sounds.

The breathy *hmmmmm* of the refrigerator.

The constant *tick-tock tick-tock* of the smiling Felix clock on the kitchen wall and its swinging tail and tennis-match eyes, off-rhythm with the grandfather clock in the living room (mental note to wind it up).

A pulpwood truck gargled past out on Underwood Road.

Sparse birdsong fluted in the October trees. She took a deep sip of the tea and closed her eyes.

Projected on the silver screen of her eyelids was a house some-where in Blackfield . . . not the Lazenbury, but some brighter, cheerier dwelling, closer to the center of town, with pearl-colored wallpaper and cherrywood furniture. Heavy traffic droned back and forth outside this other house. She walked around, inspect-ing each room until she was satisfied no one was there, and then opened her eyes. Closed them again.

This time she was walking down a street. A side street, one of those running perpendicular to the main thoroughfare. A small gaggle of children walked by, three boys and a girl. One of the boys was black, and Marilyn recognized him as the neighbor's son, the new residents of Annie's house.

The children stopped and she went to them. The girl stooped to pet Marilyn. "Aw, what a pretty kitty. Hi there, pretty-kitty," she cooed.

Meow, said the old woman. She sniffed the girl's hand and smelled Club crackers, candy, Magic Markers.

"Meow," said the girl she knew as Amanda.

"Do you speak Cat, now?" asked the fat boy.

Marilyn knew him from the trailer park down the hill from the Lazenbury. The Maynard boy. Amanda glared at him over her shoulder and gave Marilyn a few more luxurious strokes. "Pretty kitty."

Opening her eyes again, Marilyn took another sip of tea and clamped her eyelids shut. Now she was in some kind of shop, some weird type of five-and-dime maybe, if those were still around. Funny-books, plastic toys, board games, and Halloween masks were on display all over the room. She was sitting on a glass counter next to a colored man, who was typing on a sleek white laptop computer.

"Not time to feed you yet, Selina," said the man, giving Marilyn a rub around the ears. "I'll give you something when suppertime gets here, I promise." Pleasure reverberated down her spine in spite of the hand on her back. *Prrrrrow,* she said, and opened her eyes again.

Any luck? asked Mother.

The gray cat with the honey eyes had climbed back up onto the counter and was licking the last few morsels out of the can in her hands. Her mother's mind was inside, idling, listening. They were scrying in tandem. Mother was old enough, and powerful enough, to scry without the assistance of wet cat food and LSD.

Not yet. But I'll find her, don't you worry your pretty little head. Marilyn pushed the Fancy Feast away and combed her fingers through her silver hair, reveling in the acid-altered sensation of her nails sweeping across her scalp.

Dropping acid for almost forty years, and straight peyote for long before that, had inured Marilyn against its most devious effects; like most practitioners of her brand of legerdemain, she'd had the revelation a long time ago that, like a dream, the LSD's effects could be controlled, harnessed, channeled. In a dream, when you expect something to happen, it will happen. If you dream about a box, expect to find a decapitated head in that box and that's exactly what you'll find when you open it.

In that way it's a great method for distilling your own subconscious, for defragmenting one's neural pathways. Cleaning house, if you will. Searching out base desires and mental flaws and eradicating them if possible.

The lysergic acid diethylamide functioned in much the same fashion—if you expected to hallucinate something, you would hallucinate it. For a witch of Marilyn's caliber, hallucinations were a bit more . . . shall we say, *substantial* when the chemistry was altered by certain secondary ingredients. The cat food helped her channel the hallucinations, to "tune into" the stray cats of Blackfield instead of having a Pink Floyd woo-woo session. Without the aftertaste on her tongue, she could forget why she was in a fugue state and what she was attempting to do.

Inserting herself into the mind of another cat, Marilyn found herself perched in the branches of an oak somewhere downtown, treed by a black Labrador. Cat number five was under a car somewhere, devouring the cold remnants of a discarded Styrofoam box of Chinese takeout. For the umpteenth time, she mused on how much sweet-and-sour chicken looked like battered and fried mice. Another leap put her behind the wheel of a female tabby, in the middle of a frantic mating session behind the Dollar General on 9th and Thompson.

The tom's barbed penis jabbed at her rotten, long-barren womb and she almost fell off the bar stool, snapping back to the Lazenbury kitchen. "Aaraaagh!"

Problems? asked Mother.

The gray cat licked its chops and flopped over on its back, studying her face upside-down.

"No . . . no. Don't worry about me." Shaking, Marilyn caught her breath and took a deep gulp of the bitter toad tea. "While I search for Annie's daughter, I want you to get a good look at that thing down there in Annie's house. Figure out what it is, and how we get rid of it."

Who the hell are you ordering around? Reaching up, the cat snagged Marilyn's sleeve with a toenail and unraveled a loop of yarn out of her sweater. *I was one of Rasputin's lovers and pupils, you know! I mixed pigments for Michelangelo! I taught—*

"I'm not in the mood for your sass, Mother. Or your history lessons."

Sass? You ain't seen sass, cookie.

"I have no doubt. Just, please, while I take care of this, do me a favor and take a look at Hairy Freako down there in the Victorian. I'll bring you up a bowl of ice cream after dinner."

Do you promise?

"Yes, yes, of course."

The tiramisu flavor? It reminds me so much of Giuseppe and his

*sister back home in Sicily. Oh, how I loved their house, with its rose
trellis and the statue of the fisherman pissing into the ocean—*

"*Yes,* the tiramisu. Now leave me be, Mother. I've work to do."
The cat got to its feet and jumped down off the counter, trotting
away.

Pointing at the stove, Marilyn gestured the teakettle into the
air. Floating over to her teacup, it poured her another helping and
then followed her knobby finger back to the cooling electric eye.

Her head sank forward, she cupped her eyes in her hands, and
Marilyn continued scrying.

12

"You asshole!" howled Pete, startling Wayne out of his daydream. He looked up from the sidewalk and almost ran into Amanda, who had stopped to pet a cat. The animal jumped in surprise and skittered down an alleyway.

"Look out where you're going, space cadet!" said Amanda, watching the cat disappear through a cluster of patchy junipers.

The four of them had come to the intersection of Wilmer and Broad and were approaching the traffic light. To the left and right was a long stretch of two-story buildings: boutiques, offices, shops, storefronts. A pet shop across the street boasted about its hamsters, kittens, turtles. Next door, a frozen-yogurt shop in pastel colors claimed more flavors than Baskin-Robbins, and a knick-knack shop carried bamboo wind chimes and frilly marionettes on tin bicycles.

Broad reminded him of the older parts of Chicago, the streets that led back to the wild-west days, but Blackfield's historical district was cleaner, almost precious in its maintenance. On the other side of the intersection, Wilmer turned into a brick road bisected by a median full of little trees, and lining it was a funnel of fancy bistros and taverns.

Pete held up his sarsaparilla. "You ruined my drink!"

"How did I do that?" asked Johnny Juan.

Pete showed him the can. Johnny leaned in to examine it. "You threw a holly berry in my Firewater!"

Wayne and Amanda clustered around Johnny to see. The girl tugged it in her direction with her long, pencil-slender fingers and he noticed her nails were green.

"I'll be dang," said Johnny, leaning back to laugh. Wayne looked down into the mouth of the can—which was no bigger than a nickel—and sure enough, a little red berry bobbed at the bottom.

Amanda smirked. "You should try out for basketball!"

"Basketball my ass!" fussed Pete. "I can't drink this now."

"Why not?" asked Amanda. "It's just a berry."

"Aren't holly berries poisonous?"

She paused and squinted up at the sky, palming her mouth in thought. "I have no idea."

Johnny shrugged. "You could try it and see. Hey, there were food tasters back in King Arthur's court and stuff. They tasted things to see if they were poisoned before they were served to the king."

"Then *you* taste it, Sir Lancelot," said Pete, thrusting the can in his direction, "and let me know if you die."

Johnny stepped back as if the can were a spider.

"You are the biggest wuss," Pete growled, balling up a fist. "Two for flinching."

"Aww." Johnny hugged himself protectively and Pete punched him twice in the shoulder, hard enough to almost knock him over. He balanced on one foot, rubbing his arm. "Jesus! Do you have to hit so hard? That's like the third time this week."

Wayne took out the ring on the ballchain around his neck. Lifting his mother's wedding band, he peered through it at the world, and at Pete's broad back.

Can you see my new friends?

Something about doing this lightened him, made him feel like he was sharing his eyes with his mom, as if the ring were a camera, transmitting some ethereal signal she could see from wherever she was now, if "wherever" was Heaven.

As Pete continued on, Wayne caught up to him. "Hey."

"Hey."

"I wanted to ask you something."

"Yeah?"

"Why do you get so upset about food?" asked Wayne.

"What do you mean?"

"Well, you told me and my dad that you don't eat much. So why do you get so upset about wasted food like the Pop-Tart and that can of Firewater?"

Pete's mouth twisted to one side in thought, or at least that's what Wayne thought, but the next words out of the boy's mouth were low and laced with emotion. "We ain't got a whole lot of money, you know? My mom does what she can, but we don't always have money . . . for things like soda and Pop-Tarts. I mean, like, there's not always food in the house, so I don't sit down and eat much, but when I do, I—" He frowned, glancing up at the sky and then at Wayne. "I don't know, Mom always told me I had to clean my plate. Kids in Africa starving and all that. So I hate to waste food, even if it's something I don't like. Like okra. Eugh."

"You guys don't have food stamp cards down here?"

"EBT? Yeah, but she won't do it. I don't know why."

"We did for a little while," said a voice behind them. Johnny. "My dad didn't want to, I think he felt like—"

"Like a failure?" asked Wayne.

"Maybe? He told my mom that he didn't come all the way to

America just so he could take a handout. Maybe your mom feels the same way."

"Pride," said Wayne.

"Yeah, well," Pete muttered, pistoning forward.

• • •

Superheroes beamed from the panes of a storefront window: Spider-Man on the left, Batman on the right, both of them in action poses, swinging through the air. Over Spidey's head was FISHER'S HOBBY SHOP, and over Batman's was COMICS, BOOKS, TOYS & GAMES.

Warm sunlight streamed in through the Spidey and Batman paintings, leaking dim and dusty gold beams into the depths of the shop. The door chime tolled like a cathedral bell in the silence; it seemed they were the only customers in at the moment other than a white cat curled into a ball on the windowsill.

"Hello?" called Amanda.

The place had a generally musty smell of disuse, the action figures nearest the front door sealed in packages bleached green by countless days facing the sun. Most days probably passed without seeing many customers, outside of regulars and the people who came for Movie Night. Shelves of games occupied the racks alongside the larger graphic novels and action figures: chess, Monopoly, Candyland, Scattergories, Apples to Apples, esoteric card games he'd never heard of. A council of Halloween masks stared down at them with empty black eyes, perched at the tops of all the shelves—Jason's hockey mask, Michael Myers's white face, a warty pig-man, a grinning devil, Pennywise the clown, Pinhead from the *Hellraiser* movies.

An athletic black man came out of a doorway stirring a milkshake. He wore a thin blue sweater hugging every muscle as tightly as a wet suit. He was a few shades darker than Wayne himself, without the warm honey cast Wayne had inherited from his mother.

"Hey, kids. How's it going?" he asked, walking over to the counter and taking up position behind a laptop.

Directly behind him was a showcase with a glass front, containing a vast array of dazzling knickknacks and mementos: signed book jackets, DVD cases, and comic covers, a Freddy Krueger claw, and a veritable army of action figures still in their blister packs. The centerpiece was an Uruk-hai cuirass, a vest of armor worn by the orcs in the *Lord of the Rings* movies, and if Wayne viewed it at the right angle he could see the silvery writing where someone had signed it with a Sharpie. Peter Jackson, it said, in haphazard cursive. The chain mail underneath seemed older than Blackfield itself.

Pete bellied up to the counter as if he were a cowboy in a saloon, putting his chubby elbows on the glass. Underneath was a carpeted display with rare cards: baseball, *Magic: The Gathering, Pokémon, Garbage Pail Kids*. "Hey, Fish. It's goin' all right, how are you?"

"About as good as good gets. Been a while, Petey boy. What brings you?" Fish chugged half the thick, sludgy milkshake in one go and put it down, waking up the computer.

"We're showing the new guy around."

"His name is Wayne. But we call him Bruce Wayne," said Johnny Juan, clapping his diminutive friend on the shoulder. "Him and his dad just moved here from . . . ?"

"Chicago."

"Welcome to the middle of nowhere, Batman," said the man. "My name is Fisher. Fisher Ellis." He offered a hand to shake. "Everybody calls me Fish."

Wayne shook it. "Wayne Parkin."

"Sweet name. Well, welcome to my Place of Stuff," said Fish, gesturing around the shop with a sweeping hand. He leaned over the laptop and started typing furiously. "I've got to do a little work. If you need anything, gimme a holler."

Wandering away, Pete and Johnny took to a table of boxed comic books, cultural geologists flipping through sedimentary layers of superhero history. Amanda simply stood next to the counter, her arms folded, looking blandly at the stuff behind the counter. At first Wayne thought about browsing the action figures, but he wanted to know more about Fish and the shop. The fact it was so empty of people was nagging him.

"So what are you doin'?" Wayne asked, pointing at the computer. "For work. On the computer. Do you—" The question felt rude, but he couldn't think of any other way to put it. "Do you *sell* anything? I mean, it doesn't really look like many people come in here."

Fish smiled. "I'm actually a director of IT for a postal company."

Turning the laptop around, he flashed the kids a screen full of cryptic text. Wayne thought it looked like the green code from *The Matrix* turned sideways. "I work from home, doing programming and things like that. 'Home,' in this instance, being my hobby shop. It lets me be here at the shop and still do work for these guys." Wagging a finger around the room, he explained, "This stuff is really for sale, but, yeah, I don't do much business. It's more like . . . like my personal stuff-room, you know? . . . You ever heard of George Carlin?"

Wayne couldn't say he was familiar.

"Well, old Carlin was a comedian, did a lot of stand-up. Not exactly family-friendly material, right? But smart. Anyway, he had a bit about making money and buying stuff. 'A house is just a place to put stuff,' he'd say. 'Bigger houses are *more room*, to put *more stuff*.' So here it is. This is my House of Stuff." He picked up the milkshake and toasted the air with the cup, gesturing around with it. "If I'm going to have all this Stuff, people might as well see it. What good is Stuff if nobody knows you got it?" He downed the rest of the shake. "Besides, I like the company. The shop keeps me social and out of my apartment."

"Oh!" gasped Amanda, darting over to one of the displays and picking up an action figure package. "I didn't know you had *Adventure Time*."

The white cat jumped up on the counter and went to stick its nose in Fish's cup, but he took it away and stroked the cat's back. "No ma'am, not for you. You already get enough protein, you don't need any more."

"I want to have a shop like this one day," said Wayne.

"You look like the kind of man who would take care of it. Treat it right."

A sheepish pride blossomed in Wayne's chest at being called a man, and a grin crept across his face. "It's really awesome. Maybe when you get tired of running this place and retire, *I* can inherit it."

Fish studied him for a long moment, then tipped the cup at him. "Tell you what. How do you feel about working up here after school a couple days a week? You could stand right here at the counter for an hour or two while I catch up on my code work, and on Thursdays you can help me get set up for Movie Night. Maybe I can start doing 'em on the weekends, too."

"Are you for real?" asked Wayne, incredulous. "That would be so cool!"

"All you gotta do is guess what superhero I'm thinking of." Fish touched a fingertip to his temple. "It's my favorite superhero. You get three guesses. Marvel character."

Wayne eyed the front window. "Spider-Man?"

"No, but you're on the right side of the industry. Ain't neither of them guys up there on the windows, though."

"Can I get a hint?"

"Umm. Grass." Fish tapped on the glass counter in thought. "Grass, frogs, and avocados. What do those three things have in common?"

Wayne considered them in turn, picturing them in his mind, chewing on his lip in concentration. "They're all green?"

Fish nodded deferentially.

"Green Lantern?"

"Nope. That's DC, dude."

"The Hulk?"

Pounding his fist on the edge of the counter in feigned defeat, Fish pointed at him and said, "You got it. Man, I knew I made that too easy. What was I thinking?"

Wayne threw his fists in the air and Pete golf-clapped. "To be fair," he said, "there's only like two green superheroes, and one of 'em is DC."

"Swamp Thing. Martian Manhunter. Beast Boy. She-Hulk. Gamora. You wanna go for a deep cut, you got Savage Dragon. You gotta do your research, man."

"Shoot, you know a lot about comic books."

Fish smirked. "Okay. Bonus points if you can tell me what makes the Incredible Hulk so incredible. Why the Hulk is my favorite."

The man behind the counter was chiseled but slim, with a triangular neck and an overhanging shelf of muscle across his chest. He looked sort of like a superhero himself. *Easy one,* thought Wayne, confident in his answer. "Because he's so strong."

"He *is* strong. But that's not why he's incredible."

"Because he's so big?"

"Nope," said Fish, leaning on the counter, his dark eyes pinning Wayne to the spot. "It's because the Hulk *adapts.*" Flexing his bulging arms, he explained. "The madder Hulk gets, the stronger Hulk gets. It's the stress, y'know, it's what makes him mad. The rage is just a by-product."

Fish spoke with the magnetic, didactic focus of a self-help guru, his words clear and precise. Between every sentence, he paused for a beat to let his words sink in. His energetic hands did as much speaking as his mouth did, cupping and flinging every third word. "Everybody has to deal with stress. Hulk deals with it by becoming *stronger* than the stress. He soaks up the emotional energy around him and channels it into his strength, uses it to go one step above the problem at hand.

"You hit him with a hundred tons of force?" He punched at the air, slapping his bicep to give the strike a theatrical *oomph.* "Hulk hits you with *two* hundred tons of force. He's not my favorite be-cause he's strong. He's my favorite because he never lets a challenge beat him, he's always ready to go one step farther than the other guy."

"Yeah. Yeah!" Wayne nodded. "I get you. I get you."

His father was pretty much the only adult Wayne ever had con-versations with that felt as intellectually equal as this one, with this cultivated, channeled man and his superhero fixation, and now he felt a bit antsy—almost patronized, except he knew Fish was being earnest. It was a bit awkward, like being drafted into a stage performance in front of all his friends, but he liked it. Made him feel ten years older.

"Absolutely, you dig it?" Fish peered at his computer screen and rattled off a burst of typing. "And that's my motto, man. Adapt and overcome. When life gives you a problem, you gotta adapt and be stronger, you know? Be the Hulk. Be better. Be bigger. Be badder."

• • •

Adapt and overcome. After they left the comic shop, Wayne couldn't get it out of his head. *Be the Hulk. Be better than the problem.* He thought this brilliant new proverb, and the eloquent, intelligent, cat-petting, code-breaking, comic-shop-owning man who called himself Fish, was the best thing since the invention of the wheel.

He even *felt* stronger, his feet lighter, as he bounced along behind Pete and Johnny Juan, occasionally flexing his chest and biceps. After the warmth of the shop, the crisp wind hurt his nose, but something about the gamma-ray pep rally made it smell sweeter.

"What are you doing?" Amanda asked him as he was crossing his arms in a bodybuilder flex. She had fallen behind, and now tagged along in the rear. "Is your shirt too small?"

"No?" He made an indignant face and put his hands in his pockets.

Pete turned left and trundled down the sidewalk to a short, quaint hump of a bridge with rusted girders and simple steel banisters. Standing beside it, they could see down into the canal. A musky fish-smell coiled up from where water trickled along the bottom some eight, nine, ten feet down.

The channel itself was a square aqueduct with a flat bottom some fifteen feet wide, made of pebbly dark concrete dyed green by algae and moss. Sandbars of dirt and rocks collected along the walls.

Pete scanned the street, reassured himself no one was watching, and hopped down to a concrete platform with a grunt. The others reluctantly followed suit.

PVC pipes ran along the underside of the bridge, painted with jibber-jabber graffiti. Pete ducked under them and walked beside the thin ribbon of water at their feet. There was barely a current; Wayne could only see it if he bent over to examine the stream, the sky reflecting off of the wobbling quicksilver.

Under the bridge, Amanda's voice reverberated, hollow, intimate. "Are you sure this is safe?"

Corn-fed Pete regarded her with obvious amusement, wheezing through his nose. "Of *course* it's not safe. Fun things hardly ever are." Their excursion definitely qualified as "fun," though Wayne was getting tired and his feet hurt. This was probably the most exercise he'd gotten in a long time. But then, adventure was *supposed* to hurt, wasn't it? Adapt and overcome.

Soon the novelty was gone and they were marching along the bottom of the channel as placidly as they had the sidewalk. Wayne squinted up at the stark blue sky. The canal cut down the middle of several city blocks, between the buildings to the north and south. This deep in the cut he felt as if he were walking a trail along the lowermost narrows of the Grand Canyon, framed by darkness. The real Grand Canyon, however, wouldn't be this marred by graffiti: RANDY FREEMAN WAS HERE 07/22/2007. YEE-THO-RAH. A cartoonish rendering of a veiny penis and testicles, crude pubic hair corkscrewing from the speedbag scrotum underneath. DIAMOND AND TRAVUS, ♡4-EVA.

As Pete led them farther and farther, the water picked up eddies seeping out of the concrete until the floor was rippling glass that clapped under their shoes. Splat, splat, splat.

The canal angled to the left and became deeper, with a dip in the middle, and a gaping black storm drain low in the wall continuously gurgled water into the trough, creating a fast-moving brook. They walked along the side of the ditch then, their ankles turned so they could traverse the incline like billy goats, and sometimes Amanda would steady herself with a hand on the concrete. Some part of Wayne expected one of them to slip and fall into the water, sliding away and out of sight, screaming and flailing, but it never happened.

The buildings became shorter and shorter until the steel banisters along the top of the channel became a chain-link fence, and the crackerjack *WHZZ, WHZZ* of a power-wrench howled down to them from some mechanic's garage overhead. *PSST, PSSSSST,* the pit-viper hiss of a paint-sprayer.

Stands of hickory and ivy and something with broad green leaves sprouted up from the base of the wall, where drifts of sand and trash accumulated. When the children shouldered past them, tiny birds shifted in the foliage, chirping and rustling.

Rumbling water became louder and louder until the children came to the end of the aqueduct and found the river, a wide band of darkness sparkling under the cold afternoon sun. The concrete sloped and the walls flared out like a spout, river-water licking and lapping up onto the stony floor and leaving smears of slimy brown algae.

Pete turned right and clambered up a short grassy hill, pushing past the end of the chain-link fence.

At the top of the rise, Wayne could finally see over the walls of the canal. They had walked east out of the main historical district and they could no longer see it, only the backs of various buildings and groves of hickory and oak.

On the other side of the river, far to the west, an apartment building was half-obscured behind the tree line.

"Where to now, Dora the Explorer?" asked Amanda.

"Down the river to the pipe, and then you cross it to the other side." Their leader set off across the riverbank, stumbling across the uneven grass. Wayne glanced at Amanda, who gave him a noncommittal *whatever* face, coughed into her hands, and fell into step behind Pete.

The pipe turned out to be close enough they could see it as soon as they went over the hill. In the background to the east, after-work traffic shushed back and forth across a long concrete bridge.

A pile of smashed bricks lay under a froth of dry brown brush. Johnny Juan picked up a piece, flinging it sideways into the river. *K'ploonk.* "I'm kinda getting tired, guys. My feet really hurt."

"You *wanted* to come," said Wayne. "You don't even live out here."

Johnny scratched his face and shrugged. "I know."

Taking off his glasses, Wayne stopped to buff them on his shirt and the world around him turned into a smear of colors. When he put them back on, Pete was already heading for the river.

To Wayne's relief, the pipe was two or three feet across, just big enough he wouldn't have been able to get his arms around it. Pete and Amanda had no trouble with it at all—the big guy put out his arms and heel-toed across it like a tightrope walker, only stopping once halfway across to bend over at the waist, pinwheeling his arms to keep his balance.

"Watch out!" shrilled Amanda.

Pete sneered at her and straightened, throwing out his belly. "Man, I got this. See how a pro does it."

He flipped them all the finger, and wobbled the rest of the way across. When he got to the other side he threw himself on the grass and sat down to watch them make fools of themselves, using the bank as a windbreak.

Amanda stormed down the hill, stepped onto the pipe, and

gracefully strolled the entire length of it as easily as if she were on a sidewalk, her long legs scissoring right across.

"Wow," said Wayne.

"Ballet," explained Johnny Juan. "Her dad takes her every Saturday to the ballet studio over on my side of town, the one in the building that used to be a garage or a hangar or something."

"How did you know *that?*"

Johnny waggled his eyebrows. "It's right next door to my family's restaurant, Puesta Del Sol." Turning back to the river, he gave a deep, steeling sigh, and flexed his shoulders. "Guess I'll go across next. See you on the flip side."

The boy stepped onto the big sky-blue pipe and started off across the narrow water. About one-third of the way across, he lost his balance and bent over at the waist, his ass in the air and one arm thrown out to the side. The other hand was pressed against the top of the pipe. Johnny quivered there, twitching back and forth trying to find his center of gravity, and then straightened up again and shuffled forward, hunkered down with his hands out like a man trying to catch a mouse. As soon as he reached the opposite side he threw himself onto the grass and clambered away from the water on all fours.

"Your turn, Batman," Amanda shouted through her hands as Wayne climbed down to the bottom of the riverbank.

Up close, the pipe seemed a lot slimmer than it had from the berm, maybe only a foot and a half across, *easily* small enough to wrap his arms around and touch his fingers. Wayne put a foot on the plastic curve and something inside him quailed from the hollow thump.

The others all sat on the far bank, watching him expectantly. *Adapt and overcome.* His reputation hung on this moment, he knew down deep. It wasn't the first time Wayne had been forced to be brave in order to fit in.

Be the Hulk, he thought, standing on the utilities pipe over the Cataloosa River as Blackfield slipped into evening.

Pete, Amanda, and Johnny Juan sat on the grass watching him. *Adapt and overcome.* A band of rushing quicksilver streamed by underneath him, thirty or forty feet across, clear enough he could see shelves of greasy brown stone under the surface.

"Hell are you doing?" said Pete. The water looked deep. Over his head, at least. "Snap out of it, fool!"

Be bigger. Be badder.

Man, peer pressure sucks.

Wayne was halfway across, his arms straight out to either side, his hips swaying and twitching to maintain his balance. "I'm comin', I gotta—" he started to say, and then he slipped. One leg slid into thin air and Wayne sat down hard, the storm pipe flexing underneath and bouncing him a few inches. Suddenly he was lying on his belly in terror, straddling it, holding on with both hands. The fall had happened so fast he couldn't remember anything between standing-there and lying-there.

"You okay?" someone called.

Water cackled past the toes of his shoes. Now the burn came, the hot leaden bellyache of blunt force to the testicles.

He sat up, hugging the pipe with his knees. "Yeah," he shouted over the coursing water, wincing up at the sky. He'd hit his chin on the pipe too, banging his teeth together, and now a headache was germinating at the base of his skull. He slid forward, inching across on his butt. "Uuuggh! I smacked my nuts is all."

Pete gave a Nelson-laugh. "*Ha*-ha!"

Once everybody was safely on the other side, Pete wallowed back to his feet and steamered off across a huge gravel clearing. Now that he'd had a moment to sit and rest for a minute, he seemed to have gotten a second wind, and he was really hustling.

Dry grass, like brush you'd see at the edge of the desert, made a crunchy lacework in the chalky white gravel. Clouds had moved in while they were traversing the Broad Avenue canal, and the bright sun was now a smear behind shreds of white, sapping the children's shadows of substance.

"So what were you talkin' about this morning?" Amanda asked, her face pinching up in a suspicious way, squinting. "When you said you had breakfast with a ghost."

"My mom died of cancer. This was hers." Wayne took out the ring around his neck. "Dad and me, we always keep a place for her at the kitchen table. We carry her everywhere we go, Aunt Marcelina says, and Dad says she came down from Chicago with us." He put the ring to his eye and ogled Amanda through it.

She smiled wistfully. "That's sweet. I'm sorry about your mom."

"It's okay. It's been awhile. Sometimes I feel like I don't remember as much about her as I did yesterday." He tucked the ring back into his shirt. "I don't like that. I don't want to forget her."

"I don't think you will." The girl reached over and squeezed his shoulder. Wayne returned the smile and pushed his glasses up on the bridge of his nose.

Scraggly pine trees made a cathedral of the forest around them. The tree line was thick with undergrowth, but Pete picked out a bald spot in the vegetation where rust-colored needles were a carpet under the bushes. Strung across the path was a rusty old barbed-wire fence, presided over by a NO TRESPASSING sign nailed to a tree and shot full of holes.

Pete stepped on the bottom strand of wire and lifted the top, opening a passage for them. Wayne expected Amanda to say something about the sign, but she never did.

As soon as they stepped into the woods, the day faded into a nether-light, streaming weakly through the pine boughs.

The kids moved deeper until they'd left the constant rumble-and-hiss of the highway behind for the forest's cloistered hush. They walked for what must have been half an hour, traipsing through leafy foliage and across patches of crumbly yellow gravel, climbing over fallen trees mulchy with termite-rot.

At one point they passed a little valley with steep banks, trees standing precariously on the edge with their roots clawing at thin air. Deep and dark, the pit was full of garbage, old garbage in sun-rotten bags, spilling mush and flaky paper onto the ground. Two new-looking bicycles, their wheels bent and their tires flat. A nude, one-legged Barbie-doll. Beer bottles and cans by the legion, glistening brown and black and white in the straw.

"See?" asked Pete. "Wasn't this better than walking down the street where creepers can pick you up?"

A peculiar feeling of placelessness had come over Wayne— without tall buildings to use as landmarks and reference points, he had lost his sense of direction amidst the endlessly identical trees. He enjoyed being out in nature, but he had developed a creeping sense of panic at not knowing where he was.

"Not really." Amanda's gait had become slow and indolent, and she had crossed her arms, her shoulders scrunched against a creeping chill.

Until then, Wayne hadn't noticed the afternoon had gotten colder. It was also darker, though they still had plenty of light left. He peered up at the smudge of white sun through the trees and judged it was probably on the verge of nightfall.

She tucked her hair behind her ear. "Would have been faster and safer to ride home with our parents. Or heck, on the school bus, even."

Pete's face fell, his expression going from tired, determined, and content down the other end of the spectrum to hurt and exhausted. "Well, I only wanted to *show* you guys something, you know? And I wanted to show the New Guy here around."

The corner of Wayne's mouth tucked up in a smile. "I appreciate it. I never been hiking before. It's nice." He took a deep breath. "It smells nice. *Pine* smells nice. I like it out here."

Pete shrugged, as if to say, *See?*

"Let's just hurry up and get home before it gets dark, okay?" Amanda shouldered past them and walked down the trail in her stormy, gangly way, her glossy black braid swinging from the back of her head. "I think we're close enough now it doesn't matter."

The trail had widened and was now quite visible, a thinness

meandering across the woods, occasionally meeting a side trail. Pine gave way to oak and naked dogwood, and little brooks zagged across their path, giving the kids something to jump over, stepping from stone to stone. Tiny silver fish darted through the brackish water.

Wayne had lapsed into a daydream, staring at his feet, when Johnny Juan said, "Whoa. Creepy as hell."

"Oh my God," breathed Amanda.

Deep in the trees, approximately the size of a supermarket shopping cart, was a clown's face.

13

Rust stains streaked down from the clown's giant eyes and mouth as if it were bleeding from the inside. On closer inspection, Wayne saw it was a sort of cart, a roller-coaster car or part of a carousel.

"Is this your surprise?" asked Amanda.

"No," said Pete, shaking his head and walking away. "That's cool, but it's not what I wanted to show you."

Pine needles and briars choked the passenger seat of the clown-face car. The mess was dark, tangled, ominous. Wayne wanted to get away from it, so he overtook Pete and jogged down the trail.

"Wait up," said Johnny.

Wayne went down a short slope and found a break in the trees where the last dregs of sunlight slanted in from a clearing. He stepped over a half-buried train track and emerged into what might have been one of the coolest things he had ever seen.

The stark umbrella-skeleton of a hulking Spider ride threw stripes of shadow over them, its suspended cars rusting quietly in the white sun. He had come out onto what appeared to be a go-kart track, a paved oval about ten feet wide and painted green. Grass and milkweed thrust up through cracks.

"Ho-lee Moses." The forest stood vigil over the ruins of an abandoned amusement park. A tree grew up through the middle of a small roller-coaster track, shadowing more rusted-out clown-cars and a broken scaffolding no taller than an adult man.

His friends crunched up out of the woods and stood next to him.

"Now *that's* cool," said Johnny.

Amanda picked a careful path across the buckled road. "I had no idea this was out here. You found this last summer?"

Pete forged ahead, leading them through an aluminum garage at one end of the track. The ground was oily and nothing grew, which made for easy walking. "Yeah. I came out here to, ahh . . . look for Bigfoot. My mom said this is the old fairgrounds. It's sup-posed to be one of those travelin' amusement park things—you know, how they go from city to city, settin' up in mall parking lots and stuff. But she said this one, the people set it up, and then they disappeared."

"Disappeared?" Wayne's neck prickled. A go-kart was over-turned against the wall, its axle bent, its guts pulled out. Parts lay strewn around it.

Leading them through the heart of the overgrown carnival, Pete lurched over the dead weeds, trampling briars, sticks cracking under his shoes. "Yeah. She said it happened back in the eighties. Before any of us were born."

Gradually the brush gave way to open gravel and dirt. "Mom said the city tried to open it anyway, and it ran for like a year, but they couldn't make any money on it and it was too expensive to clear it out. So they left it here."

A long arcade leaned over a bushy promenade, its game booths frothing with hickory and blackberry bushes. HIT THE PINS! POP THE BALLOONS! THROW A DART! WIN A PRIZE!

"Y'all don't tell her we were out here. She said not to come back. It's dangerous here." Pete gazed up at a ten-foot board standing at the end of the concourse, with a round bell at the top. "Is this what I think it is?"

Wayne came closer. "Hey, yeah. It's one of those strong-man tester things. Where you hit the thing with the hammer and the slider hits the bell." He grinned up at his big friend. "Man, I bet you could knock the crap out of this thing."

"Let's find the hammer," said Amanda.

Wandering in separate directions, the children searched through the dry grass and weeds. Johnny and Amanda went to root around under the Spider, while Pete went behind the north side of the arcade. Wayne kept going west, and found himself in an intersection between a funhouse and a caved-in concession stand. The funhouse was sooty black, heavily damaged by fire and over-grown with creepy ivy, so he didn't bother going in.

The marquee over the concession stand read FUNNEL CAKES, SNO-CONES, CANDY APPLES. The sign underneath the sales counter told him he was in WEAVER'S WONDERLAND, and it was FUN FOR ALL AGES!

Weaver. Must be the person who built and abandoned this place, he thought, cupping his face against the cloudy windows. The concession stand was empty except for a chest freezer with the lid open, nasty with black gunk. *Wonder what happened to him.* Wayne couldn't imagine anybody willingly walking away from owning their very own amusement park.

When he looked away, his eyes were caught by a giant contrap-tion down the right-hand street.

Like a flying saucer crashed to Earth, a huge purple Gravi-tron rested in a bed of brush, its door wide open to reveal a dark mouth. Strips of dead bulbs marched in rib-cage rows down its sides and down the frames supporting it from above. Wayne ventured up the textured steel ramp into the hollow machine. Curved black walls were lined with padded seats that, in the run-down darkness, could have been gurneys rather than seats meant for park patrons.

A Formica coffee table stood near the back of the Gravitron chamber, the woodgrain skin rubbed away at the corners. Several half-melted red and white candles stood in brass candelabras around a white bowl.

Wayne crept closer. The bowl was full of some black substance . . . or perhaps it was the shadows playing a trick on him, he couldn't tell; the cavernous dark of the machine's interior made it hard to see.

Picking up the bowl, he tilted it toward the light. Whatever it was, the black stuff in the bowl smelled foul: pennies, cigarettes, burnt hair. The inside of the bowl was black but dry—burned out, the contents had been cooked. He turned it upside-down to look at the bottom (MADE IN CHINA, maybe?) and saw the jagged rim of a pair of nostrils, and the two guileless eye sockets of a human skull. The teeth had been sawed away under the nose.

"Uhh!" he exclaimed, snatching his hands away.

The hollow skull hit the carpeted floor with a thump.

He felt like he ought to scream. Seemed like the logical thing to do, to draw a great big breath, open his mouth, and belt out the loudest shriek he could muster, but his lungs were too small and he couldn't get purchase on the air, as if the Gravitron's door had closed and Martians were sucking out all the oxygen.

"Uhh," he said again, backing away.

KSSS! A blast of air came out of the floor behind him and he leapt away in fright, shouting, almost falling over the coffee table.

Finding his feet, Wayne saw it wasn't air—it was a *snake,* dear God it was a long fat snake, an olive-brown firehose, draped across the black carpet in swoopy cursive. Darker markings like Hershey's Kisses ran down its smooth, flabby sides. The snake had reared up and now watched him warily, its fat jowls puffing inside its pink mouth, fangs bared.

Damn, thought Wayne, *what do I do?*

"*HELP!*" he screamed, or that's what he tried to do, but it came out a whispery squeak, flitting through the constricted tin whistle of his throat.

Coiling protectively in the center of the Gravitron, the snake kept hissing at Wayne in that low nail-in-the-tire way, barely audible. It lay between him and the front door of the carnival ride, between the boy and any chance of escape.

"Get out of here!" Wayne snatched up a candelabra and hurled it at the snake.

The candle and candelabra hit the floor and broke into two pieces, whipping over the snake's head. *Fsssk!* The reptile struck at it as it went by, punching out and withdrawing again.

Wayne stumbled up on top of the creaking-cracking table and pressed himself against the Gravitron wall. The padded gurney-seat behind him was wet and stank of mold.

"*Go aw—*" he began to scream, but the snake slithered after him, climbing up. Before he could get away, it jabbed in and bit him on the left leg just below his knee, *fsst!*, fangs stapling through his jeans into the soft meat of his calf.

Startled and confused, Wayne soft-shoed backward off the table in a tumble of candles, skidding, collapsing into the floor. His knees and shoulder reverberated against the wooden platform with a kettle-drum *boom-boom.*

Coiling on the table, the snake peered up out of the bowl of its chubby chocolate-kisses body, puffy pink yawning, the tip of its tail wriggling as if it had rattles to shake.

Knife-blades from the sun swarmed and clashed under Wayne's skin, fighting each other in the flesh behind the bite, cutting him to ribbons from the inside. The pain was unlike anything he had ever experienced in his life—*burning, pinching, stabbing, angry,* it was hot coals and hornets and rusty nails all mixed together, scraping the bone clean with rending red teeth.

He wrenched back the leg of his jeans expecting to find a white bone protruding from his brown skin, but there were only two puncture-wounds, beading raspberry blood.

Cold numbness and needles took over his left foot, prickling his toes, his heel. His calf was beginning to swell.

Tongue, too big for his mouth. Throat, closing up. He turned over on his back and goldfish-gawped at dry air, tears in his eyes. The boxing glove pressing against the roof of his mouth tasted like batteries.

"*Heeehp!*" he wheezed as loud as he could manage, his lips tingling, and fought for air. His shirt was ten sizes too small, constricting his lungs in belts of cotton. "*Huuuk—huuuuuk—*"

BOOM, BOOM, BOOM, somebody came running up the ramp into the Gravitron. A barbarian giant plastered the far wall in shadow, filling the doorway with his body, and in his thick hands was a mallet with a striker-head as big as a mailbox.

Pete lingered for about two seconds, taking in the scene, and then he charged across the Gravitron and brought the strength-test hammer down on the snake, smashing it so hard the table trampolined the reptile into the air. Someone—*a girl?*—screamed, but to Wayne it was the muffled keening of a kitten.

The ceiling fell slowly away piece by piece, unmasking an abyss of shimmering red stars.

Big old Pete, good old Pete, Petey-boy, the Incredible Pete, he demolished both table and snake, swearing at top volume, unleashing every swear and curse he knew, even as the blood-galaxy uncovered itself above his head. The huge hammer came down on the snake again and again with an industrial, echoing rhythm.

The night sky glittered with rubies that darted back and forth, mingling like goldfish in a pond. Wayne couldn't understand any of Pete's shouting through the cotton in his ears. It was an AM broadcast on a bad signal.

Silky foam seethed out between Wayne's lips and ran across his cheeks. His stomach churned, but he didn't have the strength to turn over.

A force lifted the boy up—*Aliens,* he thought, as he rose toward that malevolent universe, *they're taking me away into their purple spaceship, they're gonna cut me up and do tests on me*—and then he was gone.

14

Dinner was done and eaten, the plates were stacked in the sink, and Robin and Kenway were in the garage downstairs playing cornhole.

It was about as boring as you'd probably think it was, but Robin had a good time humoring the big blond lug. Throwing with her left hand instead of her right made it look like she couldn't aim for shit, it was nice to have him right behind her, big bear-man mitts on her forearms, guiding her through repetitive underhand motions.

"Here, you want more forward momentum," he was saying over the smell of his cologne, swinging her arm back and forth. His beard tickled her ear. His breath carried the dank pocket-change scent of beer. "You don't want to lob it straight up into the air."

"Like this?" Robin asked, lunging forward and flinging the beanbag toward the cornhole board. It slapped against the wood and slid right off the back end onto the floor.

"Not quite as hard. Just kinda . . . chuck it."

She chucked it. The beanbag whacked into the crevice at the bottom where the board lay on the floor. *Why don't you just fling it straight into the hole? After all that knife-throwing and hatchet-throwing, you know you can. Or are you afraid you'll hurt his feelings?*

"You'll get it." Kenway went around gathering them all up.

"Fun," Robin said, lying through her teeth as she helped. They deposited the beanbags back on the drafting table, but she kept one of them, fidgeting with it. "You know, I've got an idea of something you might like."

"Oh yeah?"

She tossed the beanbag onto the table. "Come with me."

She led him through the dark vinyl studio with all its computers and printers and half-glimpsed figures pasted to the walls, pushing through the front door. Down the sidewalk, toward the dentist's parking lot. Her plumbing van. Robin unlocked the back door and threw it open, climbing inside. Behind the seats was a small collection of "boffers," practice swords made with PVC piping and foam pool noodles, all wrapped in duct tape.

"Really?" asked Kenway, as she handed him one. "I didn't know you were into LARPing."

"What?"

"LARP. You don't know what LARP is?"

"No," she said, pacing around the parking lot, flourishing her own foam sword.

"A couple of my buddies in the military were into it. Live-Action Role Play. Bunch of folks dress up like knights and wizards and shit, and go out in the woods to role-play and beat the hell out of each other with these things."

"Sounds like a laugh riot." Robin sighed. "Sorry, between getting the *Clockwork Orange* treatment at the mental hospital and getting the *Full Metal Jacket* treatment from the guy that broke me out, I didn't get much pop culture in my life. Until I struck out and started doing my witch stuff."

"How many movies have you seen since the 1980s?"

"I plead the Fifth." She dove at the big man with a clumsy swing. "En garde!"

He scooted backward, whipping the boffer sword to the left, catching her blade just above his hilt. An awkward move, an underhand parry just barely strong enough to stop her blade.

She slapped him on the shoulder with the boffer and he half-heartedly tried to knock it aside with his elbow.

"I haven't seen a whole lot," she admitted. "Haven't really had time to catch up on movies or play video games. Just train. Heinrich had a VCR and a few movies on tape. *Fist of Fury. Cleopatra Jones. The 36th Chamber of Shaolin. Drunken Master. Foxy Brown.* He was into that older stuff. I think the newest movie I've seen is *Kill Bill.*"

"Why am I not surprised?"

She smacked him on the leg, but Kenway didn't flinch.

"Come on, play with me," she said, smacking him again. "You're not gonna hurt me. And if you do, I promise I won't hold it against you."

• • •

After they burned a few hundred calories whacking each other with pool noodles, the two of them sat on the tailgate of his pickup truck watching the sun go down. Kenway dug around in a cooler full of ice water, coming up with two beer bottles, opened them both on the edge of the tailgate, and handed one to Robin. A crow stood on top of the power pole in the corner of the parking lot, eyeing them quietly.

"So you really do this, then?" Kenway asked, after the crow had flown away and the sunset had crept below the rim of buildings across the street. The sky was a soft gradient of orange and purple clouds, and the moon was already visible behind them, a gray coffee-cup stain on a blue paper twilight. "Hunt down witches?"

"Yeah."

He took a swig of beer. "You like what you do?"

"Beats a poke in the eye with a sharp stick." She looked down at her hands, chuckling. Calluses on her palms, and scars across her knuckles. "Which has almost happened a time or two, actually." She looked up at him, her smile refusing to fade. "I like you."

"I like you too. You're pretty cool."

"I mean. . . ."

"By which I mean you're *really fucking cool*."

"I don't know." She kicked her legs and drank some beer. Bitter, metallic, with just a hint of banana on the back end. "You make me feel normal. I haven't had that in a long time. Feel like I've known you forever, and I've never met a guy that made me feel that way—normally I just intimidate all the guys I try to date. Or they just want to talk about boring, inconsequential shit. Whatever boring stuff they're doing at work. Or drama they're in the middle of—their neighbor, their family, their coworkers. Who freaking cares? There are immortal hags out there kidnapping and eating kids, and sucking the life out of entire towns, and I'm the only one out there fightin' 'em, and Bob thinks I care someone's eating his lunch out of the break room fridge, or he got in an argument with some asshole customer about gun control laws."

"That's what you get for dating muggles."

"Muggles?"

"Civilians. John Q. Public." He emphasized each term with a toss of his hand. "Maybe you *needed* to go out with somebody like me. We're both—"

"Kinda fucked up?"

Kenway laughed.

"I'm sorry, I didn't mean—" she said, trailing off. She added in a singsong voice, "If you're fucked up and you know it, clap your hands."

"I was going to say 'fighters,' like, we both know what it's like to be in the shit, you know?" Kenway shrugged. "Kind of thing can drive a wedge between you and the rest of humanity. Once you've seen the kind of things we've seen, done the kind of things we've done, it puts you on a whole 'nother level. Makes it hard to relate."

"Makes you a ghost?"

"Or an alien, maybe. Some ancient extradimensional being just too old and too weird for people's boring bullshit. Or maybe like we went to Narnia, had a bunch of adventures, and now we're back on Earth, but now we're part elf or something, and we've got this magic sword, and we know what it's like to fight centaurs, and, just, nobody around you can understand that shit, so you keep it to yourself, and you hold it inside you so tightly it twists you, makes you weird."

"Makes you wild. Like a wild animal."

He cocked his head.

"A wild animal," she repeated, "we're feral, y'know, we're not domesticated anymore, we're not tame. The shit, the suck, the fighting, it changed us. Made us wild animals. We're wolves in a land of dogs. We belong out there, and people can sense it."

"Maybe."

"Kinda fucked up."

Kenway laughed, and they both said in unison, "Kinda fucked up." He shook his head. "Wolves in a land of dogs," he laughed. "You are so full of shit. You've been making those YouTube videos for too long, you're starting to sound like a bad B-movie horror writer."

Robin butted him with a playful shoulder.

He gave her a sidelong look. "You *let* me win when we were playing cornhole, didn't you?"

"I must plead the Fifth once again, your honor."

The sun sank a little bit more, until the moon began to take over in earnest, gilding the sky with diamonds. She wondered if she should start considering the decision to stay or drive back to Miguel's.

"I didn't tell you the whole truth of why I came here," said Kenway. He spoke away from her, toward the sky, as if confessing to the stars. "And why I stayed. If you're gonna tell me your story, I might as well tell you mine."

Cool anticipation trickled through her at recognizing the veiled pain on his face.

"I was—*am* a combat medic. Sixty-eight Whiskey. That's the role I filled overseas. When I lost my leg, it was my buddy Hendry, Chris Hendry, pulled me out of that vehicle and put one of my own tourniquets on me. He was in the vehicle behind us. First one to get there."

Kenway rubbed his nose, pulling on it as if he were about to take a deep breath and dunk himself. He massaged his mouth, the beard grinding in his hand like dry grass. Fidgeting, wool-gathering. "But he couldn't save everybody in there. Just me. Really messed him up he couldn't save the others. After we got home, he didn't do so hot. Had a lot of nightmares that year. Hard Christmas."

"Next summer I came out here to see how he was doing. He was living in Blackfield and working at the mill. Had a Vicodin habit he was trying to kick, said he hurt his back in the, ahh—the incident. He had a job but it was on the rocks. No girlfriend, as far as I know. I got the idea in my head to take him out on the lake for a week, see if I could get him straightened up, right? He wasn't too bad off yet. Not bad enough for rehab, I think. Maybe I caught him in time."

As he spoke, he twirled the beer bottle on its butt, staring down at it. His voice was low, introspective.

"We spent a couple days out on a pontoon boat, fishing, telling stories, had a good time. He looked good. He was laughing and making jokes. I thought he might be leveling out. Then one morning—that Wednesday—I got up, made coffee, and I was making breakfast when I went in to wake him up, and when I put my hand on him he was fuckin' cold."

Ice ran down Robin's spine. She didn't know what to do, or what to say, and suddenly this enormous man seemed so vulnerable and dark. He became an emotional hot potato in her hands.

"It was ninety-five degrees that morning, and like, almost noon when I went in there. He was cold, colder than ninety-five degrees. I remember the temperature because of that giant round thermometer on the cabin porch. How do you get colder than that? He felt like somebody stole him and replaced him with a ham. Right there, in that bedroom, I thought he was playing a prank on me and had put something under his blankets. And he was hiding in the closet, waiting to jump out and laugh at me."

The stupid visual made him smirk darkly, but then he retreated into himself again.

"He brought the Vicodin to the cabin. Nothing left in the bottle." Kenway shrugged slowly. "I reckon he died during the night. Probably took it all before he went to bed." Closed his eyes, pressed the bottle against his mouth and tilted his head back, letting the very last drop of beer trickle down the glass onto his tongue.

Kenway put the bottle down and licked his lips, holding the bottle in both hands and staring down at it as if it were a precious heirloom. "I made breakfast and drank coffee while the man that saved my life was dead in the next room. And I—*me, a fucking combat medic!*—I didn't do shit about it."

"Oh my God," said Robin.

Kenway sat up straight and rolled his neck, squeezing his shoulder. "And I've been here ever since. That was about three years ago." He shot the bottle into a nearby Dumpster with a bang and a rumble. "I don't know, it just didn't seem right to leave, you know? Felt like I was turnin' my back on him. Walkin' away from him. I couldn't do it."

Thoughts of hugging him occurred to her, but actually doing it seemed inappropriate. Instead, she reached over and squeezed his hand.

His eyes met hers and he smiled sadly.

"I've been over all my woulda-coulda-shouldas," he said, patting her hand. The palm of his bear-paw was rough, leathery. "You spend a lot of time in your head when you're painting. I try to distract my mind with music, or I have TV on in the background, but I think—ahh hell, this . . . this isn't really great after-dinner conversation, is it? I don't know why I had to tell you that messed-up story. You . . . I dunno, you seem like a good listener."

She smiled up at him. "I do a lot of talking to a camera. I like having someone to listen to for a change."

15

Sent at 9:36pm
B1GR3D: hey

Received at 9:42pm
pizzam4n: what u want stepchild
B1GR3D: nice pictures. U look good
pizzam4n: thanks
pizzam4n: you don't look so bad yourself, ol man. I am
*   diggin that red hair. Always wanted me a wild irish rose*
B1GR3D: old man? haha
B1GR3D: what you doin
pizzam4n: gettin off work, u?
B1GR3D: bored
B1GR3D: i want sum of that goodlookin body
pizzam4n: boy you wouldnt know what to do with it
B1GR3D: I bet I can figure it out. Why dont u swing by

> *on the way home an let me hit it*
> *pizzam4n: let u hit it? Lol*
> *pizzam4n: oh ho ho you aint even gonna buy me dinner*
>   *first. I see how it is*
> *B1GR3D: if you want dinner I got plenty of food here.*
>   *hell I'll cook u a steak if you want. damn good steak.*
>   *Bake potato, whole 9 yards*
> *pizzam4n: you know the way to a mans heart, don't you?*
> *B1GR3D: I sure do.*

• • •

Black Velvet grumbled into the parking lot of Riverview Terrace Apartments, Joel Ellis behind the wheel, his cell phone clutched in one hand. The iPhone's screen illuminated his face with B1GR3D's address. *This redneck better be a good cook,* he thought, peering through the windshield at the apartment numbers, looking for 427. *I ain't fixin' to put myself in some stranger-danger for no cheap-ass meat.*

Building Four was in the back of the complex, a brownstone bulwark against the dark woodline. The Monte Carlo eased into a slot, washing 424's windows with bright yellow headlight, and the engine cut off. Joel got out and scanned the row of doorways.

Eyes peered through the blinds in 427's window.

There you are. He slipped his phone into his pocket, locked his car, and sauntered up the sidewalk. 427's door opened and a man stepped out, considerably taller than he expected, with a slender neck and a jawline that could cut glass.

"Hey there," said the man. He was dressed conservatively, in a flannel button-up with the sleeves rolled, and well-fit jeans.

"Sup, stepchild. You must be Big Red."

B1GR3D smiled and gave a bashful chuckle. "That I am."

This was always the hardest part, the awkward introductory phase, where they were still feeling out each other's body language and weighing their own regrets and needs, trying to get comfortable and break the ice or find a reason to leave and forget it ever happened.

"Well, come on in."

"Thank-yuh." Joel stepped inside.

The tiny apartment was meticulously clean. Hanging on the walls were impressionistic paintings of wildlife posing dramatically in the forest—deer, foxes, mice, wolves. Large prints, from the look of it, no brushstrokes. Joel touched one of them. Thin cardboard. A ten-dollar Walmart poster. Other than a black sofa, there was only a desk with a bulky gray laptop on it and a flatscreen TV on a squat, altar-like entertainment center.

Joel sat on the sofa as Red went into the kitchen, and it crackled under his body. A slipcover encased the futon in clear protective plastic. Aluminum shafts that served as its legs stood on wooden medallions, like coasters.

To protect the carpet, he supposed.

"This remind me of my grandmama," he said, brushing his fingertips over it. He could see himself in the TV screen as clearly as if it were a mirror. "Every piece of furniture in her house was covered in plastic. The couch, the mattresses, there was even a floormat in the living room on top of the carpet."

"I like a clean, healthy house," said Red's voice. "I grew up with filthy people, neatness suits me."

Machinery whirred to life in another room. As Red returned with two glasses, a robot hockey-puck came humming out of a dark hallway and vacuumed the carpet in front of the couch. "Roomba," said Joel, as Red handed him a drink. His new friend had the craggy hands of a workin' man. "Always wanted one of those."

"It's handy."

Joel sniffed the water glass and took an exploratory sip. Whiskey, and it went down smoother than soda. Hardly any burn at all, with a vague maple undertone, so faint he wondered if the honey-color was playing tricks on his tongue. "Damn, nice," he said, holding the glass up so he could see through it.

"Got the steaks on out back." Red walked away. Joel swirled the whiskey, washed it all down his throat, and followed him through the kitchen, pouring himself another couple of fingers on the way.

"Out back" was a concrete patio about the size of a walk-in closet, with two plastic lawn chairs and a huge grill. A lone lantern-style porch light brightened the scene, and a damp phantom of October breathed across the wet grass. At the edge of Red's tiny yard was a wilderness of pines, quiet and still and impenetrable in its darkness.

The grill was obviously where most of Red's money went—a top-of-the-line charcoal-fired beast with wood-slat leaf tables on both sides. He opened the top and smoke billowed out, two levels of grills scissoring open like the trays in a tackle box.

On the bottom grill two porterhouse steaks, charred black and Satanic-red, sizzled angrily over a bed of glowing coals. Nestled between them were a pair of potatoes wrapped in tin foil.

Joel settled into one of the lawn chairs while Red used a pair of tongs to place spears of asparagus around the steaks, and four medallions of buttered Italian bread on the upper shelf. The aroma streaming out of the cooker was immense, an enveloping sauna of rich salt. Joel wanted to take off his shirt and bathe in the savory steam, absorb it like a sponge.

"Outstanding."

Red smiled over his shoulder and flipped the steaks. *Kssss.* "I used to be a cook, on a boat."

"Yeah?"

"Yep. Used to live in Maine. Near the ocean. My father worked on fishin' boats all my life and when I graduated high school, he wanted me to follow in his footsteps. But I wasn't into that. Dangerous work. Boring. You lose fingers. Fall overboard. Break your legs." He tapped his head with the hinge of the tongs. "Not enough of a challenge up here. *But,* it was what my father wanted, and there wasn't any convincing him otherwise. After I looked and looked for work at home, I finally had to admit to myself I was going to have to take up the family business and catch fish for a living."

Joel sipped his whiskey, listening raptly—or, at least, the best approximation he could manage.

"So, I hooked up with this crew goin' out that season and went out to sea." Red flipped the bread, piece by piece. "Unfortunately, I wasn't cut out for it after all. Those guys really shit on me. But, here's the funny part, I turned out to be a pretty good cook. So they stashed me in the galley and put me to work makin' dinner. That was actually where I shined."

"Ah." *Sniff.* "So what you doing now?"

Red wagged the tongs at him reproachfully. "Can't tell you that. I'm sorry."

"If you told me, you'd have to kill me?" It was a joke, but Joel's face went cold anyway.

Red smirked, snorted through his nose. "Let's just say I'm kind of a big shot around town, and if word got out that I'm, uhh—"

"Gay?"

"Well, heh. I actually swing both ways, but yeah. And you know how it is in these small-minded little quarterback-hero southern towns. My name wouldn't make a very valuable currency any-more, put it that way."

"Yeah, yeah. I catch what you pitchin'."

"*Do* you?" Red went past him into the kitchen, squeezing his knee on the way by. "You're a catcher, hmm?"

"Why, you tryin' to score? Cause I'm lookin' for a batter, baby. With a big ol' bat."

The former mess cook came back with plates and tonged the food onto them, then closed the grill lid and went back into the kitchen for a bottle of steak sauce and the rest of the whiskey.

Glorious, the steaks were absolutely glorious, worthy of being remembered in song, they didn't even *need* the A.1. Joel and Red sat on the porch eating quietly, staring out at the twilight forest behind the building.

"So what do you do?" asked Red.

"I cook and run the register at Miguel's Pizza up in the mountains. Up there at the bottom of the ridge from Rocktown." Joel bit the end off of an asparagus spear. "You ever go rock climbin'?"

"Nah. Never saw the appeal."

"Yeh," said Joel. The moon was an orange-wedge behind the trees. "Me neither."

Taking out his phone, he checked to see what time it was. Quarter to eleven. Man, he never got sleepy this early, after work he was usually up until two, three in the morning. Joel put down his fork and screwed a fist into one eye.

"Tired?" asked Red.

"A little bit."

"Maybe you should take a vacation day. Play hookey." Red grinned. "You can play hookey here with me."

"Hookey? You think I'm a hooker, hooker?"

Red laughed and sawed off a piece of steak. "You tell me."

Joel's good-natured snort turned into a yawn. He slumped in his chair, feeling more and more comfortable by the minute, until his plate was on top of his crotch and he was squinting at it, slowly cutting off bites and putting them into his mouth.

"Oh," he said, dropping his fork with a clatter.

He tried to sit up, pushing with a heel, but his foot slid. Bracing himself with his elbows, he wriggled up a few inches and twisted to collect his fork up off the ground. It was like trying to pick up a stuffed bear with a claw machine: loose, weak, fumbly. The fork seemed immaterial until he managed to put a finger on it. "Whassup here." Tines scraped across the concrete.

"Having trouble, pizza-man?" asked Red.

"Yeah, shit, somethin' wrong with me."

Whiskey must have been a little more powerful than I gave it credit for, Joel mused, wrapping a fist around the fork and picking it up.

Goddamn, but he was so exhausted. The kind of bone-tired exhausted when you got up early but you ain't done nothin' all day and you want to lay down at three in the afternoon and take a nap and sleep all day and not really eat anything and when you wake up you're like *what year is it*—

He deposited the fork on the plate in his lap and rubbed his eyes. His fingers felt like they belonged to someone else and his head was half-full of water, spinning and swaying as he tried to get a fix on Red's face.

"I think . . . I think I drank too much."

"Maybe. This stuff is smooth. Sneaks up on you. Hey, why were you calling me 'stepchild' earlier?"

Joel waggled a handful of fingers at his own head, then at Red's, then at his own again. "Cause the hair. Red hair. You know—what they say, whip you like a red-headed stepchild."

"I see. You want to whip me?"

"Kinda. Maybe. Maybe *you* can whip *me*." Joel lifted his plate in both hands and shimmied upward in his chair, trying to sit up straight. The remains of his dinner slid off into the floor, his fork ringing across the concrete again in a mess of potato-mush and bits of asparagus. "Shit."

"I'll get it," said Red, putting his plate on the grill and rising from his chair.

"I got it, I got it."

Leaning forward, Joel reached for the food to pick it up with his hand and put it back on the plate, but to his surprise the backyard, grass, rocks, and all pivoted up and hit him in the face.

16

Robin opened her eyes and realized she'd fallen asleep editing video. Her laptop was open in front of her, sitting on a piece of wood she'd scavenged from the garage downstairs. Bright moonlight fell at a slant through the giant floor-to-ceiling windows, illuminating the dark studio apartment with a soft blue-gray glow. For a few seconds, she thought she was back in Heinrich's hidey-hole lair back in Hammertown. But instead of kung-fu posters and a desert, the walls were hung with impressionist paintings and the windows looked out on a red-brick wall, the back of a hardware store.

On the nightstand by the bed, a digital clock with burning red numbers said it was half past three in the morning. Robin stretched luxuriously, enjoying the feeling of the fleece blankets and flannel sheets against her skin. First time in ages she'd been able to sleep without nightmares. She felt like a million bucks, even if it was the middle of the night.

Kenway slept on one of the benches, cushioned by an array of throw pillows, a vague form under a too-thin blanket, traced by the flickering light of the TV.

She briefly entertained the idea of coaxing him into the bed, but let the thought fade. Rolling out of bed, she searched underneath it and discovered cabinets, and inside them she found a quilt. She took it over to the bench and unfolded it over Kenway, draping it over his supine form. He slept in his jeans, with his fingers interlaced over his belly in a very self-satisfied Winnie the Pooh way, his prosthetic leg removed and standing vigil next to him. He didn't snore, but every time he exhaled, he blew it through his lips with a *pewwww, pewww* sound. Robin chuckled to herself as she tucked the quilt in around him.

A cane lay across the coffee table, alongside a matte-black handgun. She bent forward to peer at it in the low light and saw a magazine pressed into the magazine well. The safety was on.

Wandering over to the huge floor-to-ceiling window, she stood by the cold glass and studied the alleyway below, hugging herself against the chill. The stars above were a shotgun-blast of diamonds on a cape of indigo velvet. The alleyway was a bottomless black canyon, featureless, abyssal.

No one lurked out there in the darkness, as far as she could tell, but that didn't banish the feeling of being watched.

An immense stage curtain hung from the ceiling by the window. She felt around the edge of the heavy fabric and found a rope. Creeping across the room, she did her best to quietly pull the curtain closed, and somewhere in the corner, a pulley rattled and squeaked softly, feeding her rope until the window was covered.

Without the moonlight or the city-glow, the apartment was engulfed in nothingness, cut only by the red numerals of the alarm clock. She tiptoed back to bed and slid under the covers again, the sheets silky and warm against her heels. Her face sank into the pillow and her body seemed to collapse in on itself, her muscles relaxing.

Sleep claimed her almost immediately.

The tree dream.

Again, she sat at the breakfast table with her mother Annie. For some reason, this time it was the dead of night.

Solid shadow rested heavily against the kitchen windows, twisting what was usually a warm, comforting memory into a sinister mutant version of itself. The only light in the kitchen was an electric green phosphorescence coming from the digital numerals on the microwave clock, turning her childhood kitchen into some secret dream-room of shadows and emerald chrome.

"You know there ain't no talk of magic in this house, ma'am." Annie folded her newspaper and set it aside, cradling long-cold coffee in both hands. Her voice was a soft, furtive mutter, as if she were trying not to be overheard. "Magic is wrong. Magic goes against God. And in this house, God's rules come before man's now. We been over this."

"Yes, Mama." Regardless of the dreadful, nonsensical darkness, Robin had already forgotten it was a dream, in that irresistible way our minds always convince us the impossible is real.

"You're more than welcome to read your Harry Potter book, but I won't have any talk about magic. Okay?"

"Okay, Mama."

"A book is just a book. It ain't real."

Dream-Robin sucked on her lip for a moment. She summoned a little courage and asked, "If magic ain't real, why does God not want it in our house?"

Annie gave her that exasperated don't-be-a-dummy scowl from under her eyebrows. "I didn't say magic wasn't real. I was saying Harry Potter isn't real. You can read them as long as you understand the difference between reality and fiction. Harry does 'good magic,' and that's okay—he's a good little boy—but in real life, good magic doesn't exist. In real life, honey, all magic is bad."

"Yes, Mama."

Found you, said a low voice from the hallway.

The floor creaked under their feet, and something heavy and hulking stood right behind Robin. In her dream-form, a willowy waif-child not even in the throes of puberty, the thing behind her chair seemed exponentially larger than she'd ever known it before.

Hot breath breezed over her ear. Rotting meat and the astringent scent of star anise assaulted her nostrils. *I've been looking for you for so long.*

Welcome home.

Flies buzzed on her mother's face.

Robin awoke in a panic, heart fighting the inside of her rib cage. When she opened her eyes, the bed was frosted in the same sick green glow.

White vapor curled from her mouth. The room seemed as if it were ten, twenty degrees colder, as if the heat had been sucked out and replaced by the vacuum of outer space. Even the bed was cold, under the blankets, and not like the coolness of its untouched perimeters, but a frigid January chill that burned like naked steel against her bare skin.

Slowly, she turned to look over her shoulder, and found herself face to face with the huge window curtain. The green glow came from behind it, shining straight through the rough screen of heavy burlap, lighting the whole thing up.

No. Not again. Robin lay in the cold bed, staring, terror pushing acid up her throat. *He's back there, hiding, watching me, grinning again.*

He's not a hallucination, is he?

The only way she was going to stop this and find some path back to sleep would be to confront this waking nightmare. She was going to have to dispel the vision by meeting it head-on—the only thing that ever worked to make the creature go away.

The creature. Why don't you call him what he is? she thought, shivering. *That man in Alabama knew his name. Your mother knew who he is.*

He's come looking for you again.

He was waiting.

And in the end, after the therapy and pills, turns out it was never mental illness at all. Just like everything else about you, everything else you've done in your adult life, the "fictional" YouTube videos, your rapier wit, your road-warrior wardrobe, it was smoke and mirrors, duct tape and paper clips rigged up to hide the truth. From everybody, including yourself.

She reached out with a shaking hand and clutched the edge of the curtain, hoping she wouldn't have to see the magician's secret on the other side. *It's not a curse from some raggedy-ass witch in a backwater Alabama shithole, either.*

She pulled it aside. Metal rings scraped somewhere high above with a tambourine sibilance, revealing the source of the light.

It's not a brain tumor causing your frontal lobe to short-circuit.

Two huge green eyes stared down at her from a massive head. The Red Lord stood over her, with muscular orangutan arms and crooked canine legs with too many joints. Shaggy hair covered it in a pelt of flame-red, moss-green, ink-black.

No, he's real. As real as the nose on your face.

And he was standing right next to the bed.

This was the closest she'd ever been to the creature. Every time she'd tried to get close to it, the Red Lord would disappear, leaving her empty-handed and frustrated, but now, this time, here it was, big as life, standing in Kenway's apartment, close enough to touch, but she couldn't move, she couldn't let go of the curtain, her hand wouldn't respond to her brain, she couldn't let go and run, run screaming out of the room and down the stairs into the street, *but it was reaching up to touch her with one of those long shaggy stinking arms, stinking of the hidden grave, of wet moldy earth, and it had too many fingers and the fingers had too many joints,*

whispering

and as it moved, the Red Lord creaked like old leather, like a wicker basket,

and that hand crept closer to hers,

whispering

and those fingers were tipped in hornlike claws, curving spikes, reaching for her, reaching past her trembling hand, reaching for her face

claws brushed her cheek

whispering

(w e l c o m e h o m e)

(w e l c o m e b a c k h o m e)

The floor lamp next to the couch came on with a *click*. "Jesus what the shit are you screaming ab—" Kenway started to ask.

His voice inserted a key into Robin's brain and her body unlocked.

As she regained control of herself, the Red Lord fell toward her, collapsed *across* the bed and *across* her body, and disintegrated over her like a column of red smoke, or perhaps the thing had never been there at all—and where it had fallen was now a mountain of knotted hair—no, not hair, *spiders, five thousand* of them, *ten thousand of them,* tiny venomous-looking crawlers with banded brown legs and peanut-shaped bodies.

The bed and Robin herself were covered in them, crawling all over each other, creating the

whispering

sound like fine wax paper, or perhaps Bible pages, being rubbed together. Robin scrambled up out of the bed, kicking out from under the sheets. "Jesus! Jesus fuck!" she cried, worming out onto the floor in a tumble of spiders, toppling onto her shoulder with a bang, dragging the alarm clock with her.

Arachnids crawled all over her, delicate legs tickling up her shoulders, across her chest, over her face. Bristly gossamer feelers on her lips, on her eyelids.

"WHAT THE HELL WAS THAT!" Kenway sat straight up on the couch.

"MUH," Robin bellowed, in the throes of a crazed fit, flailing and kicking on the floor, tangled in sheets. "*UUGGGH!*"

Hobbling into the bathroom with the cane, Kenway came back with a can of hairspray and pulled a lighter from his pocket. He aimed both at the bed, *snik! snik! snik!*, ejecting a cone of roaring flame, sweeping it back and forth, roasting as many spiders as possible. The cane fell over and the veteran stood there on one foot like some crazed combination of a dragon and a flamingo.

"Please let this be an illusion," Robin pleaded, as she got to her feet. The duvet, sheets, pillow, and all burst into flame.

Some of the spiders—looking very much like brown recluses, or what she supposed brown recluses looked like—came tumbling over the side of the flaming mattress and scuttled across the floor. She squished them with her bare feet, grinding them into the hardwood floor, slick goo and angular toothpicks between her toes. The air stank of burning arachnids and burning mattress, a thin high chemical smoke that somehow smelled like cooked lobster and burnt leaves and singed hair and roasting latex. And to Robin's surprised disgust, a hint of caramel.

The big veteran kept roasting them with the hairspray flamethrower, blowing a column of fire up and down and back and forth across the bed, swearing the entire time. Robin found the switch for the ventilation, starting a fan in the ceiling, trying to suck out the reek.

"'Stinguisher under the kitchen sink!" shouted Kenway. The bed had become a roaring inferno, filling the apartment with an eye-burning fog.

Robin ran into the kitchen and opened the cabinet under the sink. A cherry-red tank stood behind a collection of cleaning supplies. She raked them out of the way and dragged the fire extinguisher out, ripped the pin out of the handle, and lugged it over to the bed to spray the fire with foam.

• • •

Eventually, between the two of them, they had burned or stomped as many spiders as they could manage, and the fire had been put

out. The bed was a charred mess, and the floor was slimed with
spider-pulp. Both of them backed into the kitchen to recuperate,
sitting on the floor, shaking with adrenaline. Robin's feet were
caked in guts. Kenway sat hunched over, his one remaining leg
coiled under him like a cobra ready to strike or bolt, his arms
tensed, still gripping the lighter and hairspray.

"What the actual fuck," he hissed. "Why is my apartment full
of spiders, Robin?" His head turned, and his brilliant blue eyes
burned into her own. "What was that green-eyed thing standing by
the bed?"

Goosebumps thrilled up and down Robin's arms.

"You *saw* it?" she asked, astonished. "*You saw the Red Lord?*"

"Hell yeah, I saw the, 'the Red Lord.'" He coughed, making a
sour face. "Or, at least, I saw *something*, it was lighting up the room
like a goddamn Christmas tree." He eyed their reflections in the
window, as if he expected the glass to explode. "Why did it turn
into spiders? What the hell *is* it?"

"You asking me?"

"It's *your* bullshit," he said, his tone veering into accusatory.
"You telling me you don't know anything about it?" He crabwalked
backward a few feet to the end of the kitchen island and reached
over his head for a pack of cigarettes. He tapped one out and lit it
with the lighter, and sat there leaning against the cabinet, smoking
it, his hands shaking. "Freakiest shit I have ever seen. What the
fuck did you bring here?"

"Hell, I don't know! I thought it was a hallucination!"

"*That's* why you were taking those pills?" His face had turned
legit white, making his ginger-blond beard look almost ashen-
brown. "Jesus Christ whole-wheat toast, maybe I should be taking
them too."

After a while, somehow, some way, Robin's heartbeat started to
slow down, and she could feel her muscles relaxing. She got up and
climbed onto the kitchen island, washing her spider-encrusted feet
in the sink. Kenway didn't get up. When she finished, she got back

down on the floor and sat next to him. The cigarette smoke bothered her a bit, but she didn't mind.

"Sorry I was an asshole about that—" Kenway gestured toward the remains of the mattress. "Whatever that was."

"It's cool. I understand."

"You deal with this kind of shit on the regular?" he asked, digging an empty Sprite can out of a nearby trash bin and ashing the cigarette into it.

A lone spider wandered across the hardwood floor in front of them. Robin grabbed an issue of *Field and Stream* off the island counter, rolled it into a tube, and smashed the spider with it.

"You know, I was going to read that," said Kenway. "Eventually."

Robin unrolled the magazine and held it up to look at the flattened spider. "Sorry." She offered it to him. When he made a face, she rolled it up and pushed it into the garbage. "Anyway, you keep askin' me that. Sounds like you're slowly starting to believe."

"I'm getting there. How do you do it?" he finished the cigarette and dropped it into the can. "I'd be fit for the loony bin in a week."

"They say if you eat a live frog first thing in the morning, nothin' worse can happen to you for the rest of the day. Well, I started off in the loony bin, so what in the world is bad enough to send me back?" Robin scoffed. "This ain't nothing. At least it wasn't snakes."

"I'll take snakes over spiders."

The two of them sat for a while, watching the mattress smolder, trying to will their hands to stop shaking. The stink of burnt spiders and melted memory foam still hung in the air.

Welcome home.

17

"Ugh." Joel opened his grainy eyes to find himself in some kind of basement, or a garage or something, a grungy space full of junk.

For some reason, the room was upside down. Water dripped somewhere.

Drip. Drip. Drip.

Everything was cloaked in shadow, except for a piss-yellow fluorescent bulb inside the upper half of a workbench. Tools and engine parts lined the walls and scattered across the floor, and at the far end of the room was a giant wooden cutout, a spray-painted portrait of the Creature from the Black Lagoon.

A long plastic marquee leaned sideways against the wall, a dingy white antique. ARE YOU TOO COOL FOR SCHOOL?, it asked cheerfully, next to a cartoon coyote holding a glass with flames licking up out of it. DRINK FIREWATER SARSAPARILLA!

"Whhfffk."

Joel's head was pounding and drool ran up his cheeks, collecting on his forehead. When he tried to rub his face, he found his hands were cuffed together, and the cuffs were chained to the floor.

Drip. Drip. Drip.

"Mmmmff."

Cotton pressed against his tongue, and something tight was bound around his face and the back of his neck. He was wearing a gag.

Looking down (or up, as the case may be) he saw he was hanging from the ceiling by chains around his ankles. All his clothes were gone except for his underwear, a blue cotton banana-hammock. Subterranean chill raised goosebumps on his naked thighs.

Jesus Christ, his worst sensationalist fears had come true—somebody he met on the Internet for sex had abducted him.

Was Red a cannibal?

Oh God, your cheap ass gonna get ate up, just cause you don't wanna buy your own steak. He twisted and jerked, trying to see more of the room, trying to ignore the dripping water. Revolving slowly to the left, he saw he wasn't the only person hanging out, so to speak. A white guy, also dressed only in his Hanes, ankles chained to the ceiling. He was facing the wall, bruises all over his shoulders as if he'd been beaten unconscious.

"Hey," said Joel through the gag, *hhnnngh.* Swaying his head from side to side, he swung his center of gravity back and forth, pulling on the chain around his cuffs. He managed to bump the guy with his shoulder, causing him to wobble and turn slowly on his chain.

When his fellow abductee-in-arms turned all the way around, Joel almost pissed his hammock.

The man was dead—*very* dead, his throat cut, his neck a slack grin stringy with red-black fibers, the crag of his larynx glinting in the worktable's light, framed by yellow fat like scrambled eggs. A sheet of dried blood ran up his purple face, collecting on the top of his head, where it was dripping on the dark floor.

He'd been bled dry like a pig.

Drip. Drip. Drip.

"Aww, awww, no," said Joel. *Where you at, Robin Martine? Where you at, sis? Oh God, please come find me. Your brother from another mother has royally fucked up this time.*

He remembered the sound of evening cicadas, that eternal electric drone.

He remembered slashes of orange and red sunset blazing through the treetops, shattered fire in the air. He remembered the ice of the cool evening breeze on his fevered face, his swollen skin. He remembered the sound and the weight of footsteps that were not his own—ponderous, heavy, pounding the earth like a blacksmith's hammer, slow and steady wins the race.

But most of all, he remembered being carried by a monster.

Clutching his burning body were these impossibly strong arms, thick and hard and veiny, smooth, cold, so like the stony arms of an ogre. Wayne expected to hear the battle-chant of Sauron's army of Uruk-hai all around him, and the clank and clash of iron swords, and battle cries in unintelligible tongues. But the face looming so close to his own, gargantuan though it seemed, was not a cruel beast from *Lord of the Rings*. No, it was the face of an old woman.

Spirals of black hair framed her face, shot through with darts of steel-gray. Her cheeks were round, her chin and nose and forehead wide, her mouth a thin, miserly whip-slash. "You been bitten by a snake," said the ogre-woman, in a grunty Cajun accent. Her teeth were the mottled yellow keys of an abandoned piano in a haunted house. "We gon' get you some help, boy, just you see."

Someone slathered ice on his leg. Wayne flinched.

"Now, calm yourself, wiggle-worm," another voice, a pinched, wizened crow-voice. "I'm puttin' something on that snakebite that'll do you real good, arright? It'll draw out the poisons, so you can—"

And then he was on a gurney, yellow lights flashing in his face. "I think he's having an allergic reaction," said a voice to his left: a woman, but this one young.

Ambulance.

The room shook. A siren rang out somewhere outside, rising, falling, yodeling. "Can you hear me?" a man asked. White, dressed in a blue polo shirt, with an ink pen behind his ear.

"Yeah." Wayne coughed weakly. His throat whistled as he spoke.

"What color was it?"

"Color?" he asked, confused. The lights were so bright.

"The snake that bit you, son. The snake, what did it look like? Did it make a noise like a rattle?"

"Copperhead," said the woman. "One of the other boys killed it. We have it."

When he opened his eyes again, he found himself in a cold, dark room under a too-thin blanket that felt to his leg as if it were made of barbed wire. The only light came from a nearby door, seeping in around the bottom, giving shape to dark angles. After a moment of disoriented, delirious eyerolling, he concluded he was in a hospital room.

Someone was asleep in the chair next to the bed. Wayne shifted to that side and discovered Leon, his rumpled army-surplus jacket folded up under his cheek.

As soon as he saw his father, something inside Wayne broke, a brittle eggshell crumpling deep inside of him, and tears sprang to his eyes. His throat burned with shame and embarrassment. *I bet I scared you so bad,* he thought, grimacing. *I am so sorry. I am so sorry I asked you to let me walk home.*

"Daddy," he said to the dim figure, but all that came out was a breathy squeal.

Leon snored.

Discouraged, Wayne lifted the covers and examined his left foot, the soft cotton sliding across his sensitive knee like the roughest burlap. At least a tiny part of his mind expected it to simply be gone—hacked off with a bonesaw and stapled shut, wound about with a bloodstained bandage. But other than tenderness and mild swelling, the extremity was present and accounted for. The bandage around his calf was tight but clean.

Too many horror movies.

He lay back down and again considered trying to rouse his father, but in the end he decided it would be better to let him sleep. The ol' man probably had a hard night, and without his patent-pending liquid courage, it must have been twice as difficult.

A clamp on his finger radiated a feverish red light, and a wire ran from it to an outlet in the wall over his head. A pair of flatscreens mounted to the wall next to the bed displayed a whole litany of inscrutable numbers and the ever-familiar heartbeat line of an ECG. The lightning-bolt of his heart beeped slow and stately. At first he was afraid taking it off would set off some kind of chirping alarm, wake up the whole hospital and summon a nurse. But when he screwed up his nerve and pulled it from his finger, nothing happened except the glowing blue seismograph turned to a flat line and all the numbers disappeared.

A Styrofoam container lay on a table by the bathroom door. Probably something to eat in there. Cold or hot, he didn't care. He glanced at his sleeping father again and slid out of the bed. Under his left foot, the floor was searingly cold. Limping across the room, the boy found a dispenser on the wall and managed to squirt some sanitizer foam into his hands. As he rubbed them together, his stomach gnarled up and growled, and he wondered how long it had been since he'd eaten lunch the day before. He was starving.

In a chair underneath the TV were his shoes, and in one of his shoes was his mother's wedding band. He slipped the cold chain around his neck.

Underneath the chair was a black gym bag. Wayne opened it and rooted around in it. Fresh clothes. Probably his own.

He thought about putting something on, but the idea he might need to stay in his gown for some reason or another made him reluctant, so he left it alone. He took the Styrofoam container—half a club sandwich, three soggy onion rings—and stood at the foot of his bed and watched his father sleep, still racked with shame.

I just know you been scared as hell all night. I'm so sorry. I had no idea there would be a snake in there.

Really, though, he was lying to himself.

Of course he'd been afraid of stumbling across a snake. It was why he'd hustled to get away from the weedy clown car, wasn't it, all full of snaky-looking brush and sticks. But he'd just walked right on into that Gravitron, hadn't he, without a care in the world.

And God in heaven! The bills would be astronomical, he just knew it.

On top of everything else, his dad was going to have to pay the hospital a kajillion dollars because Wayne was so stupid. He remembered reading about antivenin in Science class. The exotic names of the drugs had sounded so expensive.

This was my fault. His hand instinctively went to the ring dangling against his chest. He felt puny, unworthy. Raising the ring to his eye, he studied his father through the ring, looking for the familiar comfort of the protective metal hoop. *I knew it was dangerous and I did it anyway. I am so stupid. I'm a stupid kid. A stupid baby. I deserve to be grounded. I deserve to be locked up in my tower and never let out.*

"I'm sorry, Dad," he squeaked.

Leon just snored. A wooden door, like the kind you'd see in an old house, stood behind Leon's chair, leading out of the room. Paint flaked from its surface.

Wayne blinked.

Three-oh-six.

The ring dropped from his eye and the rusty door vanished.

Astonished, he shuffled over to where he'd seen it and put his hand against the wall. Cold cinder block, painted gray, nothing else. Gently feeling the wall with both hands, Wayne searched for the door he'd seen, but there was no indication it'd been there at all—no doorframe, no knob, no nothin'.

He stepped back a pace and looked through the gold wedding-band monocle again.

There it was again, big as life, and solid.

The doorframe was the green of grass, of frogs and avocados.

Three-oh-six. It was happening again. The door in the wall. He got a mental flash of himself craning to look upward through his father's windshield at the motel room door over his head, the door that disappeared, the door he never told his father about, with its 306 in gold lettering.

Three-oh-six.

But this one wasn't a motel room door. Looked like it belonged to an old house. He stepped close and put his hand against it. Instead of the cold block wall, he pressed his palm to wood, rough and jagged with paint, as warm as if the sun were hitting it from the other side. The doorknob throbbed in his hand, hot but not painfully so, invitingly, radiating from within like the hood of a car on a sunny day.

He turned the knob. The latch disengaged with a click.

Wayne threw a glance over his shoulder. Leon was still asleep. Probably a sleeping pill—his father was given to using medication like Benadryl and Tylenol PM to knock himself out when he was having a bad night. And this definitely qualified as a "bad night."

Opening the door, he wasn't sure what he would find on the other side . . . but it sure wasn't his own house.

Dark and deep, the Victorian at 1168 Underwood Road gaped before him. All he could see was a blotch of the floor and a bit of the wall, illuminated by a weak, aquatic light from above. He was looking at the second-floor landing, from the perspective of the doorway leading up to the cupola.

Hunger still gnawed at his insides. Maybe . . .

Wayne glanced at his father again. He didn't know what was going on, but if he'd been given some strange superpower by being bitten by a snake, he ought to take advantage of it and duck into the house for a bowl of Fruity Pebbles. And with great power comes great responsibility, you know, so he'd grab Leon a couple of his energy bars while he was in there.

Madness, said some rational voice deep in the back of his mind, less in words than in pure, essential feeling. *This is madness.*

Hmm. No, he mused, peering through the wedding band. *No, this is a dream. That's exactly what this is.* Light coming in under the hospital suite door glinted on its gold surface. He let it drop to his chest, hanging from the necklace. *I'm still lying in my bed over there, sleeping and dreaming, and this is a dream.*

The door remained, still open, still revealing the interior of the Victorian. *Well, I guess if this is a dream, I might as well dream on.*

Steeling himself, Wayne stepped into the darkened house.

It eased shut behind him. *Click.*

• • •

Wayne's heart leapt and he spun around, but the door was still there. He tried the doorknob. It wasn't locked.

Relieved, he looked around the landing. Something was subtly off about the house, but he couldn't quite put his finger on it. He reached behind his back to pinch his gown shut and made his way down the stairs.

The foyer was quiet. A little table stood against the banister at the bottom, and on it was a black rotary telephone, something Wayne had only seen in old movies. *Why did Dad buy an old tele-phone?*

As he thought about it, he realized what was different about the house.

The walls were supposed to be blue, dusky raincloud-blue. In-stead, they were green, the pale fifties-green of spearmint gum and the floors at his old school in Chicago, the green that belonged with salmon-pink on the flank of a Cadillac convertible parked at a drive-in movie.

Wayne picked up the receiver and put it against his ear. No dial tone.

He stuck his finger in the rotary dial and turned it. The earpiece made a subtle *tikkatikkatikkatik* sound, but nothing else happened. Listening to the faint rattling, his eyes wandered over to the left and he noticed the front door was a different color. Wayne hung up the phone and went over to check it out, his bare feet padding on the soft, intricate runner carpet. The front door was white, the bottom chewed up by time and neglect, the paint coming off to uncover rusty metal. A placard in the middle said WOMEN.

A restroom door? Wayne's hand found his face and he rubbed his forehead in confusion.

Too strange. Time to get to the kitchen, get what he came for, and get back to the hospital. He would talk to Leon when he woke up later, and see what was going on, but for right now he just wanted to get something to eat and get off of his increasingly tender foot. Steaming along on this dream-logic train, Wayne limped down the dark hallway and hooked right into the kitchen, stopping short.

Pale, dirty light filtered in through the window over the sink, like sunbeams coming through the scummy surface of a pond. This sickly glow drew the contours and corners of a black kitchen— black walls, black ceiling, the stove was black, the paint bubbling and peeling. He touched the stove, and his fingertip came away with a paste of damp soot.

One winter when he was in second grade, maybe, Wayne caught chicken pox and had to stay with his Aunt Marcelina. She'd turned on the stove to boil water for a cup of hot chocolate, but it had been the wrong eye, searing the painted tin eye-cover on top of it. The foul smell of burnt paint had hung in the air for weeks, like a curse on Marcelina's apartment.

This same acrid stink now lingered in the black kitchen.

Wayne opened a few cabinets, searching for his cereal. Nothing in them except for canned food with old-looking labels and brand names he didn't recognize, many of them with dented sides. The cabinet where they kept the drinking glasses had a box of cherry Pop-Tarts and a box of Life, but he didn't like cherry and had never tried Life, so he left them alone.

"What is goin' *on,* man?" he asked the strange kitchen.

The floor creaked in the living room, the slow tectonic croak of a ship's deck.

Wayne's head snapped up and he fled to the other side of the table, which was not their small round wooden table, but a large Formica oval with metal trim, like something out of a diner. It was thick, and bulky, and felt protective.

"Who's there?"

No answer. His heart fluttered in his chest.

"Pete?" he asked the darkness. "Zat you?"

Waiting for a voice, Wayne stood behind the table for a long minute. None came. He opened the silverware drawer, found hand-towels, opened another drawer, found a jumble of random utensils. No weapons to be had.

Weak ocean-floor sunlight whispered into the living room as well, bandaged by the sheer white curtains. The suggestion of a brown sofa lurked next to the rumor of a coffee table resembling a pirate's chest.

Wayne chewed his cheek, eyeing a weird wooden TV with a rabbit-ear antenna and a bulging gray screen, accompanied by a panel of numbered dials. Creepy wood-framed pictures lined the walls: praying children with bulbous Casper heads and shiny blond hair, painted on black velvet.

He leaned over and was reaching for the television's power button when something inhaled behind him, a ragged wet *grararararuhh* that made him think of engines and dragons.

Ice raced down his legs and arms, his mouth falling open in terror.

Behind him, a mass of greasy, rumpled hair was wedged into the back corner where the watery sunlight faded into shadow. Green owl-eyes opened in a massive head that brushed the ceiling like a grown man in a child's playhouse.

Rararararararuhhh . . .

The beast leaned away from the wall, reaching for Wayne with orangutan arms and too many fingers, smelling of filth, of old blood, of death.

The boy ran.

Leading out of the kitchen and out of the house, the back door was metallic gray, patchy with rust. A sign near the top said NO ADMITTANCE—EMPLOYEES ONLY! He shoved it open, running through it into what should have been the backyard, but instead was a dark indoor space, swampy with the stink of old motor oil.

Turning to face the monster, Wayne found only a blank wall of corrugated aluminum.

He was alone.

Tears made cold tracks down his cheeks. He ground them away with a wrist and sank to his hands and knees, shaking and nauseous. The constricting bandage around his swelling leg was killing him and his left foot buzzed with pins and needles.

Chains rattled on the other side of the wall. Wayne stood up.

Sun-bleached kart bodies rusted quietly in the shadows, strewn with broken engine parts. Signs made out of plywood and sheet metal leaned against the wall in piles. The first one was a menacing cartoon of a clown. VISIT HOOT'S FUNHOUSE! GET LOST IN OUR HALL OF MIRRORS! The back door of the strange green version of his house had brought him to what appeared to be some kind of mechanic's garage, the cement floor dark and greasy under his bare feet.

A huge roll-up garage door dominated one wall. Moonlight slipped underneath the bottom panel.

Another sign, this one as big as a barn door, welcomed him to Weaver's Wonderland, and beside that was painted a picture of a mom and a dad walking into an amusement park, a little girl sitting on her father's shoulders.

The clanking of chains and muffled growling echoed from a black doorway. "Grrnngh!" growled something from the other room. "Hhhngh—*thp thp thp puh, puh*—HELP!"

Goosebumps prickled Wayne's skin. He peeked inside.

Planter hooks had been screwed into the wall by the door, stuck through the links of three chains. One of them lay useless underneath, but the other two ran across the room to ceiling pulleys.

Two men hung upside-down from them, a black guy and a white guy, both of them naked except for their skivvies.

The one in the thong was squirming and undulating furiously, jerking on the chains binding his hands to the floor. A cloth gag dangled around his neck. "Jesus Lord help me, get me the hell out of here," he pleaded, and noticed Wayne peering through the doorway. "Oh God, oh God, get me *down,* get me *outta here,* you gotta get me out of here, *please.*"

Wayne ventured into the room. ARE YOU TOO COOL FOR SCHOOL? asked the coyote on the sign. "What's goin' on?"

"I been kidnapped, this man has kidnapped me, I don't know if he put something in my drink, or put something in my steak, but he knocked my ass out and when I woke up I was chained up in here and right now I need you to go over there and unhook me so I can get down and I need you to do it right now. Right now right now right now."

Taking hold of the chain, Wayne tried to pull the man up to give himself enough slack to pull the hook out of the link, but he was just too heavy. The gritty floor bit into the sensitive sole of his left foot.

"I can't do it." Panic overtook him and he started weeping again, his throat burning. "I got bit by a snake on my foot and I'm so tired. I been in the hospital—"

"Honey, what's your name?" asked the man.

"Wayne."

"Mine is *Jo-elle*. Okay, Wayne baby, Wayne, take the chain in both your hands. See how the hook curves?" The chain had been pulled down onto the point of a hook on the floor. "I want you to take the chain in both hands and push it off the hook. Can you do that?"

Bracing himself, Wayne got under the chain and pushed. Jo-elle's weight made it seem impossible at first, but when he put his hands close to the hook and pushed as hard as he could, throwing his whole body into a series of shoves, the link began to scrape free.

The sleepy growl of a four-stroke motor grew outside the building, reminding Wayne of the golf carts the security guys drove at the mall back in Chicago.

Jo-elle shook with fear. "Oh Jesus, hurry up, he's back, God almighty, he's back."

Shove, shove, shove. *Almost there.* Wayne renewed his grip on the chain and ignored the tingling-prickling in his swollen leg. The filthy floor caked dried motor-oil between his toes. *Tink!* The chain slipped free and whipped through the pulley like slurping spaghetti, making a loud clatter. Jo-elle fell on his head, swearing in pain.

Outside, the golf cart engine shut off.

Jo-elle scrambled to his feet, freeing his cuffs from the hook screwed into the cement and wriggling out of the chain wrapped around his ankles. "We got to go, we got to go."

"What about the other guy?" Wayne asked, pointing at the man still chained to the ceiling. His bruised back was to them.

"He's dead, baby, there ain't nothin' we can do." Jo-elle took off into the other room, staggering in circles and looking around wildly. "How did you get *in* here? Where did you come from?"

Wayne held up his mother's wedding band. "You're gonna laugh at me, but I think I made a door. Or maybe I found one."

"You made—*what?*" Jo-elle winced in confusion. "You *made* a door? How do you 'make' a door?" He waved off the coming explanation. "Just show me the way out so we can get—"

"But there's a monster—"

"What?"

Keys jingling in the workshop. Door unlocking.

"A monster in my house—" Wayne began to say, and recoiled as Jo-elle lunged for him, grabbed him by the head, and gazed into his face.

"We got to *go*. We got to go *now*."

The door in the workshop opened, and someone thumped across the oily floor in boots, tossing a keychain full of keys on the worktable. Hollow *thunk* of some sort of plastic container. Gas can? The rattle of chains.

A raspy voice. "Hey, how'd you get down?"

Jo-elle ran over and slammed the door, swearing under his breath, bracing himself against it. The handle rattled.

"There ain't no way out of there, pizza-man," said the killer's muffled voice. "You might as well come on out. I'd lock you in there and let you starve, but I kinda need to bleed you like your buddy in here." He coughed, cleared his throat. "Nothin' personal, you know. It's my job. Well, part of it. Blood-collecting. The people I work for, they need it for the garden. Always blood for the garden."

Boots scuffing on cement: the man walked away. The bump and clatter of tools being rummaged through, assembled. "It never ends, it never ends."

"You ain't got to do this, Red," said Jo-elle.

"Sure I do." The killer paused. "You know what? Call me the Serpent. That's what the papers back in New York used to call me.

I like it. My friends called me Snake when I was little, but 'Serpent' sounds so . . . I dunno, *Biblical*, doesn't it? Man, it just rolls off the tongue."

Everything went quiet.

Hiss, a burst of noise came out of the door-crack as the Serpent spat through, his lips against the jamb.

Jo-elle twitched, almost losing his leverage on the door. "You let me out, and I ain't tell nobody, man," he said. "I swear. You let me go and it'll be like this never happened. We both go our own way and it's all good."

The Serpent laughed. "Fat chance, homo. You've seen my face. Not gonna happen."

"Homo—?" Jo-elle's face darkened. "You mean . . . ?"

"Oh hell naw. I don't swing that way, pizza-man. You kidding me? I mean, yeah, I done some things I ain't proud of to put food on the table, but deep down I'm as straight as a . . ." The killer drummed fingers on the door. "Help me out here, what's something really straight? You know, other than 'not you.'"

"An arrow? I don't—"

"Be original!"

Something pistoned hard against the door, *BANG!*, and Jo-elle jumped away. "Ow!"

A nail protruded from the door's surface, dripping blood.

Taking advantage of the moment, the Serpent kicked the door so hard one of the plywood signs fell over. The sign behind it was a painting of a sweating glass of lemonade.

WHEN LIFE HANDS YOU LEMONS, GIVE EM BACK—OURS IS BETTER!

Wayne pressed the gold ring to his eye.

Adapt and overcome.

Nothing about Jo-elle's end of the room was special, but when he turned to the back wall, there it was again, the doorway back to the green house with the burned kitchen. *Be bigger. Be stronger.* He was going to have to brave that strange dark place with its giant hairy creature. *It's got to be better than this Serpent person. I know he's going to kill me, but I don't know what the monster wants.*

"The evil you know" versus "the evil you don't." Adapt and overcome.

Summoning up all the courage he could find, his body cold and trembling in deepest terror, Wayne opened the strange door. Beyond, the hollow Victorian promised nothing but darkness and silence.

"The hell—?" Jo-elle was staring at him.

BANG! Another nail shot through the door, appearing between his fingers as if by magic. He snatched his hand away, cursing. The Serpent gave the door another kick and it flew open, squealing.

Scooping up the boy, Jo-elle fled through the door into the Victorian. Wayne got a quick glimpse of a shock of the killer's red hair, beady eyes, a scrawny throat, and then the door slammed shut behind them, plunging them into blue-green twilight.

The afterimage of the killer's face resonated in Wayne's mental eye. Seemed so familiar. Where had he seen that face before?

Jo-elle breathed, "Where are we . . . ?"

They were back in the burned kitchen. Wayne pressed against the man's clammy side, ignoring his sweatiness and the fact all he wore was a pair of bikini underwear. Jo-elle was solidly built—if a little soft around the midsection—and that was all that mattered. "It's supposed to be my house," he explained in a pained whisper, "but for some reason it's painted green instead of blue. And . . . and there's some kind of monster in here."

Peeling him off, Jo-elle squinted at Wayne. "A monster?"

"It's big and hairy. It's like . . . I guess it's like a Bigfoot."

"You got a Sasquatch. In your house."

"I'm not sure this is my house." Wayne pressed a finger to his lips. "Shhh, or it's going to hear us and come after us."

"It is, or it isn't. How can it *be* your house *and not be* your house?" Jo-elle blinked in recognition. "Wait. *Wait.* I *know* this house. I've sat at this table before. This is Annie Martine's house.

She used to babysit me and my brother when I was a little boy like you."

Now that he was out of danger, Jo-elle seemed to favor his right foot, using the kitchen counter as a crutch as he left the room. Out in the hallway, he supported himself on the armrest of a chair. "Yeah, this most definitely Annie's house. You mean you livin' here? I didn't even know it was still for sale. I figured it would be fallin' apart by now."

"Is Annie Martine the witch that died here?"

Jo-elle eyed him. "Where you hear that?"

"My friend Pete told me." Wayne stopped to rub his leg. The gauze wound around his left knee was so tight he couldn't stand it, and his ankle felt plump, tender, like a big warm sausage. "He lives over in the trailer park. He said her husband pushed her down the stairs."

"I don't know if I believe in witches, but I don't speak ill of the dead. Annie was a good woman."

He sat down in the chair. Wayne grabbed his arm and tried to pull him back up. "No, we can't stay here. It's not safe. I told you, there's a monster here."

"Just let me rest f'minute. I been upside-down for hours. My head is spinning."

"No!"

"Little man, just cause I'm sittin' here in a clearance-rack thong don't mean I ain't gonna slap you. I hurt myself falling on the floor, and you making it worse." Jo-elle took his hand away, rubbing his wrist.

Wayne scowled and headed for the stairs. "Okay, then . . . I'll leave you here. You should—"

Deep, guttural breathing rumbled along the hallway, *grarara-rararauuuh,* and the floorboards groaned.

"You on *y'own!*" said Wayne, running for the foyer.

As soon as he got there, the hulking green-eyed shadow reached out of the living room doorway with those long, hairy arms.

"*Oh!*" shrieked Jo-elle. "*What the Christ!*"

Halfway up the switchback staircase, Wayne paused to make sure he wasn't alone, and he wasn't, because the lamp-eyed creature was crawling up the wall and across the ceiling at him like some kind of huge horrible spider-bear. Wayne screamed and fought to get up to the second floor, slipping, clawing at the steps, banging his knees.

Inhaling, the creature made a deep crooning foghorn noise—*Hhhrrroooohh!*—and crabbed over the edge of the landing.

When Wayne reached the top of the stairs, it was already there waiting, crawling over the banister. "Oh!" he just had time to shout, and then the creature was on him, mumbling, wet, reeking of mold and garbage. The thing's mouth widened, a pit cracking open a long head like a watermelon, and rows of slimy teeth glistened in that eerie sea-light from above. It leaned forward and took Wayne's entire head in its jaws.

A leathery tongue pressed against his eyebrow, hot breath washing his face. He could hear a muffled whispering-crinkling noise from deep in its throat, like a candy wrapper in a pocket.

Clang!

The monster straightened, growling at Jo-elle, who stood over it with the rotary phone in one hand. "It's for *you*, bitch!" He brought the phone cradle down on that shaggy head again. *Clang!*

Grateful for the distraction, Wayne clambered on his hands and knees across the landing.

Since the monster had cut him off before he could reach the cupola door leading back to the hospital and Leon, he fled down the hallway to the upstairs bathroom. Flinging the door open, Wayne was surprised and dismayed to find only a bathtub and a toilet.

He looked back just in time to see the deformed Sasquatch pin Jo-elle to the floor and rake fingernails across his bare chest. Blood splattered up the wall.

Gathering his feet, Jo-elle leg-pressed the creature's chest, almost lifting it into the air, and pried himself free, loping after Wayne on all fours. They crowded into the bathroom and Jo-elle shut the door, locking the knob, as if that would help.

BANG! The thing outside threw itself against the door. A cup of moldy toothbrushes toppled into the sink.

Mysterious night lay opaque against the windowpane like black felt. The window over the tub was painted shut. "Now what?" asked Wayne, on the verge of hysterics. He ripped open the mirror.

Instead of a medicine cabinet, a dark room gaped inside, viewed from a high angle some ten feet in the air. Huge plate-glass windows to the left showered the room in soft gray moonbeams. The red numerals of a digital alarm clock burned in the black.

Wayne climbed up on the sink and through the medicine cabinet. "Come on!"

On the other side, he stood on top of a refrigerator, in a room that smelled like cheap shrimp and burnt hair. He climbed down onto the counter, stumbling over some bulky kitchen-thing, and jumped down to linoleum. His new thong-bedecked friend leapt down after him and fell, swearing about his ankle.

The crawlspace they'd escaped through slammed shut, becoming a painting. In fact, now that he'd noticed them, Wayne saw the wall was covered in paintings.

Bleeding on the floor, poor Jo-elle had a mini-breakdown. "Mother of God and home of the brave, what in *the* hell *was* that?"

The kitchen lights came on, dazzling them both.

A blond man with a crutch under one arm and a pistol in the other trained his gun-barrel on them. A small, pretty woman with a Mohawk stood next to him. Wayne's eyes trickled down until they came to rest on the blond's left leg, which ended in a nub just below the knee.

"Joel?" asked the man.

Joel squinted. "Kenway?"

"The hell you doing in my kitchen at—" Kenway glanced at the microwave, ejecting the magazine from the pistol and racking the slide. A bullet flipped out and he caught it in his other hand. "—Five in the morning? . . . Butt-ass naked? In handcuffs?"

"What's it look like, hero?" demanded Joel, panting and grimacing, his hand over the lacerations on his chest. "I needed to borrow a cup of sugar."

19

"And that's how we ended up here," said the kid. They were all clustered around the island in the kitchen, wide awake. Robin's camera still stood at the end of the counter, recording his tale. Kenway made them all omelets and coffee while Joel and Wayne told their stories. His eyebrows stayed high and his forehead furrowed through most of it, but to his credit he never challenged them or made any disbelieving noises.

Wayne had traded his hospital gown for a sweater and a pair of jeans from Robin. They were feminine and a couple sizes too big, but they did the trick.

With some alcohol, Neosporin, a bandage, and a bottle of breakfast stout, Joel was sore and whiny but otherwise good as new. He'd only been nicked by the nail through the door, and his cuts weren't as bad as they looked—more scratches than anything else, not quite enough to need stitches. He was wearing one of Kenway's shirts and a pair of his jeans—a pair of skinny jeans the big vet had received as a gift last Christmas and just hadn't been able to bring himself to wear.

Robin walked around the apartment, looking through the boy's ring like Sherlock Holmes with his magnifying glass, trying to detect anomalies. No such luck. It seemed whatever the ring was capable of, only its owner was able to take advantage of it.

An engraving inside the ring said, *Together We'll Always Find a Way.*

This was significant. Words hold power, and Robin knew from experience that text—whether engraved or printed—could absorb and retain, or channel, that power.

"I need to call my dad and let him know I'm all right," said Wayne. "If he's awake now, he's probably really worried. Probably wondering where I am." He sighed. "I don't have my cell phone or I'd text him."

Pouring herself a cup of coffee, Robin joined them at the island. She gave him her cell phone and his ring, and he typed in his dad's number, pressing the phone to his ear. "What troubles me the most," Robin said to Kenway, "is the Sasquatch-monster they saw in my old house is . . . well, I've been seeing it for a long time. It's that thing I've been calling the Red Lord. Always thought it was a hallucination—a part of my psychosis and my PTSD. I don't know what to think about three other people seeing it too." Robin sat there picking at an omelet, carving off little bites and eating them in a daze of deep thought.

"*Saw it?*" squawked Joel. "*Fucker tried to kill me!*"

"I'm pretty sure you're not psychotic, or whatever," said Kenway. "Psychosis doesn't shit spiders all over my bed like some kind of Satanic slot machine."

"I'm with friends, Dad," Wayne was saying, trying to lay down some damage control. They could hear the mosquito-buzz of Leon Parkin shouting through the phone. "Yes, friends. No, not Pete. I'm fine, I'm fine. Something happened in the room and I ended up somewhere else. I mean, I don't know. It was weird. Yes." His face scrunched up on one side and he screwed the heel of his hand into his eye sleepily. "Dad, I can explain it better when you're chilled out, okay?" A tear rolled down his face. "Hey. Hey, I'm sorry. For making you worry." The boy turned away from them, hugging himself, trying not to sob outright. "Do you forgive me?" Several quiet seconds passed. "I love you too, Dad."

"Hey," said Kenway. "Tell him we're gonna take you back to the hospital as soon as we get done eating."

Wayne did so. "I'm sorry for making you worry," he reiterated, his voice breaking. "Are you doin' okay? Dad, you ain't drinkin' nothin', are you? . . . Don't worry about me if that makes it harder. Yeah. I just don't want . . . y'know?" He hung up and gave the phone back to Robin.

She took a sip of coffee and asked them, "So you said the walls were green when you went into the old Underwood house?"

"The kitchen was burnt slap up," said Joel. "And your mama's old diner table was in there, too."

"My mom painted the walls green when I was a kid. When they prosecuted my dad and I became a ward of the state, the city fixed it up and painted it blue."

"Other than it bein' burnt, it looked like it did when we was kids." Joel gingerly explored the bandage taped to his chest, an adhesive combat bandage from Kenway's old combat medic supplies, like a big square Band-Aid. "Man, this makes me glad I shave."

Wayne made a face. "You shave your chest? . . . Do you shave your legs and *everything?*"

"I don't really consider this an appropriate topic for breakfast conversation." Joel winced in mock offense and he tossed one leg over a knee, sitting back with his beer. "You always this rude?"

"So *weird.*"

"Little man, don't be sassing your elders."

Kenway scoffed. "You just got away from a blood-stealing serial killer and fought off a monster in a nightmare version of your house, and you think a guy that shaves his legs is weird?"

• • •

After gulping down breakfast, they loaded into Kenway's truck and headed to the hospital. Robin rode in the back, wearing a thick jacket with the hood pulled over her head to protect her from the wind. It was a little after six in the morning, according to her phone—and the autumn air bit her face.

She squinted in the gale, holding the GoPro out, filming the scenery as it blew past. This would make good B-roll. She wanted to monologue, but the snapping of the wind would make it impossible to hear.

As they pulled into the parking lot of Blackfield Medical, Leon Parkin came striding out the front door, followed by an old woman in a raggedy petticoat that seemed to be made out of old potato sacks and swatches from the clearance fabric section of Walmart. Kenway was barely out of the driver's seat when Leon marched up and started raining blows on him, cornering him inside the truck door.

Everyone exploded into movement, shouting, running to stop him. Joel and Robin got them separated and Leon threw his elbows, trying to shake them off. "Y'all motherfuckers take my son?" he raved, seething in the middle of their circle. White vapor coiled from his mouth. "Who *are* you? What *is* this?"

"Now wait a minute—" Kenway began, putting up his hands. Blood trickled from his nose. Leon charged him again and Joel and Robin wrestled him away.

Wayne got out and ran to his dad. Leon clutched him against his side. "Get inside, son."

"But Dad—"

"Get your ass inside and I'll be in there in a minute."

The boy looked up with a stern face that belonged on a grown man and pushed away. "Dad, I left on my own. It was an accident."

"*What* did I tell you?"

"No!" said Wayne, clenching his fists and shivering. He

was limping again, his left foot a faint shade of purple. "I been helping—I've been dealing, with you, and things, you know, for long enough, Dad, and you owe me. I've always been there. *Always.* Even when you weren't." They all stared in amazement at the boy's near-shouting tone. "So right now, *I need you to listen!*"

Stunned, Leon's face softened as he seemed to see his son, really *see* him, his eyes wandering up and down Wayne's outfit.

"We *both* lost her, Dad. I hurt too. You know that?"

Leon nodded. "Yeah. Yeah, man . . . yeah," as if he were coming out of a trance, and he stooped to gather Wayne up in a huge hug. The old woman clutched the collar of her heavy patchwork coat, her stringy hair whipping around. Her face was pinched into a vapid smile until she caught Robin's stare.

Recognition flashed in the old woman's eyes. "Why don't we all go inside and sort this out somewhere warm, yes?"

● ● ●

"My name is Karen. Karen Weaver," she said to Wayne, leading them to a back corner of an isolated waiting room. "Believe it or not, I actually live right across the street from you, in the big Mexican church-house. Me and my friend Theresa were out hunting mushrooms by the old fairgrounds when I heard your friends screaming you'd been bitten by a mean old snake."

Ah, damn. It's one of the Lazenbury coven. Robin followed them, her GoPro clipped to a jacket pocket, recording the conversation. Children's books and old magazines littered an end table, and behind them an aquarium burbled peacefully.

"What kind of snake?" asked Joel.

Weaver smiled. "Well, that big kid—Peter, was it? He did a real number on it with that mallet, but from what I saw it looked like a copperhead. Anyway, I put a special salve on you, a poultice, I suppose, that worked to nullify and draw out most of that venom, and then Theresa carried you out to the road." With a giggle, she added, "For an old lady, she's as strong as a warthog." She bent to watch the fish darting back and forth in the aquarium, talking to the glass. "One of your friends got your cell phone and called 911 for you—Johnny, I suppose his name was." Weaver wagged a finger at Wayne. "A very dear little boy, you ought to thank him, and Peter, for their heroics. They're quite exceptional for children these days."

Turning to Kenway, Leon rubbed his head. "Hey, look, man . . . I'm sorry about the whole, you know, punch in the face and all—"

The vet had produced a paint-smeared handkerchief from somewhere, and was holding it to his nose. "Unnerstandable," he said, checking the fabric. His nose had stopped leaking. "Enh, I been through worse, trust me."

Kneeling to get eye-to-eye with his son, Leon said, "Now, tell me what happened. You said you would explain everything. I want to know the truth."

Wayne's eyebrows scrunched. "When have I lied to you—"

Leon smirked dryly.

"—in the last week?" Before his dad could answer, Wayne took out the ring and showed it to him. "It was this."

Leon took it in his thumb and forefinger, at the end of the chain still around the boy's neck. "Your mother's wedding band?" His features softened, his eyes wistful. "I didn't know you were wearing this."

"I been wearin' it for . . . well, ever since Mom. I found it in the cupholder in your car and I took it." Wayne held it up to his eye. "I woke up in my hospital room, got up and got Mom's ring out of my stuff, and when I came back to my bed I looked through it and saw a door in the wall where there wasn't one before."

Karen Weaver's eyes darted over to Wayne's face, and narrowed, and she seemed to be paying much more rapt attention to him. The old woman twitched as if she were about to reach for the ring in his hand and ask about it, but she hesitated—out of fear, or propriety, Robin wasn't sure. But there was no mistaking the look on the witch's face as Weaver stared, eyes bouncing from ring to boy to ring—tense, poised interest.

Greed, almost, glinting underneath her bushy eyebrows.

The boy went on to describe the strange past-version of the Underwood house, and the bizarre owl-headed Sasquatch, and rescuing Joel from the Serpent.

"A killer?" Leon stiffened. "You saw a *dead guy?*"

Joel spoke up. "I was chained up in a garage somewhere next to a dude with a cut throat. This red-headed guy had knocked me out and I guess he was drainin' people for their blood. Said something about 'blood for the garden.' He was about to stick me like a pig too, until y'boy here showed up outta nowhere and saved my sexy ass."

"And you saw this weird dark version of our house too?"

"Yes sir, I did." Joel peeled back the lapel of the jacket he'd borrowed from Kenway, exposing his bandaged chest. "And that monster damn near opened me up."

The old woman coughed once, twice, then started hacking into a lacy cloth and struggled to breathe.

That ring, thought Robin. *Does she sense something about it?*

Is it supernatural?

"You okay?" asked Kenway.

"Oh, yes, yes," choked Weaver, waving him off. "It's getting that time of year when it gets dry outside. And I've got a bit of congestion. Nothing, really. I'm going to get some water, if that's all right with you-all." She tipped her hat deferentially and sauntered out of the room.

I need to find out what she knows. Robin got up and excused herself as well, following the old woman. *The Parkin family could be in danger if she wants the kid's ring.*

Still crouping and wheezing into her napkin, Weaver glided down the hallway and around the corner. Robin followed, striding into a small hallway that contained a drinking fountain and the doors leading into the three restrooms—a men's room, a women's room, and a gender-neutral family restroom.

At the end of the hall was a utility closet, the door gently easing closed on its hydraulic arm.

The hell you going in there for? Robin moved past the restroom. She pulled the door open and slipped through into the utility closet, pushing it shut.

To her left were several floor-to-ceiling racks piled high with clean linens, to her right were three washer-dryer combo machines, one of which was drying a load with a warm, steady *rumble-bang-tumble.* In the back of the room were more steel shelving units, these packed with cleaning chemicals, scrub-brushes, sponges, and green scrub pads. Beyond that was a chain-link enclosure through which Robin could see some sort of sleek machine with a digital readout. A hot water boiler, perhaps.

The gate was unlocked; she pulled it open and stepped into the enclosure. Opposite the boiler, she found a deep industrial sink and a big soap-scummed mirror. A mop bucket stood sentinel, full of milky gray water.

No witch. Robin sighed.

Where did you go?

She went to the sink and poured a double-handful of water, washed the sleep out of her eyes, and straightened back up, toweling her face dry with her T-shirt. When she opened her eyes again, the old woman's reflection stood behind her own.

Robin gasped and spun to face her.

"I know who you are," said the crone, backing her against the mop-sink.

"You do?"

"Oh, yes, of course. You're huge on the Internet, you know." Weaver grinned, flashing peanut-colored teeth and black gums. Her breath smelled like skunky weed. "You're the witch-hunter on that Malus Domestica channel, aren't you? Oh, I've been sub-scribed to you for ages. I even have a few of your T-shirts." She threw her hands up in mock exasperation, her gaudy rings glittering in the fluorescent lights. "My friends, they don't think much of you, but I think you're a very brave young lady to do what you do. I'm a huge fan."

"You believe in witches, then." *Smooth. You're the fucking smoothest. Trying to act like you don't already know she's a witch.* Her breathing quickened, and suddenly she realized her inner monologue was Heinrich's reproachful voice, echoing in the channels of her brain. *Chick, she's been waiting for you, she's on top of this, she knows, she knows you know she knows, and—*

"*Believe* in them?" Weaver laughed. "My dear, I *am* one."

"You're one of the Lazenbury House coven."

"Ah, it looks like you done your homework." The witch wrung her hands. "Are you here to, ahh, *slay* us too, then? Stop playing coy. I know why you're in town."

Swallowing, Robin put a little steel in her spine and stepped into Weaver's personal space. "You murdered my mother and turned her into a dryad. If you been watching my videos, you know I been doing this for a couple of years now—" She jerked the collar of her shirt down. Tattooed on her sternum, just below the pit of her throat, was the protective Viking rune, the *algiz*. "—so I've learned a few things from Heinrich."

"Heinrich—?" Weaver was unimpressed. "Honey, Heinrich Hammer is a fool," she said sweetly, encouragingly. "The only reason he ain't dead yet is because he quit huntin' us years ago. He's made a puppet of you, a henchman, a bloodhound to hide behind and exact his mad, mean crusade against us without having to risk his own life. You know, you should be proud of yourself. You've accomplished more than *he* ever did."

The witch traced the symbol with a painted claw. "Now, this is very pretty, dear, quite a lovely tattoo, but it won't save you. Your little Viking protection rune may protect you against being made a familiar, but it won't protect you from the rest of our bag of tricks."

"I saw you looking at the boy's ring."

"I was, I was," said Weaver. "Very interesting—secret doors? A house stuck in the past? A monster? Are you thinking what I'm thinking, girl?"

"Illusion magic?"

"I'm not sure. I don't think so—being a master of Illusion and all, I know my own magic when I see it. I think it's something else. Conjuration, perhaps. I dabble in Conjuration, you know—it's one of my lesser Gifts. You know, speaking of Gifts . . ." Weaver laid a flat palm on Robin's cleavage, and she sidled away from the cold hand, sliding her butt along the edge of the sink.

Following, the witch migrated her hand from Robin's left breast and then to her belly. Her fingertips were cold as December, even through the cloth. "Oh, dove, I think I feel something kicking. Don't you?"

Robin pushed her away. "Get off me."

"Wait a minute," said Weaver, snatching her hand away. "Did you say *dryad*? *Mother*?" Her rheumy eyes widened and she swept in, staring into Robin's face. "Are you . . . ? Could you be? *Annie Martine's daughter*? Oh, how you've grown, my dear. How lovely you are now! I knew a few years ago you were sprung out of the nuthouse, Marilyn said as much, but we had no idea where you went! Oh, who could have guessed such a beautiful girl could have come from such a homely woman?"

"*Don't talk about my mother*," growled Robin, and she let out a mild cough. Maybe she was coming down with a cold too—bit of a tickle in her chest. "She may have been a witch, but she was a good person, and better than any of you. You had no—*cough*—no right—"

"Who knows rights better than you, eh Malus? Malus Domestica, YouTube star, traveling the roads, living the American dream, killing innocent witches by the fourscore. You wouldn't know your right from your left." Weaver emphasized *right* and *left* with palsied fists, then marched off in that sweeping, handsy Gargamel way of hers, reaching for the door handle.

Before she could leave, Robin had a fistful of her coat. "You better leave those people alone. Stay away from—*cough*—the Parkins. And tell Marilyn I'll be—*cough, cough*—making a house call." She pulled the witch close and said through gritted teeth, "You three can prepare all you want, but—*cooouugh, cough*—I've gotten a lot of practice doing what I'm gonna do to the four of you. Believe *that.*"

Silence fell over them as the dryer stopped tumbling and the machine shut off. The threat devolved into a coughing fit, and she gasped for air. Her lungs felt like they were full of down feathers, itching and wispy.

"You don't know your mother as well as you think you do. I'm pretty sure Annie Martine is responsible for whatever creature Marilyn found out there in your mama's old house. The one them black folks is living in now."

"Wait, you mean—*cough, cough*—that's not yours?"

"That thing is a little above my pay grade, as powerful as I am. And if your mother had magic that powerful, then it's a good thing we killed her dead as shit." Weaver opened the utility room door and wrenched her sleeve out of the girl's hand, her expression one of genuine concern. "You don't know what you're gettin' yourself into. Stay away from the Lazenbury House, let us take the Conjuration ring, and we'll leave you be. Get out of Blackfield and I'll . . . I'll convince Marilyn not to come after you, yes, that's what I'll do. Stick around and we'll kill you dead too."

With that, the witch slipped out the door. Robin wanted to retort, but she couldn't stop coughing and catch her breath long enough to speak. The cavity of her chest was alive with fluttering-itching-whispering. A lump in her throat. She made long, drawn-out *huuuckkkk* sounds as if she were trying to muster up a loogie, and some wet little wad popped up into her mouth, lying on her tongue like a swallowed cigarette butt.

Robin staggered over to the industrial sink, coughing as she went, and spat it into the basin.

A dead moth.

"Ugh," she said, and coughed again.

This time the tickling sensation intensified, rushing up her windpipe, and when she coughed again a cloud of fat fluttery moths burst from the depths of her lungs.

Their tiny legs fought for purchase on the roof of her mouth, filling her throat. The ones that managed to escape fell into the sink and battered the mirror, dragging their saliva-wet bodies across the dirty glass, leaving smears of bitter wing-powder.

Bits of insect were caught in her teeth. Her stomach rumbled and gnarled, and her mouth flooded with salty spit. She was going to puke.

Wheezing, sucking wind, fighting to breathe, Robin braced her hands on the edge of the sink. Tears clung to the rims of her eyelids. The convulsion came without preamble, as it always does, and she loudly and rudely unleashed a torrent of sour vomit into the mop sink.

"Guh," she gasped, staring down into a brown slurry of coffee and eggs and dead moths.

Rummaging through the shelving units, she found a roll of paper towels. Ripped off a handful and scrubbed her tongue with it in disgust. The sensation of having moths in her mouth was unbearable—after chasing the supernatural for several years there wasn't much on this planet Robin was still afraid of, but insects never failed to make her skin crawl. That's most likely why the witches usually utilized them against her. They somehow just *knew* what got your goat, and they beat you over the head with it.

Shivers danced down her back, turning into a pins-and-needles prickly feeling, goosebumps running across her shoulder blades and down her arms. The hair stood up on her wrists and the backs of her hands. She hugged herself against the chill, wringing her hands.

Itchy, *so itchy,* suddenly she was scratching her hands, and then her arms, the goosebumps had become this helpless, crazy-making itchiness. It wouldn't go away but it felt so good, it was so satisfying, Jesus, she was digging miniature orgasms out of her skin like a paleontologist unearthing fossils. Her fingernails left burning streaks down her forearms. She unbuttoned her jeans and pushed them down to her knees, scratching her legs.

Opening her eyes, she looked down. Her arms were covered in pimples. Dozens—no, *hundreds*—of whiteheads. Not only were they on her arms, but they'd spread to her thighs, too. "What the hell?"

This is wrong, she thought, slowly turning her arms this way and that, inspecting the surprise acne. *Something is wrong. Something is really wrong here.* She dug at one of the largest whiteheads, picking at it until it came loose in a tiny plug of wax.

Two little red-green eyes stared up at her.

Horror made her scalp crawl as a housefly wriggled up out of the pore in her skin and struggled to its feet.

The fly rubbed its forelegs all over its head as its wet, glassy wings unraveled, drying and hardening. Robin slapped it away. "No. No no no *no.*" Her boots clomped a jig of panicky disgust on the tile floor. This dislodged several other whiteheads on her thighs, and she fell against the wall, her back sliding down the rough cinder block. More flies pushed and floundered up out of her skin. "No, no, no, *no, no.*" As the flies emerged they left holes, stretched and hollow like toothmarks, and within seconds, her arms were covered in a honeycomb of gaping pores. Her thighs resembled the surface of a sponge, freckled with holes.

Dead flies littered the floor around her, rolled into wet bits by her frantic slapping and rubbing. Hundreds of them buzzed and droned around her head, crawling on the shelving units and white linens. She pressed her palms to her face again and tried to will it all away, tried to picture the *algiz* rune in an attempt to pull a mental shell over her mind.

That's it—maybe it's an illusion. Maybe I can think it away. Acne littered her cheeks with lumps. The pimples on her forehead squirmed restlessly under her fingers. *I think I can, I think I can, I think I can, I think I can. The little engine that could, goddammit, let it be an illusion and not an actual conjuration. Let it just be a visual suggestion, don't let these flies be real—*

Robin opened her eyes to silence.

No flies. She checked out her arms, expecting the holes to linger, but they were gone.

Relief crashed into her system, such blessed relief she fell over and lay on the cold cement floor. She stumbled back to the sink and washed her mouth out, washed her arms, washed her face.

The GoPro on her jacket was still recording. "Weaver," she said to her subscribers, checking for acne in the mirror. She shuddered, pulling the camera off and pointing it at her own face. "She's an Illusion witch. I hate Illusion magic so much. *So freaking much.* I am so going to kick *her* ass first."

When she was finally convinced the vision was out of her system, she washed her hands, washed her mouth out again.

As she stood bent over into the sink, sharp fingernails trailed delicately along her upper arm. A cold, hard hand cupped the soft point of her shoulder, thumb and index finger encircling the back of her neck, wiry hair brushing her skin, a huge hand, the hand of a man reaching for a little girl.

The corner of her eye. The mirror above her head.

A glimpse of red.

Coarse red hair.

Her heart seemed to pause in her chest, a breath caught halfway into her mouth. *IT'S HIM IT'S THE RED LORD HE'S TOUCHING ME HE'S TOUCHING ME—*

Robin stood straight, turning, backing against the sink.

She was alone.

She let out a frustrated growl that broke at the end, turned into a high, angry shriek. That *had* to be another one of Weaver's illusions. The witch knew about the monster. Did she know what it looked like? She'd said it didn't belong to the coven, said it must have been conjured by Annie.

No. There's no way. Robin stared at her face in the sink, with mild alarm at how much older she suddenly looked. Must have aged ten years in the last half hour. *Took me years to accept Mom was a witch at all, much less be able to conjure something like the Red Lord. Like Weaver said, it's above her pay grade. If Mom could magic something like that, the coven would have never gotten the drop on her.*

Right?

Besides—that thing had been terrorizing Robin for a while now. *Why would Mom sic something like that on her own daughter?*

No, she thought, and spat again. *Illusion or not, that thing belongs to the coven.*

She dug in her pocket and took out the bottle of aripiprazole. Screwed it open and took two of them. *No more bugs.* Gave it a second thought, steeled herself and slipped a third into her mouth, and swallowed them all with a gulp of water from the mop sink. She wasn't a big fan of loading up on anti-hallucination meds, but sometimes you just have to bring out the big guns.

There may be bugs on some of you mugs, but there ain't no bugs on me.

• • •

At such an early morning hour, the roads were nearly dead, and the ride back to the apartment was much warmer inside the cab of the truck. She stared out the window as she rode, her mind sorting through options, the GoPro aimed out the window collecting B-roll footage. Joel rode in the middle, the gearshift protruding between his knees.

The protective *algiz* rune on her chest had been mostly sufficient until now, defending her from all manner of energy, ricocheting it back into its source. It still worked on familiarization and possession, which was its primary purpose, but Weaver's moths-and-flies-and-maybe-the-Red-Lord illusion . . . well, it had been a bit of a shock.

But why should I be surprised? After all, according to Heinrich, the Cutty coven is the most powerful in America.

And now it is one of the last. Under his tutelage, she had roamed the continent, hunting down every witch she could find in the Lower Forty-Eight, and a couple in Canada. Nineteen of them, from Neva Chandler, the self-proclaimed King of Alabama, to Gail Symes, who called herself the Oracle of the Sands. There were still hundreds of minor witches out there—newbies, idiots, little girls who had no idea their hearts had been sacrificed to Ereshkigal, and those like Neva, vapor-locked mummies too run-down to migrate out of their own ghetto—but most of them were too embedded, too well-hidden, or so weak they might as well have been your normal everyday hippie.

The witches had no real hierarchy. They had no structured government. Most of them had divvied up the country as the first presidents were buying it piece by piece from the Mexicans and the Spanish, and ripping it from the hands of the Native Americans.

Ever since, they moved from town to town every couple of decades, eradicating the weak ones or dueling each other like Highlanders. Robin had never witnessed a witch-duel, but it must be a sight to see.

The truck stopped for a red light. Without the radio on, the atmosphere inside was quiet and contemplative.

She turned the camera around and pointed it at Joel. "I think you should stay a couple nights somewhere else. Maybe at Kenny's place. Y'know, in case the killer knows where you live."

Joel wore one of Kenway's old gray exercise shirts, ARMY across the chest. His face broke into a warm, grateful smile when she mentioned protection, and it gave her a motherly pang. Suddenly she wanted to gather him up in her arms and carry him over the threshold into Kenway's apartment like a new bride, which was a very strange sensation. She almost laughed, which—considering the last thing she said was *in case the killer knows where you live*—struck her as the worst possible thing to do.

"I'll be aight," he told her, "Got my mama's old shotgun at the house. I don't think he knows where I live anyway." Pointing at the camera, he added, "How you gonna put me on YouTube, and I ain't fixed up at all? I look like I been through a wood chipper."

"You look fine."

"At least give me a ride back there and let me take a shower." Joel tugged the chest of the huge T-shirt out. "This thing like a tent on me. And, no offense, hero, but your clothes are all beat to hell."

On the other side of the intersection was a McDonald's. They crossed the road and pulled into the parking lot. Robin offered Kenway her debit card, but his face conveyed reluctance. "Go ahead," she said, urging him on with the card in her hand. "You know I'm good for it. I'm stayin' in your apartment, after all. I owe you anyway."

While Kenway ordered them coffee with a discontented grumble, Robin took out her cell phone and dialed a number. It rang several times, but no one picked up. A recorded voice told her the owner of the number hadn't set up his voicemail yet, so she couldn't even leave him a message.

"Dammit," she told the mechanical voice. "Heinrich, when will you ever get with the times?"

This wouldn't be the first time Robin might be forced to go after a formidable witch alone. She peeled back the lapel of her shirt, looking not only at the *algiz* on her chest but the stab-wound scar at the top of her right breast. The Oracle of the Sands had been a hell of a fight—Symes had been hiding out in one of the smaller, dinkier, run down casinos on the outskirts of Vegas. Robin had gone in masquerading as one of the customers, but as soon as the Oracle realized she was there (thanks to a particularly eagle-eyed pit boss and an armada of surveillance cameras), every customer in sight lost their minds. Suddenly the casino was full of crazed cat-people out for her blood, and Robin barely made it out with her life.

The only reason she was still alive was because of the cavalry—Heinrich had busted in at the last minute and provided the distraction she needed to escape. It had cost him, though. A .45 round to the guts. That had been a harrowing couple of days. She found out after the fact Symes had gassed a cage full of house cats in a specialized panic room in her penthouse suite. A familiar-bomb, basically. As soon as it had gone off, almost every customer in the casino went feral.

Joel borrowed Robin's cell phone and tapped a number into it. "Hello? Blackfield Police Department?" he said, pressing it to his ear. "I gotta talk to y'all about something, and you gonna want to hear this. I think I just got rescued from a serial killer."

He paused. "Yeah, I'll wait."

Kenway handed out the coffee and pulled back into traffic.

"Hello there, Mr. Officer," Joel said, hugging himself. "I almost got killed by some maniac, and I thought y'all would like to know about it. Yeah, he drugged me and when I woke up I was chained to the ceiling next to a dead guy. Yeah. Yeah, I got out. No, he said he was going to bleed me dry, because he needed 'blood for the garden.' No, I have no idea what that means. No, the only enemies I got live in glass bottles. Yeah, glass bottles. As in alcohol. It was a joke." He sipped coffee. "You want me to come up there and file a statement? A report? Aight. I'll be up there in a little bit. I got to go get my car and some clean clothes."

"What you gonna do now, Hollywood?" asked Kenway.

"After we take Joel to the police station, I want to head out to my old house and formally introduce myself to Mr. Parkin," said Robin, glaring daggers out the window. "If there's really a monster in there, I think my mother had something to do with it, but I'm sure there was a good reason. And I want to take a closer look at that ring. The witches seem to be interested in it, and Weaver looks like she's willing to kill to get it."

"So you think it's really magic?"

"Yes. Weaver said it might have Conjuration magic in it. Or on it. Or however that crap works." She leaned over to eye him. "Also, don't call me Hollywood."

"Point of order," said Joel, holding up a finger.

"Hmm?"

"I need to get my car. Black Velvet is not at my house."

"Where is it?" asked Kenway.

"I drove Velvet to my booty call with the mysterious Mr. Big Red last night." Joel massaged his face with both hands, talking through his fingers. "I left it parked in front of the serial killer's apartment."

20

The stethoscope was cold on Wayne's back. A latex-gloved hand cupped the curve of his ribs as he breathed in, out, in, out. "Do me a favor and breathe *real* deep," said the doctor. Morning sunlight streamed in through the window, throwing bars of gold over Leon. He stood at the end of the bed, his arms folded imperiously, his eyes red and squinty.

Wayne filled his lungs with the hospital's minty-sweet air and expelled it slowly.

"Hrrm. This is weird," said the doctor.

"What's weird?" asked Leon.

"Well . . ." The doctor took a Dum Dums sucker out of her lab-coat pocket. She was a diminutive woman with clever, vulpine eyes and a hazel complexion. As she spoke, she emphasized her words with the sucker. The name tag on her lab coat read DR. MARISSA BAKER. "We gave your son a dose of antivenin last night when he got here, but I've got to say, this is the fastest I've ever seen anybody recover from a snakebite."

She gave the sucker to Wayne, then lifted the boy's left leg with gentle hands and placed it on the bed. "The swelling's gone down precipitously." The bandage had been removed so the bite could be examined. "Very little discoloration, there's no necrosis or infection at all in or around the punctures. I don't know what this lady Mrs. Weaver put on you before they brought you here, but whatever it was, it must have been some kind of miracle salve."

Wayne unwrapped the cream soda Dum Dum and stuck it in his mouth.

"Obviously I've never been one for homeopathic bunkus," said Marissa, picking up a clipboard and clicking an ink pen. "But judging by the effect this had on your son, Mr. Parkin, maybe it's time to start believing."

"Maybe she's one of those crazy religious snake-handlers you hear about in this neck of the woods."

Marissa grunted.

They hadn't told the hospital about Wayne's strange absence in the middle of the night. As far as the ward's nurses were concerned, Leon had fallen asleep and his son had unadvisedly wandered out to the parking lot for some fresh air. This explained why the soles of Wayne's feet were dirty, and Marissa didn't seem to even be aware anything had happened, so they didn't trouble her with it. Which was good, because he really didn't want to have to tell the story again.

"So he's gonna be fine?" asked Leon.

Marissa nodded. "*Oh* yeah," she said to the clipboard, writing. "He's more than okay—all things considered, he's fantastic. A week or two taking it easy, maybe stay off that foot as much as possible, and he'll be good as new. And that's a liberal estimate. Honestly, I think he ought to stay here another night for observation, but in truth he's not really gonna get any better day-to-day care here than he would at home." She winked. "And there's no Xbox here either."

"Point taken."

"Any pain?" asked the doctor, gently feeling the flesh around the bite. "On a scale from one to ten, ten being the worst pain you ever felt?"

"One?" said Wayne. "I mean, I guess it just feels like a bruise."

That seemed to satisfy her. "Like I said, he can stay here another night if you're on pins and needles about his condition, but if you want to take him home, I'm not going to put my foot down. To the best of my knowledge, he's through the worst of it. Usually a bite from a copperhead isn't much to an adult man—most of the time it doesn't even warrant antivenin—but to a child his size and frame, it can be serious. Your son actually had an allergic reaction, which is why he'd initially gone into anaphylactic shock and gone unconscious. But whatever Mrs. Weaver did eliminated that factor. She saved your son's life."

Leon picked up his jacket. "My insurance is probably turning over in its grave. I guess we'll head on home. Maybe give you guys a call or run him up here if anything happens."

Marissa peeled off her glove and dropped it into a wastebasket. "I'll have someone bring you a wheelchair . . . and then I guess I'm going to go turn in my resignation and take up faith-healing."

• • •

As the elevator door eased shut, Wayne reached out and tugged his father's sleeve. Puzzlement came over Leon's face.

"You know I'm not lyin', right?" Wayne looked up from the wheelchair. "About the door in the wall . . . and the monster. Jo-elle was there. He saw it all."

He had changed into the fresh clothes from the bag he'd seen under the chair the night before. Wayne wondered if he'd see the pretty girl with the shaved head again, so he could give her her clothes back. It'd felt supremely strange wearing them . . . but admittedly he had liked it, because they smelled like her.

Leon leaned against the wall. The lights in the elevator were stark but dim, turning his skin from its usual healthy umber to a greenish beetle-black. "I don't know what to believe, son. You ain't got a very good track record."

Wayne glumly sucked his upper lip.

"I thought we were gonna—I thought this was gonna be a fresh start, Wayne. For both of us. I thought we were done with street shit. I brought you to the country, got you away from the wannabe gang kids in Chicago, and . . . you got me away from Johnnie Walker and Jack Daniels."

"I'm tellin' the truth."

Leon watched his face. "Yeah."

Reaching into Wayne's shirt-collar, he pulled out the ring. It lay on the pale of his fingers, twinkling dull in the elevator lights. "I didn't even know you *had* this. How long you been walking around with it? Did I even say you could have it?"

"I got it that day you and Aunt Marcelina talked about moving to Georgia. That night I tucked you in the bed after you sat and watched the ball game and finished off that bottle you had hid in that basket Mom put on top of the bookshelf." Wayne made no move to take the ring away or even lean back, only stared up at his father. Adrenaline thrummed in his veins. *Be stronger. Adapt and overcome.* "Anyway, I found it in your cupholder and I took it. Put it on my chain. I call it your stupid tax."

"Stupid tax," said Leon, slowly, gently, suspensefully tucking the ring back into his son's shirt, shaking his head as if in disbelief.

Kinda says something you didn't even realize I had it.

The bizarre notion occurred to Wayne he was about to get hit in the face, which had blessedly never happened before. Leon might have had a drinking problem, but even in his worst moments, he never struck his son. He may have put a couple holes in the walls, but that was the extent of his furor.

Leon winced, rubbing his chest as if he were having a heart attack. He leaned against the wall and pressed the Lobby button.

"You okay?"

"Yeah." He gasped and gave a slow sigh. "Pulled a muscle
clockin' that dude in the snoot."

"He's all right, you know," said Wayne.

"Maybe."

"Was that the first time you ever punched a guy?"

Leon cracked a crooked grin. "Heh, yeah."

"You hit him hard as hell."

"Language, man," said Leon, getting behind the wheelchair as
the door clunked open.

He pushed Wayne down the hall and into the waiting room,
leaving him in front of a television while he went to the receptionist to process out. The TV was playing the local sports scores,
which were Greek to Wayne. He took the opportunity to polish
his glasses, feeling like a gigantic nerd. Luckily, it was still early in
the morning, so the lobby was relatively quiet except for the gurgle
of the aquarium. A man and two women sat in the waiting area,
reading magazines.

Leon asked incredulously, "What do you mean, it's taken
care of?"

Wayne turned the wheelchair to look. His father scratched his
head in confusion, rotating an upside-down clipboard so he could
read it. "Karen?" he asked, pressing a fingertip to the paper. "That
old lady?"

The receptionist smiled. "Yes sir. She paid you up in full."

"Just the co-pay, right?" He added with a mutter, "Is there even
a co-pay for something like this?"

"No sir, Mrs. Weaver paid everything in full. She was the one
who brought him in, and she took responsibility for his care, so
your insurance is totally irrelevant."

Leon's hand crept up to his mouth and he rubbed his mustache,
either contemplating or trying to put his brain back together.

"How . . . how much was the bill?" He flipped through paperwork and actually ducked in surprise as if he'd been shot at. *"Thirty thousand dollars?"* His eyes were bowling balls. "How was *that* thirty thousand dollars? All they did was give him a shot and keep him overnight!"

The receptionist helped him look through the papers. "Right here . . . the CroFab antivenin, twenty thousand a vial, plus the medical procedure, the room, workups, all—see this?"

"I see it, I don't believe it."

"Well, it's not *quite* thirty thousand."

"Close enough, twenty and some change." Leon signed where signatures were needed, but he shook his head as he did so. "A *hell* of a lot of change. How is an ambulance ride worth several thousand dollars?"

The receptionist smiled. "It's a bit of a sticker shock, but look at it this way, Mr. Parkin: thanks to your new friend, it's totally out of your hands, and out of your wallet." Taking back the clipboard, she went to work typing up the information. "Sounds like you've got the biggest thank-you card of your life to write."

• • •

Leon was quiet crossing town in the morning rush-hour chaos. Wasn't exactly Chicago-busy, but everybody drove like they were in a funeral procession. He chewed his lip, so deep in thought the glacial flow didn't even elicit his usual fussing and complaints. Wayne was glad. At the moment, he was savoring the relative peace and quiet of the car after sitting in the hospital all morning.

"That Weaver lady said she lives in the hacienda across the highway," said Leon. "I think we ought to go over there and say thanks. Maybe invite her over for dinner. What do you think?"

"Sure." Wayne fidgeted with the crutch in his lap.

"The doc says you should be fine in, like, a week. You won't be on that crutch long."

They rode on, neither of them saying much of anything. The

Subaru was gliding up Highway 9 into the hills when Wayne happened to glance at his father and saw a tear slip down his cheek.

Leon swiped it away and saw he'd been caught. "Thought I was gonna lose you yesterday, man."

Wayne smiled. "Adapt and overcome."

"Where'd you hear that?"

"The guy at the comic store in town." He remembered the job offer from Fisher. "Oh! He gave me a job helping him run his comic shop after school!"

Leon grinned. "Pretty cool. Gonna have you running the register, or . . . ?"

"Yeah, I think so. And helping him do his Thursday Movie Nights or something."

"All right, my son's a workaday man now."

"I can walk there from school in the afternoons. It's only a few blocks down."

"As long as you don't go back in those woods."

"Nope." Wayne drew it out long and deep: "*Noooooooope. Nooooope.*" Leon joined in and they made a frog-chorus of Nopes.

As the Victorian sidled into sight, Leon thumped the steering wheel. The U-Haul truck still sat in their driveway. "Shit—! With all the drama I forgot to take the truck back yesterday." He pulled in next to it. "Hopefully they're open on Saturdays. Think you can chill here at the house while I take care of that?"

"Sure."

Wayne got out of the car and put his weight on the crutch, shoving the door shut with his snakebit foot. He was at the bottom of the stoop when he realized he was about to go back into the house where he saw the owlhead Sasquatch thing, and a cold wet blanket of oppressive fear fell over him.

Leon unlocked the front door and looked over his shoulder as it eased open. "Hey, you all right?"

Some dark part of Wayne expected to see the monster standing in the foyer behind his father, peering over his shoulder. The steps in front of him exuded some repellent force, as if they were magnets and his shoe-soles were made of metal.

"Remember how I told you I saw that monster in our house when I went through the door in the wall?"

Annoyed concern flashed across Leon's face. "Yeah. I get it, man." He came back down to the front walk and gave his keys to his son. Wayne felt a bit patronized, but he accepted them. "Tell you what. I'm gonna leave my keys with you. You can be my wheelman. I'll go check the house and if I come running out, you start the car."

Taking the tire iron out of the Subaru, Leon crept into the house.

Out in the middle of the expansive front lawn, the boy stared up at the windows, looking for shadows, glowing eyes, twitching curtains, the vaguest hint something other than his father was lurking inside. The siding was raincloud-blue again, which mitigated some of his fear.

Shoes scuffed behind him. Wayne twitched.

Pete and Amanda were coming across the highway from the trailer park, followed by little Katie Fryhover, who was carrying a plastic kite with a picture of Sully from the movie *Monsters, Inc.* on it.

"Hey, man," said Pete. "You're out of the hospital already?"

Amanda broke into a run and wordlessly gathered Wayne up in a hug, pressing his face against the cool vinyl of her windbreaker. She was wearing some kind of perfume that reminded him of pancakes.

"We've been worried as hell, Batman," said Pete, his hands crammed in his jacket pockets. "Figured you were gonna be up there for at least another week."

"Doctor said I was doing really good. Said the main reason I was even there was because I had an allergic reaction."

Pete stared at his feet. "That's good. I mean, not that you had an allergic reaction. It was good it wasn't something serious. I mean, that it wasn't the venom itself?"

"I know what you mean. Hey," said Wayne, pointing at him with his crutch. "I saw what you did before I passed out. I saw you hit that snake with that hammer." The smile spreading across his face belied the burn flowering in his throat. "Man, you got balls." He let out a hoarse laugh. "Thank you. For smacking that snake."

Pete looked up, one corner of his mouth quirked up in a half-smile. "Just wish I could have gotten there before it bit you."

Wayne spread his arms, putting his weight on his good leg. "I'm fine," he said, holding up the crutch. "I'm fine, you know? Everything aight." He tucked it under his arm and leaned on it. "Just gotta take it easy and stay off it for like, a week."

"Sounds like time to bone up on your PlayStation skills."

"Heh heh, you said bone."

Amanda was meticulously wiping tears out of her eyelashes with her fingertips, trying not to ruin her mascara. "You kids are a bunch of nerds."

"What did you do with the hammer, anyway?"

"I took it home." Pete jerked a thumb back at the trailer park. "When my mom saw the blood on it, she didn't want it in the house, but when she heard what I did with it, she let me do whatever I wanted as long as I took it out back and scrubbed it good with some bleach." He laughed. "Actually, when she saw me coming with it, she thought I hit somebody with it. I got in trouble for going to the fairgrounds again, but—"

The front door of the Victorian scraped shut and Leon came down to join them, his phone to his ear. "And I wanted to know if you could give me a ride home from the U-Haul place," he was saying. "I'll give you gas money. Yeah. Yeah, the one on Quincy. Okay, thanks." He hung up the cell and stuck it in his pocket. "I checked every room in the house, including the cupola. One-one-six-eight is officially monster-free," he said, taking his keys off of Wayne, the tire iron dangling by his thigh. "Hey, y'all. What's up?"

Pete pointed at the tire iron. "What's that for?"

Leon held it up and regarded it as if it had magically appeared in his hand. "Oh, this? I'll let Master Wayne tell y'all about this. I got to go run an errand. I'll be back in a little bit. You guys hang out in the house or something, I'll bring back pizza." He left the tire iron in his car and climbed into the U-Haul truck. Starting the engine, he rolled the window down and pointed at the kids. "And by 'something' I don't mean go out in the woods and get bit by a snake again."

"You got nothin' to worry about there," said Pete, saluting. "Bruce Wayne is safe with us."

"That's what I'm afraid of. Y'all be good." Leon saluted them and backed the cumbersome truck out of the driveway. After grinding a few gears, he managed to get it into first and trundle down the road and out of sight.

Katie Fryhover looked like a windsurfer, trying to control the kite in her hands. "You got bitted by a nake?"

"I'm babysitting her until her grandmother gets home," said Amanda. "Is it okay if she comes in too? She's a good kid, real quiet. She don't get into anything."

"Yeah, of course," said Wayne, but he didn't lead them into the house. Instead, he lingered there on the lawn, absentmindedly rubbing the aluminum shaft of his crutch, staring at Katie as she fought the wind.

"Sooo . . ." Pete stared at Wayne's shoes, then met his eyes. "What was up with the tire tool? Your dad said something about a monster?"

"Y'all gonna laugh at me," said Wayne, crutching over to the front porch. The October breeze was brisk, chilling the toes of his left foot (which was only wrapped in a tight elastic bandage) but it was nothing compared to the chill he got when he looked at the house's sheer white curtains.

The others followed and sat down on the stoop alongside him. Katie tucked her kite into the corner between the porch and the stoop, behind a bush.

"I'm not." Amanda still stood on the stepping-stones in front of them, trying to keep her balance on the edge of one stone.

"Me neither," said Pete.

"Me needer!" said Katie.

Wayne turned sideways and sat back against the stoop banister. He didn't like having his back to the house. "I think my mom's ring might be magic," he said, taking the wedding band out of his shirt and off his neck.

"*Magic?*" Katie shouted. Her mouth fell open, her eyes wide. "Like a *widzerd?*"

"Not really like a wizard. I don't know. It started when I woke up in the hospital." He launched into yet another rendition of the story, going on through the garage rescue straight on to falling through the painting into Kenway Griffin's kitchen. He also told them about the free-standing door in the lunchroom wall, the hotel room door two stories off the ground.

Three-oh-six.

"Dude, that's crazy," said Pete. "I mean, *that's* crazy, what you *said*, I'm not saying *you're* crazy, just that, y'know, what you *said* was crazy."

Wayne nodded, looking down at the ring in the palm of his hand. "I know what you're sayin'. It does sound crazy."

"So you said a Sasquatch? In your house?"

"I don't think it was a Sasquatch." The crutch rested on Wayne's shoulder, feeling like a rifle. He lifted it up and pretended so, pressing the armpit pad against his shoulder as if it were a stock and aiming down the side of it. "But it kinda looked like one. Except it didn't look like a gorilla. It had a big head like a hoot-owl and glowin' green eyes, and fingers kinda like Freddy Krueger."

"Wow," said Amanda. She hopscotched from stone to stone,

counting numbers under her breath. "No wonder you don't want to go in the house. I wouldn't want to either."

Pete got up and fetched Leon Parkin's tire tool from the Subaru, then marched up the steps and opened the front door. "Let's get it over with," he said in mock exasperation.

"Didn't Wayne's dad already say the house was clear?" asked Amanda.

"He didn't go in with the ring." Pete swung the tire tool like a Vaudevillian twirling his cane.

"Good point."

Putting his necklace back on and tucking the ring into his shirt, Wayne was reluctant. "Are you sure this is a good idea?"

Pete made a face and walked away into the Victorian. "You can't stay on the front porch forever. Your dad's not gonna let you sleep out here." He leaned back, peeking out. "You comin', or not?"

Wayne sighed and followed him inside.

The house was quiet and dark, but at least the walls were still blue. Wayne crutched into the kitchen to make sure the table was their round wooden one, as opposed to the faux-diner table with the metal trim. The room was unburnt, as well.

"Shh," he said, flashing his palms at the others. The floor creaked and popped as they crept from room to room. "Stop movin' for a second and listen."

They all froze, even little Katie Fryhover.

Click. Click. Click. Click. The clock on the kitchen wall ticked. Wind rushed against the side of the house, breaking like a tide. A few birds sang outside, distant and muffled through the walls.

Katie sniffed wetly.

Taking out the ring, Wayne put it to his eye and peered through it. To his relief, the kitchen and the table in it remained the same.

"I don't—"

Hhhhrrrrrrooooooooo! An eerie howling sound came from the living room, pouring ice down his spine.

Two heartbeats later, the front door slammed shut. *BLAM!*

Katie and Amanda both screamed, running for the front door and wrenching it open. Wayne limped along right behind them, toting his crutch like a briefcase, and all three children sprinted out onto the grass. They were halfway across the front lawn when Pete yelled after them.

"It was the wind, you idiots!" He stood on the porch, waving the tire iron. "The wind blew the door shut!"

• • •

Once Pete had talked them back in, they went about their search for Owlhead (as they'd taken to calling it) with a little more levity, sweeping each room. Wayne would throw open a door and Pete would step in, the tire iron up in both fists like a Jedi with a lightsaber. By the time they had canvassed the entire house, they were up in the cupola and in pretty calm spirits.

"You can see everything up here," said Amanda, her nose almost touching the north window. "I can even see my house, and Pete's. They're both in the back of Chevalier Village."

"Where's *my* house?" asked Katie, climbing up onto the wide sill.

"Right behind that one." Amanda braced her with a hand, pointing through the glass at a little white terrier sitting by the drive to the Alamo house. "Be careful, don't lean against the window. See Champ down there, layin' in the grass?"

Pete climbed up and stood on the sill, the top of his head against the arch of the windowframe. "Hey, I didn't realize you could see the fairgrounds from here."

"Really?" Wayne joined him.

Rising over the forest far to the south were the tallest buildings of Blackfield, tiny windowed spikes jutting up from the trees. The huge thirteen-floor Blackfield University Library scraped sky way in the back. The sand-colored cathedral spires of Walker Memorial. The nameless twelve-story office building with the fire-damaged penthouse floor. Much closer, off to his left, Wayne could see the suggestion of shapes just visible over the leaves and scraggly black trees—the highest hump of a roller-coaster, the peak of a free-fall tower. A smear of color that might be the front of the funhouse.

"We were that close?" he asked, marveling. They had certainly walked a long way home . . . and they'd almost made it.

"Yep." Pete climbed down and sat on the bed. "Man, those women who found us were creepy as hell. Never seen them up close. That Theresa lady was strong." He flexed an arm and squeezed his bicep, speaking in a bad Russian accent. "Strong like bull."

Amanda said over her shoulder, "*Yeah* she was. Super-strong for an old lady. She carried Wayne all the way down the fairground road out to the highway where the ambulance could find him."

"Like half a mile."

Turning on his TV and PlayStation, Wayne sat next to him. A videogame started up and he went into a virtual garage, absentmindedly cycling through customization options on the muscle car he'd been grooming all month. Anonymous rap-rock whispered from the speakers.

After an awkwardly long couple of minutes, Pete said, "That's a badass Mustang."

"Thanks." Wayne fiddled with the car some more, and then his curiosity finally nibbled at him a little too hard. "So that one lady . . . I think she said her name was Karen. She said she lives in the big house across the street."

"All three of them do." Getting down from the windowsill, Amanda sat on the floor in front of the TV with Katie and the two of them leafed through one of his comic books. It was a newer *Spider-Man*, and he'd read it a hundred times, so Wayne didn't jump to its defense. "They all live in the same house together. They're not sisters, though, I don't think." She cupped her hands over Katie's ears and said, "People in Chevalier say they're lesbians."

Wayne's forehead scrunched up and he looked to Pete for confirmation. The other boy shrugged as if to say, *It is what it is.*

"She paid my whole hospital bill."

Amanda looked up. "That was nice of her."

"Think my dad said it was like thirty thousand dollars."

Pete stage-whispered, "Sweeeet Jesus."

"Sweeeet Jeedzus," echoed Katie. "Can I draw? Do you got any paper and crayons?"

"I think there's some paper in my dad's printer." Wayne stared at the TV screen as he talked. The video game was a balm to his nerves. "I don't have any crayons, but my dad's got some markers, if he didn't leave 'em at school." He handed the controller off to Pete and clomped downstairs. He was on the landing before he discovered two things: (1) he'd forgotten his crutch, and (2) he was by himself. Suddenly he felt very small and alone.

Luckily he didn't have to go all the way to the first floor. Making his way down the hall, Wayne pushed the door to his father's bedroom and watched it swing slowly open, revealing the room and everything it contained a couple inches at a time.

A tall wooden dresser from Aunt Marcelina . . . a window . . . Dad's pressboard desk from Walmart . . . several liquor-store boxes still full of their stuff . . . a window . . . Dad's bed . . .

No Owlhead looming in the corner.

Muscles slowly relaxed he didn't realize were locked solid. He remembered to breathe again.

It was going to be a long day.

Lunchtime traffic shushed past as Robin and Kenway ushered Joel onto the front porch of a bungalow-style house, perched on a hill overlooking downtown Blackfield. Through the screen of trees below the house, Robin could see an ocean of rooftops.

Instead of dropping him off, they stopped by to pick up some clean clothes. Kenway didn't seem to mind playing chauffeur all day; he didn't have anything better to do, especially since it was a Saturday.

"Hey, you wouldn't mind checkin' the place out for me, would you, hero?" asked Joel, unlocking the door.

The veteran looked like a barbarian as he climbed the front steps behind the line cook, six feet of blond hair and muscle crammed into a Powerwolf T-shirt. He moved into the house and stood motionless in the foyer, listening, his fists clenched, his eyes wandering slowly over the old-fashioned decor and flowery wallpaper.

"So is—" began Robin, but Kenway held up a hand.

He checked behind the front door and pulled a baseball bat out of the umbrella stand, but paused in surprise when it sparkled in the sunlight. The business end was covered in fake diamonds. "You Bedazzled a baseball bat?"

Joel shrugged sheepishly.

Shaking his head, Kenway stalked into the living room with the twinkling Slugger, and on into the kitchen. Joel went to his dish drain and pulled out a bread knife. Put the bread knife back, pulled out a silvery hammer. A meat tenderizer.

"You two stay here," said Kenway, and he left through a doorway.

Robin scowled. "I can take care of myself, Major Dad. I'm probably more dangerous at hand-to-hand than you are. You forget the ass-whooping I gave you so soon? Or the video I showed you?"

"Nobody could forget *that*," he replied from the hallway.

"What video?" asked Joel. "I ain't seen no video."

"I showed him the video of my first kill—the Witch-King of Alabama."

"Huh. How many witches you done killed, anyway?"

"About twenty."

"You killed twen-ty witches. Twennnnnty! Ah-ah-ah-ah-ah."

She smirked at his impression of the Count. "*About* twenty. Nineteen, maybe? I've kicked the shit out of a lot more people than that, though."

"You stone-cold, sister."

As her eyes sank onto the tabletop, Robin saw a plethora of carved graffiti—JOEL, that weird angular S you see everywhere, doodles of cartoon characters, boxes with squiggly lines drawn through them (the impossible puzzle, she realized with a start), and to Robin's mild surprise, dozens and dozens of *algiz* runes, a legion of four-lobed Ys.

When she looked up from the madness, she found Joel watching her. He was looking at the *algiz* rune on her chest, the Y with the extra lobe in the middle.

"What is that?" asked Joel.

"Protective rune from the Elder Futhark alphabet. Together with certain incantations, the Vikings used it to shield themselves and their homes from witches. It's kind of a supernatural bullet-proof vest. Witches use symbols like this to channel and catalyze their Gift. It don't imbue me with any powers."

"Gift?"

"Their power. That's what they call it. They don't like callin' it magic, and I don't either." She noticed herself code-switching back into their country-talk again. *At's what tey call it. Ayon't like callin' it magic, 'n Ion't either.* Normally the twang only came out when her blood was up and she was facing down a witch, but around Joel it was like speaking a second language.

"Why not?"

"Magic is," she began, "something wizards and magicians do in fantasy movies and on stages in Vegas, you know? Magic is . . . David Copperfield and David Blaine. Card tricks, cutting women in half, pulling rabbits out of hats, kids' birthday parties. I don't like callin' it magic. After seeing how evil and dark it is, I don't like associating it with my mother Annie, even if it takes pedantry to separate and distance her from what the witches like the La-zenbury coven do. Yeah, Mom was a witch . . . and she did some bad things—to me, to others . . . but that don't mean she got to be lumped into the same gang."

"What *is* this magic, anyway?" asked Joel. "This ain't no Harry Potter shit, from what I can tell. I ain't heard nobody hollerin' about Wingardium Leviosa or ridin' around on a broom."

"The acolytes of Ereshkigal—*true* witches—ain't so whimsical, and it goes a lot deeper. They channel the essence of the spirit world itself, guiding it with language, and intensifyin' it with sheer will." She pointed at the rune on her chest. "Using language to guide it works both ways, fortunately. We can't produce it like they can, but we can manipulate their energy. Think of their power as a laser, and words and symbols as mirrors and lenses. I can't create it, but I can bend it."

"Who is Ereshkigal?"

"The Mesopotamian goddess of death, witchcraft, crossroads, doors, and necromancy. The Greeks called her Hecate. She's worshipped by modern Wiccans and neopagans. Ereshkigal is the source of all their power." An ancient white Macbook lay on the table between them. She slid it over and opened it. "You wanna see the video I'm talking about? The Witch-King of Alabama?"

"Does the Pope shit in the woods?"

Robin winced in mock disgust. "I'll take that as a yes."

While she waited for the laptop to boot up, Joel opened the fridge and took out a beer, opening it saber-style with a single swipe of the meat tenderizer. He handed the bottle to Robin and opened another one for himself. She turned it up and downed half of it as she waited for YouTube to load. "Where you learn a trick like that?" she asked, and punctuated the question with a bone-rattling belch.

Joel made a face, then sashayed over and stood next to her, so he could see the computer screen. "I ain't *always* been a pizza-boy."

"Anyway," Robin said, navigating to her video channel, "I was going to say earlier, this is your mother's house?" She clicked on the Alabama video, turned the resolution up, and waited for it to buffer a bit. The Wi-Fi was slow, so it was going to take a minute. She silently thanked whatever God was up there she didn't have to upload videos on this line.

"Yep," said Joel.

With its speckly-green Formica countertops and avocado appliances, the kitchen was a picture-perfect representation of what it must have looked like when Joel and Fish were boys. "My brother Fish don't like livin' here, though. That's why he moved into the back of his comic shop. He says this house remind him too much of Mama."

"What happened to your mother? You make it sound like it was so bad it made you end up on medication."

"She was on the anti-psychotics, I was on the anti-depressants."

"What happened?"

"Your moms happened."

"What?" *Annie? What on earth could she possibly have done to break Joel's family down the middle?* Robin barely remembered them, much less her mother interacting with them enough to cause that kind of damage. "What are you talking about?"

"It was the witches."

"What would they possibly want with *your* mother?"

"I don't mean they put a spell on her or nothing," Joel continued, "but it was . . . you know, her knowing they killed your mama Annie, her paranoia about 'em got worse. Night terrors sometimes, maybe three or four times a month. Got worse and worse. She started sleeping in the living room because she didn't like being in her bedroom—she said there was a 'man made out of cobwebs' in her closet—but then she painted the living room windows because she thought somebody was watching her sleep.

"Accused Fish of stealing her money, accused me of stealing from her too. Spoons. She accused me of stealing her fuckin' spoons. Can you believe that? Anyway, she went batshit at the end. Completely lost her mind. Started lumping Annie in with the witches, said she was afraid of all of 'em. She thought they were gonna cut her tongue like they cut Annie's."

"What?" Robin's brow furrowed. "Ain't nobody cut Mom's tongue, she was born that way. Birth defect." Annie Martine wasn't the loveliest of women, but her petite Audrey Hepburn frame and heart-shaped face gave her an ethereal, elven quality people couldn't seem to resist.

In that brutally honest fashion of curious children, Robin had asked her several times over the years why her tongue was the way it was.

Annie gave her a different tale each time. *I stuck it out at a crab and he pinched it,* she'd say, or *I was running with scissors and tripped and, well, snip snip!* and sometimes, *I tried to kiss a turtle and he bit me,* and the last time she claimed she'd stuck it in a light socket. Once Robin had even hauled out her toy doctor bag and asked to examine Annie's tongue with a magnifying glass. A jagged red scar about an inch long bifurcated the very tip, twisting it.

Most strangers who heard Annie speak assumed she was deaf and spoke loudly to her, carefully enunciating their words. But she was never offended. She dryly looked up at whoever was speaking to her and said, "I'm not deaf," and then stuck out her tongue. Robin hated the way they would recoil in horror at her twisted scar, but Mama always laughed gaily and carried on as if it were nothing but a bawdy joke.

Joel leaned back against the kitchen counter, folding his arms. "Anyway, my moms wouldn't even go outside," he continued. "She developed—what they call it, when you're afraid of the outdoors?"

"Acrophobia?" Robin squinted. "No, that's a fear of heights. Agoraphobia, that's it."

"Developed agoraphobia. She lived there at the house for about a year, me here taking care of her, and then I eventually had to put her in the home. I couldn't do it no more."

"I'm sorry to hear that."

"I'm so glad she didn't do all that when I was *little* little—can you imagine how much that would have jacked up a little boy? And she wouldn't have been in any kind of condition to raise the two of us. There's no telling where I'd be now."

Enough of the YouTube video had loaded Robin decided it was time to hit the play button. "Roll that beautiful bean footage," she said, and . . . *click*. However, instead of her first battle, it displayed a black screen and a message: *An error occurred. Please try again later.*

"What the hell?" She looked up at Joel. "Your Internet is hot garbage."

He shrugged. "It's an old house, lady. What do you want from me?"

"Where is your router?"

He shrugged even deeper. "Beats the hell out of me."

Robin scowled at him.

"Okay, you got me fair and square. I'm stealing Wi-Fi from the guy living behind me. I ain't got my own Internet. So sue me."

She made a snarly face at him. "I should," she mock-threatened, and reloaded the website to try buffering the video again. "Take two. Maybe I can get this to go through before the connection craps out."

The two of them languished in the stillness, listening to the subtle creaking and popping of Kenway creeping around upstairs.

"He sure is taking a long time," said Joel.

Robin opened her hands, raising them from the laptop keyboard as if offering her answer as a surprise. "I reckon he's very thorough when it comes to security. You want him to search this place top to bottom, right? Ain't no creeps hiding in the closet after we leave."

Joel shuddered. "Yeah, good point."

Something shattered upstairs with a crash.

"Sorry," called Kenway.

Joel's hand slipped over his face and he pinched the bridge of his nose. His eyes darted around the room as if he were looking for a new topic to gab about, and he gestured with his beer bottle at symbols carved all over the kitchen table. "This *algiz* Viking thing. Does it work?"

"Not as much as it used to back in the day, but yeah. Why you ask?"

"Because my moms drew it and painted it all over our house. This right here ain't even half of it. Hundreds of 'em, in every room. Sharpie, paint, ketchup, Nesquik syrup, shit, blood. Muh-fuckin' ants for days. Place stunk. Took ages to clean it all up after she went into the home."

"Yuck."

"Does the protection, ahh, does it get more powerful the more you put the symbol on the thing?" he asked, punctuating with that rolling hand-gesture, and so on and so forth. "Like, on your chest, or on your walls? Or—" He made an expansive motion to indicate the symbols carved all over the kitchen table.

"You asking me if it stacks? I don't know," said Robin. "Can't say for sure. Ain't like there's scientific tests been done on this stuff. But if it does get more powerful that way, then it sound like you got the safest house in Blackfield."

"Heh. Wish I could have told her that."

"You still can."

"She died in the home a little while after she went in. Massive stroke."

Reluctant to give him another impotent apology, Robin opted for, "Wish I could have been here to explain things to her, and you, or even just to be there for you. Sound like Fisher wasn't there in the way you needed him."

"He thought the whole thing with the witches was bullshit." Joel scoffed. "Weirdest thing, man, the guy that collects action figures and old fantasy and horror movies, he the one don't believe in this supernatural stuff. Ain't that a hot mess? But yeah, he was out of there as fast as his little legs could carry him. Left as soon as he graduated high school, went to college on a football scholarship. Computer stuff. IT, that kind of thing. Now he works from home here in town. Telecommutes."

"Fancy."

"Yeah, it's aight. You'd think he'd get a big-ass house out in the country around here, but no, he lives in a loft apartment over his comic book store. I guess he's trying to save up all that money he can. He always was the ant type, and me the grasshopper, I guess."

"What about you?" asked Robin. "Did you go to college?"

"What college? On what scholarship?" Joel gave a genuine laugh. "Nah, after Mr. Barnett, I bounced around town doin' this and that. Takin' care of my moms, mostly. Fish helped, at least financially. He picked up what her insurance couldn't carry. Since I lived in the house with Mama, I didn't have to pay no rent, so at least I had that goin' for me.

"Sittin' up in your little attic bedroom, playin' with dolls and shit," said Joel, in a wistful tone. "You prolly played with me more than Fish did. Man, we didn't have no worries back in them days, did we?"

Robin shook her head, smiling a bittersweet smile.

The video was ready. She hit play, and the sound of her voice floated out of the speakers as her two-years-younger face appeared on the screen. "Been trackin' this one for weeks." The two of them stood there in the quiet kitchen, drinking beer and watching her fight Neva Chandler.

"You will die," the man said again, reaching through her van window, reaching through a window in time, reaching into her chest and clutching whatever nerve governs fear in the human body. "The Red Lord will find you."

Welcome home.

Robin shivered. Finished her beer, considered going for another one. When the video ended, Joel shook his head and walked away, tossing the beer bottle in the recycling bin.

"What?"

He shook his head again. "I don't know how you do it."

"It was hard at first. I had a hard time, in the beginning. Between Heinrich's brutal training and the blood-curdling paranormal things I saw facin' the witches, I almost wanted to go back to the mental hospital. I didn't go completely out of my mind when I was in the loony bin, but the shit I saw, and the shit I had to do, after I got out, it just about broke me."

Peering into the cabinets as if he were looking for something, Joel busied himself puttering around the kitchen. "I'm so hungry I could eat a farmer's ass through a park bench."

"What?"

"I'm so hungry I could eat a knuckle sandwich and go back for the fingers."

Robin burst out laughing. "Where in the hell did you hear that?"

"Shit my moms used to say. I think she got it from her granddad back in the day." Finally he found a jar of peanut butter and a half-pack of saltines. "What kinda shit you seen?" Joel asked, sitting back down.

"I met a witch that could go out-of-body and jump into other people's bodies."

Joel recoiled. "What? Like *Quantum Leap*?"

"Yeah. She had to touch them first. It was crazy as hell watchin' her move through a subway—I met this witch in New York City, by the way—and it was like watching a train full of people do the Wave. Except instead of standing up and raising their hands, these people sitting elbow-to-elbow would turn and look at me one after the other with this creepy, pissed-off look."

"How did you fight her, sis?" The pizza chef slathered peanut butter on crackers. "How you even fight something like that?"

"I couldn't attack her directly. She was jumping around inside of innocent people; she abducted kids and puppeteered the innocent hosts, made 'em take the kids to dead-drop points, like out in the industrial parks or in the subway tunnels, and leave them for her coven to retrieve. If I managed to catch her and try to fight her, she would find some way to jump out and leave me standing there ready to beat the shit out of somebody that never even seen me before." Robin stole one of his crackers and crammed it into her mouth. "What I had to do was, I had to figure out where her original body was at, and kill that."

"How did you figure that out?"

"I let her kidnap a kid, then I followed her proxy host into the subway system and ambushed the coven when they got there. From there I just had to work my way into the center of the coven's lair to kill the Matron. Along with three other witches and about two dozen henchmen. My guy Heinrich helped me with that one. He did not appreciate having to walk through sewer water."

Joel stared at her for a long moment, his eyes studying her face, a half-slathered cracker on the table in front of him.

Finally he said, "I'm glad you're back in town. It's like having my sister back. You *do* feel like the only person I know that truly gets me. And knowing you're the resident professor on this shit makes me feel a lot better about all of it."

"I'm glad." She smiled and stole the cracker. "The more time I spend with you, the more you feel like the brother I never had. I'm glad I came back, even if it was just to reconnect with you."

Joel shook like he'd gotten a chill and went back to peanut-buttering crackers. "If we keep on with this Hallmark Channel shit, my teeth are gonna rot right out of my head."

Kenway returned, the Bedazzled ball bat resting on his shoulder.

"The coast is clear," he said, laying the bat across the table. "Thought I saw somebody. Turned out to be a really big mirror that for some dumbass reason was inside of a goddamn closet."

"Seven years bad luck, Sergeant Slaughter." Joel got up and pushed his chair under the table. "And now I'mma go change out these clothes into something a little more me. And . . . look for a broom to clean up broken glass."

Kenway winced and mouthed *Sorry* as he passed.

When he came back downstairs, he was tying a silk do-rag around his head, dragging a cloud of tart perfume. Skinny jeans, black boots, and a spaghetti-strap top. "You should polish your boots," said Kenway. "I used to wear some like that. I can show you how to spit-polish them so shiny you can see yourself in 'em."

Joel looked down. "I'll skip the spit, but I do appreciates ye."

"So are we gonna go pick up his car by ourselves, or do we want to get a cop to follow us down there?" asked Robin.

"I fear for my car," said Joel. "Ain't no tellin' what he's done with it. But I fear for myself a little bit more. I think if I'm gonna go knockin' on a serial killer's door, I want a trigger-happy cop there with me."

• • •

The officer on duty at the police station took them into the break room and made a cup of coffee while Joel gave him a statement.

Kenway and Robin sat at a hand-me-down trestle table from the local school that folded up in the middle and had attached stools.

"So you say he had you tied upside down by your feet," the cop echoed for clarification.

Lieutenant Bowker was a tall, corn-fed man. The back of his neck cradled his shaved skull in a fat roll. Stirring his coffee, he came over to the table and sat down with a clipboard. "And he had another man tied up there? You say this killer was . . . collecting blood for a 'garden'?"

"Yeah." Joel sat with his fingers templed under his nose. The studs in his ears twinkled in the fluorescents.

"Now, are you *sure*—" Bowker lifted a sheet of paper to peek underneath, let it fall. "—this wasn't just some kind of sexual fetish game gone wrong? Maybe things got a little out of hand and maybe you misconstrued the, ahh, the situation, so to speak. I mean, people get roofied all the time, and stuff like this happens. Not to diminish that kind of thing, you know, but, ahh . . . murder is kind of in a whole 'nother ballpark."

Joel had already detailed the series of events that led to waking up in the garage—talking to B1GR3D online about dinner and sex, meeting him at his apartment, getting halfway through a steak and passing out.

He closed his eyes as if in restraint, and a few seconds later, opened them. "Yes. I'm more than sure it wasn't a sex game. There was a man who was dead as shit, and all of his blood was in a plastic bucket. Not a little bit of blood. All of the blood from his body was in the bucket."

"Now, he, ahh . . . ." Bowker wrote some more. "You said you escaped. How did you 'escape'? Seems like it would be hard to get out of a hogtie like that. Especially in fuzzy cuffs."

"I didn't say the cuffs were fuzzy."

"Ah, right." Bowker crossed out some text.

"I squeezed one of my hands out the cuffs—they weren't put on tight enough—and I got myself down while he was gone." The cuffs themselves had, in reality, been removed with Kenway's bolt cutters and were now rusting quietly at the bottom of the Dumpster behind his studio. "I ran through the woods until I got to the road, where Mr. Kenway here found me walkin' down the highway."

"What about the other man?" asked Bowker. "The other one that was tied up. You just left him there?"

"He was dead. Nothing I could do."

"How d'you know?"

"Because his throat was cut." Joel drew a finger across his neck, and his voice became urgent, exasperated. "Blood was runnin' up to the top of the man's head *and drippin' on the motherfuckin' floor.*"

Bowker leaned back warily. "Well now there ain't no need to get excited, Mr. Ellis."

"*There ain't—*" Joel stopped himself before he could become fully livid, and spoke in measured tones, bracketing each point with his hands. "I almost got *killed,* and you want to mess around. Ain't you supposed to protect and serve?" He sat up straight and boggled at some spot on the wall with a dazed look. "Oh, hell. I must've forgot where I was at. I'm Black in a *got-*damn police station." His eyes focused lasers of sarcasm on Bowker's pink face. "What was *I* thinking? Maybe I should've kept the cuffs on."

Adrenaline dripped into Robin's system at the way this meeting was going.

The officer pursed his lips, flustered, his face darkening. He glanced over at Kenway and the snarling, hooded wolf-man stretched taut across his broad chest. "We ain't got to go *there,* Mr. Ellis," grunted Bowker. "I'm honestly tryin' to help you in good faith. Now I don't much care one way or the other what your proclivities are, and I'm real sorry you must have got the wrong idea here." He twiddled the ink pen between his stubby fingers and went back to writing, his tone hardening, losing that good-ol-boy apathy. "Can you tell me what this man looked like?"

302 · S. A. HUNT

"He had red hair."

"Anything else?"

"Yeah, he was real skinny, had a skinny throat and skinny arms, but he was—he was *sinewy,* you know? The strong kind of skinny. Big hands." Joel traced the edge of his jawbone. "Had a real sharp jaw. Nose like a beak, big nostrils. Itty-bitty beady eyes, dark eyes."

Bowker wrote for a long time, pausing every so often.

"Anything you can tell me about where this man was holding you?" He fidgeted, rubbing his nose, scratching his cheek. "Do you remember any details about where you were detained?"

"Yeah. Yeah . . . lot of signs and pictures and stuff leaning against the walls. Like, advertising signage. Stuff about Firewater sarsa-parilla, a big picture of the Loch Ness—no, I mean, the Creature from the Black Lagoon. I think there was something with a clown. I saw something about Wonderland. Welcome to Wonderland?"

"Weaver's Wonderland?"

"That's it."

Bowker sighed in a way that seemed like dejection to Robin. Or perhaps disappointment. "Sounds like the old fairgrounds out in the woods off the highway." The pen tapped the clipboard. Reaching up to the radio on his shoulder, he keyed the mike. "Hey, Mike. This is Eric. Can I get a ten-twenty?" They all sat staring at each other expectantly for an awkward moment.

"I just got done with lunch and now me and Opie are uptown goin' south down Hickman," said a static-chewed voice. "Ten-eight."

"Want you to do me a favor." Bowker examined the clipboard. "We ain't got a key to the gate out there at the fairgrounds, do we?"

"The city probably does, somewhere, God knows where," said the radio. "But that don't stop me from getting out of my cruiser and walking around it. What's goin' on?"

"I'm taking a statement from a fella says he escaped from invol-untary confinement in that location. He was put there by someone he describes as a serial killer." Bowker coughed into his fist and keyed his mike again. "I want you to head up there and see if you can find anything shady."

"Ten-four."

Bowker sat there, breathing through his teeth and staring at the clipboard. Robin could almost hear his gears grinding. "Okay," he said, rising up out of his seat and adjusting his patrol belt. "Gonna go get this keyed into the system. I'll be right back."

As soon as he left, Joel leaned over to Robin and Kenway. "These redneck-ass small-town cowboys," he growled under his breath.

Robin hugged herself. The break room was cold, it seemed, colder than the actual October day outside. *Must be the slab floor,* she thought. "He gon' send those two cops out there by themselves? To look for a serial killer?"

"He probably ain't even believe there *is* a killer. He probably still just thinks it was a—" Joel made air-quotes with his fingers. "—sex game."

The conversation dwindled into silence, and Robin finished off the last of her coffee, putting the empty cup into a trash can that was already full of garbage. Digging some quarters out of her pocket, she went to the snack machine and browsed the junk food inside.

"How long it take?" asked Joel.

"You know these country boys," said Kenway, poking at the table with his index fingers. "Hunt and peck typists."

Bowker stepped into the break room and Kenway looked up from his impersonation of the man's keyboarding skills, casually leaning back and folding his arms, nothing to see here. The officer paused awkwardly, then sat down and shuffled a stack of papers against the table.

"Okay." He folded his arms and leaned on his elbows, speaking confidentially. "I've got the report filed. You're on the books." He twiddled the pen between his forefingers again. "How come it took you so long to come down here and talk to somebody?"

"I don't know." Joel sat back and anxiously picked at his fingernails. "Guess I was so freaked out and glad to be away from it, going to the cops didn't really occur to me." Of course, he glossed over the necessity of getting Wayne back to his father at the hospital, the explanation of which would have thrown a real wrench into the situation.

"Fair enough."

"Besides." Joel pointed at his face. "I'm black *and* gay. Goin' to the cops ain't gon' be my first instinct."

Bowker gave it some thought and tapped the pen on the table. "Mr. Ellis, we here don't discriminate, okay?" He pointed at his own face, to the military haircut. "Now, I may *look* like Cletus T. Slowboat, third in line at the Asshole Parade, but I want to assure you, you're as important to me and everybody else here as the next guy." He glanced at Robin. "Or gal."

Joel nodded quietly. "Okay." He bit down on a tight smile. "All right. Aight, we're cool."

"Now, you said you met him at *his* apartment. I'm assuming your vehicle is still over there on the property, if this 'Big Red' hasn't moved it to another location." Bowker fetched a huge sigh. "What I'm gonna do is, I'm going to follow you-all over there to his apartment and we're gonna kill two birds with one stone—get your car and see if this fella is at home."

* * *

The closer they got to Riverview Terrace Apartments, the antsier Joel became until he cracked the window and bummed a cigarette off of Kenway. Robin sat in the middle, the twenty-sided-die gearshift between her knees. She reached over and took his hand. "It's gonna be okay, bro," she said, smiling. They were shoulder to shoulder. "You're gonna be safe and you're gonna get your car back."

As soon as they came around the corner of the building and started seeing the 400 block, Joel threw his head back and swore in anguish.

Black Velvet was gone.

"I'm not surprised," said Kenway. "It's probably at the bottom of Lake Craddock."

Robin shot him a look, and he winced.

"You better hush your mouth," Joel told him. "I'd sooner you take the Lord's name in vain than insinuate somebody's hurt my baby." He slipped into a loud and vehement string of curses, his fists clenched. "I just *had* that sound system put in there. This is some grade-A bullshit." The truck curved to a stop in front of the 400 block and Bowker's cruiser slid into a space next to them.

They all got out, except for Joel, who stayed in the Chevy. As soon as Robin shut the door, he locked her out.

The bitter, clean smell of cut grass lingered in the air.

Bowker knocked on Red's door. "Police." No answer. He knocked again, this time more insistently. After there was again no answer, he went to the front office to fetch the property manager and get a key. Robin pressed the rims of her hands to the apartment's window and peered through them, trying to see past the blinds, but they were turned so the cracks between the vinyl slats afforded no visibility at all.

Even though she knew full well the front door was locked, she took hold of the knob and tried to turn it.

(gotta go gotta get out pack it up go go go)

She snatched her hand back.

That was strange.

Disembodied smells filled her nostrils: expended gunpowder, sizzling steak. The green scent of cut grass became stronger. She stepped away, cautiously, as if she'd encountered a beehive, and was overcome by the sudden and intense need to flee, mixed with a cold cloak of guilt. Not remorseful guilt, but only the clear recognition of culpability; she felt chastised. No: *chased.* Abstract words flickered in her head, Polaroids of excited fear.

(stupid let your guard down shoulda done em both)

"What was *that* about?" asked Kenway. "You jerked like you touched a live wire."

"I don't know." She looked at the palm of her hand. *Residual paranormal power? Am I picking up on it?* If so, it was the first time anything like that had ever happened. She wasn't even sure if it was a thing that *could* happen—the witches were the only ones with any paranormal ability, weren't they? The sigils and runes decorating her body deflected paranormal energy like a sort of metaphysical armor, but other than the hallucinations of the owl-headed Sasquatch, Robin had never been privy to any kind of paranormal sensitivity. The sigils were an umbrella, but she had never felt the rain itself before. It was a bit like discovering a new sense.

Maybe her sigils being overpowered by Weaver at the hospital had left her sensitive, like sunlight on a burn. Maybe . . . maybe it was the proximity to Cutty. The creases in Robin's palm shined in the sun as she flexed her hand. Was Cutty so powerful her power overflowed into the streets?

Could simply being the daughter of a witch mean Robin could siphon off surplus power like some kind of psychic vampire? She had certainly wondered over the years whether she had inherited some modest fraction of whatever paranormal talent lay within her mother Annie. As far as Robin knew, witchcraft began with a singular ritual, and had nothing biologically to do with the witch herself—it was all on the paranormal side of the equation, spiritual, exterior to genetics, initiated by the symbolic sacrifice of the heart to Ereshkigal.

Witchcraft did not live in your DNA.

This might even be why she'd been seeing the Red Lord more and more since getting closer to Blackfield. *Maybe it's—maybe the Red Lord is like their patron. No, that's not right. Witches derive their power from Ereshkigal. Maybe it's their amplifier. Is that even a thing? No doubt Heinrich would have mentioned it in our studies back in Hammertown.*

He doesn't know everything, she told herself.

Maybe it's their pet. Maybe they knew I would come back to Mom's house one day, so they stuck a monster in there as a trap. Weaver had said the Red Lord didn't belong to them, but it wouldn't be the first time a witch had lied to her face. *They're all full of shit. Shit and shadows.*

If the coven didn't conjure it and didn't make her hallucinate it, and Annie didn't,

(*"We don't talk about magic in this house," dream-Annie had told her over their dream-breakfast a thousand times in half the motels in the Midwest*)

then who did?

Maybe—That little voice in the back of her mind, a little Jiminy Cricket, a tiny Doubting Thomas.

Maybe what?

Kenway was still staring at her, alarm slowly overtaking his face. She realized she was mouthing her internal monologue to herself, and the heat of embarrassment coiled up her neck into her face, glowing in the curve of her jaw. *Maybe your mother did conjure that thing.*

And it scared her so bad she swore off witchcraft forever.

She checked her cell phone. *Call me back, Heinrich, damn you. I need to pick your brain.*

. . . Heinrich.

Did Heinrich put it there?

No, she told the cricket. *He's about as magical as ten hours of fuckin' C-SPAN.*

"You okay there, Pedro?" asked Kenway. "Doing some long division?"

She snorted. "I'm fine."

Eliminate the impossible, said the Sherlock Holmes standing next to her mental Jiminy Cricket, *and whatever remains, however improbable, must be the truth.*

Okay. So—

Hallucinations don't scratch gouges in bathroom doors.

So it's not a hallucination.

Whether Mom could or couldn't—and I have no reason to think she could—she wouldn't conjure something that would terrorize her own daughter for as long as this thing has, and completely ignore the witches and their Groundskeeper Willie.

So it's not Mom's.

Heinrich couldn't conjure something this powerful. He can barely get his dick out of his pants, much less pull a rabbit out of a hat. Hell, I'm more magic than he is.

So it's not Heinrich's.

Then it's real. And it has to be from the coven.

"Elementary, dear Watson!" she said to herself.

"I think you need to lay off the caffeine," said Kenway. "I'm grounding you from Starbucks for a week."

She glared at him. "Do you *want* to see me cut somebody?"

"Okay, a day then. I think your eye is twitching."

"What?"

Interrupting her impromptu impression of Travis Bickle, Lieutenant Bowker came back with the property manager, a limping stump of a man with big staring eyes and a salt-and-pepper beard. His golden bouffant was parted in the center like a monkey's ass. The name embroidered on his shirt was ROGER.

The manager unlocked the door and stepped aside for Bowker, who strode in with his hand on the butt of his pistol.

"Well, damn," said the officer.

The living room was completely devoid of furniture—of anything, really, that said a human had been living here until last night. The walls were bare, and the spotlessly clean carpet wasn't even marred by the footprints of a sofa's legs.

No appliances stood on the counters. No food in the cabinets, no food in the fridge except for a single Arby's sauce packet in the crisper.

Bowker came out of the bedroom. "Can you tell me who the apartment is leased to?"

"Yeah, sure." Roger stared at the clipboard in his hand. "Says here it's a fella by the name of Richard Sutterman." He looked up and shrugged. "I don't get back here much other than to check on old Mr. Brand in 432. Always havin' to snake his toilet out, sewage backin' up into his bathtub and whatnot. I don't recall what this Sutterman looks like."

Startling Robin, Joel leaned against the front door's frame. He must have mustered enough courage to get out of the truck.

Bowker asked him, "That name mean anything to you?"

"Never heard it before in my life."

Bowker rubbed his face in exasperation and tossed a hand. "I can head back to the station and look through the database, or maybe go talk to the county clerk and see if he can find any info more concrete on this Sutterman fella, but . . ." His offer tapered off, the unspoken admission hanging in the air. *It ain't much to go on.*

Psychic whispers still lingered in the air, tracing cobweb fingers along the rims of Robin's ears.

She got a faint mental flash of a vial, and a hand using a hypodermic needle to draw out a tiny bit of the contents. Then she flashed on an image of that same needle being injected into a grilled steak. She also got a flash of a word—*Yee-Tho-Rah*—but had no idea what it meant.

"Come on, the trail's cold for now," she said, sidling past Joel. The GoPro on her chest gulped footage. "I got some editing to do while I think, and then I want to go have a look at my old house."

22

Leon had rented a couple of movies from Redbox—one of the *Avengers* movies, a sci-fi movie with starships and aliens with extremely gnarly faces, and whatever the latest Nicolas Cage flick was. Except for Wayne, the kids all sat in the living room eating pizza and watching the movies, Katie lying on the floor drawing her pictures.

The sun settled on the purple-gold horizon, fleeing from a speckle of stars, and the summer's last serenade of frogs and crickets trilled in the trees.

The kids had gone home to get permission from their parents to spend the evening at 1168. Katie's grandmother had been more than happy to have the night off, and started filling a hot bath before Amanda even left. Pete's mother and Amanda's dad, on the other hand, came over to get the lay of the land.

Pete's mom Linda sat on the stoop, hunkered over a cigarette.

She was tiny and mousy with a husky radio-DJ voice and a twitchy, good-natured personality.

"Yeah, that's fine," she was saying to Leon. "Pete needs good friends. I'm proud of that guy, what he did with that big ol' hammer. He can be kinda moody sometimes, and he swears a lot, but he'll surprise you. He takes care of people he likes, he really does. He's a good kid." She had apologized profusely for Pete taking the kids to the fairgrounds, and she did it again for good measure. "I told him not to go back up there, but, you know, he does what he wants. Not that he's a rebel, he . . . he's an independent kid, yeah?"

"I understand, totally," said Leon. "Wayne's got a bit of a wild streak himself sometimes. After his mom died, he went through a rebellious phase, tried to run with a couple of bad kids back in Chicago. I had to tell him what's what a couple of times."

Amanda's dad Warren hulked over the slim, spindly Leon. Blond curls tumbled out from under his do-rag like an extra from *Sons of Anarchy.* His neat beard was laced with white. "Really?" he asked, leaning against the wall with his fingertips in his jeans pockets. "*That* little guy?"

Leon chuckled. "Yeah, believe it or not. When his mom died, I didn't take it so well. Got to drinking a lot. Wayne got a little rebellious—or maybe just lonely—tried to make friends, fell in with the wrong crowd. Little bastard named Lawrence, him and a couple of his hardhead buddies. They talked him into one too many things and he got picked up skipping school. Luckily it happened to be a cop who worked with my dad back in the day, so he knew us. Brought him to me at work because it was so late there wasn't no point takin' him to class."

He glanced at Wayne, who sat in the porch swing behind him. "That was the day my sister Marcy talked me into moving down here. Neither one of us was handling it. We had to get out of there."

"Welp," said Amanda's dad, checking his watch. "I got work at four in the morning, so I'm gonna pack it in for the night. Y'all take it easy, brother." His heavy black biker boots clomped down the front steps. Pausing on the lawn, Warren chuckled. "I'd tell you to look after my little girl, but to be honest she's the one takes care of us." Leon saluted him as he sauntered off into the velvet purple twilight.

Linda stayed behind, finishing her cigarette. "Why aintcha in there watchin' the movie with the other kids?" she asked Wayne.

He shrugged. "I don't know. I just wanted to see the sunset." He didn't want to admit he was still afraid to spend time in the house.

Royal colors made a masterpiece of the western sky. Linda took it all in. "Yeah, I see what you mean. They are nice down here in the south, ain't they? The sunrises are even better." She smiled at him. "I still remember the very first sunrise I ever saw when I got clean. My husband Tommy come and carried me home from the hospital. I sat in the parking lot of a gas station and cried my eyes out over it."

"I did the same thing on Wayne's birthday last month," said Leon, yawning. "Well, I didn't really sob, but . . . you know, I went through like half a box of Kleenex."

"How long's it been?"

"How long's what been?"

"Since you quit drinking."

Leon tilted his head. "How did you know I was drinking?"

"You said so a minute ago."

His look of surprised confusion broke into a grin. "I guess I did. Man, it's been a long day. I need some sleep." He sighed. "Figure a couple of months."

"You figure?"

"I didn't drink long enough I feel like I need to do the anniversary thing. The coins, all that." Leon took out his cell phone and fidgeted with it. "I never did go to AA. I gave my debit card to my sister and let her buy my groceries, so if I felt like I needed a drink I wouldn't have the money to run out and get something." He stared into the sunset. "It was tough, and I still get that hook pulling my insides every now and then, but . . . you know what they say. One day at a time. That's what my dad always said. He was a cop. He didn't take no flak from nobody. I guess that's where I get it. He did whatever he put his mind to, and damn the help."

"Tommy's daddy, he drank *real* hard. Drank like a fish." Linda took a long drag off her cigarette and ashed it into the grass. "He got so bad he was hallucinating. A couple of years ago it got about as bad as it was gonna get. He was seein' Vietnamese soldiers out in the woods and he said he was gonna shoot me so the 'gooks' couldn't rape me. And he didn't even know who *I* was. So Tommy got it into his head to save his daddy's life. Took him to the hospital to get him clean. He broke down so bad he ended up in a wheelchair and almost lost a leg from a staph infection."

Leon winced.

"Bout gave him brain damage. He was in a coma for near two months. It's crazy how dependent you can get on the booze. After so long, you literally can't survive without it. Going clean will kill you. So it's a good thing you got out of there while the gettin' was good." Linda put out her cigarette. "So is your dad still around?"

"No." Leon shook his head. "He died when I was seventeen."

"What happened? If you don't mind me asking."

"Pulled over the wrong car. Saw the passenger throw something out the window into the woods, and when he went to go ask about it, the passenger shot him. This was before dash cams, but his partner was there."

Horror and sympathy warred on Linda's face.

The conversation was dragging Wayne down, so he got up and went inside to face his fears, letting the screen door slap shut behind him.

Thump, thump, thump, he crutched into the living room and plopped down on the couch next to Pete. They were watching the *Avengers* movie, or at least Pete was. The girls lay on the floor making pictures; Amanda was drawing them and Katie was coloring them.

Standing next to the TV was the strength-test hammer, still pink from bloodstains even after Pete had given it a thorough scrubbing. Wayne leaned up and took a piece of tepid pizza from the box on the table, sitting back to nibble on it. He couldn't pay attention to the movies because his eyes were fixed on the far corner, opposite the TV, where he'd first seen Owlhead. The monster had been tall enough the top of its broad head brushed the ceiling, its back to the nearly empty bookshelves on that side of the room. It had reached for him with long arms, as long as he was tall, covered in copper-wire hair, streaked with the swampy green of old filth.

"I owe you, man," he said, when he'd gotten down to the crust.

Pete tore his eyes away from the screen. "What?"

"I said I owe you."

"For what?"

Wayne looked at him as if he'd grown a third eye. "Saving my life?"

Pete shrugged, squishing his chubby face with his shoulder. "It was the w—the woman, I told you. The old woman. *She* saved you, alls I did was smack the snake."

"Was you about to call that old woman a witch?"

"So what if I was?" Pete chewed his cheek. "I mean, I guess? People say they are. My mom says they used to be friends with the lady that lived in this house."

Wayne peered at his leg. "Do you think she did magic on me?"

"I don't know what magic looks like, but I don't—I-I feel like that's not it."

A faint disappointment settled over Wayne. "Oh."

Settling into the couch, he pulled his knees up to his chest and tried to lose himself in the movie. His eyes were growing heavy when he heard his father shout outside.

"Ay! *The hell* you think you doin'?"

All the kids scrambled up and went to the windows, Wayne looking through the screen door.

Apparently Linda had gone home while they were watching the

movie, because she was no longer on the stoop. Instead, three people had come marching out of the night, approaching the house. He recognized them as the big blond Viking dude, the girl with the Mohawk, and the pizza guy he'd saved from the serial killer.

"We don't want no trouble, Mr. Parkin," the woman was saying. "We just wanted to check on your son and talk to him about what he saw in his hospital room."

Without her bulky jacket, Robin was slender and small, with narrow hips and a long, graceful, otteresque neck, but Wayne had the feeling surprising strength lurked in her wiry body. Veins stood out on her forearms. She was wearing a nylon chest harness, and a small camera was mounted between her breasts.

"I appreciate you finding him after he wandered off, but I don't know you from Adam," said Leon. "And frankly I'm not sure I'm comfortable with any of this. What he saw was a hallucination brought on by shock, and that's the end of the story."

"You know that ain't true."

The blond man shrugged. "He's got another witness says he was there for the whole thing."

"Yo," said Joel, his thumbs in his jeans pockets.

"I know that guy even less." Leon paced slowly, talking with animated hands. "How do I know *he* didn't lure Wayne out of the hospital room while I was asleep and run off with him?"

The pizza-guy recoiled in mortified anger. "The fuck?"

"I didn't—I didn't, well, I mean—"

"You think just because I'm gay, I'm some kind of child molester?"

"No. No, of course not, I wouldn't—"

To Wayne's dismay, his father had come up with the worst-case scenario. Something urged him to step into this and defuse it the best he could. "That's not how it went, Dad," he said, pushing the door open and stepping outside without his crutch. "Joel is all right. And you know it."

Leon simply pointed at him with a *shut your mouth* finger,

daggers in his eyes. Wayne quailed at first, his eyebrows rising, but he stood his ground.

"I squared up to a fuckin' demon to get him off your son," said Joel. "You need to—" He bit back further retort, wheeling away from the confrontation as if making to leave. "Sis, I didn't come here to be accused of being a pedophile."

"Your son is a good kid," said Robin, calming Joel with a hand to his shoulder. "And sharp as a tack. I feel like he deserves the benefit of the doubt. He wouldn't be defending a kidnapper, would he?"

Folding his arms, Leon seethed at the three interlopers for a long moment.

Then his eyes drifted over to Wayne, who was trying his hardest to project a vibe of honesty. "I'm a teacher, man," he finally said, a look of defeat coming over his face. He leaned over and rested his hands on his knees as if he were about to vomit, then straightened up, his hands meeting. He slowly cracked each one of his knuckles as he talked. "I'm a teacher, and what if I just can't get on board with this story, of-of-of doors that aren't supposed to be there, and monsters in shadow-houses? I need empirical evidence, goddammit. I believe in the scientific method, you know? Theories, hypotheses, experimentation. Like the doctor at the hospital said, this is hoodoo. And I don't go to church because I don't believe in hoodoo."

"This has nothing to do with a lack of religious faith," said Kenway. Realization dawned in his eyes and he spoke to Robin. "Wait, if these witches take their powers from the goddess of the underworld, does that mean God is real? And Heaven, and Hell, and all that?"

Robin shook her head. "Ereshkigal is the goddess of the afterlife, the spiritual realm, not the 'underworld,' because there *ain't* no underworld. Heaven and Hell are states of mind in the void of the afterlife, not physical locations. The classical Hell and its nine Circles Dante Alighieri described in *The Divine Comedy* don't exist. Heaven is sublime contentment. Hell is sublime regret."

This was all gibberish to Wayne. Comedy? This didn't sound funny at all.

Kenway waved away all that poetic mumbo-jumbo, pressing the point. "What about God, though?"

"There *is* a force, I believe, but it ain't the belligerent all-knowing Old Testament sky-wizard so many people think it is. God—or Allah, or Ahura Mazda, or Jehovah, all different names for the same thing—it's not an old bearded man in a toga and sandals, it's a word for the attracting force of unconditional love itself. It can be the strongest force in the universe if you let it."

Kenway's laugh echoed off the side of the house. "That was uncharacteristically sentimental of you, lady."

"More Hallmark shit," joked Joel. "I thought we was past this."

Leon took a deep breath and blew out a long, exasperated sigh. "Maybe I should talk to you the next time I feel like I need a shot of Jack. When I lost my wife, I lost my belief in this stuff. If God exists, He's a real nasty piece of work."

Robin grinned crookedly. "I sound like a TV evangelist. But it's true. At least, that's the conclusion I've gathered in the couple of years I've been doin' this. You kinda get a feel for the supernatural when you deal with it on a regular basis. But I don't really traffic in churchy matters, Mr. Parkin. My job is a little darker than all that."

"Darker?" Leon went over and sat on the stoop, and Wayne joined him. His father slipped an arm around his shoulders. "What, you mean like an exorcist or something?"

"Of a sort. I hunt witches."

"I didn't think you looked like the convent type. A witch-hunter? I thought that went out of style with bonnets and butter churns."

"Those were delusional Puritans in Salem times, Mr. Parkin. Using superstition and dogma to eliminate anybody they didn't like and suppress femininity and sexual freedom. I'm sure you've heard that refrain many times, being a teacher."

"I'm a literature teacher, not history. And you can call me Leon." He pointed at the camera on Robin's chest. "Are you filming this?"

She nodded, detaching it from her harness and handing it to Kenway. He aimed it at her and she gave him the finger. "I run a YouTube channel about my travels. Do you mind me filming?"

Leon hesitated. "I guess not."

"So how are you feeling, Wayne?" asked Robin. The woman's tone was clinical, interview-like. He got the feeling she shed her normal irreverent, profanity-laced drawl for the videos.

"A lot better. Whatever Miss Weaver put on me was—" Wayne almost said *was magic,* and amended himself. "—like, a miracle. The doctor said so. And she even paid my hospital bill. Almost thirty thousand dollars."

Joel and Kenway whistled in unison. "Hot damn," said the pizzaman.

"I am forever in her debt," said Leon. "The hospital would have been chasing me for that money until the day I died. She saved both our lives."

"I've got a little secret I never got to tell you back at Kenway's apartment," said Robin. "This used to be my house. I grew up here, and I slept in the room up there—" She pointed at the uppermost tower looming over them, the windows dark. "—in the cupola."

"That's my room now," said Wayne.

"I hope you love it as much as I did. Felt like a princess in a castle."

Wayne's mouth tucked to one side in a coy, assessing way. "Was your mama the one that died here?"

"Yes. Yes, she was."

"My mama died too. This ring I showed you earlier was hers." He took out the gold wedding band around his neck and showed it to her, the inscription sparkling in the dull yellow light of the wall sconce. *Together We'll Always Find a Way.* He was glad Dad let him keep it; he felt naked without it.

"I'm sorry," said Robin.

"Me too."

She paused, an uncomfortable warmth on her face, as if consolations were unusual for her.

"It was cancer," said Leon. "Throat cancer. She was getting better, but then they let her get an infection and it spread to her lungs. She went downhill fast. Like the song, it's been just the two of us ever since." He hugged Wayne tight. "So you used to live here. What were you talking about, your mom dying here?"

"My father, he . . . murdered my mother, here in this house." Turning, Robin pointed up at the Lazenbury. The huge house loomed over them in the background, a black square jutting into the night sky. "And it's them, those women up there in the mission-house, that made him do it."

Wayne stared. "Are they really witches?"

"Yes. Very dangerous and very old witches."

"I can't believe I'm buying into this shit, but I'm going to ask anyway. Does this mean you're here to, what?" asked Leon. "Kill them?"

She stared at the stepping-stone under her foot. "I don't refer to it so crassly, Mr. Parkin. But yes, I'm here to neutralize them."

"Neutralize."

"Yes. Would you prefer the term 'gank'? I'm here to gank 'em. Like I said, they're dangerous."

"You sound like an enforcer with the mob or something." Leon rubbed his forehead, his eyes darting around at the grass as if he were trying to read it. He tossed a hand up for emphasis. "Anyway, I don't know if I can condone a 'ganking,' Miss, ahh—"

"Robin. Robin Martine."

"Miss Martine. They saved my son's life. They paid for his hospital visit. They've barely said one word to us, much less brought over a basket of poisoned apples. Surely they can't be *all* bad, can they? They're three little old ladies, for Christ's sake."

Robin stared at the stoop in thought.

When she looked up again, her face was dark, her eyes piercing. "They're pitting you against me, Mr. Parkin. This whole thing— the snakebite, Weaver paying your bill, all of it—they're bribing you into service as a human shield. They know I'll hesitate because of you."

"Sounds like crap," said Leon. "How could they orchestrate my son getting bitten by a snake?"

Robin regarded Wayne. "How did you kids end up at the fair-grounds, anyway? Whose idea was it to go out there?"

He didn't say anything at first, for fear of incriminating Pete. But then he got the idea to pull a Spartacus and said, "It was me. It was my idea. Somebody told me about the f—"

"Oh, bull," said Pete, pushing the door open and coming out-side. "It was *my* idea, ma'am. I wanted to show 'em my secret way home nobody knows about. I take the Broad Avenue canal down to the river and then there's deer trails that go up and through the fairgrounds. They come out behind this house, back there in the trees."

"Hmmm." Robin took out a Sharpie. "Take off your shirt."

"Take off my shirt?"

"Yes."

"Why?"

"You'll see in a minute," she said, coming up onto the porch and uncapping the marker. Pete wriggled out of his shirt and stood there with it bunched up in one hand. Robin zeroed in on his chest and drew a symbol in the middle. "What's your name, by the way?"

"Pete."

"Nice to meet you, Pete. Thank you for letting me draw on you."

He looked down at the marker, scrunching his second chin. "Why did you draw on me?"

"Do you feel funny?" Robin looked up at him; she was still hunched over with the heel of her hand on his left boob.

"Other than the fact I took off my shirt and you're drawing weird stuff on me? Not really."

"The symbol I drew is an *algiz* rune."

Leon made a face. "Did I just hear you say 'owl jizz'?"

Standing back, Robin massaged the bridge of her nose, closing her eyes. "No, '*all-jeez.*' Ancient Norse protective symbol that blocks or dampens supernatural influence . . . like the witches' power."

Pete tried to angle his head for a better look at the symbol, making a scrunched-up face. "Is something supposed to be happening?"

"Yes."

She seemed disappointed at first, but then a new zeal took over and she capped the Sharpie. "But it doesn't look like what I expected is going to happen. So you can put your shirt back on. I guess you taking the kids to the fairgrounds was just a coincidence."

"So maybe Karen Weaver really *did* do what she did out of the goodness of her heart," said Leon. "I'm thinking of going up there in the morning and inviting her to Sunday dinner as thanks." He watched his hands worry at each other. "It's not exactly thirty thousand dollars worth of thanks, but it's the best I got."

"What did you expect to happen?" asked Joel. "His head to spin, him to start puking out pea soup?"

"I'll tell you later, if you really, *really* want to know," Robin told him, and turned to Wayne's father. "I would steer clear of those women from now on, honestly. They're bad juju. In fact, everybody needs an *algiz* while I'm here and I've got a Sharpie in my hand. And don't wash that off, by the way."

"You're not drawing voodoo bullshit on my son."

Wayne pushed himself to his feet. "I don't mind. You can draw on me," he said, unbuttoning his shirt. "What is this symbol supposed to do? I know you said it's 'protective,' but what does that mean?"

Leon took his wrist and tried to pull him back down, his eyes steely. "No. You're not getting mixed up in this."

"I'm *already* mixed up in it."

Wayne tugged back the leg of his jeans to expose the snakebite. The only visible evidence he'd ever been bitten were two tiny scars halfway between his knee and his ankle. If he compared both legs side by side he could see the difference—the bitten one was almost imperceptibly larger because of the swelling—but at a glance, it was as if he'd never been bitten at all.

Robin stared at the living room window, where Amanda and little Katie Fryhover were peering over the back of the sofa. "Mr. Parkin, if I can prove your son saw a monster in your house, if I can show you this whole dog-and-pony-show isn't just TV bullshit or snake-oil chicanery, will you trust me?"

All of the children's eyes were suddenly as big as cantaloupes.

"You wanted theories, hypotheses, and experimentation, didn't you? The scientific method?" she asked, sauntering closer until they were standing within arm's length of each other, the woman gazing up into his face. "Well, I can give it to you."

Leon took out his cell phone, turned it right-side up, and examined it with a sigh.

"It's eight-thirty on a Saturday night, I ain't got a date, there ain't nothing to drink in the house, and I ain't slept worth a damn in three days." He put his phone back in his pocket and threw his hands up in resignation. "Why the hell not?"

23

To Robin's disappointment, there was no psychic blowback as she walked into her childhood home. The house had no aura of paranormal energy. To her eyes, it was what it had always been: a lonely, drafty gingerbread with memories hanging in the corners like cobwebs.

She looked down at the GoPro strapped to her chest, pointing it up at her face to see if the red Record light was on. It was.

Good. Footage good, fire bad.

Regardless of what Kenway had said about her mental stability, she had been dealing with hallucinatory psychosis for the majority of a decade. At this point, between the terrible first few months of nightmares about her mother dying in her arms, and the therapy sessions that became traumatic in and of themselves, she felt like she knew what was a hallucination and what wasn't. In fact, in many cases the med cocktail had helped overwhelm illusions induced by witchcraft. The colony of newbie witches she'd encountered in Oregon last August—a backwoods death-cult commune led by a 110-year-old woman calling herself Susie-Q—had tried to trick her into believing she was in the middle of a roaring forest fire, but an emergency thirty milligrams of Abilify had sufficiently untied her brain.

Something about pharmaceutically de-sensitizing herself seemed to lessen the effects of the witches' visions. Following a regular low-level dosage regimen actually served to inoculate her against their illusions to the extent she could sense their falseness. It was a bit like seeing the Matrix—with the anti-psychotics in her system, she could see a "fraying" around the edges of their false images, a rough-hewn texture that made the illusions look cheap, as if they had been constructed out of papier-mâché and macaroni. This made it easier to find inconsistencies that made it easier to peel the illusion back.

Checking her phone, she silently cursed herself for missing her medication deadline. She'd been so focused on getting the videos edited and put up and so anxious about going back to Underwood Road she'd forgotten all about it.

"Hey, buddy?" said Robin, adjusting her camera harness straps.

"Yeah?" Leon's arms were folded and his face was a stone mask. He looked like a cop waiting for her to try something funny.

"Can I get a glass of water?"

Leon nodded to Wayne, and the kid got up and went into the kitchen. Robin followed and found Wayne pouring some tap water into a red Solo cup. *Take two 5mg tablets by mouth every day,* the directions on the side of the bottle said. Her pill bottle only had a handful of doses left in it. She would have to look for another prescription soon. She had been titrating down, rationing them at one five-milligram tablet a day, trying to make them last. The prescription was always hard to get, because she was so outwardly high-functioning. The last doctor, the asshole in Memphis, he'd been an uphill battle. "I'm sorry, ma'am, the medication's side effects—ischemic stroke, seizures, the risk of anaphylactic shock . . . I mean, two hundred and forty pills? I can't advocate prescribing this much on a whim."

"Attention whore," the nurse at the mental hospital had called her. Anderson. Head Nurse Anderson. How could she forget that harpy's name? "You just want the pills because they make you feel special. There's nothing wrong with you. You're faking it; mental illness isn't even a disability to you, is it? It's a badge of honor. To you, it's a license to be a shit." *Attention whore.* And now she had a YouTube channel with millions of subscribers.

Pushing one tablet between her lips, she gulped it down with some metallic-tasting water. *Maybe you were right, Anderson,* she thought, shuddering. *Maybe you were right.*

She peered down into the pill bottle.

"Fuck it," she told her YouTube audience, "time for the nuclear option. Time to put up or shut up, Slender-Squatch." She tipped the whole thing into her mouth and painfully gulped all the pills down. Forty milligrams and half a glass of water, down the gullet. "If the Red Lord is a witchcraft hallucination, it's a powerful one. We'll do this like we did in Klamath Falls, won't we, and we'll see how that works. A few days' worth of anti-psychotics at once should tell me whether or not that thing is a psychiatric Harvey the Rabbit or the paranormal rabbit-man from *Donnie Darko.*"

Empty orange bottle. White pill-dust lined the bottle's inner curves. *Why are you wearing that stupid man suit?*

Wayne stared at her, his jaw set. "Are you okay?" When he went around to the other side of the kitchen it seemed like a preemptive gesture, as if he wanted to put the table between them.

"I'm fine," she said, leaving the red cup in the sink. "Have a headache, is all. Thank you for the water."

They regarded each other from across the room.

(t h e r i i i i n g)

A voice, deep, muffled, coming from somewhere obscure.

Sounded like Darth Vader on quaaludes, talking through a pillow directly into her right ear.

"You're welcome," said the boy, and he stumbled back into the living room, giving her the side-eye as he went. Robin hugged herself, letting her eyes wander around the familiar-but-not-familiar kitchen. What she remembered as green was now blue, and next to the replaced appliances it gave her an odd sensation of Capgras delusion, as if she were talking to an old friend wearing a mask.

Holding up her GoPro, she stared into the lens and sighed, giving it a meaningful look. The show wasn't just about the things she faced, it was about her. That's what the viewers were there for. Come for the monsters, stay for the girl. But this time, she couldn't find the words to encapsulate the way she felt in this alien home.

So she capped off those bottled-up feelings with her ringmaster top-hat. "You guys out there in Internet-Land ready for a show?"

When she came back to the living room, the children sat on the sofa watching her raptly, and there was a feeling of ominous ceremony in the air, as if they were preparing for a séance. Leon was propped against the bookshelves next to the television, his arms still folded impatiently, and Kenway leaned in the foyer doorway.

"The creature you saw in that shadow-version of your house," Robin said, wringing her hands as she paced in front of the TV, "I've been seeing it off and on for a couple of years now." She debated telling them about the psychosis, but the look on Leon's face told her it would erode his trust. "I *think* it's the same thing, anyway. Whatever it is, I've been seeing it more since I came back to Blackfield. Since this is my old house, I think it has something to do with me."

"What do you think it is?" asked Wayne.

"I don't know. Hallucination? Ghost? Demon? But I'd like to try to find it and get a better look at it."

He shook his head emphatically. The expression of terror on his face was genuine. "Oh, no, you *don't* want to see it. Owlhead is scary as hell."

"The boy speaketh the truth," said Joel. "That thing will make you piss."

Pete spoke up. "Your mother was a witch, wasn't she, ma'am?"

"Yes." *Brisk way to bring it up, but yes.*

"Maybe it's here because of her."

"I don't know," she said again, and sighed deep. "Well, if we're going to get on with it, there's no time like now. Wayne, do you have your mother's ring with you?"

He took the wedding band out of his shirt, took the chain off his neck, and handed it to her. Robin held it up to the ceiling fan light. "The inscription on the inside of the ring says *Together We'll Always Find a Way*. Words and symbols can bend or break the witches' power, and what the inscription says is important. 'Together we'll always find a way.' Think about it. The connotations of words are what have an effect on their hexes, curses, and spells, and what is this saying?"

(t h e r i n g r i n g t h e r i n g g i v e i t)

The slow guttural voice crept in around the edges of the conversation, under their words, like a television in another room. Robin took a deep breath and tried to ignore it, tried to will the aripiprazole to start working.

Pete raised a hand. "What does 'connotation' mean?"

"The way a word makes you feel. How does the word 'video game' make you feel?"

"It makes me feel happy? I guess?"

"But it's just a word for a box of circuits and wires."

He shrugged sheepishly. "I really like video games. They make me happy."

"A video game is only a box of circuits and wires, but the word makes you happy because you have fun with them—and that happiness is the connotation. It's the deeper meaning of the word. If I said, 'Let's go play video games,' in your mind you're gonna be gearing up to go have fun, right?"

He nodded, rapt.

"So what does the phrase 'find a way' mean to you?"

"To literally find a way," said Joel. "Wayne accidentally found a way with the ring—an actual way, a doorway. A doorway leading to the garage where I was hanging."

"Yes. And that's how it works. The meanings of words, whether it's Viking runes, English calligraphy, or Japanese kanji, affect Ereshkigal's power." Robin went back to pacing. "I've been thinking about this. When Wayne's father mortgaged the house, he also bought—"

"Renting," said Leon.

"Hmm?"

"I'm just renting the house. From the realty company. They're renting it out."

"Oh." A pang of dismay, or perhaps inferiority, flickered through her, as if merely renting the house instead of buying it outright devalued it, and by proxy, Robin and her family as well.

Leon sat on an ottoman, templing his fingers. "You were saying?"

"What I was going to say is, now that you and Wayne live here, you're part of the residual energy of the house." She held the ring up to her eye and looked through it, turning in a slow circle, searching the faces throughout the room. "And that includes your belongings, like this ring. From what I can tell, the engraving is channeling my mother's latent energy."

"What if I gave them a blender with 'Let Nothing Stop You' engraved on it?" asked Kenway. "Would that mean they'd have a blender that could blend anything? Even steel?"

Robin gave him a stern glance over the ring. "It doesn't work that way. The symbols have to have emotional or cultural meaning. The older languages, like the Elder Futhark rune on Pete's chest, naturally have more power than modern-day English. But you can augment English by lending the words importance, or gravity. Like this ring. The engraving lends the ring weight. Makes it an artifact. But only to the person to whom the engraving has meaning."

"It meant a lot to me and Haruko," said Leon. He held up his left hand, flashing the mate to the wedding band. "She actually made these rings herself. Forged them from stainless steel. She made her own jewelry, sold it on websites like Etsy, and in Chinatown." He dug in his shirt-collar and pulled out a tiny metal pendant depicting three spirals joined in the center. "She made this too. It's a 'triskelion,' a Celtic symbol that represents the act of learning, of moving forward. She made it for me when I started teaching school kids. Said it would inspire me."

Her eyes lost their edge and she smiled softly. "Was that your wife's name? Haruko?"

"Yep. Haruko Nakasone. Formerly of Nakasone's Knick-Knacks."

Made them herself? thought Robin. Something about this sparked a question in the back of her mind, but she couldn't quite put her finger on quite what it was. Wayne's mom couldn't have been a witch—witches' power came from their heart road, their *libbu harrani*, not an external source. But she could feel some aspect to this, something she couldn't quite find the shape of, like unfamiliar furniture in a dark room.

Mental note to do some research when she got back to Heinrich's hideout and the piles of stolen esoterica books there. "It's very pretty."

"I met her at a party in Chicago when I first started going for my bachelor's degree at UIC. I was teaching English classes in Chinatown at the time." His face lightened with a wistful grin. "I knew she was the one when she started showing up for classes as an excuse to come talk to me."

"Is jewelry the only thing she liked to create?"

"The ghosts, Dad," said Wayne.

Leon stared at him as if he'd spoken an alien language, and then his eyes darted over to Robin. "Yeah, uhh. Thanks for reminding me, son. Yeah, she also painted *yōkai*." He hesitated, rubbing his jaw for a moment, with a lost look on his face. His eyes scanned the room, darting along the few still-unpacked boxes remaining around the room. He opened one of them, then another, and took out what looked like a medieval scroll. "She painted yōkai, but she didn't really sell those. I mean, she did, technically, but for like a thousand bucks apiece, which means she didn't sell a whole lot of them outside of the art fair."

Unfurling the scroll, Leon gradually revealed an intricate painting of a woman in a flowing white dress.

Robin tried not to scream.

"Whoa," said Pete.

"*Super* gross," said Amanda. "I mean, it's nice. Beautiful painting. But super gross."

"Yōkai are Japanese ghosts," Leon was saying. "Back in the day—and by that I mean feudal Japan—people would commission these creepy ghost paintings and hang them by the front door of their home to scare away intruders."

Gracefully depicted on the thin sheet of canvas, the woman in white seemed to have been caught in the act of turning away from the viewer, as if about to walk away, but the longer one studied it, the more one saw she was in a shy, guarded position, as if trying to shield herself from prying eyes. And for good reason, because her skin was as pale as a fish-belly, and her face was distorted into a gap-faced scream. The yōkai's mouth drooped open like a sack and her eyes seemed to *unravel,* all of her features running down her face like a wax figure in the sun until the eye sockets and mouth began to blend into one hollow C-shaped cavern.

"This one," said Leon, "is called *Drowned Woman.*"

No words battled in Robin's throat or mind as she stared at the wall-hanging, only a patternless, frantic static.

"Hey, if you ever want to sell those, dude," Kenway said, "I know a guy into stuff like that, met him when I started trying to sell my art. He's got an office in Atlanta. You could do something like a memorial art show or something. If the idea of keeping the proceeds makes you feel gross, you could donate the money to a charity you think Haruko would have approved of."

Please just roll the painting up and put it away. Please God please.
It was everything Robin could do to keep from fleeing the room.

Mr. Parkin did just that, leaving the scroll on the cold hearth, and Robin felt the knot at the core of her body come undone. First, she realized her fingernails were digging into her palms, and then secondly she realized she had fingernails, and hadn't bitten them down to the quick as usual. Nothing like staying busy to keep you out of a bad habit.

"How—" Joel started to say, and hesitated. "How come you don't have any pictures of Haruko?"

Leon twisted to look at the bookshelves behind the TV. There were books, of course; a scattering of knickknacks, a trophy with a little man on top swinging a bat at a Tee Ball post, a small crystal award with the word *Poetry* etched front and center on the plaque. Framed photos of Leon accepting certificates, shaking hands. Wayne with other children, candid scenes of Wayne and Leon, class photos.

"I dunno." He picked at his eyebrow as if he wanted to hide his eyes behind his hand. "I guess they're still packed up in my room with the other boxes. It's just easier that way. Somebody told me once, 'If you got time to think, you got time to drink.' And I try not to let myself sit and think about certain things."

Sighing in irritation, Robin inspected the room with the ring up to her eye again. Nothing special leapt out at her, no doorways made themselves apparent in the walls of the living room. She wandered out into the foyer hallway, and the children scrambled off the sofa to follow her. She ended up in the kitchen, turning in a slow circle again.

"This is where I found the door to the garage," said Wayne, pointing at the back wall.

Robin faced the wall, but saw nothing out of the ordinary.

"What about the rest of the engraving?" asked Amanda. "It says '*Together* We'll Always Find a Way.' What if it's only Wayne who can do it?"

"Worth a shot." She handed the ring back to its owner.

Wayne put it up to his eye, and for a long second she almost convinced herself he could see the door. But then he relaxed, his hands sinking to his sides, and he frowned at her. "Nope. I don't see nothin'."

"Maybe it don't work when you're actually *in* the house," offered Pete. "Maybe it only works when you're somewhere else and you want to come *here*."

Robin had to admit, that made sense.

With a sigh, Leon took off his wedding band. "What about this one?" It took a bit of twisting and pulling to get it loose. "Maybe if—"

As soon as it came off, a shine emanated from inside, a faint javelin of white light jutting out of the hoop of the ring.

Tiny motes of brighter light sparked out of the epicenter of the glow, slow-motion welding slag drifting outward like dust in a sunbeam. Leon blinked, speechless. "Oh hell naw," said Joel, eyes and mouth gaping. "Y'all, that's some *Lord of the Rings* shit."

Katie Fryhover grinned a snaggletoothed grin. "Preeeetty."

"*That's* different," said Robin. "How come you haven't seen that before?"

"This is the first time I've taken this ring off." Leon put the ring on the kitchen table as if he were afraid to touch it, standing it on edge. The ring turned by itself and the light-javelin flared. Now it was two feet long and hard to look directly at, a miniature star compressed to a smear the width of a human finger. Their shadows wheeled and swooped around the room, capering across the wallpaper, diving into the cabinets.

"I have some real important questions I wish I could ask your wife, Mr. Parkin," said Robin, trying not to stare into the light.

"You and me both, ma'am."

"It's a compass," breathed Amanda, peering through her fingers.

Leon picked up the ring and the javelin faded to a mere whisper.

"I can feel it tugging," he said, holding it up. "Like a magnetized compass needle." He rotated on the spot and the javelin faded down to a vague blur hovering in the C of his thumb and forefinger. He turned the other way and the javelin grew again, spearing over his shoulder and out in front of him.

A bitter ozone-stink floated in the air. Robin put her palm in front of the light. It wasn't hot at all. The back of her hand glowed orange, the finger-bones dark shadows in veiny flesh, sprouting from her wrist.

"Nothin' to it but to do it, I guess," said Leon, and he marched out of the kitchen.

Out in the hallway, the javelin faded, even though he was still facing the same direction. Leon turned to his left and the ring flared again. He walked toward the foyer. The ring led them to the second floor, the kids clomping up the stairs behind him as if he were the Pied Piper.

"Here," Leon told them, opening the door to the cupola.

The only thing on the other side was the stairway hooking up into the shaft's spiral. Wayne held Haruko's ring up to his eye. This must not have had an effect, because he closed the door and opened it again. Closed it, opened it. "I don't know, there's nothing."

Leon's ring was still pointing at the door. He went upstairs, Robin, Pete, and Wayne following. "I'll be down here," said Joel. "If y'all run across that shaggy bastard, I don't want any part of it."

With four people standing in it, the cupola was unusually crowded. Examining the room with his ring, Wayne turned every which way, looking up at the ceiling, looking out all the windows, even squeezing between Robin and Pete to check under the bed.

Now the javelin of light pointed down the stairs. "Come on," said Robin, herding Wayne down them. At the bottom, she closed the door leading out to the landing (wincing apologetically to Kenway, Joel, and the girls as she did so) and braced the boy with a hand on his shoulder. "Now yours. Open the door."

Wayne eyed the door through the monocle of Haruko's ring and turned the doorknob. It scraped and creaked as if it were a thousand years old. He pushed the door open, revealing not their friends standing on the upstairs landing, but an archway full of deepest darkness.

• • •

A breath of frigid air wafted out, curling around their knees, chilling their hands. Groaning from the depths of the shadow-house was the immense galleon-creak of shifting timbers, as if the earth below that strange foundation was constantly moving.

Robin sat down and Leon settled behind her, putting his ring back on. "I'm not going in there," said Wayne, staying on his feet, as if he would bolt at any moment.

She adjusted the GoPro on her chest rig. This was going to require a Spielberg-worthy framing.

"Hopefully you won't have to." She drummed her fingernails on the doorframe, lightly at first, then a little more insistently. "Here it is, buddy," she said, her voice soft, as if perhaps she were speaking to herself more than anything on the other side. "Here we are. Come show your face. I know you're in there." The dark doorway yawned apathetically for a long several seconds, as if it had nothing to prove to her. She leaned forward, trying to get a better look at the faint light down the hallway.

Bursting out of the shadows, a shaggy arm reached through the door, claws flexing a hair's-breadth from her face.

"Oh!" Robin threw herself backward against Leon's shins, and Wayne screamed, running up the stairs into the cupola. Pete let out a shrill shout.

Before she could properly react, the coppery hair all over the arm burst into flames, *WHOOSH,* as readily as if it were drenched in gasoline. The arm withdrew and the fire diminished in the watery darkness, a single flame licking one last time.

A pair of bright green eyes blinked sluggishly, each one the size of a softball.

Grrrrururururuhuhuh, rumbled Owlhead.

His wet, ragged respiration reminded Robin of a tiger, or perhaps a dragon in a movie, but muffled, heavy, languid.

"You," she breathed, staring. "It *is* you."

The Red Lord from her dreams.

Owlhead *was* the Red Lord. And he was here, he was solid, he was *real,* and he wasn't a hallucination. He wasn't going to vanish into a pile of spiders this time. The forty milligrams of aripiprazole anti-psychotic didn't do shit to him.

(g i v e m e)

"No," she said, and realized she was still cowering against Leon's feet, halfway up the stairs. She sat down, but didn't lean forward. She stared into the Red Lord's great green eyes, and tried to will her heart to stop pounding. Thundering, really—rapidly, like the hummingbird drumbeat of some speed-metal song. "I got some questions. I got you here now. You fucking *real,* you're *tangible,* you're *here,* and I'm going to ask you some questions."

No voice reverberated in the corner of her mind.

"You there?"

Grrrrururururuhuhuh.

She checked over her shoulder. Wayne was still upstairs—he wanted no part of this, and she didn't blame him. Leon's face would have been as white as milk if he could go pale, but his open mouth and wide eyes were more than enough evidence of his terror.

He didn't leave, though, she had to give him that. Neither did Pete, though he had moved halfway up the stairs, watching around the corner.

"What *are* you?" Robin asked the empty doorway.

Grrrrururururuhuhuh.

Robin had never addressed anything like this before. She tried to remain assertive. Her hands trembled and her insides quaked, but it wasn't entirely from fear. She felt like she'd drank six pots of coffee. The aripiprazole had kicked in, and it had shifted her body into a strange gear. Five-wheel-drive. "No. You answer my questions. You been houndin' me for ages. I ain't slept worth a shit in weeks, thanks to you. And now I'm gonna get some information out of you, goddammit. I wanna know what and who the fuck you are."

(s o h u n g r y)

"Hungry?" Owlhead's eyes were like green Christmas baubles with lights inside them. "What do you eat?"

An image squirted into Robin's mind, indistinct, piecemeal, a cloud of clues like a half-finished jigsaw puzzle. Her subconscious fluttered around the edges, trying to make sense of the shards, and she caught glimpses

liver-spotted hands, wielding a knife,
coming around a boy's throat, slash

of various things, faces,

a curtain of blood

places . . . no names, but

tiny graves in the woods

a distinct motif she thought
she could sort through . . .

broomstick leaning in the corner
flickering firelight, bubble and
gurgle of boiling water

Marilyn Cutty's birdlike smirk swam in the gloom. Robin leaned forward, disregarding the fact she was within arm's reach of the creature again. "*Cutty?* You eat witches?"

No answer.

The stairway creaked slowly. Robin looked up and saw Wayne creeping down, his eyes curious. She threw out a trembling hand. "No! Stay upstairs! Keep the ring up there, away from the door."

Grrrurururuhuhuh.

(t h e r i n g t h e r i n g)

"Why you want the ring? Does it protect you? Does it allow you to get out that house?"

Grrrrurururuhuhuh. Owlhead blinked slowly.

"If it eats witches," Wayne said from the cupola, "ask it why it tried to bite my damn head off."

A hand slipped over Robin's shoulder. Leon in the corner of her eye. "Are you psychic or something? How is that thing talking to you? I don't hear nothing but the breathing."

"I don't know," she admitted. "I don't know!"

Heinrich. She really needed to talk to him, but he wasn't answering his phone. He had a bad habit of doing that.

"Why are you here?" she asked the eyes. "Who brought you here?"

Grrrrurururuhuhuh, breathed Owlhead.

Sensory echoes welled out of the darkness, like heat distorting the air over a fire. When the ripples broke over her mind's eye, she saw her mother's face. "Mom?" Robin stared. "Did my mother have something to do with bringing you here?"

The green eyes closed, vanishing, extinguishing.

Frustration. She could feel swells of frustration rolling out of the doorway, washing against the stairs like the surf at high tide. The Red Lord wanted something, but she couldn't tell what. *The ring, of course, but something else. What else?* "You want to tell me something? What you want me to know?"

Then it hit her. *Name. Name.* "I need a name." And she leaned in, peering deep into the dark. "What is your name?"

To his credit Leon was right beside her, eyes focused on that black rectangle at the bottom of the stairs. "What is your name?" he asked. "And why are you in this house?"

They hesitated, craning forward, listening, watching, straining to divine some kind of answer from the door. They saw nothing except for a lightless gap, an empty, absent blackness.

"Is it gone?" Wayne, at the top of the stairs, leaning around the corner. "I don't see anything. What was that noise it made? Sounded like a growl."

An answer was forming in Robin's mouth as a great shaggy arm thrust out from the doorway and took hold of Leon Parkin's foot. Long, knob-knuckled fingers wrapped around his ankle and jerked it out from under him.

Before they could react, Leon banged down the stairs on his back. Instead of a scream, he let out a strangled hoot. "*Ooh!*"

"*Dad!*" screamed Wayne.

"*Help!*"

Bracing herself against the wall, Robin fumbled for Leon's hands as he slid toward the doorway on his ass. "*I got you!*" She took his left arm with both hands, but her fingers caught in the cuff of his work shirt, a white dress shirt, and the cuff link button popped off with a staccato ripping noise. She lost him with her right hand, but her left still had his wrist.

The Red Lord's arm burst into flames with a *WHOOSH!* and a halo of bright, shimmering fire. Colors prismed in a half-circle around the flame.

By now everyone was screaming and the stairwell descended into pure chaos. Leon got one foot under him and managed to crouch on it, the other leg out behind him in an awkward fencing lunge, but the burning arm jerked him backward and the two of them fell against the wall, shoulders slamming against the clapboard with a woody crunch.

Fingers slid through Robin's hands. At the last second, her eyes darted up and locked onto the man's sweat-glossed face, where she saw pure, unadulterated terror in his eyes. "It's got me," he stammered.

Leon banged once against the doorframe and slipped into the dark.

"God-fucking-*dammit*," shouted Robin, and without a fraction of hesitation she charged into the doorway after him.

• • •

Dizziness overcame her as she stumbled into the dark Other-House. Suddenly it all came back as she knelt there on the second-floor landing—this was *her* house. Not the house Leon and Wayne had claimed, but her childhood home. Under her feet was the threadbare rug Jason Martine had bought at a yard sale when Robin was twelve. Set against the wall was the creaky old wicker vamp chair her grandmother Edith had passed down to her mother Annie. Their family pictures hung on the wall. But it was all overlaid with this sinister, desolate darkness only given shape by some strange glow that shimmered and rippled across the walls and floors like a flashlight on cave-water.

"*Help!*" bellowed Leon, sliding across the floor, kicking madly at the fist wrapped around his leg. The Red Lord was still on fire as he walked down the landing toward the stairs, a hoary red cave troll wreathed in flame, still dragging Wayne's father, the white flames casting a silvery shine.

In the holy firelight, Robin could see more clearly the house that had once belonged to her family. Cobwebs draped over the furniture like bridal veils, and buntings of hideous gossamer hung from the rafters. Dust turned everything a sullen shade of gray.

Tucked into the back of her jeans was the silver dagger she'd used on Neva Chandler. *The Osdathregar. The Purifier. If this thing works on witches, it should work on whatever this is.* She charged after them and past Leon, plunging the dagger into the Red Lord's arm. He let go of the man with a terrifying noise, a metallic roar like an oil tanker running aground, and rounded on Robin. The Red Lord clubbed her with his flaming hand.

Something popped like bubble-wrap in her chest as she cartwheeled over Leon and collided with the wall. Framed pictures fell, smashing on the floor.

Scrambling onto his hands and knees, then on his feet, Leon fled.

The Red Lord did not give chase. Instead, he committed to confronting the woman who had stabbed him with the silver dagger, the mysterious blade Heinrich had called the Osdathregar, the weapon Heinrich seemed to treasure above all the other weapons in his armory. Stomping toward Robin, the Red Lord reached down and took her by the arm, snatching her up off the floor. His other hand closed on her throat, and he slammed her against the wall, pinning her by the neck.

The room spun. The darkness narrowed, trying to converge on her face, as if it couldn't wait to swallow her whole. Those glowing green traffic-light eyes were mere inches from her own, each eyeball the size of her fist, set in spiraling eye sockets as big as dinner plates, in a head the size of a television set. Robin gazed into them and saw nothing but the empty, feral rage of an animal driven to lunacy by imprisonment.

White fire still licked from the arm pinning her against the wall, but as she watched, the flames extinguished themselves, as if the darkness were asbestos, smothering them to death.

"Why have you been stalking me? Watching me? Taunting me?" choked Robin. Her feet pedaled uselessly at the air. "What is so special about me?"

The beast's other hand came up, palming her forehead, the heel of his palm covering her eyes. In that brief moment, her mother's face swam out of the darkness again, coming through in grainy patches, like a bad signal on FM radio.

"I can't breathe." She punched at the arm and the hand around her throat, throwing hook after hook into his forearm and wrist. The flesh under all that hair was as hard as bone, unyielding and solid. "You asshole. Either kill me or tell me what I need to know. One or the other."

He said nothing, just kept trying to force the image of Annie Martine into her head, like hammering a wedge into a tree stump. It felt like he was splitting her brain down the middle trying to jam something through a hole in the brick wall of aripiprazole in her system.

"Okay," she spat, reaching for his body with her free hand. Her skull felt like it had ten gallons of water sloshing around in it.

Tangling her fingers in the shaggy hair coating his chest, Robin pulled with everything she had and thrust the silver dagger, driving it deep into the creature's chest.

And her mind split open like a coconut.

24

Light flares in the inky void, resolving into a face. Annie Martine materializes, illuminated by candles, fading in from black. Gradually, the scene makes itself clear: her mother is kneeling in a dirt-floored, stone-walled room, surrounded by thousands of stumpy white candles—on the floor, arrayed along the walls, standing in floor brackets.

Annie mutters to herself, her eyes closed. The incantations she's saying are too low for Robin to make out. She is almost nude, clothed only in a pair of Hanes boyshorts, nubile, her late-teens body sleek and glittering with beads of sweat. Occult symbols have been painted in key positions on her body with some dark paste like melted chocolate. Not blood. Some kind of mixture. They look like brush-painted kanji, but . . . wrong, somehow. Upside-down, maybe. Too many parts, not enough curves.

A round diagram six feet across has been drawn on the floor with chalk, a ring of incomprehensible symbols. A man lies in the center of the runic circle, stripped naked, his paunch sweaty, his balding scalp glistening in the candlelight. His arms and legs are outstretched like the Vitruvian Man, his wrists and ankles tied to steel tent-stakes, driven into the earth. He wakes up, blinking, looking around worriedly.

A folded dishtowel lies across his groin, obscuring his genitals.

"Where am I?" he asks.

Annie finishes muttering and looks up at him from under her brows. She is undebatably angry, but it is a long-simmering rage, ripe, reptile-cold. "You're in my cellar, Edgar."

"Why am I naked? What is this?"

"This is a ritual. I've chosen you as my sacrifice." Annie stands up, presenting the full glory of her lithe, petite body.

Her dark hair is feathered and parted in the middle, and it makes everything feel like a scene excerpted from a horror movie from the eighties, even though this vignette had to have taken place in the early nineties. The only thing missing is a synth score from John Carpenter. Robin gets the distinct feeling this vision is a stolen hand-me-down memory, a psychic telephone game—the Red Lord took this scene from the past, lifted it from her mother somehow, and passed it on to her daughter.

(An inheritance, then?)

(Well, better late than never, I suppose.)

"Sacrifice?" He angles his head up, peering over his belly. "What the hell are you going on about?"

"Shut your mouth." Annie walks slowly around the runic circle, pacing like a predator. He watches her, his eyes trickling up and down her sweat-slick body, and the lust hiding behind the terror in his eyes is disgusting.

"Listen, I'm willing—"

"I know about the children," says Annie.

Edgar Weaver immediately stops talking.

The girl-woman makes a complete revolution around the circle before she speaks again. "The amusement park you built in the woods with your wife's money."

"Weaver's Wonderland."

"Whatever you want to call it."

"Those kids are trash," Edgar says at first, then seems to realize he's spoken harshly, frowning, biting back his words. "They come from broken homes, poor homes, dead homes. No one's going to miss them. Nobody's even going to look for them, we got Blackfield in our pocket. We have men in the police department."

"Someone will miss them." Annie picks up a kitchen knife from the floor and points at him with it. Liquid fire dances on the blade. "I found out what you and Cutty are up to. The tree. You know the trees are unnatural. Disallowed—"

Edgar laughs nervously. "The dryads? Everyone has them."

"No. Only the ones willing to kill for them. That's—"

"They're the only way you can live on, you idiot. You want to die like one of us mortals?"

She scowls. "Fell magic. You know that—"

"You want to fall apart at eighty years old? The heart-road makes you immortal, but it doesn't keep you from aging. It doesn't make you ageless. The dryad keeps you from mummifying."

"And I know that. Cutty knows that."

"Cutty doesn't care." His chuckling grows in confidence. "Marilyn is just over three hundred years old. She was around when they signed the Declaration of Inde-fuckin'-pendence! Can you grasp that? Can you even wrap your pretty little head around it? Cutty's been crafting nag shi since long before you were born. She does what she wants. That's the consequence of self-government, isn't it? 'The honor system.' Ha! There's no honor among thieves, and even less among witches."

"What would you know about witches . . . man?" She says "man" as if it is a derogatory term, like "imbecile" or "outsider." It doesn't affect him, because he's heard it a hundred times.

"I know Cutty and my wife are going to kill you if you hurt me."

Annie gestures to the runic circle, drawing a broad oval in the air *with the tip of the knife. "Do you know what this is, Edgar? My new friends know a lot about us. And about—"*

"It's bullshit. You don't know anything." He spits at her, but most of it only speckles his own legs. "You and your so-called friends, Annie, you don't know shit. I don't know what you're planning, but when you're done, the coven is going to kill you. No—they're going to flatten you. Squash you like a bug. Fledgling. You're a baby witch.

"The nag shi came from the Dream-Witch Yidhra, she's the first one to have made them—she was the Prometheus who showed them how it was done. And they'll kill you to protect it."

"Not if I kill them." Annie smiles.

"And how, pray tell, do you intend on doing that? Cutty's too powerful. They all are. Even my wife's got forty years on you."

"I found a way."

"The only thing capable of killing a witch as old as Cutty is a demon. And nobody's brought a demon into the material world in two millennia. Not since the Christ Sanctification locked the door on Hell two thousand years ago."

She stands over him, smiling knowingly. A drop of sweat trickles down her belly, zagging through the fine hairs like a bolt of lightning.

Edgar's angry expression sours and his eyes dart around the room, widening in revelation. "Wait—that's what this is?" He flexes his arms, straining against the ropes, kicking. "You think you're going to summon a demon? You think you're going to call up Satan and sic him on your neighbors?" Now he's flailing, pulling at the ropes as hard as he can. The anger melts away, replaced by crazed, fearful giggling. "You're crazy as hell. Who the hell do you think you are?"

Annie steps over Edgar's thrashing legs and takes a knee between his thighs, crouching over his pelvis. She hovers over him in a three-point stance, her black hair spilling around her face, burying her eyes in shadow.

"What good is immortality with a price like this?" she asks him, tracing curlicues in his chest hair with the tip of the knife. "A blood

price? Innocent blood? Come on, Eddie. Even if I condoned the crafting of nag shi, they've been watered with the blood of criminals before. Murderers, thieves, rapists. Not children. Not that it's any—"

"Plenty of children." Edgar smiled. "What do you think the Count-
ess Bathory did with all those virgins?" He shook his head sadly. "The
virgins are best, y'know. They're like Miracle-Gro. You can't make fi-
let mignon with dollar-store beef, and you can't grow a nag shi worth
a damn with the blood of a rapist. The soul inside the tree, it responds
badly to evil blood. You know that."

"If you're trying to talk me out of this, you're doing a spectacularly
bad job of it."

Straightening, Annie leans back, tilts her face to the hidden heavens. She's obviously heard enough. Words in a dead language Robin
doesn't recognize stream out of her mouth in a muttering tone. She
lifts the knife toward the ceiling, the incantation rising, changing to
a different language, becoming faster, louder, a rapid-fire litany of
gibberish. Suddenly Robin realizes what she's speaking now.

German. Annie is shrieking in German.

Where would her mother learn a German ritual?

Edgar looks as if he's trying to press himself against the dirt hard
enough to sink into it, trying to will himself away from this lunatic
woman-child. Annie's eyes roll back, her eyelids parting to show only
the white sclera.

"What the hell?" the man under her pleads. "Stop! Please! Stop
this crazy shit! We can talk about this! I swear to God, I'll talk to my
wife, see if I can get 'em to dig up the tree, I'll—"

Her head sinks forward and her irises roll down out of her eye
sockets again. But she's not looking at him, she's looking at a point
somewhere far behind him, somewhere deep in the soil. Annie brings
the knife down, but not into his chest like he expects, not yet, no,
not yet, she opens her mouth and slips the tip of the blade into her
mouth like a spoon. The steel scrapes against her teeth as she opens
her mouth wide.

Annie presses the blade-point against the floor of her mouth, turns *it up so she's holding it like a bridal bouquet, and flicks it up and out. The knife penetrates her tongue and rips it open up the middle, splattering Edgar's face and chest with blood.*

He flinches, squinching one eye. "Jesus Christ. You're insane."

Crimson wells in her mouth and spills over her teeth, down her chest and between her breasts. Annie leans forward, trying to speak, trying to continue the incantation, choking on the blood. It collects on his chest in a hot puddle. "Uckkkk, ffnnnggkk, uurkk."

Her eyes: they're almost all white, except for pinprick black pupils.

Now she raises the knife and drives it through his rib cage into his heart. Edgar seizes up, hissing through his teeth. Veins stand out on his neck as he pulls at the ropes again, fists clenched, knuckles white.

One final breath huffs out of his lungs and he goes limp, the light draining from his eyes. Annie leans on the knife, the strength going out of her, and it sinks up to the hilt in his flesh, more blood pulsing from the wound. She stays that way for half a minute, her eyes closed, willing the dizziness to go away. Blood continues to trickle out of her mouth. It is everywhere, now a pool collecting under Edgar.

What snaps her out of her reverie is the sick bbbrraaaap *of Edgar's corpse as it relaxes and lets go of the gas still in his system. The fart reverberates in the dirt chamber.*

"Jevuf, Eg," Annie complains, getting up.

The cellar spins. The girl spits a stream of blood through her teeth like a farmer. She slides the knife out of the body's chest and stands back, nausea churning cold in her guts. She collapses to her knees, sitting down, the dirt cold against her skin.

Nothing seems to be happening. She scowls at the dead man and sweat rolls down her face. Did she just kill a man and disfigure herself for nothing? No, there is a reason: Edgar was a horrible person who did horrible things, and he deserves this. And if she hadn't done it, someone else would have. He had it coming.

Wait.

Something's going on. The corpse is different.

She gets up on her hands and knees and crawls over to Edgar's side.

The wound she made with the knife—it's turning black, rotting, withering like a bad apple. It's larger, too, easily three inches long, where the knife-blade had only been an inch wide.

The darker it gets, the worse the wound smells. The odor of anise, of licorice and absinthe, and the smell of sulfur too, rotten eggs, rises out of it. The flesh around the hole withers and turns black, radiating outward in black veins, as if infected with darkness. It's caving in, a depression falling through like burning paper into a hollow cavity in Edgar's chest. Annie slinks away, her eyes locked on the spreading, sinking blackness. The body is eroding through the middle, deteriorating from the inside out, not so much hollowed but becoming the growing hole itself.

Fear streaks through the girl, and her future daughter, at this bizarre, terrible turn of events.

Underneath her, the ground shudders. Annie's hands instinctively snatch away and she crabwalks backward until her shoulders smack into the stone wall. The dirt stirs slowly, like a blanket over the tossing and turning of a sleeping giant. Dust clouds down from the ceiling. A dozen lit candles topple over, rolling around on the floor. Some of them go out in the blood with a crisp, venomous hiss.

"Oh, my God, what did I do?" Annie asks herself, her voice a strained whisper.

Edgar's remains (if one can call them that at this point) seem to be sinking into the dirt floor, as if his blood is acid and it's eating a crater in the soil, a crater confined by the shape of the symbols chalked around him. His torso is now a black hole demarcated by four disembodied limbs and a head.

The hole grows in depth and diameter until whatever's left of him slides or tumbles down into the darkness, leaving a pit six feet wide in the middle of the room.

Everything falls dead silent.

Dank, cold air layers over the rim of the pit, licking boldly, invitingly at Annie's hands.

Hesitant at first, she crawls toward it and peers over the edge.

The blood pooling in her mouth still runs down her chin, and now it strings syrup-thick straight down into the new abyss. Down it goes, where it stops, nobody knows. The darkness appears to be infinite.

"What in the name of God," she says, but the words are addled by her ripped tongue and come out garbled.

Something is moving down there.

Without warning, the darkness rushes up and she bowls over backward, scrambling to get away. It rushes against the floorboard ceiling, pooling between the joists, falling upward like water. It doesn't seem to have any real mass, and makes no sound at all as it fills the room— it's more of a gas, a billowing fog that turns the wood as black as ebony and leeches the color from the Georgia-red dirt.

This was a bad idea.

Annie flops over and runs for the cellar stairs, scrambling up the board risers toward the door, catching a splinter in the palm of her right hand, but there is something crawling out of the pit, something ponderously heavy and seething, and when she looks over her shoulder she sees two green eyes: Chinese lanterns the color of grass, of frogs and avocados, glowing dully in the dark.

Grrrrururururuhuhuh.

A clawed hand with too many fingers grips her ankle, and drags Annie Martine back into the depths of the basement. The staircase's risers dig into her back as she falls, scraping skin from her leg and shoulder, and she lands facedown in the dirt.

As she stares over her shoulder, Robin's mother screams.

Crouched at her feet is an incredible and terrifying sight, a hulking creature covered in shaggy hair the color of blood and comprised almost wholly of gangly limbs. It looks down at her with brilliant green eyes set in a gargantuan head and gives her that drowned-engine growl again. Grrrrururururuhuhuh.

"Yes," gasps Annie, as if in response to some unheard question. "I summoned you here to make a deal."

The Red Lord's head tilts, but he says nothing, if talking were ever part of his skill set. He reaches forward with one terrible claw again and grasps Annie's ankle, dragging her away, crawling backward, dragging her toward the pit in the middle of the cellar. The packed earth stains her naked body red and brown.

Annie screams, "No! I did the ritual! You have to listen to what I say! This is a deal! I called you here to protect me from the coven!"

The Red Lord pauses. He lets go of her, resting on his haunches, and begins to slowly pace around the room on all fours like an anxious panther. As he moves, his hips and shoulders roll in unnatural ways, over-extending and rotating in their sockets as if they are less part of a natural skeletal order and more a mocking approximation of some living being.

The entire time, he stares at her with those terrible green eyes.

"With this entrapment spell, I have imprisoned you here in my home, author of discords, sixty-third spirit, lord in the abyss, governor of thirty legions of damned souls," says Annie. Her words remain muddled by her injured tongue, but the meaning is clear. "You will protect this house from the oracle Marilyn Cutty, the skinchanger Theresa LaQuices, and the conjurer Karen Weaver, and their Matron, the oracle they call Mother. You will not allow the four of them inside this house. Within these walls, you will not allow them to do harm to me."

Saying nothing, doing nothing, the Red Lord crouches by the pit. He seems to be waiting for her to say more. Annie must be receiving the same sort of mind-voice Robin had been hearing the past few days, though now it must carry a word of agreement to her terms, because Annie appears to relax, or at least a grim form of relief passes across her face.

"Now what is your demand in exchange for my wishes?" she asks, her voice breaking. "I was told you would require something as payment for your services."

The Red Lord blinks, head tilting ever so slightly.

Annie gasps, a subtle breath of the close, foul air of the cellar. "Oh, God. You can't be . . ." She shakes her head, covering her face with her hands. When she looks up at the creature again, her next words come out in a sobbing howl. "But the goddess has taken my heart from me!"

From her vantage point somewhere in the darkness, Robin watches the two of them size each other up. The Red Lord crawls toward her mother in a slow, self-assured fashion, eyes always locked on her face, vivid green in a colorless room. Facing this horrible thing, Annie tries to regain whatever composure she'd had before, but it's all she can do to keep from screaming herself hoarse.

Scrambling backward, she turns and claws up the stairs, hand and foot at first, banging against the wall, and then running, pounding up and up to the door at the top. She wrenches it open to find her own kitchen, but something is wrong. There are still no colors, no electricity. The night outside the windows is more than night—it is an absence, a nothingness. She doesn't have to open it to see and to know the house, or at least this facet of it, exists in the vast vacuum of the underworld.

She didn't pull the beast into our world.

He pulled the house into his.

All of this realization happens in a fraction of a second as Annie bursts from the cellar door and crashes into the doo-wop diner table, slamming it into the kitchen cabinet and overturning two of the chairs. Frantic, terrified, she goes to her belly and crawls underneath the table, curling into a fetal ball in the shadow. She bought the table two years ago at a yard sale in Summerville, thinking it would look good in their kitchen, with its aluminum trim and steel legs and sparkly green surface, not knowing she would one day be using it as a shield between herself and some hulking monstrosity from another plane of existence.

The cellar door, even though it was already black, fills with a deeper darkness. Green light splits it as two lambent eyes open.

The Red Lord slinks into the kitchen.

Panic overtakes her. Annie clambers to her feet and runs.

She pounds down the hallway rug toward the front door, sparing a second to glance through the archway into the living room. Black and white too, an ominous shadow-lair straight out of an Alfred Hitchcock movie. Some shimmering light illuminates the walls in there, like a handful of broken glass. The windows are black squares.

To her surprise, the front door opens easily. Annie flees the house.

But she doesn't get far. As soon as she steps onto the front porch, she can plainly see there will be no escaping.

Beyond the porch railing is an abyss as deep and yawning black as a starless night. Annie sees this at a run and tries to stop herself, grasping at the banister as her feet find stairs, but she slips, goes down on her ass, slides halfway down the stoop, and then her bare feet are dangling out into space. The lawn is a Mariana Trench.

From somewhere far below comes a strange sound: the dissonant noise of competing flutes. Annie Martine hangs by her hands from the front steps of her house, dangling over a long fall into a mad, infinite nothing.

Looming over her is the Red Lord.

At first Robin thinks he is going to peel her away from the steps and pitch her screaming into the whistling dark, but he takes hold of Annie's upper arm and drags her to safety, depositing her on the porch with all the care of tossing a bag of dirty laundry, elbows and ass banging on the boards.

The dirt-streaked woman lies on her back, gasping for breath. "No," she says, pushing herself backward with her heels. "Even if I wanted to, it doesn't work that way. Not anymore. Crossing back into the sanctified land afterward might kill me. Poison me."

She knows, though, and Robin suspects, the Red Lord would never let her get away, never let her get out of the deal, whatever it is. Once you've summoned a demon and asked your favor—and at this point, Robin was dead sure it was a demon—you satisfy his demands, or you die.

25

A familiar voice cut through the vision-dream: strained and distant, a muffled growl from a thousand miles away. Slowly, faintly, Robin understood there were boards behind her head, no longer wallboards but floorboards, and she was lying on her back, her teeth clenched, her fists tight, her legs folded painfully underneath her as if she'd passed out in the middle of a guitar-solo knee slide. The silver Osdathregar dagger was squeezed in one hand, her knuckles aching.

"I got you, kid," said the voice again.

Hands grasped her wrists and the floor slithered under her. Someone dragged her through the darkness. Tremors coursed through her as though her very bones were vibrating, and the bitter taste of steel blossomed in her mouth, and the acrid smell of burning rubber filled her nostrils.

Her teeth chattered. The world went away again.

• • •

Figures stood around her, a looming tribunal of ominous shapes. Robin awoke with a reflexive gasp, scuttling backward, her heart stomping against her ribs.

More demons.

Instinctively she brandished the silver dagger at them.

"Whoa there, Stabby," said one of the figures.

She lay on a duvet in a chilly room where gray-blue morning light limped through the curtains. The master bedroom, her parents' bedroom—no, now the man's room, the boy's father. Leon? Yeah, that was his name.

"Good morning." Mr. Parkin himself stood over her, and Kenway next to him. The digital clock on the nightstand said it was a quarter to eight. Robin turned over and held her aching head, curling into the fetal position. For a weird second, the rough blanket underneath her felt like a dirt floor, and she could still smell the dank, musty, dungeony forgotten-ness of the cellar. Her back, her head, and her elbows felt like she'd seen the business end of a Cadillac.

Joel sat in a chair by the bed. He rubbed his face with his hands and folded his arms. "You scared the hell out of me, girl."

"She scared *you?*" Kenway sat on the mattress next to her, face etched with horror and worry. One hand clutched something so tightly she thought he might break it.

"What happened?" she asked.

"You stabbed it," said Leon. "You stabbed the monster. After it ran away, I started dragging you out of there and I think you had a seizure."

"A big one." Joel leaned closer. "You were freakin' out, boo, you threw up, started doin' the jitterbug." He did an impression of her seizure, his back stiffening, his arms locked against his sides and his eyes rolled back. Looked like Frankenstein being electrocuted.

Must have been a *grand mal.* First she could remember ever

having. There had been a few *petit mal* the last couple of years—a few minutes of lost time here and there as she'd zoned out. One of them she'd actually caught on videotape. A spooky twenty minutes of watching herself stare into space. But she'd never had a shivering, tap-dancing, knock-you-on-your-ass episode before.

Of course, she'd never swallowed eight times the recommended dose of aripiprazole before, either. But at least she knew now the Red Lord wasn't a figment of her imagination, and it wasn't Illusion magic from Karen Weaver.

"Scary," she noted.

"No *shit*." Kenway leaned close.

One beefy hand came up, and in it was the empty Abilify bottle.

"Kid said you took the entire thing," he said, his voice grim, gritty, low. "What were you thinking, Robin? What were you trying to do?"

"If I overdose on aripiprazole, I can power through witchcraft illusions," Robin told him defensively, her hands scrunching the blanket into fists. "It's an emergency tactic. Anti-psychotic drugs versus psychosis-inducing magic. It's like using nitrous in a street race. It makes sense to me, and it's worked before."

"Bullshit," said Kenway. He stood up and pitched the bottle overhand across the room. It ricocheted off the wall and hit the floor with a clatter, rolling under the bed. "You know, the next time you decide to overdose on your meds, let me know. So I can fuck off somewhere else and I won't find you dead the next morning."

That said, he left the room.

Shame burned Robin's face. Neither Leon nor Joel said anything, but the way they were shoe-gazing told her she had indeed fucked up.

Her GoPro camera and harness lay in a pile on the nightstand. The Record light wasn't on. She snatched it up and was about to ask about it, but Joel spoke first, "Don't worry, it was still recording when we pulled you out. Cut off a half-hour ago. I reckon you got the footage you was looking for."

Relief wrestled with shame and loss.

A bolt of pain next to her right ear made her wince. "Down there. In the cellar, my mother did some kind of a ritual, when she was young, and it summoned that monster, that demon thing. Trapped it with a spell from German Judeo-Christian witchcraft or exorcist hoodoo or something, I don't know what. Sounded like a Celine Dion cover of 'Du Hast Mich.'"

Leon frowned. "*That's* what that Looney Tunes hair-monster was? A demon. For sure. There's a demon. In my house."

She dragged herself up and sat against the headboard. "I saw it. In my mind. Like a letter from the past, you know? Like I was watching an old videotape, except the VCR . . . it was in my head, and the tape was shitty and dirty but I could still see. Mom was trying to stop them, barricade the doors, to block the other witches from coming into the house to kill her. She was trying to summon a demon, but instead of making it manifest here, she accidentally created another—I don't know, it's like she cleaved off a second copy of the house. This dark copy, or some kind of dark flip-side. Or maybe she didn't, maybe it was the demon that created it. But that's where the demon manifested, and that's where it was trapped. She imprisoned it there."

The bedroom fell silent as their brains churned, processing this new information.

A half-cup of coffee on the nightstand next to the clock was pushing a rich aroma into the air, and Robin couldn't stand it any longer. She rubbed her temples, her eyes cutting sidelong at the cup like a jonesing junkie. "I need a cup of that and I need it ASAP."

• • •

She comforted herself with the familiar ritual of rinsing out the last of the coffee and making a fresh pot, going through methodical motions: fetching the bag of frozen Dunkin Donuts in the freezer (helps it keep longer, so sayeth the Leonard), dosing out the proper portion (three scoopfuls to a full pot of water), pouring water into the Mr. Coffee's reservoir.

Click. She pressed the button and stood there at the counter, staring at the machine until it began to gurgle. Tendrils of steam crept out from under the lid.

"Hey," said Joel, eliciting a twitch.

Her eyes moved first, and then her head. She blinked—slowly, balefully, like a lizard, she thought—and said, "What's up," sounding perhaps a little more nonchalant than she felt at the moment. Maybe there was still a bit of the Abilify buzzing in her system; she could feel the floor pressing hard against the soles of her feet, and the room was colder than it ought to be, traced in the damp early-morning chill that made you feel small and thin and vulnerable, like a newborn chick too far from its warm nest. She was a naked wire, thrumming with anxious electricity.

"You okay?" Joel leaned in. Steam bathed their faces. "You took a nasty fall, according to the Professional back there. And that seizure thing? Got me worried, bruh, for real."

Leon the Professional, thought Robin. She could always appreciate a good movie joke. One of Heinrich's favorite flicks. When she started on this road to revenge, she liked to envision herself as the Natalie Portman to Heinrich's Jean Reno—his protégé, his shadow, *sa fille de substitution.* "Yeah," she said, not looking up from the slowly filling coffee carafe. "I'm fine. I mean, I slept. A little, at least. I just need a cup of coffee and I'm ready to rock."

"You overdosed and had a seizure. Are you sure you don't need to go to the emergency room?"

"No. I done this before."

"Oh, okay. And what happened then?"

"It didn't knock me out, but I staggered around the woods for like an hour, tryin' to will the ground to stop breathing under my feet."

Joel leaned back, wry disapproval scrawled on his face.

"Look, most of what happened to me last night was supernatural," said Robin, parceling out each word with her hands, as if the explanation needed help getting out of her head. "The demon thing knocked me out more than the meds did. He opened a window into the past in my head. Well, I say *opened*, but it was more like he tied a vision to a brick and threw it through my brain's living room window. He showed me a stolen memory from my mom. That kind of thing don't come cheap, you know. You can't just . . . *inject* random memories into someone's brain and not expect some kind of, of, cerebral trauma, you know?"

"You saying he gave you brain damage?"

Robin licked her finger and made a check mark in the air. "Demonic brain damage. One more item off my bucket list."

"Oh, good. Is there anything else on there I should know about? Dismemberment? Defenestration? Thing they did on *Game of Thrones* where the big guy pushed his thumbs into the little guy's eyeholes until his skull exploded? Is there a five-dollar word for that?"

"If that happens, I really *will* need a bucket."

Joel loomed in close, giving her a playful scowl, eyes narrowed. "Just drink your damn coffee, princess." He walked away, shaking his head.

Their estranged companion Kenway had escaped to the back stoop to smoke a cigarette and stare at the deep Slade Township woods, with its wet, obfuscating October morning fog, wispy cumulus clouds rolling low through the trees. In Georgia, you don't really call it "the forest." The forest is a European thing, a Dungeons & Dragons thing, a storybook glen where knights ride, and bandits creep, and faeries flitter. The forest is where stories begin. No, down here in the Appalachian pines, where meth-heads murder each other over stolen power tools, where banjo-toting mutants make you squeal like a pig, where you might kick aside a pile of yellow leaves and find the moldering bones of somebody's brother or father, you call 'em *the woods,* and the woods is where stories end.

Man, Robin thought, spooning sugar into a mug. *Aripiprazole hangovers make me corny as fuck. Write drunk, indeed.*

Her head swam. Nausea burned in the swell of her jaw, as if there were venom in her salivary glands, just waiting to poison someone's blood. She looked up from her careful caffeine alchemy and found Joel staring up at her, sitting at the table. They were the only two people in the kitchen.

"What?" she asked, spoon poised in midair.

He shrugged and sat back. *Nothing,* said his expression, *nothing at all.* But he continued to stare at her.

"If you gon' say something, say it."

"You know he's mad at you." Joel folded his arms. "You know you fucked him up."

Robin poured creamer into the mug, and coffee on top, and threw her hands wide in a *what-can-you-do* way. "It was bound to happen sooner or later. I'm just surprised it took so long. Normally everybody just wanna nail me against a wall and disappear, and as soon as the medication comes out, the disappearin' part usually comes first." She stirred the coffee with a cold chuckle. "At least *something* gets to come first."

"No," said Joel, holding up a finger. "No jokes here, comedian. You don't get to let him into your life, learn his secrets, and use them against him. That is a good man out there. He ain't the disappearin' type. It's time to stop sabotaging your own happiness. Yeah, I can see it in your eyes. You think you're broken, you think you don't deserve somebody good, and when you see a good thing comin', you start playin' it all by ear because who gives a fuck, right? It's all going to turn to shit anyway, right? Well, just fuckin' stop."

"Thanks, Mom."

Joel snorted. "Hey, if the heels fit."

They lingered there in a kitchen for a long time, Joel sitting at the table like Human Resources holding a job interview, Robin leaning against the counter holding a cup of coffee under her face, sauna steam curling across her lips and chin.

"You know what happened with that army friend of his."

"I know."

"How can you do that to him?"

"I wasn't thinkin'."

"No, you wasn't." Joel got up and poured himself a cup of coffee. The teacher's coffeemaker was a big one made for an office, a twelve-cup cauldron. Probably a hand-me-down from some teachers' lounge, fired and replaced by a Keurig.

"I ain't ask for this, you know. You set me up with him."

"I've known him long enough to know he's the same kind of screwed up you are. You both got eyes like knives. You two go together like chocolate and—"

(the shit, the suck, the fighting, it changed us. Made us wild animals)

"Peanut butter?"

"I was gonna say 'soy sauce,' but yeah, peanut butter, that works."

Their banter was interrupted by a knock at the front door.

Joel's grim smile disappeared and he eased out of his chair, his head hunched down. "You expectin' visitors?" he asked, glancing at the window over the sink.

"No." Robin started toward the hallway leading to the foyer, but Katie Fryhover stepped into the doorway.

"Witch-lady is outside." The little girl knuckled one eye sleepily. "Why is she wearing a bunch of rags?"

Sidling past the little girl, Robin crossed the hallway and slipped into the downstairs bathroom, a cramped half-bath with a toilet and a sink. The walls were tiled in a dizzying motif of hornet-yellow sunflowers. "Go see what she wants, Mr. Parkin," Robin said through the half-open door, briefly recognizing how weird it was to carry a cup of coffee into the bathroom. She put it on top of the hamper. "Don't let her know we're here."

Joel sidled inside, squeezing between them. Robin stood in the corner behind the sink, pushing a wastebasket out of the way. "If she sees me, she gonna know you're here," he said to her, closing the toilet's lid and sitting on it. Joel tried to close the door, but there was a soft knock. He opened it a crack.

"I need to use the bathroom," Katie whispered through the gap.

The pizza-chef palmed the top of her head and tugged her into the bathroom, closing the door for good. Robin clutched the little girl against her knees. "Shh," she murmured, looking down at Katie's upside-down face with her finger across her lips. "Gotta be quiet, okay, honey? We can't let the witch-lady know we're in here, or she'll turn us into bugs."

"I don't wanda be a bug," Katie murmured back, shaking her head slowly.

"Then be as quiet as you possibly can."

In perfect unison, Joel turned off the bathroom light and Leon opened the front door.

"Good morning."

"Good morning from the Welcome Wagon!" hooted Karen Weaver. "I was out 'n about, and I wanted to stop by and see how your boy was doing."

"Actually, I'm glad you came by. I was going to come up and see you today."

"Is that so?"

"Come on in, ma'am . . . feels a little clammy out there. I'd hate for you to catch your death of cold."

"Too true, too true." Weaver's boots thumped on the entryway rug and knocked on the hardwood floor. The front door closed with a soft click and the two of them went into the living room, which made them a little harder to hear.

In the bathroom, Robin was dead silent and motionless, straining to listen. She tried her damnedest not to cough.

"Well, hello there, kiddos! Oh, a sleepover! How wonderful!"

"What's this?" asked Leon.

"Oh, it's an icebox cake. I thought the boy would appreciate a sweet treat while he convalesces." The rustle of paper. "Look through the glass dish—see how the cake is marbled underneath? You bake the cake and pour Jell-O mix into it, and let it soak in the fridge. The Jell-O sets inside the cake."

Some strange sensation of hunger echoed in Robin's bones, reverberating from deep in the center of the house as if the creaky Victorian itself were tired of nails and mice and wanted something fresh. A half-presence lurked out there with them, the same eerie weight you sense when you know someone's home with you but you haven't seen them yet.

Owlhead, she thought. *You can smell the witch, can't you?*

When she closed her eyes, she could almost hear his ragged, leonine breathing. And he wasn't hungering for icebox cake.

"Wow, that's really nice of you. Sounds great. After breakfast, maybe, I'd love some."

"Yes, yes, after breakfast, of course, of course. Here, I'll stash it in your Frigidaire." The brittle rapping of Weaver's boots clattered down the hallway toward the kitchen and the bathroom. Robin realized she was scrunching up the little girl's shirt and let go. Weaver kept going and hung a right into the kitchen and paused. "Why does it smell like perfume in here?"

"Been burning incense," said Leon. "Nice expensive stuff from the head shop down there by the Payless Shoes. Thought it might warm the house up a little. Housewarming, you might say."

"Good call, good call. I burn frankincense myself." Opening the fridge, Weaver hooted. "Boy oh boy oh boy. I can tell you're a bachelor, sir. Heavens. Ain't nothing but takeout, leftovers, and condiments! Cold pizza indeed! Reckon I'm going to have to treat you gang more often." The heavy Pyrex dish thumped onto the metal rack inside and she closed it up.

"Sort of what I wanted to talk to you about, actually," said Leon, right on the other side of the bathroom door.

"Oh, we got all the time in the world for small talk." Weaver came back out into the hallway and paused. Her breezy bulk was almost palpable through the door, like a winter wind through an autumn window. A faint ratcheting noise was followed by a gush of warm air from the vent next to Robin's toes. "So drafty in this old house, ain't it?" asked Weaver. "Come on, let's turn up the heat a bit. Don't want the boy to catch a cold on top of a snakebite, hmm?"

The witch thumped back into the living room and clapped once, rasping her dry old hands together. Robin's mind produced a mental image of a housefly furiously rubbing its forelegs against each other. She shuddered.

"How are you feelin', dear boy? How's that leg a' yours?"

Wayne mumbled something not quite audible.

"Very good, very good. Sounds like the poultice did the trick, hmm? Drew the poison right out of you as easy as . . . well, dirt out of a carpet! It's the salt, you know, that does the trick. You toss in a few secret ingredients and it'll draw the venom right out of the bite."

(b i t e y o u , w a n t t o b i t e y o u)

Starvation surged in Robin's chest, dropping into the pit of her belly, and for a terrifying second she thought her stomach was going to growl out loud. Owlhead wanted the old woman, and bad. She could feel it. But without a display of prestidigitation on Weaver's part, the demon couldn't find her. It was attuned to her arcane energies.

"People's got lots of mean things to say about our country remedies and old wives' tricks," Weaver was saying, "but when they work—and they always do—oh, those folks shut their traps, they shut 'em right up."

Leon took the opportunity to jump in. "Mrs. Weaver—"

"Call me Karen."

"Karen, then . . . I just—"

"Or, you can call me Grandma if you like. Granny, Grammama, Mee-Maw, I come a-runnin' to 'bout any of those."

"'Mee-Maw'? I wanted to thank you for what you did at the

hospital. For . . . for footing Wayne's hospital bill. I don't—I don't even know how to voice my gratitude enough. You have no idea how much you helped me out. I mean, almost thirty thousand dollars? As a high school teacher, that's like a year's pay for me."

The witch tittered. "Wasn't no trouble, no trouble at all. You save up a lot of money livin' with two other old goats in a crumblin' pile in the ass-end of nowhere. Chicken coops're cheap, and we're all hens down that way."

"I see." Leon scoffed politely. "Well, there's not much I can do to repay you, at least for the time being, but I, uhh . . . I wanted to invite you over for dinner. My treat. It's the least I can do for the lady that saved my son's life and me a ton of heartache."

"How lovely of you. I'd be delighted. But your kitchen is awfully small . . . and ain't exactly geared to the gills. Now, our kitchen, on the other hand, well. You could roast a buffalo in that sucker, hooves and all, and dress it up no worse than Wolfgang Puck himself! And it's been quite a long time since we've had any company up there. Yessirree."

Silence lingered for a few seconds, and then Weaver went on talking.

"Make a deal with you, Mr. Parkin. You put together what you want for dinner—steaks, chicken, lamb, whatever you fancy. Bring it on up to the house. We'll sizzle it up fine and dandy with some veggies and baked tubers and yeast rolls, hmm?"

"Yeah, okay. Sounds good to me."

The uncertainty in Leon's voice made that a bald-faced lie Weaver would have to be an idiot to miss.

"You seem reluctant, buddy. What's the matter?"

"I hate to impose."

"It's the stories, ain't it? The tall tales about us being a bunch of witches. Bubble-bubble-toil-and-trouble and all that. I expect the folks over there in the trailer park been tellin' you tales out of school." Weaver chuckled dismissively, airily. "Take a gander at my face, hon. What color is my skin? Green? . . . No? And where's the wart on my nose? My pilgrim hat and buckled shoes? My bristly dustbroom and black pussycat?"

Another stretch of quiet, and then Leon said with a soft laugh, "Okay, yeah. I get the point. Sometimes I'm bad about letting what people say get to me. Not quite gullible, but—"

"Too trusting?"

"I guess? I guess you could say so."

Pete cut in. "The heck is a tuber?"

"A potato, my man," said Weaver. "An obsolete word for a potato, from an obsolete potato of an old woman."

Nobody laughed. Weaver continued to talk, unfazed. "Trust is a good thing, Mr. Parkin. A good thing. I think this world could use a bit more of it. Without it, where would we be? Kids don't hardly get to play outside these days, do they? They just sit in the house with their Internet and video games because the world out there scares the hell out of them. We don't trust them around strangers anymore. We don't trust Halloween candy anymore, for Pete's sake, and as an alleged witch I can tell you without a doubt that's a crying shame."

Robin could only think of her mother pinning Weaver's husband to the floor two decades ago. Edgar, the real-life boogeyman, making children disappear out of his homegrown Six Flags. She had no doubt Weaver was complicit in the racket. *Hypocrite hag,* she thought, squeezing little Katie's shoulders. The girl squirmed. She pressed her hand over Katie's mouth before she could complain. *Sorry, sorry—don't squeal! We'll all be shitting bumblebees if she finds us in here!*

"Anyway," said Weaver, "I need to get back to the ranch. I got a dress I've been working on for a month or so now and I'm starting to get down to the wire on my deadline. These young ladies these days, they don't have any patience for craftsmanship."

"A dress?"

"Oh, yeeeah. I design and make wedding dresses and sell 'em on the Internet. A real cottage industry, all by myself. Can you believe it? I talk down at the Internet like it's some kind of playpretty for lazy folks, but really, it's been a Godsend for an old lady like me. Why, I can visit the Great Wall of China from the comfort of my kitchen!"

The two of them headed to the front door, Leon with his slow cowboy stride, Weaver bustling along in a constant swish of fabric and a boot-heel drum solo.

"How does steak sound?" Leon asked, opening the front door.

"Like this: MOO."

The kids in the living room giggled.

"Steaks sound just fine, Mr. Parkin," said Weaver.

"Please, call me Leon."

"Ah, the lion! I like that quite a lot. You strike me as a man with a lion's courageous heart, Leon. Boy's quite lucky to have such a father. I think he takes after you."

"Thank you."

"Seven o'clock? Six? I don't want to keep the lion-cub up too late. It is a school night, after all."

"Six is fine. I'll be there."

"It's settled." Weaver's voice became a little clearer, a little louder. She must have leaned into the doorway to shout. "Have a good Sabbath, everybody! Dig that cake! There's more where that came from!"

An awkward silence followed this as the children hesitated, unsure of how to respond.

"Thank you, Miss Weaver," called Amanda.

Pete and Wayne echoed her. "Thank you, Miss Weaver."

Meanwhile, Robin could feel the witch's laser gaze through the wall, as if she had Superman's eyes. *She knows we're here. She knows, dammit.* Even though they'd parked in Chevalier Village so the plumbing van wouldn't be sitting in Leon's driveway for Cutty to see.

"You're very welcome," grinned Weaver. "Au revoir!"

The front door closed. The whole house seemed to hold its

breath for a full minute as everybody stayed locked in position, listening. Almost as if they were waiting for something.

"That is one creepy-ass old biddy," noted Joel.

Katie stirred. "I have to peeeeeee."

"All right, all right." Joel cracked the door open. Wayne's father stood by the front door, peeking through the sidelight windows. "Is she gone?"

Leon spoke over his shoulder. "Yeah. She's gone."

"Gone gone?" asked Joel. "She's off the property?"

"Yeah, she's crossing the highway right now." Leon gave them a pointed look as they came out of hiding. "Man, for a big-shot witch-hunter, you sure are hot to stay outta sight."

Robin was the last out of the bathroom, closing it behind her to give Katie some privacy. "You remember that green-eyed thing in the darkhouse?" She said 'dark house' as one word, *darkhouse*, as one would say "big-house" or "outhouse." Seemed to be evolving into her name for it. "Well, that creature may be the only thing that can kill those witches. That's how powerful they are. They'd tear through us like wet toilet paper."

"Then what made you think you'd be able to take 'em on by yourself?" asked Leon, going into the kitchen.

The water ran as he washed out the coffee mugs, staring out the window over the sink. Robin put her fists on her hips and stared darkly at the foyer rug as if she could find wisdom in the intricate red-and-blue curlicues. "Thought I might have a chance with the Osdathregar, I guess."

"Hey, guess what," said Kenway, coming in through the back door. He blew the last smoke of his cigarette as he did, the door pulling the cloud inside-out. In the awkward silence of the witch's departure, his boots sounded like hammers on the tile.

"I give up. What?"

"You got company," he said, and stepped aside.

A tall, gangly man sauntered into the kitchen and pushed his fingers into the pocket of his coat, pulling a flip-phone out and opening it. The felt gambler hat on his bald brown head, along with the black overcoat, made him look like he should be chasing an outlaw through Tombstone. The witch-hunter's eyes were inscrutable behind silver aviator shades as he showed them the phone's screen.

"I finally got into my voicemail." Heinrich pinched the cigar from between his teeth and blew a cloud of coconut-smelling smoke. "Robin Hood, how many times have I told you not to call me and interrupt my kung fu?"

Acknowledgments

Congratulations! You made it to the acknowledgments page. But your princess is in another castle.

The first person I'd like to thank is my mom—for so much, mostly being my frame of reference for what a strong woman looks like, and for giving me a place to stay while I wrote this book, and the next one. Thanks to your help I was able to sell enough self-published books to spread my wings and really, truly fly for the first time. I have a wonderful career and life now, and it's thanks to the books . . . but they never would have happened without you.

I would also like to thank my miracle-working agent, Leon Husock, for giving me my first break. He's the one I point to when I say dreams actually can come true.

And of course, my stalwart editor and friend Diana Pho at Tor Books, who laid into this manuscript with a chain saw and made it ten times better. She is an amazing person and a consummate professional, and it has been a revelation to work with her.

Last but not least, my Outlaw Army, my believers and Constant Readers who have been with me from the beginning, especially Chaser Spaeth and Katie Fryhover, who made amazing cosplay of characters from my Outlaw King series. Thank you for sticking with me this far. I love you folks so much.

Robin will return in

I COME WITH KNIVES

S. A. HUNT

Available May 2020 from Tom Doherty Associates
Read on for a preview.

1

Present Day

Forty yards back, a steel pole as big around as Michael DePalatis's arm stretched across the overgrown dirt road. Pulling the police cruiser up to the gate, he unbuckled his seatbelt and started to open the door.

"I got it." Owen checked the gate and found there was, indeed, a chain confining the gate to its mount, and a padlock secured it. Two of them, in fact.

Hypothetically they could go around it, if not for the impenetrable forest on either side. "Shit." Mike got out of the car anyway. "Looks like we're walking." He hopped over the gate, his keys jingling. The grass beat against Mike's shins, and hidden briars plucked at his socks. "When we get out of here, you might want to check yourself for ticks. Few years ago I was part of a search effort out in woods like this, and when I got home I found one on my dick."

"Oh, that's nasty," said Owen. He laughed like a kookaburra.

Conversation slipped into silence. The two men walked for what felt like half an hour, forging through tall wheatgrass and briars. Mike glanced at his partner as they walked. Officer Owen Euchiss was a scarecrow with an angular Van Gogh face. The black police uniform looked like a Halloween costume on him.

They called him Opie after the sheriff's son on *The Andy Griffith Show* because of his first two initials, which he signed on all of his traffic citations. His constant sly grin reminded Mike of kids he'd gone to school with, the little white-trash hobgoblins who would snort chalk dust on a dare and brag about tying bottle-rockets to cats' tails. Middle age had refined him a little, but the Scut Farkus was still visible under Opie's mask of dignified wrinkles.

"Ferris wheel," said Owen, snapping Mike out of his reverie. He straightened, peering into the trees.

The track they were walking down widened, grass giving way to gravel, and skeletal machines materialized through the pine boughs. They emerged into a huge clearing that was once a parking lot, and on the other side of that was an arcade lined with tumbledown amusement park rides, the frames and tracks choked with foliage.

Had to admit, the place had a sort of postapocalyptic *Logan's Run* grandeur about it. A carnival lost in time.

Not any better than a "pet sematary."

The two policemen walked aimlessly down the central avenue, heels crunching in the gravel. "What did Bowker say we're supposed to be looking for?" asked Owen.

"You heard the same thing I heard."

"'Something shady.'"

They came to a split, facing a concession stand. Owen took out his flashlight and broke off to the left, heading toward a funhouse. "I'll check over here."

Mike went right. A purple-and-gray Gravitron bulged from the woodline like an ancient UFO. Across the way was a tall umbrella-framed ride, chains dangling from the ends of each spoke like something out of *Hellraiser*. He contemplated this towering contraption and decided it had been a swing for kids, but without the seats it could have been a centrifuge where you hung slabs of beef from the chains and spun the cow blood out of them. Or maybe it was some kind of giant flogging-machine that just turned and turned and whipped and whipped.

When the rides had been damaged enough and lost so much of what identified them, they became alien and monstrous.

Third-wheel mobile homes made a village in the back, caved in by the elements. Bushes cloaked their flanks and bristled from inside. He slapped a whiny mosquito on his face.

Blood on his fingers. He wiped it on his uniform pants.

After wandering in and out of the carnie village, Mike decided none of them were in good enough shape to sustain life. He headed back into the main arcade.

At this point he had developed an idea of what Wonderland looked like from above: an elongated *I* like a cartoon dog-bone, the arcade forming the long straight part down the middle. Mike stood at the west end of the dog-bone, staring at the concession stand, and took his hat off to scratch his head.

He took the left-hand path, walking toward the funhouse. Behind the concession stand to his right was a series of roach-coaches: food trucks with busted, cloudy windows, wreathed in tall grass. A Tilt-a-Whirl, an honest-to-God Tilt-a-Whirl. Bushes and a tree thrust up through the ride, dislodging plates of metal and upending the seashell-shaped cars. A wooden shed with two doors stood behind the Tilt-a-Whirl, quite obviously an improvised latrine.

Here, the treeline marked the end of Wonderland. A chain-link fence tried to separate fun from forest, but sagged over, trampled by some long-gone woodland animal. Tucked between the Tilt-a-Whirl and the smashed fence was a pair of gray-green military Quonset huts. At the end of one of them stood a door with no window in it, secured with a padlock. NO ADMITTANCE—EMPLOYEES ONLY!

"The hell?" Mike lifted the padlock. No more than a couple of years old. Schlage. As he tried the doorknob, the entire wall flexed subtly with a muffled creak. Old plywood? He pressed his palms against the door and pushed. The striker plate crackled and the wall bowed inward several inches.

"Geronimo," he grunted, and stomp-kicked the door. The entire wall shook.

Another kick set the door crooked in the frame. The third kick ripped the striker out and the whole door twisted to the inside, the hinge breaking loose.

Inside was pure, jet-black, car-full-of-assholes darkness. Dust made soup of the air. Mike took out his flashlight and turned it on, holding it by his temple, and stepped into the hut. A workbench stood against the wall to his right, and a dozen buckets and empty milk jugs were piled in the corner, all of them stained pink. Wooden signs and pictures were stacked against the walls:

VISIT HOOT'S FUNHOUSE!

ARE YOU TOO COOL FOR SCHOOL? DRINK FIREWATER SARSAPARILLA!

GET LOST IN OUR HALL OF MIRRORS!

Three hooks jutted up from the bare cement floor in the middle of the room. Chains were attached to them, and the chains led up to three pulleys.

Old blood stained the floor around the hooks.

"Ah, hell," said Mike, drawing his pistol.

On the other side of the workbench was a door. He gave the stains a wide berth, sidling along the wall.

Flashlight in one hand and pistol in the other, he crossed his wrists Hollywood-style and pushed the door open with his elbow. Beyond, the polished black body of a Monte Carlo reflected his Maglite beam.

POW! Something exploded in the eerie stillness.

A bolt of lightning hit Mike in the ass. Electricity crackled down the Taser's flimsy wires, *tak-tak-tak-tak,* racing down the backs of his thighs, and he hit the floor bleating like a goat. The pistol in his hand fired into the wall between his jitterbugging feet, blinding him with a white flash.

"You *had* to come in here, didn't you?" asked the silhouette in the doorway, tossing the Taser aside and plucking the pistol out of Mike's hands. Chains rattled through a pulley and coiled around his ankles. Strong, sinewy hands hauled him up by the feet and suspended him above the floor. One of those white five-gallon buckets slid into view underneath his forehead, knocking his useless arms out of the way, and then his hands were jerked up behind his back and he was locked up in his own cuffs, dangling like Houdini about to be lowered into a glass booth full of water. "This is what I should have done to that faggot, instead of lettin' him hang around," said a man's voice, reminiscent of Opie but growlier, deeper, more articulate. "But I got his fuckin' car now. Sweet ride, ain't it? Did you see it in there?"

Mike's heart lunged at the *snick* of a blade being flicked out of a box-cutter.

"No, *please!*" he managed to grunt.

"You live, you learn, I guess." The man cut a deep fish-gill *V* in Mike's neck, two quick slashes from his collarbone to his chin.

Both his carotid and his jugular squirted up his cheeks and over his eyes, beading in his hair. The pain came a full second later, a searing cattle-brand pincering his throat. Mike gurgled, sputtered, trying to ask questions, deliver threats and pleas, but there was nobody in the garage to hear him.

The door slammed shut, leaving Michael in musty darkness.

Heinrich's eyes were intense—not wide and starey eyes, but the small, flinty eyes of a Black Clint Eastwood. He'd grown a beard at some point, and it was as gray as brushed steel. He was a big man—not burly or stocky, but long-trunked and long-limbed, with a commanding, arboreal presence. Robin's witch-hunting mentor looked like a bounty hunter from the Civil War.

To her eternal surprise, the old man took his coffee as sweet as a granny. She studied his face as he folded his sunglasses neatly, hanging them from the collar of his shirt.

"I watched the video you posted the other day and knew you were heading back to Georgia. Hopped in the car and hauled ass out here. That's why I haven't been answering the phone—I've been on the road." They all sat around the kitchen table in the Victorian house at 1168 Underwood, nursing cups of Folger's and listening to Heinrich recount how he caught up to his protégé. Robin was still a bit dazed from the previous night's encounter with what the kids called "Owlhead," the ensuing vision she'd had of her much younger mother summoning it, and the antipsychotic meds she'd overdosed on in an attempt to dispel what she'd thought was a hallucination.

Her GoPro camera lay on the counter next to the coffee maker, recording their impromptu palaver. "Did you come out here to help me," Robin asked, "or stop me?"

Taking off his gambler hat with a measured motion, Heinrich placed it in the center of the table, revealing his glossy brown head. He regarded her with a flat stare, Kenway and Leon sitting quietly to either side, and ignored the question. Instead, he asked, "What are the side effects?"

"Ischemic stroke. Anaphylactic shock." She looked out the window at a slate-gray sky. "Seizures."

Heinrich rolled his head in wry agreement. "Where there's smoke, there's fire. You had a seizure last night, according to these men," he said, giving the eyeshadowed Joel an assessing up-and-down. The pizza-man eyeballed him right back, folding his arms indignantly. "Maybe you *do* need to ease off."

"I don't think you need any more," Kenway said in a flat growl.

"I *have* been cutting back." Robin frowned. "But I need them to stop the hallucinations."

"No, you don't."

"Hallucinations?" asked Leon. "You mean this kind of thing has happened before?" He glanced toward the hallway door, as if his son Wayne were standing there. She could see the protective-ness written all over his face. Embarrassment she hadn't experienced in a long time made her face burn. She probably wouldn't have felt this way if Wayne weren't involved; she could almost hear Leon thinking of ways to keep him away from her.

"On top of the illusions that the witches can plant in your mind, I've been seeing strange things for a very long time," she told him. "Night terrors. Nightmares that might be memories—"

(—*Go ahead and look,* buzzed a stretched-out face—)

She visibly flinched, and a little coffee spilled on the table. Robin mopped at it with the sleeve of her hoodie. "—Memories that might be nightmares. And the owl-headed thing."

"Well, I think we proved Owlhead ain't a hallucination. I saw it with my own eyes. Maybe all that other shit is real too." Leon's taut expression loosened a little. "Maybe you're not crazy after all."

"We'll discuss your meds later." Heinrich took out a cigar and leaned forward with his elbows on the table, examining it at length as if it were the bullet destined to end his life. "I'm sure there's some other antipsychotic that won't fuck you up so much." He didn't offer one to anybody else, even though he knew Robin was a smoker. "Anyway. I ain't here to be your pharmacist, and I sure as hell ain't here to stop you. I ain't never been able to stop you before."

"Speaking of psychotic, we talked to a member of the coven. The young third one, Weaver."

"What about?" He stuck the slender cigar between his lips and dug a matchbook out of his shirt pocket, the Royal Hawaiian wagging as he spoke. Robin knew what it would be before she even saw the label: Vanilla Coconut. He cupped the cigar with a hand and lit it, shook the match out, and dropped it into the dregs of his coffee. "You two catch up on life 'n shit? Quiche recipes, grandkids, who's fuckin who on *The Young and the Restless*?"

"She put an illusion on me and left me in a hospital laundry, hallucinating bugs crawling out of my skin. How did you get in without her seeing you?"

Disgust passed across Leon's face, tinged with sympathy.

"I parked in the trailer park and hung out there for a while to watch the house." Heinrich took a deep draw, the cherry flaring, and blew smoke at the ceiling. The rich smell of coconuts floated in a dragon of blue smoke, turning the kitchen into a dingy cabana. "Waited for her to go in the house, went around the side."

Robin started to take a sip and put the mug back down. "Weaver told me I'm a puppet. Your henchman, your human shield." *Your personal Jesus,* interjected some weird neuron in her brain. "Said you groomed me to be a witchhunter so you could quit the game and pull a D. B. Cooper." She leaned over her coffee. "You didn't teach me how to fight so I could avenge my mother, did you? You did it so you could hide in your fortress in Texas, and let *me* do all your dirty work."

"I'm turning sixty-six this year." Heinrich ashed the cigar into his coffee mug. It was white and had a picture of Snoopy on it, fast asleep on the roof of his doghouse. "I can't fight the good fight forever. Somebody's gotta take over, and you were ready to be sculpted, a block of marble ready for Michelangelo's chisel."

Robin battled the urge to throw her coffee in his face. "I'm not your bitch." She took a deep shaky breath and let it out in a sigh.

"She told *your* tall dusty ass," interjected Joel, clutching a cup of coffee.

"You were never meant to be." Heinrich ashed his cigar again and leaned back. "They're turning you against me, Robin. Fragmenting the opposition. If you're gonna make the decision to come back here and fight, you're gonna have to keep your head together. Don't let Weaver tie you up in knots. That's what she's good at. They've all three of them got specialties, and hers is getting inside that dyed-up volleyball you call a head. Remember how I told you back in the day how they'll use tricks and lies to keep you from getting close? Well, this is it."

"Maybe." She sipped coffee, trying to read the expression on Kenway's face. The anger over the Abilify was new. It wasn't scary, but it left her feeling cold and hollow inside.

Heinrich stared at the table, woolgathering.

"I saw a little girl with a lot of hurt and hate in her heart." The old man's voice was torn between defensiveness, compassion, and anger. "I seen good people turn to shit trying to burn it all out with drugs. When I found out Annie had a daughter and she was in the mental hospital, I knew I had to get to you before the streets did. Or worse, you tried to fight Cutty with no preparation." He took another draw and talked the smoke out. "Bein' homeless ain't no joke. The hell you think you'd be if I hadn't taken you in?"

Reaching across the table as quick as a cobra, he grabbed Robin's wrist and turned it, held it up to the dim morning light. The pink rope of scar tissue running down the inside of her wrist shimmered with a faint opalescence.

Fresh concern came over Joel's face at the sight of the scars. She wrenched her arm out of the old man's hand, his fingertips slipping shut on empty air.

"You'd be dead in a gutter," said Heinrich, pointing at her with the two fingers pincering the cigar, "*that's* where your skinny white-girl ass would be. So listen to your heart and use your head, Robin Hood. Ain't nobody against you but them. Don't let 'em talk you in circles. That's their first trick. You know that. You know better. I didn't take you in and teach you what I know for you to fall for their bullshit."

The sun continued to fill the kitchen with morning light. "I saw my mother," Robin said eventually. "In a dream, when I had my seizure."

She recounted the contact with Owlhead and the demon's stolen vision from start to finish, from the ritual Annie performed on Weaver's husband to the demon crawling out of the hole. Leon choked on his coffee, and got up to fetch a paper towel to mop it up off his shirt. "There's a hellhole in my goddamn basement?"

"I don't know what it is, specifically, but—" Robin started to say.

"No, that's exactly what it is," said Heinrich. "Sounds like what happened was, Annie thought she had sacrificed Edgar Weaver to draw a demon into our world to kill Cutty, but what she did was sign a blood contract that allowed Hell to annex the house."

"In plain English, please," said Kenway.

Heinrich swept a hand down his face, pulling at his cheeks. His lower eyelids were rimmed in red; he obviously hadn't slept. "Basically, like Puerto Rico is a territory of the United States, this house is now a territory of Hell. It has been for about two decades. I imagine it's why ain't nobody lived in it since Annie died." He pointed toward the living room. "The dark version of it that little boy in there found with his mama's ring? That's the Hell-side of this house."

Everyone stared at Robin, making her want to shrivel up. "I thought you said there wasn't a Hell," said Kenway.

The old witchhunter grimaced, tossing a hand. Ashes dusted the tabletop. "Of *course* there's a Hell." Heinrich swept them off onto the floor. "Is she filling y'all's heads with her Dalai Lama God-is-love-and-Hell-is-regret bullshit?"

They smirked at him. Robin gave him the finger.

"There for a while last year she got real deep into Nichiren Buddhism," said Heinrich. "She even had me chanting *Nam Myoho Renge Kyo* over and over again, doin' yoga and shit and eatin' rabbit-food. *Me—!* The last time *I* did the Downward Dog, I got crabs and a night in jail."

"Y'all nasty," said Joel.

"The demon," said Heinrich, getting up from the table. "The hallucinations. Owlhead was drawing you here." He paced slowly up and down the foyer hallway, one hand in his pocket, the other holding the cigar to his mouth. "He wants you here for some reason."

"But why *now?*" asked Robin. "I've always seen him, but it's only been every now and then. The first nineteen years of my life, I saw him four times. Once when I was as young as that little girl in there, once in middle school, and twice in the mental hospital. The last two years, I've seen him at least fifteen times. It's like he's leading me here. What's special about now?"

"You turned eighteen. Came of age. Maybe he thinks you've passed some kind of threshold that would make it possible for you to let him manifest in our world? You are the daughter of the woman that summoned him, after all. Maybe there's a link somewhere."

"If he's looking for a virgin, he's barking up the wrong girl."

Heinrich laughed.

"And if he wants me to let him loose, I ain't doing that. I wouldn't even know how." She eyed the cigar smoke in the air.

"You're the research wonk—do you know if there's another part to that ritual beyond cleaving off a shadow-clone of the house to imprison him in?"

The old man shrugged. "Hell, I don't know, I'd have to look at the materials she used."

"What *are* demons, anyway?" asked Joel. "That thing with the owl-head didn't look like any demon *I've* ever seen. I would've expected, y'know, the usual—cloven hooves, pitchfork, horns, the whole nine yards. Not a dilapidated animatronic owl from a haunted pizzeria."

"Demons, at their simplest," explained Heinrich, "are viruses."

"I ain't pickin' up what you're throwin' down."

"All right, a virus is basically a piece of DNA wrapped in protein. You could say it's dead, but it would have to have lived to be dead, and it's never been alive. But it *wants* to be alive. And the only way a virus can assume some semblance of life is by infecting a living being. I like to think of it as a Terminator—a facsimile of life that's never been alive itself, wrapped in meat." He sighed and took the cigar out of his mouth, staring at it as he rolled it in his fingers. "The way it's been explained to me is, there are two kinds of souls. The souls that come out of Creation's oven well-formed and functioning find their way into a living body at some point. The souls that come out deformed don't get a body. They sorta float around out there in the dark, in the void of Purgatory. Demons are those two-faced, waterheaded, heart-on-the-outside, too-fucked-up-to-live souls. And the only way they can reach the same level of life *we* enjoy is to possess a living body, the same way a virus possesses a living cell."

"You say 'Creation's oven,'" said Leon, wiping his hands dry with a towel as he came back to the foyer. "So you're tellin' me there's an actual God up there, cranking out souls in His spiritual bakery?"

Heinrich guffawed, leaning back to laugh at the ceiling.

"That's the million-dollar question, ain't it?" He stubbed the cigar out on the sole of his boot. "Welcome to the clergy."